You
Gotta
Have Balls

You
Gotta
Have Balls

LILY BRETT

wm
WILLIAM MORROW
An Imprint of HarperCollins*Publishers*

This book is a work of fiction. References to real people, events, establishments, organizations, or locales are intended only to provide a sense of authenticity, and are used fictitiously. All other characters, and all incidents and dialogue, are drawn from the author's imagination and are not to be construed as real.

FIRST EDITION

Designed by Sarah Maya Gubkin

Printed on acid-free paper

Library of Congress Cataloging-in-Publication Data

Brett, Lily, 1946–
    You gotta have balls / Lily Brett.—1st ed.
        p. cm.
    ISBN-13: 978-0-06-050569-1 (acid-free paper)
    ISBN-10: 0-06-050569-9
    1. Women—Societies and clubs—Fiction. 2. Women—New York (State)—Fiction. 3. Female friendship—Fiction. 4. Writing services—Fiction. 5. New York (N.Y.)—Fiction. 6. Letter writing—Fiction. 7. Conversation—Fiction.   I. Title.

PR9619.3.B693Y68 2006
813'.54—dc22   2005051109

06   07   08   09   10   JTC/QWF   10   9   8   7   6   5   4   3   2   1

For David, my sweetheart,

and

for Virginia Lloyd and her beloved husband,

John Gallagher, 1956–2004

You
Gotta
Have Balls

One

"Why are you talking about men and how smart they are?" was one of the first things Sonia Kaufman had said to Ruth Rothwax, when they met, about ten years ago. "Why are you talking about men and how smart they are? You should be talking about menopause. It's looming." It had made Ruth laugh. Ruth and Sonia were the same age. Fifty-four. Both had grown up in Australia, but had met in New York. Sonia was an intellectual property lawyer for a large law firm. Her husband was a senior partner in the same firm.

Ruth ran her own business. A letter-writing business. She had clients in New York, L.A., Chicago, Boston, and Washington, D.C. People had said, when she began Rothwax Correspondence, that it would never work. That was fifteen years ago. She now had more corporate clients than she could handle and more private clients than she wanted.

There was something very satisfying for Ruth about putting words together. Part of her satisfaction was the control it was possible to have over words. If you put words in the right order they stayed in the right order. They didn't make moves that took you by surprise. They didn't suddenly turn into strangers or take up tango lessons.

Sonia spent her working days sorting out who owned what ideas, colors, markings, thoughts, and words. Ruth thought Sonia could pay a little more attention to her own thoughts and words.

"Try some of my lamb and fennel sausage," Sonia said. "It's delicious." Ruth and Sonia were having breakfast at Coco's, on Twelfth Street.

Lamb and fennel sausage? How could Sonia eat lamb and fennel sausages for breakfast? Ruth thought.

"No thanks," she said.

"Why don't you eat properly?" Sonia said. "You've got five grains of cereal and half a dozen cubes of assorted fruit on your plate. Have some ham and eggs, or the steak and potato hash."

"You sound like my father," Ruth replied.

"There's nothing wrong with your father," Sonia said.

"There's nothing ever wrong with anyone else's father," Ruth said. "Anyway, I can't eat red meat. I associate it with burning flesh."

"Grow up," Sonia almost shouted. "So, your mother and father were in Auschwitz. My mother was in Theresienstadt and I can eat fried brains, stewed kidneys, diced liver, and assorted legs, heads, necks, and feet. You can't be fixated about the Holocaust."

"I'm not fixated," Ruth said, quietly.

Ruth thought that Sonia must be one of the few women in New York who didn't have a food disorder of sorts. The degree of the disorder could vary, but hardly any women Ruth knew had a less than complex attitude to food. Unlike men. Men went to a restaurant. Ordered what they wanted. And ate it. So did Sonia. She didn't spend an hour scrutinizing the menu in a state of anxiety and indecision. Or bemoan what she'd eaten as soon as she reached the end of the meal. Sonia just ate.

Ruth tried to defend herself. "I know a lot about food and nutrition," she said to Sonia. "There's research that suggests that eating dark chocolate can reduce your risk of blood clots and give you more relaxed blood vessels."

"You'd have to have intravenous Valium to give you relaxed blood vessels," Sonia replied. "It's not normal to know that about chocolate or to fixate on the Holocaust."

Ruth knew that normal wasn't easy to quantify. Weather charts and forecasts regularly used the word *normal*. They tracked normality. Weather charts could tell you the average daily departure from normal for the month or the year. Ruth thought she would like to be able to track the average daily departure from normal in herself.

"Lots of things aren't normal," Ruth said. "Lots of things that are normal shouldn't be normal. If you watch the nightly news, you'd think the world was run by men. And you'd be right. That's not normal. In news item after news item, middle-aged white men stride across streets, stand at podiums, or sit behind desks. They make statements and proclamations. They pontificate. They attack. They praise. They explain. Where are the women? Not in evidence. And not in power. When a woman does get into a position of power, it's a big deal. It's a big deal to have Condoleezza Rice. It was a big deal to have Golda Meir. And that was thirty-five years ago. And who is to blame?" Ruth said, a bit breathlessly, looking at Sonia.

"Men," Sonia replied.

"No," Ruth said. "Women. Men are so clearheaded. They know what they want. And they know how to get it. Their brains aren't fogged and clouded and clogged with purposeless pursuits. They're not filled with self-delusions of sweetness or notions of their own niceness, or twelve different diet plans. Women need to talk to each other. Honestly. They need to trust each other. Not shred each other. They need to share information, contacts, experiences, and intimacies."

It seemed to Ruth that intimacy, in general, had been usurped by more pressing needs. Career moves, conference calls, parenting, home décor, or home acquisition seemed to generate more heat than orgasms. And great moves mostly referred to office politics, real estate transactions, divorce negotiations, or exercise routines. Not foreplay. Or libido.

Ruth worried about her libido, herself. She thought libidos were easy to lose. Much easier to lose than gloves or umbrellas. You could keep an eye on your gloves or your umbrella. But you could misplace a libido and not know it was gone. For years. And even if you were worried about your libido, you couldn't talk about it. Libidos were not an easy subject to discuss. You couldn't chat about a missing libido in the same way you could discuss a missing dog or cat. And, on the whole, the loss would go largely unnoticed by others. Unlike weight loss. Or hair loss.

"Women need to share experiences and intimacies," Ruth said again to Sonia.

"What sort of intimacies?" said Sonia.

"All sorts," Ruth said.

"I don't know any woman who feels at ease talking about sex," Sonia replied. "Any married woman, anyway." She paused. "That's probably because they're not ecstatic about the sex they're having," she said. "Sex between married people is just another function of their existence. Like paying your bills or taking the garbage out. It's as utilitarian and pedestrian as washing the dishes. And as mechanical. Two minutes after you've started, it's all over. He's ejaculated. You've groaned. You've both momentarily forgotten what you watched on TV or what happened in the office, or that two minutes ago you wanted to slug a kid or each other. Thirty minutes later, you're asleep or back to thinking about the kid or the office. Whatever distance you traveled to overlook the unattractive socks or underpants or peculiar eating habits, is back. Whatever distance you traveled to get to each other is back. The only way to have more than that is to have a lover. That's what I did for years. I can't do that now. It's too complicated to be a wife, a mother, and a lover. I could barely manage the wife and lover parts, as it was. There was so much organization involved. You can't manage that with children. And anyway, you can't be buying cornflakes and thinking about what your lover tastes like at the same time. It's impossible."

Sonia looked distressed. Her normally orderly blunt-cut straight hair had gone awry. Bits were sticking out as though in fright.

Ruth felt disturbed. She felt sorry for Sonia. Ruth wasn't sure that sex, or its frequency, was a reliable measure of a marriage. There were so many components. She thought she had a good marriage. She knew she loved Garth. But love was such a nebulous thing. You could love someone for so many misguided reasons. So many delusions could, and did, go into love. So many distractions. And so many destructions. You could love someone because he or she helped you to feel bad or burdened or flattened or downtrodden, or safe or superior. You could love someone as a very effective substitute for loving yourself.

You could love someone as a substitute for so many things. Good and bad. How did people know why they loved who they did? She'd spent half her adult life in analysis, and so many dollars, in an effort to help her try to make sense of her own life. And she had a better grasp. She didn't have the whole picture. You'd think that for that much money you'd get the whole picture. She knew that her heart still lifted when she came home and saw Garth, at the end of the day. She thought that was probably as good a criterion as any other. As good as sex. She used to think sex had to be perfect. Perfect in its frequency. Perfect in its execution. But perfection was such a fluid state. With so many variables. If it existed at all, it had to be momentary. It seemed to Ruth that there were times when sex seemed perfect. And, Ruth thought these times were probably often enough.

"You really think men are clearheaded?" Sonia said.

"Yes," said Ruth. "Very clearheaded. Men know that it's in their own interest to support other men even though they may hate the other man's guts. Men don't scratch and bitch and claw each other. Men handle themselves with much greater dignity."

The thought of men handling themselves, with dignity or not, conjured up quite the wrong image for Ruth. She tried to blink it out of her head.

"Women are so aggressive, so competitive with each other," Ruth said. "And women love another woman's misery. They can't wait to join in and commiserate about how miserable you are. Want a lot of friends? Put on weight, get fired from your job, get cancer or maybe something less extreme like shingles or Bell's palsy. Cancer can be very taxing on a friend.

"Men have more straightforward friendships. They don't hang up phones in a huff with each other. They don't feud and not speak for months over insignificant issues. Men don't weep at something another man says. Or hate them for years because of it."

"I hate to say it," Sonia said, "but I think you're right."

"I think I'm right too," said Ruth. "Men are so smart. The average severely depressed, semi-witted, half-lobotomized man is so much smarter than most women."

Sonia started laughing.

"I've been thinking of forming a women's group," Ruth said. "A small group of smart women who'll care about each other, and collectively gain more power. For themselves. And other women."

"You're thinking about forming a women's group?" said Sonia. "Who would be in it?"

"I'm not sure," said Ruth. "You?"

The fact that she wanted to form a women's group had almost taken Ruth by surprise. She was also startled at the vehemence of her hopes and the intensity of her agenda. She hadn't yet asked any women to join, but she'd planned the first meeting carefully. And decided it would be held in her loft.

She had even written out an agenda. First, each woman would make a short introductory speech about herself, five minutes at the most. Ruth's hope was they would all talk about their lives in a way that was as intimate and honest as possible. That they would say more than what could be said or discussed at any cocktail party or dinner party. Ruth thought it would be a good idea if the women also mentioned why they had joined the group. After the introductions, there could be a question-and-discussion period, in which people could respond to what had been said. Ruth planned to suggest that the group draw up a list of subjects to be discussed at future meetings. They could allocate two subjects an evening. And allow one hour per subject.

On her agenda was a suggestion that the group put aside, say half an hour each month, for members who needed specific help. Help with contacts, advice. Help with anything. She wrote out a set of rules for the meetings and made a note to herself to call them guidelines. Ruth's rules were simple. People should not talk when someone else was speaking. All remarks should be addressed to the whole group, not to the person beside you, or a small splinter group. Ruth felt it was important for everyone to hear what everyone else was saying. And important for someone to chair each meeting. She also thought a timer would be a good idea. That way the more garrulous members wouldn't occupy the whole meeting and everyone would get a chance to speak. She thought each meeting could begin with a three-minute response to the previous meeting by each member. "Am I too dictatorial?" she wrote on the piece of paper. She had decided not to ask Sonia that question.

"How are you managing without Garth?" Sonia said.

"I think I'm managing," said Ruth.

"He's only been gone for a week," Sonia said.

"He's not gone. He's away," Ruth said. "Gone sounds very gone."

"He's gone," Sonia shouted. "He's not in the country."

Garth had left for Australia last week. Garth was a painter. He'd had exhibitions in America, Australia, England, Germany, Austria, Switzerland, France, Mexico, China, India. He was working on a large commission for a winery outside Melbourne. Three murals for the walls and an intricately patterned floor. The floor was based on one of Garth's paintings and made with thin slices of the trunk of a dead hundred-and-ten-year-old ironbark tree that were interwoven with small river stones and set into concrete.

Garth painted every day. Seven days a week. He painted during the day, and he often worked in his studio, at night. The crucial things in Garth's life, Ruth often felt, were his paintings, and her. Everything else had to share whatever space was left.

She couldn't say that about herself. She loved words. She loved composing sentences. She felt happier writing, no matter how tedious the subject matter was, than she did doing anything else. But she still had a lot of room left, for doubts, worries, anxieties, and her three children. She'd been an overly concerned mother. She often told her son that he'd have been much better off with less attention from her when he was small. It used to make him laugh. But she meant it. No one needed a mother who was always looking at you. Who hovered and inquired and discussed and listened. Relentlessly. It was entirely unhelpful.

"Do you know how lucky you are to have him?" woman after woman had said about Garth, to Ruth. "Do you really know how lucky you are?" a woman at a cocktail party kept repeating to Ruth, recently. The repetition had made Ruth feel as though she was visibly, toxically, and terminally flawed. As though she was a burden, if not an outright charity case. No one as far as she knew had ever said to Garth that he was lucky to have her. She certainly felt lucky to have Garth. He was very smart and very kind. And very funny. Maybe she was lucky to have anyone. She'd felt, as a teenager, that she never would. It was funny how those things never left you. How the fat teenager never totally disappeared. Garth often told her how lucky he was to have her. She was always grateful to him for feeling that way.

Garth would probably be away for six months. It would be the longest time they'd spent apart, in their twenty-five years together.

Garth usually quelled Ruth's anxiety. He saw most possibilities and oc-currences as full of promise. Although he'd only been gone for a week, it had seemed like a very long week to Ruth. She couldn't even really talk to him, on the phone. Garth was not good on the phone. He didn't like phones. In person, Garth was loquacious, articulate, exuberant, and affectionate. On the phone he turned into someone who resembled an accountant or an insurance clerk. A friendly accountant or clerk. He spoke to everyone in the same cheerful, brisk manner. Including Ruth. Garth sounded pleased to hear from the caller and eager to get off the line. To everyone. Ruth had learned, long ago, that it was not much use expecting to be able to discuss her work, or the kids, or her father, or anything of any length, over the phone with Garth. She missed Garth.

"I know he's not in the country," Ruth said to Sonia. She paused. "I'm trying to restrain myself from ringing him every five minutes," she said.

"Good," said Sonia.

"I'm not succeeding," said Ruth. "Yesterday I called him seven times. It's okay," Ruth said before Sonia could say anything, "I couldn't get through. I got the answering machine each time. I didn't leave a message."

Ruth felt embarrassed. She decided to put some distance between herself and the conversation about the multiple calls to Garth. She went to the bathroom.

"Shall I call you if I make any firm arrangements for a women's group?" Ruth said to Sonia as they were leaving Coco's.

"Absolutely," said Sonia.

Ruth strode along Broome Street. She loved walking. She walked everywhere she could. Walking gave her time to think. Gave her a peacefulness. "Have a good day, asshole," a woman on the corner of Mercer Street shouted at a man who'd nearly knocked her over in his haste to grab a cab. "This city is insane, crazy, loco," the woman shouted at no one in particular.

Ruth felt happy. It was still a relief to hear someone complaining about New York again. Complaining about the city used to be almost mandatory for New Yorkers. Everyone complained. Including Ruth. She complained about the noise, the traffic, the cost, the rush, the stress. Complaints about the city came to a standstill on September 11th, 2001. Complaints disappeared. In the days after September 11th, people in the streets looked heartbroken. You could see what people were feeling. You could see who they were under the masks that mask people from each other. It was almost shocking to see what person after person was feeling. The anonymity and invisibility of those around you was removed. You could see beyond the lipstick, the business suit, the briefcase, the jeans, or the Chanel coat. You could see anguish on people's faces. You could see tenderness. You could see vulnerability. You could see love. You could see who people were.

Who people were had preoccupied Ruth for a large part of her life. "You'll never know what people are capable of," her mother, Rooshka Rothwax, used to say to her, over and over again. Rooshka and Ruth's father, Edek, had spent five years imprisoned in the Łódź Ghetto, in Poland, before being transported to Auschwitz. Ruth knew that her mother really knew what people were capable of. Really knew who people were.

Business had slowed down dramatically for Rothwax Correspondence in the period immediately after September 11th. It stayed slow for weeks. Months really. It seemed to Ruth that people were expressing themselves more. By themselves. They appeared to be more in touch with their feelings. It seemed that post–September 11th, people had a greater need to be connected, more directly. To communicate in their own words. Not hers. Heads of corporations or small businesses, housewives, economists, bankers, forklift drivers, doctors, often people who'd never read a poem in their lives, were writing poetry. And their own letters. Words, it seemed to Ruth, had become more personal. Words had always been personal, for Ruth. And essential. If you grew up with parents who didn't speak much English, you understood that the right word was critical.

Ruth also thought that after September 11th, many issues that had previously seemed meaningful had become meaningless. Small and large irritations had seemed of less consequence. Almost inconsequential. Hostility, antagonism, animosity, antipathy, and impatience were visibly diminished. Neighbors spoke. Colleagues cared. Families appeared to unite. It didn't last. After three or four months, business picked up. Rothwax Correspondence was as busy as ever. Ruth had to compose many September 11th letters. Clients wanted references to the tragedy in a large number of business and personal letters. Other things also went back to normal. Or possibly deteriorated. Three years after September 11th, old prejudices were even more entrenched. Old hatreds enhanced and amplified. And intimacy between people seemed as distant and absent as it had ever been.

Ruth's intimacy with her father had increased. Eighty-seven-year-old Edek Rothwax had moved to New York from Melbourne, Australia, five months ago. He'd wanted to move. He'd wanted to live in New York. He wanted to be closer to Ruth. She'd said to him that it wouldn't be easy. That he'd be lonely in New York. That he wouldn't have his friends around him. "I got no friends," he'd replied. "Who do I see?" Ruth had listed several people. "These are not friends," Edek had said. "These are people what I play cards with."

"I am still pretty strong," Edek said. "I can help you in the business. I can still carry parcels and I can order stuff what you need. I can make things easier for you." Ruth's chest had constricted at the thought of Edek making life easier for her.

She had been right to worry about Edek making her life easier. Edek was causing disarray, if not mayhem, in the office. He had put himself in charge of what he called "the Stockings Department." Ruth had explained to him that while he may be ordering stock and doing the stocking, he couldn't really call it the Stockings Department, because that suggested stockings. "That's what I will be doing," he had replied. "Doing the stockings." Ruth had given up. Edek was unstoppable. He came to the office every day. Before Ruth. And before Max, the thirty-two-year-old woman who had worked for Ruth for almost eleven years.

Edek overordered everything. He ordered twelve cartons of paper for the laser printer. There were eight reams of paper in each carton. And five hundred sheets of paper in each ream. That added up to forty-eight thousand sheets of paper. A week later, he ordered another twelve cartons. Rothwax Correspondence didn't need that much paper. They printed only two copies of each letter, and 30 percent of the letters they wrote were written by hand. Tara McGann, a Ph.D. student at Columbia University, worked in the office, at night, handwriting the letters. She was very good. And very accurate. She never misplaced or mistakenly altered a word. Ruth hoped that Tara McGann's Ph.D. would take several more years.

Edek ordered mainly from catalogues. He loved ordering. He bought wire-bound notebooks. Hundreds of them. "I do see you do write down the points what you want to make, in such notebooks all of the time," he had said when Ruth questioned him. She didn't want to point out that she only used the wire-bound notebooks to make notes when she was not in the office. In the office, she used legal pads. White legal pads. Rothwax Correspondence would have to be a multinational corporation in order to need that number of wire-bound notebooks. And the wire-bound notebooks all had yellow pages. Ruth hated writing on yellow paper.

Ruth narrowly avoided Edek's buying custom-imprinted pens for Rothwax Correspondence. He'd come into her office to ask her what she thought would be the best wording to put on the pens. "Rothwax Correspondence for Every Person's Letters" was Edek's suggestion. "They would be very good for business, in my opinion," he had said, and looked hurt when Ruth firmly said, "No they wouldn't." Edek recovered from this within a few days. And went back to ordering. He ordered absurd things. He ordered a self-navigating sweeper vacuum cleaner. You pushed one button and it propelled itself around the floor.

"We've only got carpet in one room. And that's the storeroom," Ruth had said.

"But this machine does save you a lot of time," Edek had answered. "Nobody does have to push it. It does move by itself. This machine does know when it has finished the room." The manufacturers of the self-propelled sweeper vacuum cleaner said, on the box, that their product scooped debris better than a traditional sweeper. Ruth wondered if by traditional sweeper, they meant a broom. Edek liked to put the self-navigating sweeper vacuum on several times a day. Ruth hated the sound it made as it swept and vacuumed the storeroom.

Edek loved to be helpful. In his desire to contribute to the well-being and efficiency of Rothwax Correspondence, he rearranged things. He plugged the fax machine into the company's main phone line. The resulting confusion lasted almost two days, the first time he did it. He unplugged the surge bars that protected two of their computers. He rearranged several filing drawers and, among other things, erased a slew of messages from the answering machine. He interrupted Ruth, often. Yesterday, Edek asked her if they had run out of staples yet, just as she had thought of a good line for the greeting-card line she had just branched out into. She didn't want to tell Edek that they had enough staples to staple every one of the forty-eight thousand Hewlett-Packard laser jet pages he'd bought, to the other forty-eight thousand Hewlett-Packard laser jet pages she knew would be arriving any minute.

"No, we don't need any staples yet," Ruth had said to Edek. The line she had in her head had evaporated. It was to have gone after the line, "Congratulations. Ditching him is so much better than ditching yourself."

This was to go into a greeting-card subcategory Ruth had called "Women." It was part of a much larger category she called "Relationships," which also had subcategories called "Big Moves," "Think Twice," and "Good Moves." And sub-subcategories of "Marriage," "Divorce," "The Boss," "The Colleague," "The Partner," "The Job," "The Decision," "Consequences," "The Relatives," "Pets," "Neighbors," and "Decisions."

Her father interrupting her train of thought was not one of the most worrying aspects of the addition of Edek Rothwax to the offices of Rothwax Correspondence. One day Ruth had made the mistake of asking Edek to deliver a batch of letters to one of her very wealthy clients. "Is the boss in?" Edek had asked the boss's assistant, when he'd arrived with the letters. "I am Ruthie Rothwax's father," he'd added. "I am Ruthie Rothwax's father," Edek had said, again, when the client himself came out of his office. After chatting for a minute or two, Edek asked the client, Mr. Bregman of Bregman Capital Ventures, if he'd ever been to Israel. Mr. Bregman said no. Edek then explained that most Australian Jews had visited Israel. Edek had explained, and not succinctly, how Australians gave more money per capita to Israel than Jews in any other country. And that a very large percentage of Australian Jews had visited Israel. And only a very small percentage of American Jews had ever been there. "I think that all Jews have big responsibility to visit Israel," had been Edek's closing statement. Ruth had heard all of this from Mr. Bregman's assistant, who had called to say the letters had been delivered. Ruth was surprised at the call. Few clients called to acknowledge the delivery of letters. Certainly not Mr. Bregman.

"Did your father deliver them?" Mr. Bregman's assistant had asked Ruth.

"Yes," said Ruth.

"Oh, good," the assistant said. "We thought he might have been an impostor." Then Ruth had heard the rest of the details.

"I'll lose him as a client," Ruth had said to Edek when Edek had returned to the office. "And we're not trying to change the world."

"What are we doing?" Edek had said.

"We're making a living," Ruth said. "We're earning money."

"We got already enough money," Edek had replied.

Ruth didn't want to argue about that. She didn't want to point out that she had supported him for years. Support that was much more expensive now that he lived in a one-bedroom apartment on Second Avenue than it was in Melbourne. Part of her thought that Edek was right. She probably did have enough money. She had enough money to own a large loft in Soho and a beach house. She had enough money to buy all the books she wanted and to go to the theater as often as she liked, and to travel.

"I'll lose him as a client," she said, again, to her father.

"Big deal," Edek had answered.

Ruth wished she could find an interest for Edek if not a hobby. Something to occupy some of his time. But he'd never really had any hobbies. None at all. Unless you included eating. Ruth didn't think eating qualified as a hobby.

Her father did enjoy a game of gin rummy. She had suggested that he join a Jewish senior citizens' organization. "What for? To play once in a while a game of cards with some *alte kackes* like me? It's better that I help you out," he'd said. "That way I can be of help to you," he'd added, in case she hadn't quite understood.

Ruth took a deep breath. She was almost at the office. She was sure her father would already be there and possibly already inquiring about lunch. During the morning, Edek would periodically ask what time was lunch. Ruth explained to him, over and over again, that Rothwax Correspondence was not like a school or a factory, where lunch hours could be fixed. They had to be flexible. They ate their lunch whenever they felt hungry, and when it was convenient.

Edek then began asking Max and Ruth what they were going to have for lunch. He would start asking this question at about 10:00 A.M. No one else in the office was thinking about lunch at 10:00 A.M. Possibly, no one else in Manhattan was thinking about lunch at 10:00 A.M. Edek liked to get the lunches. Max, who usually ordered in, was quite happy for Edek to get her lunch. It gave her a greater choice. She could now get food from Whole Foods, or the Balthazar Bakery, or even Olivier's Asian Rice Bar, which was at least ten blocks away.

Edek was prepared to walk anywhere or catch a cab to get lunch. In order to keep hot food hot, he would get a cab back even if the office was close. He liked to get lasagna or spaghetti Bolognese or macaroni and cheese from a deli on Duane Street, for himself. And this way, he could fill the container himself and get exactly as much as he wanted. "I did eat too much lasagna," or spaghetti or ravioli, he would announce to Ruth, holding his stomach when he finished his lunch. "But it was very good," he would add before swallowing several Tums or Rolaids.

When Ruth arrived at work in the morning, she would often find Edek sitting in her office looking through files. Or talking to Max. Edek would be giving Max advice. Advice about life or love, or apartments or the subway. He would tell her about his life, while she looked transfixed and ignored incoming phone calls. As soon as he saw Ruth, Edek would jump up and leave. He would run off with the same short, stubby, swift little steps he'd run with all his life. He would disappear into the storeroom. Or the bathroom, or the kitchen area. "I was just finishing," he would say as he fled. "I don't want to be a bother," he'd add. "Your father is wonderful," Max said, several times a day.

If only Ruth didn't need Max in the office, Max would be a perfect companion for Edek. They could talk all day. Max loved to talk. Max could be very long-winded about even the simplest things. For years Ruth had been telling Max to edit. "Edit, Max, edit," Ruth would say as Max used dozens too many words to explain what she was saying.

"I'll only be a minute," Max would say when she interrupted Ruth. "I'll only be a minute because I have to call Mr. X back and get the accounts out before the post office closes." Or because the locksmith was coming or the exterminator or the window cleaner. Edek didn't think Max used too many words. He listened to all of Max's words and then offered up his own.

Ruth wished Edek would meet a nice woman. Someone Jewish, maybe someone who spoke Yiddish, and, possibly, Polish. Ruth wasn't expecting Edek to meet the love of his life. He'd done that. He'd loved Rooshka dearly. For so long. Ruth just wished her father could find a companion. Someone to go to the movies with. Someone to do things with. Someone to keep him company during the day. If she could find someone to keep her father occupied during the day, then her own days would be more orderly.

But Edek wasn't interested. "I got plenty of company," he'd said several times. "I got you, that's the main thing, and I got Gut." He always pronounced Garth "Gut." "And I got Zelda and Zachary and Kate which are very good grandchildren to me. Not many people does have such good grandchildren," he added. "I got plenty of company. You do not have to worry about me. I am one hundred percent okay. I should worry about you. You do work too much. And I am very happy that I can help you with this work."

Ruth had felt flat. But she couldn't bring herself to puncture Edek's notion of his contribution to Rothwax Correspondence. When he told her he'd found manila folders or cardboard rolls on special, she just looked pleased. Or what she hoped passed for pleased. Rothwax Correspondence never used cardboard rolls. Ruth hoped they weren't very large. She told Max to tell the people who delivered them to take them straight to the basement. Ruth had had to start using the 250 square feet of basement space that came with her office. She'd never used it before.

Ruth suggested that Edek join a seniors reading group she'd heard about. It was in the East Village and affiliated with the local Temple Beth Zaadeck. Edek didn't think highly of that idea.

"Are you stupid?" he'd said.

"A reading group is a group of people who meet to discuss a book they have just read," Ruth said. "You get to hear other people's opinions and understandings and interpretations of what happened in the book."

"Do you think I am stupid?" Edek said. "Do you think I cannot understand English? What for should I join such a group where people do discuss what did happen in the book they did just read?"

Ruth looked at him. "Why don't you understand what I am saying to you?" he said with exasperation. "I do read mainly those detective books. You do know that. You been watching me read those detective books nearly your whole life. You did buy me such books many times. And Zelda does buy me even more such books than what you do." Ruth still looked blank. "What does happen in such books what I read is what does happen." Edek said. "One person does kill another person and then somebody does find out who did kill this person. Sometimes one person does blackmail another person or more than one person. In nearly every case, you do know who did do this blackmail before the book is finished. What does happen in the book is exactly what does happen. There is nothing to talk about. Maybe you can say if it is a good book or if it is a bad book but you do not need to have a special meeting to say about a book if it is good or if it is bad."

Ruth nodded and agreed with Edek. "That was not such a good idea," she said. "Maybe we should get you a masseur. A regular massage would be good for you."

"That stuff is not for me," he said, and rushed out to get some more paper clips for Max from the storeroom.

"You can't swim," Ruth said to her father, a few days later. Edek had looked at her as though she was speaking in Mandarin. "I thought you might enjoy swimming classes," she said. "They have them, in the morning, at the Ninety-second Street Y."

Edek looked at her as though she'd lost her mind. "I did never swim in my whole life," he said. "I did not want to swim when I was a young boy in Poland, why should I want to swim when I am an old man?"

It had seemed like a good idea to Ruth when it was just a thought. She'd had notions of Edek enjoying being able to swim when they went on family vacations together. It was a far-fetched, if not absurd, notion. For many reasons. For a start, Edek had fair skin and burned easily. Edek was looking at her expectantly. "You're right," she said. "Why should you want to learn how to swim?"

"Thank God you can see this," Edek said. "For such a clever girl what you are, Ruthie, you do say sometimes things what are very stupid."

"You treat your father like some parents in this city treat their kids," Sonia had said to Ruth recently. "They want to occupy and organize every moment in their kids' lives. The kids are sent to dance, swim, and ski classes. They take flute, trombone, piano, and saxophone lessons. One instrument is not enough. They learn French, Italian, Spanish, Japanese. Bilingual is no longer adequate for a kid in Manhattan today. You have to be trilingual. You have personal trainers and learn self-defense before you've begun kindergarten. And learn language skills before you can speak, and attend dance movement classes before you can stand up. You have to be able to dance, eat, swim, and speak Japanese while talking to your nanny in Spanish and your mother in English. And learn interview interaction techniques in order to get into preschool."

"Why do they learn interview interaction techniques to get into preschool?" Ruth asked.

"In order to get into the right preschool," Sonia said. "But that's not the point. The point is why are you so manipulative?"

"I'm not manipulative," Ruth said. She didn't think she was manipulative. She was just trying to run a business. And keep her father happy. At the same time.

Yesterday, after work, Edek had become very excited. "Look at that woman," he had said, pointing to a suntanned, shiny-skinned, large-busted, spike-haired, late middle-aged blonde who was walking on West Broadway. "Doesn't she look like Zofia?" Edek had exclaimed. "Not as nice as what Zofia looks but she does look very much like Zofia." Ruth and Edek had met Zofia and her friend Walentyna at the Mimoza Hotel in Kraków a year ago. It was Edek's first time in Poland in over fifty years. It was his first time in Poland since he'd been imprisoned in Auschwitz. He'd last seen his home, in Łódź, when he was twenty-three.

Edek had never expressed an interest in accompanying Ruth on one of the excessive number of previous trips she had made to Poland. He'd been bewildered by why she kept going there.

Ruth's first trip to Poland had been the first time she had seen where her parents came from. The first time she'd seen the huge apartment blocks and the small palace her father's parents owned. It was the first time she'd stood in the small courtyard her mother had studied in. Rooshka had dreamt of being a pediatrician in that courtyard. Ruth had traced and retraced the routes her mother had walked to school and back. She'd stood on the balcony of the apartment her father had grown up in. The balcony from which her father's father watched his youngest son, to make sure he was wearing his yarmulke, when he came home from school. Edek told Ruth that he always put his yarmulke on just before he turned the corner into Zakatna Street. Ruth had stood on that corner. Weeping. She had wanted to buy the grand piano, which was still in the apartment, and the sofas and the armchairs. And the bed. It was all still there.

Then quite unexpectedly over a year ago Edek had said to Ruth that he would go to Poland with her. Ruth hadn't left Edek's side, in Poland. She didn't want him to spend one second alone in Poland. She didn't want him to feel alone.

Edek and Ruth had been having breakfast in Kraków in the dining room of the Mimoza Hotel, where they were staying, when Ruth noticed Zofia and Walentyna looking at them. Ruth nodded hello to the two women. Edek looked up and smiled at them. Both women beamed back. From then on, it seemed to Ruth, Zofia and Walentyna were everywhere she and Edek went. Well, at least, everywhere in the hotel. They saw them in the elevator, on the stairs, at the reception desk, in the dining room, and in the lobby.

At the end of Edek and Ruth's second day at the Mimoza, Zofia came up to them and introduced herself, and Walentyna. Zofia addressed all her conversation to Edek. "You and your daughter must have a drink with us," she said. "You both look like very interesting people. Or maybe you and your daughter would like to come for a walk through Kraków tonight?" she said, again to Edek. "Me and Walentyna, we are from Sopot, and we have been already a few days in Kraków so we know where are nice walks in Kraków."

Edek, who was not partial to a lot of walking, unless it was with the aim of returning having eaten or purchased some food, nodded and looked at Ruth.

"We'd love to," Ruth said. "But we have a few things to do tonight, so we won't be able to join you."

"What is it what we have to do?" Edek said to Ruth.

"We have to discuss our trip to Auschwitz," Ruth said.

"We did already discuss it," Edek said.

The word *Auschwitz* silenced the two Polish women. "It is a terrible place to go," Walentyna, who was the quieter of the two, said.

"My father knows that," Ruth said.

"Maybe you would join us tomorrow?" Zofia said.

Before Edek could answer, Ruth had said, "That sounds quite possible," and taken her father's arm. "Good night," she added as she and Edek left.

"Good night," Edek called out, hurriedly, looking a bit perturbed.

"They do seem two very nice women," Edek said to Ruth.

"They're probably okay," Ruth answered, and changed the subject.

Ruth now looked at the woman Edek was pointing at, on West Broadway. She could see a slight resemblance to Zofia. Slight. This woman was much more delicate. Zofia had a more solid appearance. Zofia wasn't fat. Just solid. Very solid. She looked sturdy and robust. Zofia had very large breasts. Her breasts looked willful. Her handshake was very firm. As firm as her demeanor. The woman on West Broadway was wearing a short, tight skirt. Zofia seemed to wear only very short, very tight skirts and plunging necklines. Necklines that, from one day to the next, appeared to be plummeting dangerously. Each one lower than its predecessor.

"Why are you thinking about Zofia?" Ruth asked Edek.

"I am not thinking about Zofia," Edek replied. "I did just see a woman who did remind me of Zofia, that is all."

Ruth didn't like Zofia. She found her too pushy. Too presumptuous, too audacious. She found Zofia too everything. Ruth quite liked Zofia's friend, Walentyna, who had also had her eye on Edek but had stood no chance next to the louder, more forthright, and well-muscled Zofia, who swam in the sea in Sopot, where she lived, every morning. Summer and winter.

Ruth had thought that both women were too young for Edek, anyway. They seemed to be in their mid-sixties. And Edek was in his early eighties. Ruth had unexpectedly discovered, on her and Edek's next-to-last day in Kraków, that Zofia and Edek had had a brief liaison. Well, had slept together. Probably more than once.

"I like your father very much," Zofia said to Ruth just before Ruth and Edek left Kraków. "I think I am the woman for him."

Ruth had tried to point out to Zofia that she hardly knew Edek.

But Zofia had insistently insisted that she did. "A woman knows when a man is the man for her," Zofia said.

"My dear, dear Edek," Zofia said to Edek as Ruth and Edek were getting into the cab for the airport, "I will call you every day until you come to Sopot."

Edek laughed. Zofia stood in the street and blew kisses to Edek, until Ruth and Edek were out of sight.

Ruth reached the Sanger Building. Her office was on the tenth floor. In the elevator Ruth thought about the line of greeting cards she had started. She thought that the cards would suit a more intense consumer than the reasonably bland cards that were available now. And she thought they could be a more stable form of income in economically or politically tougher times. Her card, "Don't Be So Hard on Yourself," was already doing well. Inside the card was: "The only people who are not making mistakes are those who reside in an urn or a plot." Ruth had worried that the mention of death, however oblique, might put people off. But it hadn't. The card was selling well, as were quite a few of her other cards.

Ruth walked into the office. Her father was already there. He looked happy to see her. "My daughter is here," he announced, beaming. Ruth felt bad for feeling irritated and agitated by her father. He didn't deserve it. He was a sweet man. He wasn't doing anything wrong. He wasn't harming anyone.

Edek came into Ruth's office later that morning. "You want some lunch?" he said.

"No thanks, Dad," she said. "I haven't even had a cup of tea."

"I do know this," he said. "You did not yet come out of your office."

"Well, I've only been here for two and a quarter hours," she said.

Edek looked at her desk. "You got a lot of letters to write?"

Ruth stopped working. She'd forgotten what she was writing, anyway. She tried to distract her father. She suggested he learn the answers to the one hundred most commonly asked questions in the interviews that were conducted by the Immigration and Naturalization Service of the Department of Justice as part of the process of acquiring American citizenship. There were questions like, Who was the first president of the United States? Who is the president of the United States today? How many stars are there on our flag? What color are the stars on our flag? What is the date of Independence Day? Independence from whom? Who wrote "The Star-Spangled Banner"? How many changes or amendments are there to the Constitution? Who said, "Give me liberty or give me death"? What is the capital of your state?

There were a lot of questions. Ruth thought learning the answer to Why are there one hundred senators in the Senate? or Who was the main writer of the Declaration of Independence? and What is the name of the ship that brought the Pilgrims to America? would be a stretch for Edek, and keep him occupied for a quite a while. "Why should I know what are the answers to such questions?" Edek said. "You think I am going to remember such facts like this for a long time? A woman did tell me that you do need to be living in America for five years before you can put in the application papers to be a citizen. I am eighty-seven. You think I am going to remember the answers to such questions for five years? I will probably be dead in five years. Or one year. Or less."

Ruth gave up. "Okay, Dad," she said, and picked up her work, again.

"You want some lunch?" Edek said.

"Not yet, thanks, Dad," she said.

Ruth was grappling with a letter she didn't want to write when Edek walked back into her office. It was midafternoon and she'd already spent too much time writing this letter. She kept on working. Edek didn't say anything. He just stood and peered over her shoulder. She ignored him. She was writing a letter for a wealthy widow who liked to write directly to whoever was responsible for peeving her. In this case it was a car repair service that she felt had overcharged her for replacing the rear-vision mirror of her car. Ruth thought that the letter would probably cost her client more than the car repair.

"You are using too many words," Edek said to her, after a few minutes.

"What?" she said.

"You did write, 'The mechanic, whoever he or she was, should have,' " Edek said.

"Why is that too many words?" Ruth said.

"Can't you see?" her father replied.

"No," she said. She was tired. She didn't want this conversation. She wished Garth was in New York and she could call him and ask him to ask her father to help him in the studio. She had tried to call Garth several times in the last day or two but she hadn't managed to get through to him. And he wasn't calling her. Well, he wasn't calling her often enough. She felt a small surge of resentment at Garth for leaving her. She knew she had to stop this line of thought. She knew she had to pull herself together. Garth hadn't left her. They were still married. Still in love. He was just in Australia. A million miles away.

"You do not need to use 'or she,' " Edek said triumphantly. "When did you see a woman what is a mechanic?"

Ruth tried to explain that it was sexist to assume that a mechanic wouldn't be female. And that sexism was discrimination.

"It is not a discrimination," Edek said. "It is a fact."

"It is sexist language," Ruth said. "Like using the word *cook* for women, and the word *chef* for men."

"That is crazy," Edek said. "A chef is a man what works in a restaurant and a cook is a woman what cooks." Ruth sighed. "A chef can be a woman off coss," Edek said. Not only was she tired, she had a headache. She hadn't slept well. She was missing Garth. "Did I say that a chef cannot be a woman?" Edek said.

"You didn't say it," Ruth said, "but you implied it. It's like saying lady doctor, or woman judge or male nurse. You are implying something other than what you are saying."

"What?" Edek said. Ruth tried to explain it to her father. "It is a madness," he said, when she finished her explanation.

"It's not a madness," she said wearily. "A madness is a mental illness. This is a choice."

"This is a choice what is a madness," Edek said with glee.

"No, it's not," Ruth answered. Ruth heard herself. She sounded like a six-year-old. Why was she arguing with her father about nonsexist word usage?

"What is wrong with you, Ruthie?" Edek said. "You was never in such a bad mood with me when I did live in Australia. I think that you do work too hard. It is not so good to work too hard."

"I don't work too hard and I like my work," she said. She heard the irritability in her voice. And she felt bad. Her father was so easy to please, in so many ways. And he hadn't had an easy life. And she had. Well, compared to him.

Ruth thought that children of Holocaust survivors, particularly children of death camp survivors, probably found it almost impossible not to compare any distress they experienced with the distress their parents had experienced. And the parents' experience was, inevitably, worse. It would be hard to have experiences worse than most Jews in Nazi-occupied Europe had had. Everything had been an issue of life and death. Children of survivors couldn't compete with that. Ruth noticed that she often compared her ordinary, everyday trials and tribulations, and her more serious trials and tribulations, to the matter of life and death.

When she developed high blood pressure, she noticed that when she mentioned the different side effects of the medications she'd had to take before the right medication was found, she often added, "It's not a matter of life or death, of course." If she lost something, or missed a good business opportunity or had a disagreement with Garth, she would say, "I know it's not life and death," almost as though in order to get anything in perspective it had to be seen against a backdrop of life and death. They had had a fire, eight or nine years ago, in their SoHo loft. No one had been in the loft when the fire had started. When a neighbor had called Ruth on her cell phone and told her the news, the first thing Ruth said was, "It's not life and death."

When Ruth and Garth saw how much had been destroyed, Ruth said, "It's not life and death." Pale, and visibly shaking, she said, "It's not life and death." When they were sorting through the debris, the burnt remnants of decades of Garth's paintings, decades of the diaries she'd written, decades of photographs of her parents and her children, and wondering where she and Garth were going to live, Ruth said, "It's not a matter of life and death." For the year it took to rebuild the loft, she said, "It's not a matter of life and death," so many times, she startled herself. And Zelda, who was in college at the time, asked her not to say it again. "We all know that, Roo," Zelda had said.

Ruth didn't know why all three kids called her Roo. She'd never been called Mom, Mama, or Mother. Well, not by anyone she was related to.

"Do they feel you're not their mother?" a parent at one of the schools the kids had attended had said to her.

"They may well sometimes wish I wasn't but they do know that I am their mother," Ruth had replied.

"I didn't mean anything offensive," the woman had said.

Ruth thought it was relatively unlikely that the woman had intended the question to be a compliment. It was surprising how often people let you know exactly what their intentions were. When someone said, I don't mean to hurt you, offend you, worry you, be cruel, be unkind, be rude, you could almost count on the fact that they very shortly would. Just as you could reasonably predict that the person who said, "I'm a very honest person," may well turn out to be dishonest, or "I'm a very open person," may well be the most closed and impenetrable of human beings. Most people in a conversation directed at them, which included the phrase, hurt you, offend you, or worry you, left that conversation hurt, offended, or worried. The speaker's intention was as clear as it was successful.

Whatever her intentions may have been, Ruth felt upset whenever she upset her father. He was doing well in life. He was eighty-seven. He lived on his own. Most of his good friends had turned out to be not such good friends. Or had died. He missed Rooshka. A lot. He often wept when he mentioned her. So did Ruth. She didn't think she would ever recover from her mother's death. It was probably impossible to recover from a death, anyway.

In America there was a lot of talk about grief and loss as though they were neat, trim, fixed entities. Able to be titled, quantified, and categorized. Entities that could have beginnings and endings. Beginnings and endings that were clearly delineated and articulated. On television or radio news programs, documentaries or dramas, or even in movies you could hear declarations about being in the grieving process, followed by declarations about the period of mourning being over, the process of healing beginning, and the seeking of closure. The statements could be referring to the country, the city, the radio or television station, or an individual and their partner, colleagues, or family. People always seemed to know which stage of which process they were at. Ruth had spent so much of her life struggling to understand much smaller aspects of grief and loss. She knew she would never be able to isolate what stage she was at about anything more complex than shopping at the supermarket. Ruth seemed to spend a lot of time thinking about issues that were insoluble. She thought that that was either an inherent part of spending years in analysis, or simply being a human being. Or both.

Ruth, now, also spent a lot of time thinking about errands, tasks, transactions, enterprises, and undertakings that would occupy Edek. But the errands and tasks didn't always succeed in making Edek feel useful. Or happy. Edek looked crestfallen when things went wrong. When he got lost or brought back the wrong item. And he looked bored and listless when he had nothing to do. Several times he said he should have stayed in Australia. And not immigrated to a new country such a short time before he was going to die. Edek was not on the verge of death. He wasn't even ill. He just talked about dying a lot. He had since Ruth was a very young child. "Soon I will be in the ground," he would say. In conversation about the planning of any event more than a week away, Edek would add, "If I am still alive." He said this when he was thirty-five, forty-five, fifty-five, sixty-five, seventy-five, eighty-five. Death was always on his mind. And that was understandable when you'd spent six years of your life surrounded and immersed and drenched in death.

Edek and Rooshka were always surrounded by the dead. And Rooshka and Edek had hundreds of dead. And only themselves left living. And then Ruth. Ruth had understood what an inadequate replacement she'd been for Edek's and Rooshka's mothers and fathers and brothers and sisters and nephews and nieces and cousins, aunts and uncles. She'd understood that, from the very beginning. She'd had a palpable sense of the missing. A tangible sense of the absence. And the permanence of the absence.

She'd been born so soon after all the murder, all the horror, all the mayhem. She had escaped the murder. But she hadn't quite escaped unscathed. She hadn't escaped the horror, the chaos, the mayhem, the fear, or the terror. They had remained in Rooshka and Edek and had been transmitted to Ruth, from the time she was born. She hadn't escaped the grief and the disbelief. They, too, had become part of her present. A permanent part. And they had leached from her to her children. Diluted and more muted. But present.

Two

Ruth arrived at the Second Avenue Deli where she was meeting Edek. The restaurant had such a distinct New York Jewish deli aroma. Dill pickles mingling with chicken soup and pastrami. Ruth decided to have a cup of chamomile tea. The Second Avenue Deli didn't serve chamomile tea, so Ruth had brought her own teabag and ordered a cup of hot water. Chamomile tea calmed her digestive system. She'd eaten at the Second Avenue Deli with Edek last week and hadn't felt quite well since. She and Edek had been having dinner there two or three times a week. Just the two of them. They seemed to be eating there less frequently now. Edek appeared to have things to take care of some nights after work. And Ruth had been glad of the break. Edek had missed a few days of work in the last two or three weeks, too. Those days had been so peaceful. Ruth thought that Edek had probably needed a break. Long hours in an office was tiring for anyone.

Edek loved the Second Avenue Deli. He loved the chopped liver, the chicken soup, the matzoh balls, the brisket. He loved everything on the menu. The food didn't agree with Ruth. Or she didn't agree with the food. Either way the result was uncomfortable. But Edek only wanted to eat at the Second Avenue Deli. He didn't want to eat any- where else. And it was easy for him to get to, he kept pointing out. His apartment was across the street. Everything at the Second Avenue Deli was nearly perfect, according to Edek. There was a slight exception, the gefilte fish. "The Second Avenue Deli does not have such good gefilte fish what Mum used to make," Edek had said. He'd looked miserable at the thought of Rooshka and her gefilte fish. Edek had fallen in love with Rooshka when Rooshka was thirteen. He'd adored her and he saw her as a beautiful young girl, until the day she died. He'd been dis- traught after her death. For years.

"We should go to Russ and Daughters," Edek said suddenly one night as they were leaving the office. "It is the only place what does make gefilte fish nearly like Mum's." Ruth was surprised to hear that Edek wanted to eat somewhere else.

"What about the Carnegie Deli?" Ruth suggested.

"It's not so good what Russ and Daughters is," Edek said.

"But we can't eat at Russ and Daughters," Ruth said. "There are no tables or chairs."

"We can buy the fish at Russ and Daughters and eat at my place," Edek said. "Or your place. We do pay three thousand dollars a month, what is one hundred dollars a day so that I can have somewhere to sleep and I can sit at my own table. If you did rent the loft you would get a minimum of seven thousand dollars a month."

Ruth wondered when Edek had become a real estate rental expert. His figures were more or less accurate. It wasn't hard in New York City to be knowledgeable about the price of apartment rentals. It was a subject al- most everyone was interested in. Many Manhattanites could tell you the rental price of a one-bedroom or two-bedroom apartment. Far fewer would be able to gauge the rental value of a loft. There were fewer lofts than apartments for a start, and individual lofts had many more variables than apartments and couldn't easily be compared with each other.

"For ten thousand dollars a month, we do still need to find a table and a chair in a restaurant to eat a piece of gefilte fish. It is a madness," Edek said.

Ruth didn't want to eat in the loft with Edek with Garth away. She thought she'd feel lonelier eating in the loft with Edek than she felt when she was eating there alone. And that felt lonely enough. The thought of them eating alone in Edek's apartment seemed even bleaker. She wasn't sure why. It was a perfectly nice apartment, quite spacious for New York. There was something reassuring about including the rest of the world in the dinners. The life force that restaurants contained. The waiters, the busboys, the conversations, the interactions. Ruth thought that maybe she needed to include the outside world whenever she was alone with Edek. As though things could become forlorn, bleak, and without hope very quickly. And without warning, with just the two of them.

"It is a madness," Ruth said to Edek. But Edek dropped the subject. And they continued to eat at the Second Avenue Deli.

Ruth began to take her own food and a plastic fork to the Second Avenue Deli. She took steamed vegetables in a plastic leakproof food storage bag. She balanced the plastic bag on her lap and would, surreptitiously, eat from the bag when the waiters were not looking. To deflect attention away from the food in her lap, Ruth would order a bowl of chicken soup. It was not easy to put a fork into a plastic storage bag and remove a piece of whatever vegetable was in there, and then relocate it to your mouth. Particularly without attracting attention. Bits of broccoli, fennel, celery, and an occasional Brussels sprout fell into her lap. She stabbed herself now and then with a misaimed fork, and noticed small bruises appearing on the top of her thighs.

"Why don't you eat what normal people does eat?" Edek said to her, repeatedly. "Have some chopped liver. It is a very good chopped liver."

"Normal people eat steamed vegetables and fish," Ruth said.

"You do not eat fish here," Edek replied. "You do only eat such vegetables."

"I can't put steamed fish into a plastic food storage bag," Ruth said.

"Then eat some fried fish," Edek answered. "They got very good fried fish."

"I don't like fried fish," Ruth said. "I like poached fish, steamed fish, and grilled fish—"

Edek interrupted Ruth. "You are afraid you will again be a fatty, Ruthie," he said. "That is the truth."

"No, I'm not," Ruth said. But she knew Edek was right. Even after years of analysis, on two continents, she could still think that four extra mouthfuls of anything calorific could metamorphose and reappear as triple-sized hips. And she still couldn't gauge what size she was. She could look in the mirror, something she tried, on the whole, to avoid, and decide she was twice the size she'd been earlier in the week. Or, on infrequent occasions, decide she was a little thinner. There was no rhyme or reason for those decisions, as there weren't for many things that were emotionally freighted and distorted. At least now, she didn't panic for too long. She just tried on her red coat. Her red coat was a narrow-cut coat that fitted her, just.

Ruth didn't weigh herself. She didn't like weighing herself. Jumping on and off scales was not for her. The anxiety and apprehension she experienced beforehand and the preparations she made were not worth it. She used to weigh herself in the mornings. Naked. She would make sure that she got rid of anything that could weigh her down. Anything that would add to her weight. She emptied everything it was possible to empty. She emptied her bowels, her bladder, her lungs. Weighing herself was time-consuming as well. She couldn't just weigh herself once per morning. She weighed herself numerous times in an effort to achieve the lowest possible weight. First she stood on the front of the scales, then the back section, and then both on the right and left sides. She also stood on her toes, and with her feet flat. The reading usually remained consistent.

Last week Edek had announced that he had lost four pounds since moving to New York. Edek had sounded very pleased with himself. Ruth wasn't sure how Edek had managed to lose the four pounds. She decided that it was the extra walking he'd been doing getting lunch. She had been surprised to hear about Edek's weight loss. She didn't know he thought about his weight. She didn't even know that he weighed himself. Edek had never mentioned his weight before.

Ruth was twirling her hair around her finger at a table at the back of the Second Avenue Deli. She hadn't twirled her hair around her finger for years. She realized that something was bothering her. Something about her father's behavior in the last few days was bothering her. In the last week, he'd come into the office less frequently. He had also sometimes arrived late. And left early. He said he was busy. Busy doing what, she'd asked him, several times. But his replies had revealed nothing. "I am busy," he said. Questioned further, he stuck to his guns. He was busy. "I am busy," he said. "Busy, busy, busy. What more do I have to explain?" Busy, busy, busy? Who did Edek think he was, Rupert Murdoch?

Ruth didn't know why she was so bothered by it. Hadn't she spent months wishing Edek had something to do? Something more than coming into the office all day, every day? Hadn't she wished he had a hobby or an interest or a companion? She shouldn't be bothered. She should be pleased. But she was bothered.

Ruth's cell phone rang. It was Zelda. She was pleased to hear from Zelda.

"Can you speak, Roo?" Zelda asked.

"Yes," Ruth said. "I'm waiting for Grandpa at the Second Avenue Deli."

"Not the Second Avenue Deli, again," Zelda said. "Even I'd be sick of it by now and I really like their food. Is Grandpa late?"

"Just a bit," Ruth said.

"Grandpa is never late," Zelda said, in a surprised tone. "He gets so agitated at the thought of being late. More agitated than you do."

"I know," Ruth said. "My need to be on time is much more moderate."

"It's not your need to be on time, Roo." Zelda said. "It's your need to be early. You get everywhere early. That's why we spent ten hours waiting at airports before we could board flights, when we were kids. You lied to Garth about the departure time of every flight. It took him years to catch on, and then he thought it was funny."

"Okay, Zelda, can we talk about something else? Anyway, I'm much better now."

"Not much," Zelda said. "You often call me, bored, at some airport or other. It's the only time I ever hear you bored."

Why were her children so argumentative? Both Zelda and Zachary would pursue any argument until their opponent caved in, usually from exhaustion. Kate wasn't like that. She would drop the subject after a minute or two. She didn't go into combat mode, like the other two. Kate was more like Garth, in that way. And she was Garth's biological child. Not Ruth's. Kate didn't need to win every point in every argument. Something Garth had suggested, more than once over the years, was a trait that Ruth possessed. Ruth always had the same answer. "It's just Jewish," she said. And it was. Jews always had one more point to add to any discussion, no matter how lengthy it had already been.

"What could be wrong with Grandpa?" Zelda said.

"Nothing's wrong, Zelda," Ruth said. "He's eighty-seven. He's probably becoming a bit more casual, or mellow." She didn't want Zelda to worry. She was a bit concerned about Edek being late, herself, but after years of panicking at every opportunity, Ruth was now trying to contain her concern.

"Grandpa more casual?" Zelda said. "I met him for lunch last Saturday at one P.M., the time we'd agreed to meet. I actually got there five minutes early. Grandpa was outside the restaurant, leaving me his fourth phone message in ten minutes. I got them all when I got off the subway. Each one said, 'Zelda, I just want to know where you are. It is Grandpa.' "

Ruth laughed. "As though you know hundreds of elderly Jewish men with thick, Polish, Yiddish, Australian accents who leave you multiple phone messages," she said. "I'll call him when we hang up." Ruth decided not to feel worried or bothered by Edek. He did seem happier and less agitated. Maybe he was settling into his life in New York. Maybe he was feeling fewer of the hiccups of relocation. And dislocation.

"I just called to say hello," Zelda said. "I've had such a stressful week. I had to go to the dentist, twice. Then I discovered that Lancelot has developed diabetes."

"Cats can get diabetes?" Ruth said.

"Yes," said Zelda, "and now I have to give him injections every day." She paused. "I know you don't like cats, and you don't think I should have one in my small apartment," she said.

"Zelda, let's not have that discussion now," Ruth said. "Or again. I'm not crazy about cats but it's your life and you can have ten cats if you want to." Zelda, who worked in publishing, had always been crazy about cats. And dogs.

"Okay," Zelda said. "Anyway, it's been an awful week. Really awful. A television producer yelled at me in front of one of my authors. And I hadn't done anything wrong."

Why did her children think she was the person to call in order to voice what had gone wrong? Possibly all children saw mothers as a repository for complaints. It wasn't that Ruth didn't want to hear any complaints. A couple of complaints were okay, but she wanted to hear other news. Anything that wasn't a complaint. She thought she had a five-minute threshold for listening to complaints. After that her head began to hurt. "Zelda love, I have to go. Grandpa's going to be here any second," Ruth said.

As soon as she hung up, her cell phone rang again. She thought it was Zelda, although the caller ID said "number unavailable." Zelda had a habit of ringing back with a small coda to a conversation.

"Hello, baby," Garth said. Ruth's spirits rose. She was so happy hear from Garth. She'd really missed him. She'd known she would. She hadn't looked forward to his trip to Australia. But she knew it was in her own interest to be able to tolerate Garth being away. Ruth had had a lot of trouble separating from Garth. She had trouble separating from anyone she loved.

"Hello, sweetheart," Ruth said to Garth. "I'm so happy to hear your voice. How are you?"

"I'm fine, my love," Garth said. Garth called her my love, my girl, Mrs. Kisses, my beautiful bride. He called her by these names all the time. He had for over twenty-five years. He also called her his prize. "You're sure it wasn't a booby prize?" she'd said to him numerous times. She didn't feel like anyone's prize. She felt much more like a burden.

"I've missed you," Garth said. "I've felt quite lonely without you."

Ruth felt buoyed. "I'm so pleased you miss me and feel lonely," Ruth said. "That makes me happy." She was happy and surprised that Garth had been feeling lonely without her. He was an unusually self-sufficient and self-contained person. He was gregarious and very charming, but he didn't seem to miss or need people very much.

"I've been really lonely," Ruth said. "I don't like being away from you at all. I don't like sleeping on my own. I don't like having breakfast on my own. And there's more," she added. "I don't like taking the garbage out, and I get a bit scared at night. I miss you. I even miss you at work. I know I can't pick up the phone and call you and tell you that I'm tired or I've got a headache. I can't tell you whether I've had a good shit or not in the morning. I can't just call you and tell you lots of things," she said.

Garth laughed. "How is your father?" he said.

Ruth took a deep breath. "My father is driving me nuts," she said. "I'm actually at the Second Avenue Deli waiting for him."

"Waiting for Edek?" Garth said. "Edek is never late."

"Well, he's fifteen minutes late now," Ruth said. "I feel a bit worried about him."

"I'm sure he's fine," Garth said.

"Well, he's seriously driving me nuts," Ruth said. "He criticizes everything I eat. He's buying enough office supplies to be able to run IBM. We don't need half the stuff he buys. I need a break from him. He interrupts me all the time. He's got a better suggestion for everything I do, and the way I do it. He chats to Max too much. She adores him. Everyone adores him."

It was true, everyone adored Edek. The doorman in the Sanger Building, the people who ran the local deli, Velma, who cleaned the loft and Edek's apartment once a week, the man in the news kiosk near the office, and the man who served hot dogs from the stand not too far from the kiosk. Everyone adored Edek. Zelda, Zachary, and Kate adored him. Garth adored him. Ruth had no one to complain to about Edek. If she even looked irritated by him, Zelda or Kate would say, "Grandpa is wonderful." She couldn't disagree. She thought he was wonderful, too. But he was also dementing. And irritatingly omnipresent. And annoyingly observant.

"Your father is really fabulous. He's amazing for his age," Garth said.

"I know," Ruth said. "I feel bad complaining about him." Why was she saying she felt bad about complaining? Why was she even entertaining the notion of feeling bad about complaining about anything? She'd just listed a long list of complaints. One after the other. No wonder Zelda felt comfortable calling Ruth with her complaints. Ruth was clearly the Queen of Planet Complaint.

"How are you feeling, sweetheart?" she said to Garth. "I've gone on and on about me."

"I'm fine," Garth said. "The landscape is beautiful. It's endlessly various. It has arid, dry deserts and tropical rain forests and the most stunning sculptured coastlines, and one beautiful beach after the other. There's something profound and profoundly moving about it to me."

Ruth couldn't understand Garth's attachment to landscape. Her own attachments seemed to be limited to human beings. And chocolate.

"When I think of the Australian landscape," Ruth said, "I think of being seated in the front cabin of an old truck, with my father sitting outside on the flat tray of the truck, which had no sides, and my mother next to me, in the cabin, in a state of near hysteria about the possibility of my father falling off. We were on our way to our first holiday in Australia. We were going to Chaskel Roller's guesthouse in Hepburn Springs. I was eight. I was so thrilled. It was thrilling to be going somewhere."

"I think you might like it here," Garth said. "Well, you'd like the river. You do like rivers."

"That's true," Ruth said. "If they're not too far from a hospital, a police station, and a supermarket."

Garth laughed. "Sweetheart, I think I'll say goodbye now. I know you'll want to speak to your dad." Ruth looked at her watch. They'd been talking for almost ten minutes. That was pretty good for Garth. He really hated talking on the phone.

"I'll talk to you very soon," Garth said.

"When?" she said. "I mean approximately when, I don't mean exactly when."

"I can't say," said Garth. "It's not always easy for me to get to the phone."

"Can't you just tell me roughly when you think you'll be able to call?" Ruth said. "Do you think you'll call tomorrow? Next week? Next month? Next millennium?"

"Don't make me feel bad," Garth said.

"I'm sorry," said Ruth. "Now I feel bad for making you feel bad."

Seconds after she hung up, her cell phone rang. Ruth could see it was her father.

"Dad, where are you?" she said. "I've been worried. You're never late."

"Oy, Ruthie, I am very sorry. I did know you would be worried, but I was in the subway and it was not possible to ring you."

"Where are you now?" Ruth asked.

"At home," Edek replied.

"At home?" Ruth said. "I'm at the Second Avenue Deli waiting for you. Why didn't you come here?"

"I was carrying some things which I did need to put in my apartment," Edek said.

"Okay," Ruth said. "How long will it take you to get here?"

"Ruthie darling, I did call you to tell you that I cannot come tonight to the Second Avenue Deli," said Edek.

"You can't come?" Ruth said. "Why not?"

"I got things to do," Edek said.

"Things to do?" Ruth said. "What sort of things?" she said.

"Just normal things," Edek answered.

"But what sort of normal things?" Ruth said, feeling agitated.

"Just normal things," her father said. "Normal things what normal people does do."

"Well, just tell me what one of those things is?" Ruth said.

"Ruthie," Edek said, now sounding annoyed, "this is normal. It is normal to be busy. I am busy. Like you are busy. I am busy. I am busy doing things what is normal for people what are busy."

What was her father doing? Was something wrong? Was he missing Australia? He didn't seem depressed. Or even mildly depressed. He was keeping up with his exercise. She'd asked him if he was sticking to his exercise routine a few days ago. Exercise, apart from its other beneficial effects, lifted your spirits. Ruth knew that. She didn't know where her spirits would be if she didn't exercise. Possibly in Antarctica. She had hired a personal trainer to work out with her father for an hour, three times a week, at a gym on Second Avenue, close to his apartment. Edek had had a personal trainer, in Australia, for over three years.

"Off coss I am doing the exercise," Edek said. "It is killing me."

"You're walking briskly on the treadmill?" she'd said.

"Off coss," he'd said.

"And you're doing the weight lifting?" Ruth had said.

"Off coss, off coss," Edek had said. "Off coss I am doing the weight lifting. That is why I am half dead every day. I do have to lift up such things with my arms and with my legs. I do have to push things and pull things what is not natural to push and to pull. The young man does make me do everything. And why do I do this? Because my daughter does want me to."

Ruth was used to these complaints. Edek used to voice them regularly from Australia. Ruth saw that her cell phone battery was low. "Do you want to come over to the Second Avenue Deli, just to have something quick?" she said to Edek.

"I got things to do, Ruthie, don't you understand?"

"What sort of things?" she said.

"Things what all people got to do," Edek said.

"You could have some latkes," Ruth said. "And you love their latkes."

"The latkes are not so good," Edek said. "I did have a bad stomach after these latkes the last time. And don't tell me again that I did eat too many."

Ruth was alarmed. Edek could usually be counted on to have double if not more servings of latkes, the potato pancakes he adored. Maybe there was something wrong with him?

"Is there anything wrong, Dad?" she said.

"As a matter of fact there is something wrong," Edek said. Ruth's heart sank. She felt sick.

"What is it?" she said.

"I do not want to bother you with those things," Edek said. "You are too busy with too much stress as it is."

"Please tell me what's wrong," Ruth said. "I need to know."

"I did not want to bother you," Edek said.

Ruth's heart began pounding. "Tell me now, Dad," she said.

"Okay, okay," Edek said. "It is not something you should worry about."

"Just tell me, Dad, please," Ruth pleaded. Her heart was racing. She felt quite bilious.

"Okay, okay, I will tell you," Edek said. "When I do press one key, such a very small key what is next to the key what you do press to make a space—"

Ruth interrupted him. "Is this a computer problem?" she said.

"Off coss," Edek said.

"What a relief, I thought there was something wrong with you," she said.

"Ruthie, there is nothing wrong with my heltz," Edek said. "I am very heltzy."

"Thank God," Ruth said. "I felt quite frightened."

"Ruthie, I have to go one day," Edek said. "It is a fact of life."

Ruth's whole body was limp with relief. "Tell me the problem, Dad," she said.

"Okay," Edek said. "As I did explain to you, when I do press this very small key what is next to the key what makes a space, I have big trouble."

Ruth tried to envisage what was next to the space bar, on her father's computer, or maybe on everyone's computer.

"That's the ALT key, I think," Ruth said.

"Alt?" Edek said. "Like *alte kacke*."

"Yes," Ruth said, "but shorter."

"When I do press this *alte* key, it goes highway," Edek said, with frustration. Ruth decided not to dwell on deciphering what a highway had to do with the problem.

"Why do you press the ALT key?" Ruth asked Edek.

"If I did know I was pressing this *alte* key, it would not go highway," Edek said.

"Go highway?" Ruth said.

"Go highway," Edek replied.

"Which way?" Ruth said.

"What do you mean which way?" Edek said. "Everyway. It does happen because I do press this small button by accident. And then it goes highway. I do lose everything what I am doing on the computer."

"Everything goes highway," Ruth said. She thought about it for a moment. Then it dawned on her. "Everything goes haywire?" she said.

"Everything," said Edek. "Everything goes highway."

"Okay," Ruth said. "I'll find out what we can do about that." She was not at all sure that anything could be done about it.

"Thank you very much, Ruthie," Edek said.

"When am I going to see you?" Ruth said.

"I will be at the office tomorrow," Edek said, "and I can have a cup of coffee with you. You still got some of those Wedel's chocolate?" Wedel's chocolate was made in Poland. It was hard to get in New York. Ruth bought some whenever she saw it. Her father had told her about Wedel's chocolate and Polish ham, from the time she was small. Polish ham was the best ham in the world, according to Edek, and Wedel's chocolate was out of this world. Ruth had recently heard that Wedel's had gone out of business. She thought that that couldn't possibly be true. Wedel's had been around forever. They were part of Edek's youth. The good part.

"I've still got two packets of Wedel's chocolate wafers," Ruth said.

"Okay, then maybe I will have a wafer with my coffee," Edek said. The thought of Edek having a Wedel's wafer with his coffee reassured her. There couldn't be all that much wrong with Edek if he was still making inquiries about Wedel's chocolate wafers.

Three

Ruth picked up the file on her desk. It was labeled Direct Text Paper Samples. Direct Text was the name Ruth had given her greeting-card company. Direct Text cards used no graphics. Ruth used plain, colored paper for her cards. She chose paper in different colors, in different sizes and with different textures. The cards were all color and dimension. There was nothing to distract from the text. No patterns, no drawings, no ribbons, no cutouts. She wanted the color, dimension, and texture of the paper to enhance and highlight the text. And she wanted the text to be meaningful. So much of life's text wasn't. So much of what people said to each other was insignificant.

It was surprisingly hard to say what you really felt. For everyone. That was probably why Rothwax Correspondence had done well. People wanted to communicate what they felt. People wanted to connect. The connections in greeting cards on the whole, were vapid, sanitized, and clichéd. As though they had all been processed through some emotion-exterminating detergent. The sympathy cards were so muted they could be expressing sympathy over a stain on the sofa. Birthday cards, under the guise of being humorous, were cruel, demoralizing, demeaning, and insulting. The cards for women were all to do with wrinkles and sagging breasts and a suggestion of gratitude for still hanging on. The women, not the breasts. For men, the cards concentrated on beer guts, tooth loss, and hair loss.

The cover of the birthday card Ruth had just done said:

Cash In on Your Assets

Inside the card was:

Achievement, intelligence, and maturity are at a premium.
Happy Birthday

Ruth was hoping that this card would appeal to a broad age range. She was marketing it in four different colors. Choosing the papers and the colors was the fun part of the job. Ruth had loved paper all her life. Every day after school she used to stop outside a cardboard factory in Nicholson Street, Carlton, in Melbourne, and watch the cardboard and the offcuts being bundled and stacked. She loved the sound of the cardboard being cut and the smell.

She had chosen a beautiful, burnt sienna orange for a divorce card she was working on. Divorce cards were not common, although 50 percent of all marriages were ending in divorce. That statistic seemed to have held steady for years. You could buy congratulations-on-getting-a-new-cat and congratulations-for-getting-braces cards but it was almost impossible to find a card that dealt with divorce. Ruth's card read:

Divorce Has to Feel Like the End

It's important to know that it is also a beginning.

Ruth loved working on the cards. There was something so satisfying in using very few words and getting it right. She worked late last night on two cards.

The Right Thing to Do Is What Is Right for You

What is right for you will be right for those around you.

The other card read:

Selfish Is a Stupid Word

It's healthy to think of yourself.

She had to run her cards by the marketing arm of the small company that distributed her cards. She had a feeling everyone would object to the "Selfish Is a Stupid Word" sentiment. But Ruth had always thought that *selfish* was a nebulous, meaningless word. It covered up too much. Like the word *lazy*. She'd never understood the popularity of either of these words.

Edek, who'd been chatting to Max, came into Ruth's office. He leaned over Ruth's shoulder and read, in a loud, almost formal voice, "What Is Right for You Will Be Right for Those Around You." Edek paused. "This is going to be a minefield for you," he said.

Ruth was startled. "What do you think is going to bother people about it?"

"I did not say people was going to be bothered," Edek said. "I did say it was going to be a minefield."

"Minefields are bothering and often dangerous things," Ruth said.

"This is not the minefield what I am talking about," Edek said. "I am talking about such a mine where you dig and do find things. Things what are good to find."

"That's not a minefield," Ruth said.

"That is maybe a different minefield, but it is a minefield," said Edek.

Ruth thought about it. She wondered whether a field of mines—diamond mines, gold mines—could be called a minefield. She decided to look into it later. "So you like the card?" she said.

"Very much," Edek said. "Like I did say I think it is going to be a minefield."

"Oh good," Ruth said. "I'm glad."

"I am helping you out a bit today in the office," Edek said. "Max is very happy about this. She does say there are quite a few things to do."

Ruth decided not to dwell on what jobs Max had decided Edek should do. "Thanks, Dad," she said. "Can you close the door behind you?"

"Off coss," said Edek.

Ruth put the greeting cards away. She had several letters to do. These were letters that wouldn't be able to be adapted and cut and pasted from a template she had on file. She had hundreds of these templates in scores of categories. She had whole paragraphs on file that could be used for multiple occasions. She had files on different beginnings and endings. And a computerized index that made sure that no client received letters that were too similar to that client's previous letters.

The first letter was for real estate lawyer James King. He had been a client of Ruth's for years. Yesterday he'd asked for a condolence letter to be written on behalf of himself and his dog, Gus, a Labrador, about the death of Gus's friend, also a Labrador. The letter was to the deceased dog's owner. Ruth hadn't known James King had a dog, let alone that the dog had a close friend. Ruth found it hard to understand people's intense attachments to pets. But she understood attachment. When she wrote letters about pets, and they were mostly cats or dogs, she pretended that they were people.

Ruth looked at the notes Max had prepared for her. There was Gus, James King's dog, and Willie and Scout. Who were Willie and

Scout? Which one was the deceased dog and which one was the owner? She called Max. "I'm doing the dog condolence letter for James King," she said. "Who are Willie and Scout?"

"Hang on a minute," Max said. "I think Scout is the dog and Willie is the owner. No, Willie is the dog, and Scout is the owner." Max sounded distracted.

"Is Scout the dog or Willie the dog?" Ruth said. "I've got to know."

Max paused. "The dog is Willie and the owner is Scout."

"Are you sure?" Ruth said.

"Yes," said Max.

Ruth looked at the rest of the notes. The two dogs played together in the park every day. They shared a dog walker and a dog trainer, and were both on Dr. Atkins's low-carbohydrate, high-protein diet.

She began the letter.

> *Dear Scout,*
>
> *I feel so deeply for you about the loss of your beloved Willie. Gus and I will always have Willie in our hearts. Gus will miss Willie so much. And so will I. Gus will think of Willie every day and dream of Willie at night. Their life together won't pass because Willie has passed on. The park without Willie will never be the same again for Gus or for me. But Willie will live on in our hearts as he will in your heart. Gus and I send you our most sincere condolences during this difficult and painful time. We have made a donation to the Humane Society, in Willie's name.*

Before Ruth could end the letter, she needed to know how close the two men were. She knew the dogs were close. She couldn't find any notes on how well the two men knew each other. Ruth didn't want to end the letter with a formal ending if the men were best friends. She got up and opened the door of her office.

"Max," Ruth said, "I need to know whether the dog owners were friends or acquaintances." Max opened the file. James King and Willie's owner, Scout, it appeared, were acquaintances. "They only saw each other with their dogs," Max said.

"Thanks," Ruth said.

She went back to her office and signed the letter, "With my warmest wishes."

Ruth had had a bad week. She'd tried to call Garth three times and couldn't get through to him. Each time she'd called, he'd been on the site, off the property, or the phone didn't answer. And the answering machine wasn't on. She had missed the calls he'd made to her. She'd listened to the messages he'd left and wanted to cry. She wanted to see him, to talk to him, to be held by him. She'd fought several bouts of rising panic that she would never see him again. The feeling that people could easily disappear had dogged her from childhood. That if you weren't careful everyone could disappear. For years she'd gone limp with relief when anyone she loved came back from anywhere.

In the late afternoon, Edek called. He was calling from the Lower East Side. "I am on the Essex Street," he said. "I did find a shop with perfect dill pickles and I did find a place what makes a chopped liver what is nearly so good as the chopped liver what Mum did make."

"What are you doing on the Lower East Side, Dad?" Ruth asked.

"I am just looking," Edek said. "It is a very interesting place."

"Just looking" was the phrase that stuck out. Edek never just did anything. There was always a purpose behind his actions. He never just looked or just walked.

"Dad," Ruth said. "You want to have dinner with me tonight?"

"Ruthie darling," Edek said. "I did already eat my dinner." Ruth looked at her watch. It was six o'clock. "I did eat at a new restaurant I did find on the Lower East Side," Edek said. "It is called Noah's Ark. It is on the Grand Street." Noah's Ark didn't sound Italian or Chinese or Brazilian. Noah's Ark was clearly Jewish. "Here are only Jews,"

Edek said. "Old Jews, young Jews, Jews with families. It is a very good restaurant. The food is very, very good. I did have chicken soup with kreplach and then a schnitzel. At the next table was an old Jew with a new wife. She did look Chinee." Ruth had given up explaining that it was Chinese, not Chinee. "This old Jew did look very happy with his Chinee wife. They was eating latkes and fried fish."

"What about the Second Avenue Deli?" Ruth said. "Have you given up on that?"

"I did eat there a lot, Ruth, and it is still very good, but I was already here in the neighborhood, so I did look for a restaurant and I did find Noah's Ark."

"What were you doing in the neighborhood?" Ruth said.

"Just looking," Edek said again. "I want you to come here with me one day. You can buy everything here. Very cheap. You can buy bottles of water. Sixty bottles of water for fifteen dollars. That is twenty-five cents for one bottle. Near the office I did pay a dollar fifty for this same bottle. You can buy everything, Ruthie. You can buy brassieres. Such big, big brassieres and such not-such-big brassieres."

Ruth thought Edek was probably talking about Cadman Hosiery. The window display of Cadman Hosiery looked as though it hadn't been changed in fifty years and featured what looked like quadruple-D-cup bras. There were also assorted, dilapidated, ancient mannequin body parts scattered in the window. It looked like the aftermath of a massacre, with the quadruple-D-cup-size bras as the only survivors.

Why was Edek looking at and talking about "such big, big brassieres." He didn't usually talk about bras. Who was he thinking of? Zofia? Zofia's breasts would have filled those quadruple-D cups. They were large and sturdy and pointed firmly to the way ahead. Zofia's breasts announced her presence seconds before the rest of Zofia arrived. They were impressive and intimidating breasts. They looked as though they could float a drowning man back to shore, or lift themselves into the air without the aid of propellers. Edek, Ruth knew, had

had more than a passing acquaintanceship with Zofia's breasts. Ruth looked at her own breasts. They were quite limp. Or at the very least, relaxed. Garth called them perky little breasts. But the truth was there was very little perk left.

"You could buy your brassieres at this shop," Edek continued. "The prices are very cheap. But you do probably buy your brassieres at a posh, posh brassieres shop."

"You went inside to inquire about the prices?" Ruth said.

"Yes," said Edek. "Why not? I was interested to see how much they do cost. I am interested to see what it does cost to live in a city like New York City. I do already know the subway and the cheap places to eat and the dry cleaners."

"Why would you want to know about bras?" Ruth said.

"Brassieres is just like everything else," Edek said. "Brassieres is like underpants and socks. If you do want to understand how much it does cost to live somewhere you have to look at everything."

"But I pay your bills," Ruth said.

"So what. Do you want me to start to be a big spender? Off coss not. You want to walk with me on the Lower East Side, Ruthie," Edek said. "I will take you to the pickle shop where you can buy sauerkraut and schmaltz herring, and maybe you will want to look at the brassieres shop."

Ruth hung up the phone. "My father is walking around the Lower East Side," she said to Max.

"Oh, he loves it," Max said. "He's been telling me I should move there. He says it's much cheaper than where I'm living."

"He's been telling you to move there?" Ruth said.

"Yes," said Max. "And he's right. I could get a much bigger apartment for the same rental. And I'm sick of living in a closet. He told me that there are lots of bargains there, particularly if you go below Delancey Street."

"What is my father doing?" Ruth said.

Max laughed. "Spreading his wings like you wanted him to do," she said. "It was driving you crazy, and was disrupting things, when he came into the office every day. He seems happy, and we don't have to listen to that self-navigating vacuum cleaner going around and around the storeroom anymore."

"Spreading his wings?" Ruth said. "Is he preparing to fly? What is he doing?"

"You worry about him too much," Max said. "You were worried about him the day he arrived, and now you seem even more worried."

"I'm not worried," Ruth said, "I'm concerned." But she knew that that wasn't true. She had never mastered the category of concern. She had always slipped straight into worry.

"Edek is doing what all New Yorkers do," Max said. "He's embracing his independence and he's embracing New York. I'm excited for him."

"I'll try to be," Ruth said.

Ruth was definitely not excited about the progress of her proposed women's group. She had been trying to organize a group of women. She had tried to sound casual about the agenda, the structure, and the possible subjects for discussion.

She had approached twelve women. Nine of them had declined. The remaining women had agreed, over enough e-mails to run a small country, that there should be no set subjects. And the conversation should be free-form.

One of the women suggested that a restaurant might be a better location than Ruth's loft for their meeting. And another woman suggested that the group expand its activities to other things, for example a group shopping expedition. "We may learn a lot about our strengths through shopping outings," she'd said in her e-mail. She had also suggested "the principles of communication among women" as a topic for discussion. And had added a note saying that she thought the conversation shouldn't be too personal. The principles of communication among women? What did that mean? What were the principles of communication? Talking, listening, thinking, discussing. And what was communication if it wasn't personal, Ruth thought. Lawyers, businessmen and -women, salespeople, scientists, even doctors went to seminars to learn how to personalize their communication. Couples went to couples therapy. Impersonal communication didn't seem to be very effective in any area. Ruth felt dismayed. The group was splintering before it had even begun.

Minutes after this last e-mail arrived Sonia called. "What the fuck is going on?" she said. "Restaurants? Shopping? The principles of communication? I think I'll suggest a group pedicure."

Ruth started laughing. "I wouldn't be able to do that," she said. "I'd be too self-conscious about my weird toenails."

"What's wrong with your toenails?" Sonia asked.

"Oh, they're just getting thicker and more opaque, like my dad's toenails," Ruth said. "When I was a kid I used to think his toenails were a result of brutality or malnourishment in Auschwitz."

"Not everything emanates from Auschwitz. Do you want to have dinner together on Friday?" Sonia said.

"I'd love to," said Ruth. "I've been feeling a bit miserable and lonely without Garth."

"I'd like Michael to go away for a while," Sonia said.

"Maybe you'd change your mind if he actually did," said Ruth.

"Maybe," said Sonia.

"Let's meet at seven-thirty P.M. at Vang, it's on Varick Street," Sonia said.

Ruth arrived at Vang early. Vang was one of those relatively expensive restaurants created with innocuous generic upscale architecture and interior design. This covered everything from the lighting to the table and chairs and crockery, cutlery and glassware. There was nothing offensive about anything in the restaurant. And there was nothing appealing. Ruth left her jacket and some papers on the table and went to the bathroom.

Ruth walked into the women's bathroom. She was just about to enter a cubicle when a restroom attendant, a woman in her mid-fifties, came running up to her. "Don't use that cubicle, miss," she said.

"Oh," Ruth said. "Why? Is it disgusting?"

"Yes," the restroom attendant said.

Ruth went into another cubicle. She was washing her hands when the attendant came back.

"What is it about women?" Ruth said. "They're much messier than men, aren't they?"

"Women customers are much messier and much dirtier than men," the attendant said. "Women are filthy. They urinate on the seats and on the floor, put tampons in the toilet, leave blood smears on the seat, and they don't flush."

Ruth had often been perplexed by how dirty, how disgusting, really, so many women's bathrooms, in public places, were. Women presented themselves as neat, well dressed, well groomed, well mannered. Yet in public bathrooms they seemed to have no regard for anyone else and a primal urge to spread the contents of their bowels and bladders and ovaries.

"The worst thing is if they vomit in the sink," the attendant said.

Ruth wished she hadn't started this whole conversation. "It's been nice to talk to you," Ruth said, and left.

Sonia was waiting at the table when Ruth got back. Sonia looked flustered. Upset.

"Hi," Ruth said, giving Sonia a kiss. "What's wrong?"

"I've just had a shit day at work," Sonia said. "It started off bad and got worse. Instead of the usual hundred and twenty or hundred and fifty e-mails I had almost three hundred. And then a clutch of faxes. And faxes usually have urgent deadlines. Stuff that needs to be acted on or delegated immediately. It was lucky I got in early."

"Why do you get so many e-mails?" Ruth said.

"Because intellectual property has a high caseload with many, many deadlines," Sonia said. "You're working with many different patents and trademarks and copyright issues. If you do litigation, you probably work on one case all day. Or trusts and estates. You might work on three or four cases a day. In IP you don't spend your whole day on a patent. You might spend an hour dealing with one aspect of one case, then move on to the next. IP is all about timing and deadlines and keeping on top of the deadlines. So you advance a large caseload bit by bit at the right time.

"I was fantasizing about retiring to some small village in Italy or killing the client I'd had on the phone for half the afternoon. He drives me nuts. He is really cheap. He wants a lot of work done for nothing and questions every single charge. If you question the charge, it stalls the payments. If he has a ten-thousand-dollar bill, he'll go through it and ask why he got charged for a three-dollar fax. He's used a ten-dollar charge to hold up a ten-thousand-dollar bill. He's so cheap and likes to swear at people. This afternoon he was ranting at me. 'I can't believe this fucking shit,' he was saying. 'You fuckers just drain me. I can't get any work done because all of my money is allocated to you fuckers.' 'You cocksuckers are draining me,' was the last thing he said to me."

"Was it his shouting or his obscenities that bothered you?" Ruth asked Sonia.

"Both, I think."

"Well, you swear, yourself," Ruth said.

"I only swear with friends," Sonia said. "Cocksucker sounds much less offensive when you're talking to a friend."

Ruth could see some sort of logic in that, although she couldn't articulate exactly what that logic was.

"He screams it at me," Sonia said. "Actually that's what really up-sets me. I can't yell obscenities back at him. I want to shout 'You moth-erfucking, cocksucking, worm-laden, garbage-mouth dickhead' at him. And I can't. I have to keep talking about his patent and the fact that I know his associate lives in Mexico but the documents need to be signed in New York and he has to fly his associate to New York in order to get these documents executed."

Ruth laughed. "The motherfucking, cocksucking, worm-laden routine might have been just as effective," she said.

"Yes, and had me fired," Sonia said. "You can't trash a client. You have to be nice to them because you don't want them to take their busi-ness somewhere else. And he's a big client. So I sat there in a quiet fury. But then just when I thought the day was finally over, I did something appalling."

"Oh no," Ruth said.

"You know what I did?" Sonia said. "I spilled a cup of coffee all over the desk of the most anally retentive guy in the office."

Ruth started laughing.

"It wasn't at all funny," Sonia said. "This guy is really anal. He has everything on his desk in a certain way. I can understand that. I do the same thing. But he's extreme. Another partner once moved this guy's stapler about two inches from where it was, and it was the first thing he noticed when he got back to his desk. He fixated on it. He wanted to know who moved it.

"He also likes to pick garbage up off the floor when he walks down the hall. I saw him pick up a paper clip once. As soon as he'd passed me, I threw a paper clip onto the floor. It was just in view of his office. Sure enough he came out and picked up the paper clip. One day I threw some rubber bands on the floor and I could tell they were dementing him. It was a small amusement in my day. But today wasn't amusing. I handed him a file and I was holding a cup of cof-fee. I leaned over to put the file on his desk and the coffee poured out over everything. His secretary and two paralegals who were there froze. I felt really bad. I tried to help clean it up but that made him more hysterical.

"He's probably still cleaning his desk," Sonia said. "I need a drink."

"He makes me feel quite sane and balanced," Ruth said.

"Your need for order is quite extreme," Sonia said.

"I don't think it's quite extreme," Ruth said. "It's a little extreme. Anyway, I'm trying to change. I'm sick of trying to be in control. I'm sick of monitoring everything I eat. I'm sick of being inflexible. I'm so sick of myself. Before Garth left, I wanted to have a bite of his ham and cheese sandwich." Sonia looked at her strangely. "I'm speaking literally, not metaphorically," Ruth said. "It wasn't one of Garth's body parts I wanted, it was a bite of a ham and cheese sandwich. I never eat a ham and cheese sandwich. I never eat sandwiches. I weigh up the total calorie count and the effect it could have and decide on some lower-calorie lunch. I really wanted that sandwich."

"Hey, that analysis looks as though it's finally having an effect on you."

Ruth ignored Sonia's dig. "I want to be ordinary," Ruth said. "I want to be regular. I want to be flexible."

"You want to be ordinary, regular, flexible?" Sonia said. "Then start with tonight. What are you going to eat?"

"I can't start right now," Ruth said. "I'll start tomorrow. I'll change my cereal and add some more strawberries."

"That's your idea of change?" Sonia said. "It's going to be a long, slow road."

Ruth ordered a bottle of San Pellegrino mineral water and Sonia ordered a scotch on the rocks. They both perused the menu.

"I'm going to have the veal chop," Sonia announced. "Don't have anything on spinach," she said to Ruth. "This is the new you."

"I'll have grilled shrimp," Ruth said.

"The new you is going to be hard to distinguish from the old you," said Sonia. Sonia downed her scotch in one movement and heaved a sigh of relief.

"I plan to be bolder," Ruth said. "I'm sick of having to look like I look. I'm sick of having to have my hair look right. Whatever right means to me. I wash my hair every day because I don't like the way some of my curls fuzz overnight. Then I let it dry over breakfast because it goes haywire if I dry it with a hair dryer."

"You think that much about your hair?" Sonia said. She looked carefully at Ruth's hair. "It looks like that's just the way it grows."

"To get that look," Ruth said, "takes the right shampoo, the right hair products when it's wet, the right drying method, and then different hair products once it's dry."

"And you do that every day?" Sonia said.

"Yes," said Ruth. "But I'm planning to change. I'm not going to wash it every day. I'm going to try every second day. I wish I was the sort of person who could not wash my hair for a week."

Ruth paused. "One of the women I asked to join the women's group called me today," Ruth said. "She said it would be more helpful to have a group that reeducated men so that men allowed more women to succeed. That really depressed me. Women sit around and talk about why men are holding women back. But there's an absolute silence on the subject of whether women are holding women back.

"If we don't understand that the notion of women as being all-embracing, nurturing, and compassionate is a myth, then we're doomed. Women are furiously jealous of each other. Women see other women as the enemy. We're our own enemy. We strike out against our own gender. And we use very underhanded methods. We use gossip to get rid of a rival. Lies to discredit other women. And innuendo to undermine."

"That's a very negative attitude," a woman sitting at the next table said to Ruth.

"Negative?" Ruth said. Ruth hated the word *negative*. Americans were always using the words *negative* and *positive*. Everything was either negative or positive. *Negative* and *positive* were words that were rendered meaningless and generic unless they were applied to science or medicine.

"We're not saying that women are atrocious human beings," Sonia said. "We're saying that they work against each other's interests."

"And should be working at supporting each other and trusting each other," Ruth added, turning away from the woman.

"We won't be asking her to join the women's group," Sonia said.

Sonia's veal chop and Ruth's grilled shrimp arrived.

"How's your father?" Sonia asked Ruth.

Ruth hesitated. "Something's changed," she said. "He's not in the office that often. And I'm not sure what he's doing. When I ask he says he's busy."

"Wasn't he driving you nuts in the office?" Sonia said.

"Yes," said Ruth, "but at least I knew where he was and what he was doing."

"You sound like the obsessively worried mother of a delinquent teenager," Sonia said. "Your father is not skipping school. He's not on drugs. He's not hanging out with a bad crowd. He's a mature adult. He's eighty-seven. He's probably exploring New York. He's probably out cruising."

"Cruising for women?" Ruth said.

"Yes," said Sonia, "unless he's changed his orientation and he's cruising for men."

"I don't think he's out cruising," Ruth said. "You think everyone's out cruising because that's what you'd like to do."

"I don't want to cruise," said Sonia. "I just want a lover. I wouldn't cruise. I'd think about the men I already know."

"You've got a finely calibrated plan?" said Ruth.

"No," said Sonia. "I've got a possible plan. And it's not finely calibrated. I'm still a bit torn and not at all sure that it's a good course of action."

"That's good," Ruth said.

"It probably is," said Sonia. "Because I'm married and the mother of twins. Your father is a single man. Why shouldn't he be out cruising? He's not a baby. And he's a good-looking man."

"You sum up every man?" Ruth said. "Even eighty-seven-year-olds?"

"Sure, why not?" Sonia said. "You probably never do."

"No, I don't," Ruth said. "I love Garth."

Ruth thought her answer made her seem lame and limp. Maybe loving Garth shouldn't prevent her from sizing up other men? Why did she use the word sizing? She thought. What would she be sizing? She decided not to delve into the psychological issues of possibly simple semantic decisions. And tried to keep all thoughts of her father sizing up or cruising out of her head. It wasn't easy.

"Why did we have to talk about my father?" Ruth said.

"We didn't," said Sonia.

"You brought the subject up," Ruth said.

"Did I?" Sonia said. "It must have been in order to avoid talking about how restless I feel in my marriage. I do love Michael. And I'm so much kinder to him than I used to be. When I had a lover, I loved Michael less."

Ruth wondered how Sonia could, so apparently simply, quantify the love she had for Michael then and now. It was probably gut instinct. Gut instinct about how patient you were, how tolerant you were, how affectionate and maybe how attached.

"Michael and I get on well," Sonia said. "We've always got on well. We love our girls. But there's got to be more to life than shared political values, an understanding of each other's jobs, a love for and concern about your eleven-year-old daughters, and no embarrassment in having a shit while he's shaving in the bathroom. I feel trapped. I feel as though I'm with him all the time I'm not at work. I feel trapped by the endless familiarity. I know exactly how he brushes his teeth and puts on his socks and knots his tie and scratches his head. He's really happy.

His contentment and happiness make me feel claustrophobic. I need to get away."

Ruth wondered where Sonia needed to get away to. In her own experience it was always herself she wanted to get away from. She wanted to get away to anywhere that she herself wasn't. Maybe Sonia's destination was as unclear and as unattainable?

"Even having separate beds would help," Sonia said. "We're married but why can't we sleep in our own space? Why do we have to be unconscious together? I want my own space. I don't want to leave Michael, I just want my own space. I had my own space when I had a lover."

"No, you didn't," Ruth said. "You had a diversion, a substitute, and a pack of lies that you had to keep to yourself. You were always lying to Michael. You had to. Everyone who's married and who has affairs has to lie. Was it having all those lies all to yourself that made you feel less invaded, less crowded, gave you your own space?"

"I don't know," Sonia said.

"I think having one's own space may be an internal thing," Ruth said.

"You've had so much analysis, you think everything is internal," Sonia said. "You probably think the weather and the garbage collection are internal issues."

"I do locate some of what are internal fears on the weather, which I know is external," Ruth said. "But I've given the garbage collection a miss. I just see it as the garbage collection." She paused. "You know what I think you're doing, Sonia?" she said. "I think you're looking for trouble. You must have needed the threat of trouble to have had affairs with men for so many years of your marriage to Michael."

"If I want to be analyzed I'll find an analyst," Sonia said.

"I know that feeling of wanting trouble," Ruth said. "I feel as though I'm always trawling for trouble. Particularly when things are going well. As soon as I start to feel a deep happiness, I start trawling as though I'm like some slug at the bottom of the ocean, with two giant antennae and three-hundred-and-sixty-degree-vision eyes at the ends of my antennae. The moment I sense happiness those eyeballs start swiveling. They're on a mission, a search, an almost desperate search for trouble. It usually takes me about ten seconds to locate a trouble spot. Then minutes later, I've accumulated so much trouble, the happiness has all but evaporated. I've learned, now, to pause. When something good happens, I pause and try not to run off and scavenge around for something to dislodge it."

"Is that what you've learned about yourself after shelling out hundreds of thousands of dollars in analysis?" Sonia said.

"It's quite a lot," said Ruth.

But it was not quite enough, Ruth thought to herself. She had been very distressed, almost distraught, this morning. Garth had left a message on her cell phone saying he was going to Melbourne to buy some equipment. He didn't say when he was leaving or when he was coming back. She didn't know whether he was driving or getting the train. Or where he was staying.

Her distress had turned into agitation this afternoon, and she had called him. It was 5:00 A.M. in Australia.

"I'm glad you haven't left for Melbourne," she had said in a harsher voice than she'd intended, when Garth had answered the phone.

"What's wrong, sweetheart?" Garth said, clearly alarmed by the tone of her voice.

"What's wrong is that you're going to Melbourne," Ruth said.

"What's wrong with that?" Garth said. "I have to go to Melbourne. I've run out of some things and I've got to go to the art supplies store."

"What's wrong is that you didn't tell me when you were going or when you were coming back," said Ruth.

"I'm only going for a day," Garth said.

Garth sounded irritated. He was hardly ever irritated with her. Maybe at close range her irritating qualities were blurred. Maybe distance brought them into focus. She decided to be calmer. To be more reasonable.

"It's not a big deal," Garth said.

Ruth couldn't stop herself. "It's a big deal to me," she said.

"Sweetheart, I can't call in my every move," Garth said.

"Why not?" said Ruth. She'd meant the "Why Not?" to be funny. It hadn't come out that way.

"I'm taking my father to Shelter Island for the weekend," Ruth said to Sonia as they were leaving Vang. "I haven't been there since Garth left. I haven't wanted to go there without Garth."

"I'd go anywhere without Michael," Sonia said.

"That's not funny," said Ruth.

"I didn't mean it to be funny," Sonia said.

Shelter Island was a small island ninety miles from New York. It was accessible only by ferry. The island had fifty-two miles of waterfront. It was quiet and peaceful. Houses were, on the whole, unlocked and car keys were left in the ignition. Ruth and Garth's house was half a block from the beach.

One third of the island was occupied by a nature reserve. The island had a lot of wildlife. There were a lot of frogs, and a variety of turtles. There were snapping, painted, and spotted turtles. There were deer, raccoons, red foxes, chipmunks, squirrels, muskrats, opossums, cottontail rabbits, shrews, and moles. There were over two hundred species of birds including ospreys and red-tailed hawks.

Edek hated Shelter Island. He hated it. He had been looking forward to the experience, but there was nothing, in Edek's opinion, to be experienced. He was looking for vitality, for activity, for sidewalks, shopwindows, ice cream stores, hot dog vendors, delicatessens with good stocks of chocolate. Instead, the streets were almost empty.

Ruth had warned Edek that the island was very quiet. He said he liked quiet. All he needed, he said, was a deck chair and a book. Ruth was not prepared for how much Shelter Island unsettled Edek.

"What do you like about the island?" he said to Ruth.

"The quiet," she said.

"Ruthie, you got a very quiet loft in the city," he said.

Ruth hadn't been able to interest Edek in anything. He didn't want to walk on the beach. He didn't like sand. And he couldn't swim. Edek had got through the weekend with a chair on the deck, a book, and a supply of extra dark Côte d'Or chocolate Ruth had brought with her from Economy Candy, on Rivington Street.

They were now waiting in line to drive onto the ferry to Greenport on their way back to New York. They had already been waiting for almost thirty minutes. Edek was edgy. He didn't like waiting for anything. But waiting to get off Shelter Island seemed to tax his waiting quotient. He got in and out of the car at least ten times in an effort to see if he could sight another ferry or to try and calculate how many ferries had to come and go before he and Ruth could get onto one.

Ruth planned to leave the car in the public car park in Greenport. She and Edek were booked on the 7:00 P.M. Sunrise Express bus to Manhattan. On a Sunday night this trip could be less than express. It could sometimes take three hours. Ruth had packed plenty of food and drink.

"Why don't they buy another ship?" Edek said exasperatedly. "It is stupid to have ships what does fit in such few cars. They would make a much bigger profit with such bigger ships." He sighed. "By now a normal person what lives in a normal place would be already back in New York." Ruth wasn't sure whether to defend her own normality or the normality of the island. She decided Edek might have a series of good arguments for his case, for either. She kept quiet.

"I think, anyway, we are going to be on the next ship," Edek said.

"We are, Dad," she said.

"Thank God," Edek answered.

The captain waved them onto the ferry. He motioned for Ruth to go into the far left-hand lane of the ferry. Ruth nodded, turned the wheel, and headed left. *"Oy cholera,"* Edek shouted. Ruth slammed on the brakes. *Oy cholera,* literally translated, was "Oh cholera." Colloquially, in Yiddish, it meant there was big trouble. It was a degree more heated than, "Oh shit."

"Careful, careful, careful," Edek said, in a panic. "You are driving too close to the side of the ship."

"Dad," Ruth said, "you're unnerving me, please let me get the car on the ferry."

"I am not unnerving you," Edek said. "You was already nervous when we was waiting for nearly an hour to get on the ship. You did already say, two times, that you did hope you would get the middle lane of the ship. In the middle lane you only have to drive straight."

Ruth maneuvered the car, at a snail's pace, into the left-hand lane. She was less than relaxed. She'd hardly driven in all their years in America. Something about switching sides of the road had seemed to throw a switch in her head. In New York, there was no need to drive. And that meant she could avoid looking at that particular problem. When she drove on the all-but-empty roads of Shelter Island, she concentrated with the ferocity of a cardiothoracic surgeon about to restart an implanted heart.

"What happened to you, Ruthie, you was always such a good driver," Edek said. "You have to drive more often in New York and then you will not be such a nervous driver what nearly drives into the side of a ship."

"It's not a ship," Ruth said with irritation. "It's a ferry."

"This is a boat what is on water and is driving us to the other side of the water," Edek said. "In English this is a ship." Ruth didn't reply. They had landed in Greenport.

As Ruth and Edek were boarding the bus, Ruth noticed that the exit-row seats were still free. Ruth made a dash for them. She got the two exit-row seats. She felt elated. The exit-row seats had twice as much legroom.

Edek opened his book and began to read. The book, a thriller, was called *Thicker Than Blood*. It was by someone called Don Owen. Ruth looked at Edek. He looked up. "This writer is not so good what is Loodloom," Edek said. "He is a little bit like Loodloom, but not so good." Loodloom was Robert Ludlum. Ruth thought that Don Owen was not alone in that category. "In this book there are two men what each did lose their memory," Edek said. "One of the men does think the other man is a spy. The other man does think the first man is his brother. And there is already big trouble. Already two people are dead. Both dead people was strangled." Ruth looked at the book. Edek was only up to page 40. She decided she definitely didn't want to hear any more details of *Thicker Than Blood*. She took the *New York Times* out of her bag.

A while later Ruth looked at Edek. He looked quite peaceful, immersed in *Thicker Than Blood*. She was happy that his detective fiction books allowed him to escape into someone else's horror. Allowed him a way to feel the terror and the brutality and the inexplicability of what had happened to him, in someone else's story, someone else's nightmare.

"When I do read these books," he'd said to her, many times, "I do live every moment like I am there in the book."

Edek looked up. "I think the man what thinks the other man is his brother is going to be killed," he said. "I think the other man thinks he is a spy what does have to kill the man what does think he is his brother. He does think this because there is now a third man who is from China what has told him that the man what does think he is this man's brother, is really a professional murderer what has been paid to kill the man what does think he is a spy by the spy's wife."

Ruth was momentarily confused. "Does the man who thinks he is a spy have a wife?" she said to Edek.

"He does think he has one because this man from China did tell him that his wife was in hiding because her life was in danger."

They were almost in the city now. "Is there anything at all you like about Shelter Island?" Ruth asked Edek.

"No," Edek said. "Maybe if it did have a bridge it would be better," Edek said. "Not for me, I am finished with the Shelter Island, but for other people. A ship is such a stupid idea. You do have to wait and wait. With a bridge you can drive on and you can drive off."

Ruth dropped Edek off at his apartment, in a cab. He looked exhausted. The weekend in the country had clearly worn him out.

Zelda called Ruth. "Hi Roo," she said. "I'm just calling to see if you're okay."

"Did all three of you have a conference call and decide I wasn't okay?" Ruth said. "Zachary and Kate have already called me today. They both asked me if I was okay."

Zelda laughed. "We didn't have a conference call, Roo," she said. "We had dinner together last night, and we were all a bit worried about you. We all know you haven't spent a night apart from Garth for years, and we realized we didn't know whether you were okay or not."

Ruth suddenly felt like a child. "I'm okay," she said to Zelda. "Well okay-ish."

"If you want me to come over and stay the night with you, anytime, I will," Zelda said.

"Thanks," Ruth said. "I think I'll be fine."

Ruth bought herself a piece of chicken breast roasted with lemon zest and rosemary at Gourmet Garage on her way home from work. She ate her dinner at a small table near the windows of the living area in the loft. She hadn't been able to eat her dinner at their large dining table in the six weeks since Garth had left.

Ruth woke up thinking about Garth's laugh. Garth's laugh almost exploded out of him. The laugh seemed to come from the center of his being. He would laugh so hard, his body would double up. Ruth sometimes wished she could join herself to him. Plug herself into that laugh. She sometimes sat pressed against him when he laughed like that, as though she knew that that position was the closest she was ever going to get to an unrestrained, unconstrained, wholehearted sense of joy.

Ruth and Edek were walking on the Lower East Side. It was Sunday morning. Ruth was happy to be walking with Edek. She hadn't seen him for days. In fact she'd seen very little of him in the last two weeks. They had already walked a lot this morning. They had had a really nice morning walking around the Lower East Side. They had walked along Grand Street, Hester Street, Essex Street, Ludlow, Rivington, Orchard, and Allen streets. Edek had pointed out every restaurant they passed, including a kosher pizzeria and a hamburger and french fries place. "Even the Chinee food is good," he'd said.

"How many places have you eaten at?" Ruth said.

"How should I know this?" Edek said. "I am not such a person what does count the restaurants what I do eat in. But everything is cheap. The Chinee bargain shops do sell such bargains."

Ruth was bothered. How much time was he spending on the Lower East Side? And what was he doing?

"Do you know anyone who lives in this neighborhood?" she'd asked him.

"No," he said. "But here everything is cheap. You can buy toilet paper for less than a quarter of the price what a person has to pay for toilet paper," he said.

"It's probably very thin toilet paper," Ruth said.

"It is exactly the same toilet paper what I use in my apartment," Edek said.

Ruth did like the Lower East Side. It was full of life and full of diversity. SoHo, where she lived, had had its diversity devoured by gentrification. On Rivington Street, Ruth and Edek walked past a huge painted sign on a building. The sign displayed bunches of grapes and a bottle of wine. It was an advertisement for Schapiro's Kosher Wine. Under this sign was Festival Mexicano, a Mexican restaurant. Across the road was Liu's Wash and Dry, a Chinese laundry, and a little further down the street was Botanica San Lazana, a store that sold religious paraphernalia, Jesus statuettes, candles, rosary beads, and an array of air fresheners with various saints painted on the containers.

In the surrounding streets, there were bedding stores, vintage clothing stores, hosiery and underwear stores, and Chinese stores and markets that sold preserved ducks' eggs, red bean ice cream bars, and large fish in plastic bags, called Dried Croakers. And then there were the Jewish restaurants and delis and dried fruit and nut stores and pickle shops. At Kosar's, a bakery on Grand Street, you could buy bialys, sesame sticks, garlic knots, and the same large, round onion bread disks that Ruth ate as a child.

Ruth and Edek stopped for lunch at Noah's Ark. In the middle of lunch, Edek announced that he wanted to move to the Lower East Side.

"Why?" Ruth said. "I thought you liked living on Second Avenue."

"I do like it, but I like it here much better," Edek said. "Here is more shops what I like and more restaurants what I like."

"I guess we could look for a place and try to get out of the remaining part of your lease or sublet your apartment for a short period," Ruth said.

Edek beamed. "Then you do think it is a good idea, Ruthie?" he said.

"I think that what makes you happy is a good idea," said Ruth.

"This will make me happy, for sure," Edek said.

"Are you sure?" Ruth said.

"I did just say for sure it will make me happy," Edek said.

Ruth became even more disturbed. Edek was saying he was sure he was going to be happy and he hadn't included the possibility of his imminent death, which usually preceded or followed notions of anything to do with happiness or the future.

"I got another idea," Edek said. "If we are going to go to all the trouble to find another apartment and to shift my things, maybe I should get an apartment what is a little bit bigger than the apartment what I got."

This idea of Edek's took Ruth completely by surprise. "Why do you want a bigger apartment?" she said. "Your apartment is quite big."

"That is true," Edek said. "It is not so small, but it does only have one bedroom and one other big room."

Ruth was agitated. She ate three slices of bread with her salad. She hadn't intended to eat three slices of bread. Edek had finished his mushroom and barley soup and his pastrami sandwich.

"Why do you want a bigger apartment?" she said.

"I do not want such a much bigger apartment," Edek said. "But I did think if I am going to shift to another apartment then maybe I could have an extra room. That way I could have two bedrooms not one bedroom. And the Lower East Side is cheaper than where I am. You do pay three thousand dollars a month for my one bedroom. For two thousand dollars I can get two bedrooms.

"Maybe I will have a visitor," Edek said. "Maybe someone from Melbourne will come and visit me."

"You said everyone in Melbourne was dead," Ruth said. "Well, everyone you knew."

"Not everyone," Edek said. "Topcha is not dead."

"You said she was sick and had lots of things wrong with her," Ruth said.

"Ach," said Edek. "She likes to complain. She is not so sick that she cannot come to visit me, in New York." He paused. "If you do not think it is a good idea," he said, "then that is okay with me."

"I want you to have what you want," Ruth said.

"Ruthie," Edek said, "if you do not want me to live in this area or to shift to an apartment what does have two bedrooms that is fine with me. You are the boss."

"What do you mean, I am the boss?" Ruth said. "I'm not your boss. I might be Max's boss and Tara's boss, but I'm not your boss. The Lower East Side is a great area," Ruth said.

"Zelda did say that she would like to live there herself," Edek said.

"You've already talked about this to Zelda?" Ruth said.

"Off coss," Edek said. "Zelda does ring me nearly every day. She did say that I should be able to find an apartment what has two bedrooms without too much trouble."

Ruth wondered when Zelda had developed her real estate expertise.

"There are some new condominiums, they do call them condos, what are nearly finished, on Essex Street," Edek said. "Do you want me to show you what such a condominium is? They got all the facts about exactly what the condominiums will be when they are finished."

"Okay," she said. She was curious to see what Edek was talking about.

They walked to Essex Street and stopped outside a newly constructed building between Grand and Canal streets.

"This is the building what does have the condos," Edek said.

A sign in the window of the lobby at the front of the building read, "Dedicated to a Finer Quality of Life." These condominiums had, according to the sign, a spacious layout, high ceilings, three exposures, hardwood floors, and a gourmet kitchen with a SubZero stainless steel fridgereezer and a stainless steel range. Edek didn't cook and she wasn't sure he knew what an exposure was. The apartment also had "extraordinary closets." Ruth wondered what constituted an extraordinary closet. Did the racks revolve? Was there background music? Did Puccini or Beethoven or Brahms begin when you opened the doors? There was a "rare twenty-four-hour doorman." Why would you want a rare twenty-four-hour doorman? What was wrong with a regular one? Or did rare mean he was rarely there? The apartments also had a landscaped terrace. How much landscaping could a terrace contain, Ruth thought. She read the line again. It said landscaped terrace with water irrigation system. What was that for? Were they cultivating rice? Were these terraces doubling as rice paddies?

"They've got irrigated terraces," she said to Edek. "Do you know what that means?"

"No," he said. "But it can't hurt."

Ruth called Garth. "My dad wants to move," she said. "The apartment he's got his eye on is a new condominium. It's got three exposures, a gourmet kitchen with SubZero stainless steel everything, a twenty-four-hour doorman, and a landscaped terrace with an irrigation system."

Garth started laughing. "You have to admire your dad's spirit."

"My dad's spirit?" Ruth said. "He's gone from saying that he needs nothing at all and would be happy sleeping on the floor in a corner of the loft, to wanting an apartment with high ceilings, a twenty-four-hour doorman, and a landscaped terrace with an irrigation system."

"I'm sure he doesn't know what a landscaped terrace with an irrigation system is," Garth said, still laughing.

"He doesn't," Ruth said. "But he thinks it can't be a bad thing."

"He's probably right," said Garth.

Garth was still laughing when they said goodbye. Ruth felt happy. Happy to be laughing with Garth. The last four phone calls they'd had had been a bit tense.

Ruth's head was throbbing. She reached over for the headache pills and swallowed two with some cold chamomile tea. She had some greeting cards to go through. She personally checked each letter for all of their clients before they were sent. It was so easy to make a slip, to press the wrong key. A small typo or a spelling error could have catastrophic consequences. You had to be so careful. With the slip of a finger or the twist of a wrist words and phrases were stripped of their original intent and distorted into unrecognizable and sometimes appalling questions, declarations, and statements. One slip and friend could become fiend. The public administrator could become the pubic administrator and the United States of America could become the Untied States of America. These were slips no computer spell-check could detect. A very pubic moment sounded just as feasible as a very public moment to a software program. Your massage was succinct, powerful, and effective was indiscernible to technology from Your message was succinct, powerful, and effective. Technology had its limits. It couldn't tell the difference between the fast track and the feast track.

Edek came into Ruth's office. He was carrying a large parcel. "I did buy you something which I think that you do very much need," he said.

"What have you got, Dad?" she said.

Edek unwrapped the parcel. He looked very pleased with himself. "This will make everything in the office, one hundred percent more easy," he said. "This" was an electronic desktop labeler. It came with over seven hundred different pieces of clip art that allowed you to add your own personal touch, the package said. Ruth had no idea what a piece of clip art was. Edek had also bought a box of replacement cartridges for the long-lasting, laminated, adhesive-backed labels. Edek was beaming. "Do you see what I mean?" he said. "You do use such little, thin paper labels to put on all of your files. And you got so many files. With this machine you will be able to have something much better. A label what you can read straight away and what will never come apart from the file."

Ruth pulled herself together. She couldn't explain to Edek that she'd never be able to work the machine and she'd have to employ someone just to print labels. "That's a great idea," she said. "We'll start with the largest files." Edek looked very happy.

"I will read the instructions and see if maybe I can make a few labels for you," he said.

"I love you, Dad," she said.

"I love you too, Ruthie," he said. "I was pretty sure you would be happy with this thing." Edek sat down. "What are you doing?" he said.

"I'm working on some greeting cards," she said.

"Do you think you got the same knack what you got with the letters?" Edek asked her.

"I don't know," she said. On her desk was a card that said:

Pause

Make sure you're very sure.
Five words from someone who cares.

Ruth thought that this could be a card for people contemplating changing jobs, changing gender, leaving a partner, getting married, getting divorced, not speaking to a friend or relative, or making accusations or complaints to a boss, a colleague, a neighbor, a son or daughter, a friend or a partner.

Edek looked at the card. "This is a very clever piece of advice," he said. "You do want people to think very carefully before they do do something that maybe they will regret."

On her desk was another card she was working on:

You're Right

You're doing the right thing.

This card was intended for people who were uncertain. Most people, herself included, were often uncertain about small and large issues in their lives. They were uncertain about whether they were right. Right to pursue a college degree, leave a job, move to another state, talk to their boss, their wife, their husband, their partner, their parents. Often the answer was obvious to a friend.

Edek picked up the card. "I can see what you are saying," he said. "You do want to help people to have the courage to do what they do really want to do."

"That's exactly it," Ruth said.

"It is a very good thing to help people to do the thing what they do want to do," Edek said.

Ruth looked at him. He had placed an emphasis on each word in a way that made Ruth feel he was alluding to something in particular. She looked at him again. He seemed perfectly normal.

She decided to change the subject. "The cards you can buy," she said to Edek, "all seem to lack emotion. To lack real feeling." Ruth thought that greeting cards were supposed to be a vehicle for expressing and addressing something of importance, with feeling. Ruth thought that cards should touch people, move them. Stir them.

She pulled some greeting cards out of a drawer that was jam-packed with cards she had bought at various stores.

"Look, Dad," she said. "This is a card to congratulate someone on buying a new home." "Congratulations, New Home Owner," the card said. This was above a photograph of a refrigerator. Inside, the message said, "Cool Place." To Ruth, the card looked chilling. The fridge looked cold and so did the message. "Cool Place" was fine, but not with a fridge attached to the phrase. To Ruth the card seemed insignificant. Buying a house was a significant, highly charged emotional moment for most people. Ruth thought that this was not a terrible card. So many cards were just awful. This card was just much less than it could have been. It reduced the importance of the achievement. And the exhilaration of the achievement.

"That is stupid," Edek said. "They did buy a house not a refrigerator. I think you got a big chance with this card business."

Ruth picked up another card. "Another Year Older," the card announced. "Remember it's wrinkles we worry about first but it's gratitude that gets us in the end." Gratitude for what, Ruth thought, still being alive? These cards were meant to undermine. Regardless of your achievement or your struggles you were reduced to wrinkles and gratitude. Or a beer gut and tooth and hair loss. Almost all cards for anyone over fifty had embedded in the message the fact that the person was over the hill. On the decline. Disguised as humor, the cards were insulting and offensive. They were demoralizing.

"I did never worry about wrinkles," Edek said. "Why do you think they do think that all persons are worried about wrinkles? And if a person is worried about wrinkles it is not such a nice thing to send to them a birthday card what is about wrinkles. Ruthie darling, I think you got a big point about what is wrong with the greeting cards."

"Look at this birthday card," Ruth said. Edek looked. "Many women think guys get sexier and more attractive with age," he read. He opened the card. There in bold print was, "These women are dumb."

"That is a little bit funny," Edek said.

"I don't think so," Ruth said. "I think it's mean, mean to the person who's getting the card." Ruth didn't understand why the cards had to be derogatory in order to be funny. So many of the cards were mean-spirited in an indirect way. She'd shown Zelda a batch of cards. Zelda had put it succinctly. "These are like the college friend who says, 'Those pants make your big hips look wonderful.' A minute later you say to yourself, 'Wait, why do I feel terrible?' "

The cards between men and women all seemed to emphasize conflict and division. They were reinforcing, and often exaggerating, already objectionable stereotypes about what women think of men, and what men think of women. There was a lack of directness, of affection or real emotion, and a lack of personal language. There was a divisive element that ran through so many categories of cards. Ruth was hoping to tap into the relatively small market that found these greeting cards as corrosive or sentimental or insipid as she did.

Edek had been looking through some of the cards in the drawer. "If you have got the same knack what you got with letters," he said, "I think you are going to do a lot of business with the cards."

"I hope so, Dad," she said. "Then we can all retire."

"I did already retire," Edek said. "And I am very comfortable, thanks to my daughter."

Something about that statement bothered Ruth. It was Edek saying he was very comfortable. There was something wrong with that. He hadn't added a complaint or a wish, as an addendum. He hadn't made any mention of not having much time left. He hadn't even told her she was working too hard. He'd simply said he was comfortable. And he'd said he was retired. These were very bothering and unnerving aspects of a seemingly simple statement.

"Are you all right, Dad?" she said.

"I am more than all right," Edek said.

Four

Ruth looked at her e-mail. There was an e-mail from one of her clients, a publisher, asking her if she was interested in writing a small book called *Thirty Ways to Start and End a Letter*. Months ago she had talked to the publisher about the trouble people had beginning and ending letters. People began letters with the most stilted, awkward, and inept expressions. *Re* was an abbreviation used in abundance to begin a letter. *Re* your last letter, *Re* your question, *Re* your suggestion, *Re* your invitation, *Re* your vacation. And endings were a problem, too. *Best wishes* was wildly overused. And *Best,* its abbreviation, didn't make sense. Ruth had thought that the advent of e-mail would improve people's writing skills. Instead everything was abbreviated and truncated even more. Everything but the basic information was excised. Salutations and endings had been eliminated. Ruth thought about the book suggestion. It didn't really appeal to her. She felt she'd begun and ended a lot of letters. She didn't want a new project. She wanted a calmer, quieter life.

Max buzzed her on the intercom. "There's somebody on the line,"

Max said. "She won't give me her name or tell me what she's calling about. She's insisting on speaking to you. She says she wants to give you a surprise." Ruth hated surprises. Even pleasant ones. She didn't like the notion of surprise in any form. She liked to be prepared. To know what to expect. She liked to avoid as much as she could the many things in life that were unpredictable.

"She sounds very enthusiastic," Max said.

"Okay," Ruth said. She picked up the phone. "Ruth Rothwax," she said.

"Ruthie," the person said. "Ruthie, this is Zofia."

Ruth was shocked. And confused.

"Where are you, Zofia?" she said.

"I am in Newark airport, New York," Zofia said. "And Walentyna is with me."

Ruth was stunned. How could Zofia and Walentyna be in America? At Newark airport? A thirty-minute drive away from where Ruth was sitting? How had that happened? What were they here for?

"You're at Newark airport?" Ruth said, her head reeling.

"Yes, Ruthie," Zofia said. "Me and Walentyna are in Newark airport, New York. We are very excited."

A question suddenly hit Ruth in the stomach. She felt queasy. Who had given Zofia and Walentyna her office number? The answer seemed obvious.

"We are very excited to see you again, Ruthie," Zofia said. Ruth could hear Walentyna in the background.

"We are very excited to see you," Walentyna was saying. Walentyna seemed in very good spirits. She sounded almost boisterous. She didn't sound like the quiet, overshadowed-by-Zofia person she'd been in Poland. Both women were clearly very excited.

Ruth felt ill. She opened the top drawer of her desk. She wondered if she had any Pepto-Bismol. She used to keep a small bottle of Pepto-Bismol in there for emergencies. It wasn't there now. And this was an emergency. She really felt quite ill. Why was Zofia in New York? And why was she calling her Ruthie? Zofia had said Ruthie at least half a dozen times in the few minutes they'd been on the phone. As though Ruth was her best friend. Or a close relative. That thought made her feel even worse.

"Where are you going?" she said to Zofia. "Are you on your way somewhere?"

"We are not going anywhere else," Zofia said. "We are here in New York, and, Ruthie, even here at Newark airport, New York looks just like New York."

What did she mean? Ruth wondered. What was she referring to? The crowds around the baggage carousel? The lack of porters? The popcorn vendors? What did Zofia, who lived in Sopot, a small seaside town in Poland, know about New York? For a moment Ruth wondered if this was a joke. Was Zofia really still in Sopot? That moment was brief. She could hear the sounds of airport announcements in the background. The announcements were in English.

"I meant, where are you going now? From the airport?" Ruth said.

"Oh, we are going to Edek's place of course," Zofia said. "And we will see you very soon."

Ruth hung up the phone. She just sat there. She couldn't move. Or think. Or maybe she didn't want to think. Maybe she wanted to stop the flow of thoughts and questions that were threatening to enter and crowd her head. She didn't want to call her father. She assumed he knew that Zofia and Walentyna were heading for his apartment. She didn't want to speak to him. She couldn't bear to hear what he knew about and what he didn't know about. And how long he'd known whatever it was that he knew. She sat in her office in a daze. Suddenly some of her father's behavior started to make sense. His busyness for a start. His absence from the office. His busy days and busy nights. What was he doing when he was "busy"? When he was "busy doing things what is normal for people what are busy."

Ruth wondered how long Zofia and Walentyna would be in New York for. Probably two or three weeks, she thought. Then another thought hit her. What if they planned to stay longer? She thought about Edek's interest in the Lower East Side. And his knowledge about real estate prices and apartment rentals. Surely that couldn't have anything to do with Zofia and Walentyna. Or could it? And what about his mentions of a larger apartment? What was her father intending? What was he thinking? She started to feel very shaky. She wanted to call Garth, but it was too late. He'd be asleep and she didn't want to wake him. She definitely didn't want to wake him sounding hysterical. She needed to calm down. She found a packet of Rolaids in another drawer. She chewed four of the antacid tablets. She didn't feel any better.

Ruth called Edek. "Have Zofia and Walentyna arrived at your place yet?" she said.

Edek sounded startled. "You do know they are here?" he said.

"I wouldn't be asking you if they'd arrived if I didn't know they were here," Ruth said.

She knew she sounded agitated.

"Ruthie, column down," Edek said.

"I am calm," she said.

"You are not column," Edek said. "I can hear it in your voice. How do you know that Zofia and Walentyna are in New York?" Edek asked.

"Zofia called me from the airport," Ruth said.

"Zofia did call you?" Edek said. "I did tell her not to call you before I did get a chance to talk to you."

"You've had plenty of chances to talk to me, even if you have been very busy," Ruth said.

"*Oy a broch,*" Edek said. "I did tell Zofia not to call you. I did tell her that I did need to talk to you first."

"What else did you tell her?" Ruth said, with as much sarcasm as she could muster. She still felt bilious.

"Ruthie, Ruthie, column down," Edek said.

"If you wanted me to be calm you should have told me what's going on," Ruth said.

"Nothing is going on," Edek said.

"If it's not such a big deal to you, why did you keep it from me?" Ruth said. "Why didn't you tell me about it?"

"You are all the time very busy," said Edek. "I did not want to bother you."

"Well you've bothered me much more by hiding it from me," Ruth said.

"I was not so much hiding it from you, Ruthie, I did just not tell you about it," Edek said.

Ruth decided not to argue about the semantics of that sentence. She took out two more Rolaids. "So you've been in touch with Zofia since we met her in Poland?" Ruth said. She flinched. Why had she used that phrase? There had been a lot of touching, mostly Zofia touching Edek, when they were in Poland.

"Yes," said Edek. "I did talk to her on the phone."

"How often?" Ruth said.

"Not so often," said Edek.

"Did you speak to her once or twice?" Ruth said.

"Maybe a couple more times than once or twice," Edek said.

"How many times?" said Ruth. She listened to her tone. She sounded like an irate mother.

"How should I know how many times I did speak to Zofia?" Edek said. "Do you think I do count how many times I do speak on the phone to people what I do ring?"

"So you rang Zofia?" Ruth said.

"Off coss," Edek said. "It does cost too much for Zofia to make such telephone calls. It does cost a lot of money to ring America from Poland, and it does cost not too much at all to ring Poland from America."

"Did you speak to her once a month?" Ruth said.

"Why is it important how much I did speak to her?" Edek said.

"I just want to know how much you know about what's happening," Ruth said. "I want to know what you know about why Zofia and Walentyna are in New York."

"Many people do come to New York," Edek said.

"Dad, you've avoiding telling me anything," Ruth said.

"What is there to tell?" Edek said.

"That's what I'm trying to find out," said Ruth. "I didn't even know you had had any contact with Zofia."

"I did speak to Walentyna sometimes, too," said Edek.

"Oh good," said Ruth. "That really clears things up."

"Ruthie why are you so upset?"

Ruth didn't answer. She didn't really know the answer. And the Rolaids had made her feel worse. She'd taken too many.

"Dad, how long are they here for?" she said.

"I do not know exactly," Edek said.

"Why are you being so evasive?" Ruth said. "Do you know what *evasive* means?" she added.

"Off coss," he said. "I do read it in my detective books. Many people in my detective books are such types what are evasive."

"You mean they don't answer questions," said Ruth.

"I do mean that they do not give all the answers to the question what they are being asked." Edek clearly knew what *evasive* meant.

"Do you know how long they're allowed to stay here on a visitor's visa?" Ruth said.

"No," said Edek. "I do not know this."

"So you know nothing?" said Ruth. She felt exasperated. And angry.

"I do not know nothing, Ruthie darling," Edek said. "But I do not know how long a person from Poland can stay in America on a visitor's visa."

"What do you know?" Ruth said.

"I do know that they both got green cards," said Edek.

"That's impossible," Ruth said.

"That is not impossible," said Edek, "because it did happen. Things what are impossible are things what do not happen."

Ruth was trembling. Here she was in a state of shock and her father had suddenly turned into a wordsmith delivering dictionary-like definitions.

"Zofia and Walentyna have got green cards?" Ruth said.

"Yes," said Edek.

"Oh shit," she said.

"They did get the green cards from such a lotto," said Edek.

"They won their green cards in the green-card lottery?" said Ruth.

"Yes," said Edek.

Ruth was speechless. This was starting to sound surreal. She knew several Australians who had won green cards in the annual green-card lottery run by the U.S. government. She didn't even know that Poles could enter the lottery. Not all citizens of all countries could. She felt dazed.

"They've both got green cards?" she said to Edek.

"That is what I did say," Edek said. "They both did get green cards. As a matter of fact they was both very excited."

"Who told them about the green-card lottery?" said Ruth.

"I did," said Edek. "I did tell them when I was in Poland."

"So you told them, over a year ago," Ruth said, "when you'd known them for about a week?"

"Yes," said Edek. "I did know they was both good people."

"Did you know that you might see them in New York?" Ruth said.

"I did know for sure that I would see them in New York," Edek said.

"When did you know that?" Ruth said.

"When Zofia did ring me to tell me about the green cards what they got."

"Okay, Dad," she said. "What are they doing here? And how can they afford to be here?"

"They did bring the money what they did both have in the bank," Edek said. "It is not so much money what you have, Ruthie, but there is not such a lot of people who does have such money what you got."

"I haven't got that much money," Ruth said.

"You got plenty," said Edek.

"I'm sure I've got more than Zofia and Walentyna," Ruth said.

"Off coss you have," said Edek.

"So what are they going to do here?" Ruth said.

"Zofia does want to open a business," Edek said.

"She wants to start a business in New York?" Ruth said. "What sort of business?"

"I do not know," said Edek. "And to tell you the truth Zofia does herself not know."

To tell you the truth, Edek had said. How much of the truth had he been telling her lately? Clearly very little.

"Zofia is sure she can make a business," Edek said. "Plenty of people does start a business. America is the *goldeneh medina*. It is a country what has still a lot of opportunities."

Opportunities for what? Ruth thought. Opportunities for Edek? The thought of Edek having opportunities with Zofia was very unpalatable.

"Where are they going to stay?" Ruth asked Edek.

"They will stay with me off coss," Edek said. "They do not know anybody else in New York."

"They're going to stay with you?" Ruth said. "In your apartment?"

"Yes," said Edek. "I got plenty of space."

"You haven't got that much space," Ruth said.

"They are only two people," Edek said. "When you was small we did only have two rooms and we did have Regina and Itzak and their two girls with us for quite a few months."

Quite a few months? Is that how long Edek was thinking of sharing his apartment with Zofia and Walentyna for? "That was a different time," Ruth said. "We didn't have any money and neither did Regina and Itzak."

"Zofia and Walentyna do not have such a lot of money," Edek said.

"But you hardly know them," said Ruth. "Maybe they could stay in a hotel? I think you should take your time and think about it. I don't think you should rush into anything."

"How much time do I have?" Edek said. "A bit of rushing is not too bad at my age."

Edek had to rush off the phone. Zofia and Walentyna had arrived.

Ruth felt depressed. The thought of Zofia and Walentyna's presence depressed her. She had nothing against Walentyna. Walentyna seemed to be a nice, really quite sweet, person. But Ruth didn't like Zofia. She didn't even know why she didn't like Zofia. She didn't dislike Zofia. She just didn't like her. Both of the women had adored Edek. That had been abundantly clear from the moment they'd met him, in Poland. Walentyna had been as keen to get to know Edek as Zofia had. But Walentyna hadn't stood a chance. She was no match for Zofia, who, with laserlike precision, had focused her breasts and her attention on Edek. It was Zofia who had slept with Edek. *Slept with.* What a stupid expression, Ruth thought. She was sure that there hadn't been much sleeping involved.

She tried to go back to work. But she couldn't think. She couldn't concentrate. Thoughts of Zofia and Edek filled her head. Zofia touching Edek, in Poland. Holding his hand. Encouraging him to eat. No one really needed to encourage Edek to eat. With Zofia's encouragement Edek had eaten even more than he normally did for the week they'd been in Kraków. He'd paused when he and Ruth had gone to Auschwitz. But Zofia and Walentyna had been waiting for him when Edek and Ruth had returned. With a large tray of food. A platter of sausages and cheeses and pâtés and liverwurst.

Ruth thought about the last few weeks. Some of the more puzzling aspects of Edek's behavior no longer seemed as puzzling. Edek talking about large bras on the Lower East Side now made much more sense. So did other small moments. His panic about his cell phone having been off all day. And his offhand reply about who might have been try-ing to ring him. Edek posing the possibility of his friend Topcha visit-ing him, in New York, seemed to be another ruse. Another piece of subterfuge. Ruth's head was pounding. She took two headache pills and went home early.

She wanted to call Garth. She wanted to call Garth and cry. She thought about waiting until she could sound less hysterical than she felt. She thought that that could take days. She called Garth.

"Hello, sweetheart," Garth said. "It's so nice to hear your voice."

"You won't believe what's happened," Ruth said to Garth. "Zofia and Walentyna have arrived in New York."

She told Garth the whole story. Garth wasn't horrified. He wasn't even shocked. He barely sounded disturbed. She thought that the scant whiff of disturbance she detected was probably disturbance about her. She hadn't succeeded in modifying her hysteria.

"Relax, sweetheart," Garth said.

"If I could relax I'd be somebody else," she said to Garth. She'd said this to him dozens of times. It always made him laugh, but it hadn't stopped him from telling her to relax.

Ruth began to suspect that Garth thought Zofia and Walentyna's arrival was a good thing. That made her feel even more tense. Garth had an annoying habit of seeing everything as uplifting. He could stretch most pieces of information into good news.

"At least your father will have some company," Garth said.

"The wrong sort of company," said Ruth.

"Baby, why has this put your nose out of joint?" Garth said.

"My nose is not out of joint," Ruth said. "My nose is the same shape it always was. Anyway, do noses have joints?"

"No, technically they don't have joints," Garth said.

"My nose isn't out of joint," Ruth said. "I'm just worried."

"You were worried about your father before," Garth said.

"Now I'm even more worried," she said.

Garth laughed.

"It's not funny," Ruth said. This conversation was not going in the direction she'd wanted it to.

"You wanted your father to have a hobby," Garth said.

"Zofia and Walentyna sharing my father's apartment doesn't fall into the category of having a hobby," Ruth said. "Their presence probably, if not almost certainly, has more complex consequences than any hobby, unless that hobby was bungee jumping or skydiving."

Garth started laughing again.

"You don't think this is a serious matter, do you?" Ruth said.

"Oh sweetheart," Garth said, "I don't think it's a serious matter. I think it might be a good thing."

"Good for who?" Ruth said. "Good for Zofia and Walentyna. They both get to get out of Sopot, which, despite having the longest pier in the entire Baltic region, has its limits. And Zofia gets to . . ." Ruth stopped in mid-sentence. She didn't want to explore that thought. She didn't want to think about whatever it was Zofia might get to.

"Good for your father," Garth said.

"You're no help at all," Ruth said.

"Sweetheart, you have to calm down about this," said Garth.

Why was she being told to calm down? There were some things it was perfectly reasonable to not feel calm about. And Zofia's arrival was one of those things.

In the morning when Ruth got out of bed, she felt as though she'd hardly slept. Her head hurt. And she felt exhausted. She decided not to call her father. She'd wait for him to call her. She'd called the kids last night. Not one of them was disturbed by the news.

Kate had said, "Great." "That will be so nice for Grandpa," was Zelda's response. And "Good on Grandpa," had been Zachary's reaction.

"Did you know they were coming?" Ruth had asked Zachary.

"No, but I'm assuming Grandpa did," he'd said.

Ruth was sitting in her office. She was wondering whether the short, sharp, stabbing pains in her head were symptoms of an impending stroke, when she heard a large commotion coming from just outside her office door. She opened the door. Edek, Zofia, Walentyna, and Max were standing there. They were all talking. And beaming. Zofia and Walentyna looked happy. And well. They showed no visible sign of the wear and tear of air travel or jet lag. They both looked brimming with health. Zofia was wearing a low-cut, tight, teal blue top and a dark aqua spandex skirt. The skirt was straight and tight and short. Her shoes were blue. They matched the blue of her eyes. She looked as overloaded with energy as she had in Poland. She looked intimidatingly energetic. Almost obscenely energetic. No one, Ruth thought, should have that level of energy. Zofia's skin was clear and unlined. Her breasts were firm and pointed. As if they were making an announcement. A large announcement. Her legs were unmarked, shapely, and muscled. Zofia was solid. She had solid arms, solid hips. There was nothing flabby about her solidity. She looked strong and fit.

Her too tight, too short skirt and her blond spiky hair were possibly the only signs that she had just arrived in the country. Possibly from Poland. Her hair was too yellow. A New York colorist would never leave a bleached blond yellow. The yellow would have been mellowed into a paler, less strident shade. Unless the client was young. In her teens or twenties. And Zofia wasn't. Zofia was in her sixties. Walentyna wore a cream dress, belted at the waist. The dress had a large round collar. The dress made Walentyna look even more slightly built than she was. It was too big. Too big in the shoulders. Too big in the waist, in the hips. Walentyna's neck was dwarfed by the size of the collar. But her spirit wasn't. Walentyna looked so much more animated, more excited, and more vivacious than Ruth had ever seen her, in Poland. New York, which could have a deleterious, dampening effect on some people, had clearly infused Walentyna with its vivacity.

"Hello," Ruth said, in what she hoped was a cheerful, welcoming tone. Zofia and Walentyna looked up and rushed over to greet her. Zofia grabbed and embraced Ruth with such gusto that Ruth feared her lungs would be permanently dented. She had forgotten how strong Zofia was. Strong physically. And strong in her enthusiasm.

Walentyna kissed Ruth on both cheeks. "It is very nice to see you again," she said.

Zofia looked at Ruth again. "You do not look so well, Ruthie," she said. "Is something wrong?"

Is something wrong? Ruth thought. Yes, something was definitely wrong. "No," she said, "I'm just a bit tired."

"She does work too hard," Edek said. "I did tell her that many times."

"I don't work too hard," Ruth said. "I don't work that hard. I don't work nearly as hard as a bricklayer, or any other construction worker. I don't work as hard as a dishwasher in a restaurant or a postman."

"Why are you talking about a bricklayer or a postman?" Edek said. "You did never want to be a bricklayer or a postman."

"I was just using them as examples of people who work hard," Ruth said.

"What for?" Edek said. "You did not once in your whole life say you did want to be a postman."

Ruth wished she'd agreed that she worked too hard.

"Edek darling," Zofia said. "Ruthie is just saying that she does not work as hard as some people do work."

Edek darling? Zofia had been in the country less than twenty-four hours and Edek was already *Edek darling.*

"Ruthie, me and Walentyna, we are very happy to see you," Zofia said.

Ruth smiled.

"Ruthie is very happy to see you, too," Edek said.

Tara arrived. "Terra," Edek said excitedly, "I do want you to meet my friends from Poland, Zofia and Walentyna. Zofia and Walentyna, this is Terra McGann," he said with a flourish. "Terra is a very nice girl." Tara, Max, Zofia, Walentyna, and Edek stood and chatted for a while. Ruth wasn't sure what to do. She felt superfluous. Everyone was getting on so well with everyone else. Tara looked at her watch.

"I'd better start getting some work done," she said. "Your father's friends are wonderful," Tara said as she passed Ruth. Ruth tried not to frown.

"Aren't they fabulous?" Max said, as soon as Edek, Zofia, and Walentyna had left the room.

"Are they?" said Ruth. But Max didn't hear her. Max was in the middle of a full-blown monologue about Zofia and Walentyna's fabulousness.

"They're so natural and direct," Max was saying. "You can tell they are both unpretentious." Ruth wasn't sure that Max's perceptions were all that perceptive. "I love Walentyna's clothes," Max said. "She looks like the fashion world hasn't touched her. It's so sweet." Ruth thought that far from the fashion world having passed Walentyna by, Walentyna was possibly ahead of her time. She had achieved the waif look without having to have artificially torn hemlines and expensive ripped-and-then-stitched-together bodices and sleeves and trouser legs. "I think they're both going to blend in well here," Max said. Ruth didn't want to think about Zofia and Walentyna blending in.

They probably would blend in well, Ruth thought, despite the excess of yellow in Zofia's hair. Their Polish accents wouldn't set them apart. In New York, everyone spoke with a thick accent of one sort or another. Why was she dwelling on the yellowness of Zofia's hair? There were far more compelling aspects of Zofia to dwell on than too much yellow. It was bitchy and trite of her to be critical of the color of Zofia's hair. What had happened to the principles of sisterhood and support she'd espoused to Sonia? The principles behind the women's group she had been trying to form? Those principles had disappeared the moment Zofia had appeared in New York.

She could hear Edek expounding on the virtues of the self-navigating vacuum cleaner in the background. She went back into her office. She found it hard to concentrate. This new aspect of Edek's life was much more distracting and disturbing than the carnage he'd caused being in charge of the Stockings Department.

Edek opened the door of her office and then knocked. "Can we come in to say goodbye, Ruthie?" he said. All three of them came into the office. "I did show Zofia and Walentyna the work I did do when I was in charge of the Stockings Department," Edek said.

Ruth noticed Edek's use of the past tense. He had relieved himself of the position. He'd evidently resigned as head of the Stockings Department.

"I can see that Edek is very good at this job," said Walentyna. "Me and Zofia did never see a vacuum cleaner that moves by itself."

"Probably they do not have such a vacuum cleaner, in Poland," Edek said.

"There are probably not too many people in America that have a self-navigating vacuum cleaner," said Ruth.

"Edek you are very clever," said Walentyna.

"Of course our Edek is very clever," Zofia said.

Now he was *our Edek*. This was Zofia's first day in America. Ruth felt a sense of dread at what was in store. Zofia had already moved with considerable speed. How much faster could she operate? What would she be like a month from now? Ruth looked at her father. He looked so cheerful. Almost radiant. "Look at this calculator," he said to Zofia and Walentyna, picking up the twelve-digit, two-color, heavy-duty ribbon calculator from Ruth's desk. "I did buy this calculator for the business," Edek said. "I did buy one for Ruthie and one for Max."

"Edek must be a big help to you," Walentyna said.

"Yes," said Ruth.

"Edek is a very big help," Zofia said. Zofia had paused and placed an extra emphasis on the word big. Why did half of what came out of Zofia's mouth seem so suggestive to Ruth?

Ruth went over her own last thought. Why had she phrased it like that? Why was she thinking about things that could come out of Zofia's mouth? She didn't want to think of anything coming in or out of Zofia's mouth. She decided that she was being hypersensitive or overly anxious. Or both.

"Edek is a very big help," Zofia repeated. "I know this," she said, looking up at Edek.

"Ruthie, to have such a calculator does make things a lot more easy in the office, doesn't it?" Edek said.

"Yes, it does," said Ruth.

"That is the same thing what Max did say," said Edek, looking pleased.

Edek opened one of the files on Ruth's desk. He beckoned Zofia and Walentyna over to look at the file. All three peered in. Edek flipped through the documents.

"Ruthie does write such letters for people what is rich. And she is a rich girl herself now."

"I'm not," Ruth said.

"Pheh," Edek said, dismissing her statement. "People do pay her a lot of money just to write a letter," he said to Zofia and Walentyna. "Ruthie does write a letter what looks like a letter the person did write. Only it is more clever than what a normal person can write."

"People pay money to you to write a letter?" Walentyna said to Ruth.

"People do pay her a lot of money," Edek said.

"How much?" Zofia asked.

"Hundreds of dollars," Edek said, with formality. As though he was making a public announcement.

"Hundreds of dollars," Zofia and Walentyna chorused together.

"Yes, hundreds of dollars," Edek said.

All three of them stepped back and looked at Ruth, with admiration. Edek's admiration was tinged with the sort of pride that came with ownership.

Edek nodded his head. "My daughter is very clever," he said. "Not everyone does have a daughter what is so clever."

Both of the women were nodding in agreement.

"I have to go back to work," Ruth said.

"Off coss," Edek said. "She does have many such very rich clients who do wait for letters," Edek said to Zofia and Walentyna.

An hour after Edek, Zofia, and Walentyna had left, Ruth was still in a daze.

Max called Ruth. "Mrs. Lord is on the phone," Max said. Iris Lord had been a client for years. She had been one of Ruth's very first clients. "Mrs. Lord wants a divorce card that no other clients of ours can use. She wants to own the copyright and have access to reprints."

Ruth was startled. How many divorced or likely-to-be-divorced people did Iris Lord know? Ruth liked Iris Lord. Iris Lord was in her sixties and immensely wealthy. Her ex-husband, George Lord, the heir to the Lord's Tools chain of hardware stores, had left Iris when she was fifty-nine. Iris Lord had fought, and emerged from the skirmish with $140 million.

"I don't find it hard to meet men I find attractive," Iris Lord had once said to Ruth.

Ruth thought that Iris might just be the sole woman voicing that thought in New York. New York was full of women bemoaning the dearth of attractive men.

"I meet a lot of attractive men," Iris said. "And men who find me attractive." She paused. "It's easier if you've got money. Money is an aphrodisiac. Lots of money in the bank overrides a too flabby tummy, a drooped derriere, and thighs that are marked with veins. Money almost negates the disadvantages of age. I probably have the same degree of desirability as a thirty-five-year-old with an income of six-hundred-thousand dollars."

Iris Lord came on the line. She sounded very bouncy. Ruth didn't feel at all bouncy. Ruth felt bounced about. Disoriented. Winded. And trounced. How had her father done this? Ruth thought. How had he managed to orchestrate the transplantation of Zofia and Walentyna from Sopot to Manhattan? Ruth was sure the two women couldn't have carried out the maneuver without him. She didn't think they would have made the decision to move if they hadn't had Edek to move to.

Ruth and Iris discussed the divorce card that Iris wanted to order. Iris wanted to make it broad enough to send to a variety of people. And she wanted it to feel timeless. Not dated with any contemporary references.

"Why does Mrs. Lord want so many cards?" Max said to Ruth as Max was preparing to leave for the day.

"I guess because a lot of Iris Lord's friends are getting divorced," Ruth said. "I guess you could just say a lot of people are getting divorced."

"Not your father," Max said. "He looks like he's getting attached."

"Thanks, Max," Ruth said.

Ruth lay in bed that night trying to sleep. She was trying not to think about Zofia and Walentyna and trying not to think about not falling asleep. The more you thought about the fact that you were unable to sleep, the less able to sleep you became. Ruth had experienced this more than once. She had expended a lot of energy trying not to feel anxious about her inability to sleep or about how much sleep she was missing. She lay in bed concentrating on not becoming tense about not falling asleep. She didn't want to think about Zofia, Walentyna, and Edek. She didn't want to know where they had had dinner. She didn't want to know where they had walked. She didn't want to know how they felt. She didn't want to know where they were sleeping. She knew they were in Edek's one-bedroom apartment. She didn't want to think about the sleeping arrangements in Edek's one-bedroom apartment. That one bedroom had a queen-size bed. And there was a queen-size sofa bed in the living room. Who was sleeping where? Maybe Edek had been gallant and given Zofia and Walentyna his bedroom? Maybe Edek was sleeping in the living room? Why was she thinking about where they were sleeping? Ruth looked at the clock. It was 1:45 A.M. She thought that Edek and Zofia and Walentyna were probably sleeping. A lot of people were probably sleeping. Zachary, Zelda, and Kate were probably sleeping. Sonia was probably sleeping. Half of New York was probably sleeping. She wasn't. She was wide awake.

Edek called Ruth at the office the next day. She knew she sounded curt. Even her hello was brisk.

"What is wrong with you, Ruthie?" Edek said.

"Nothing," she said. "I had a late night."

"We did go to a new restaurant last night, me and Zofia and Walentyna," Edek said. "We did go to a Yemenite restaurant. You know what is a Yemenite?"

"A Yemenite is a Jew who used to live in Yemen," Ruth said.

"Or a Jew what his family did used to live in Yemen," said Edek.

"Yes, a Jew whose ancestors were formerly resident in Yemen," Ruth said with a degree of irritation in her voice.

Edek had either overlooked her irritation or hadn't noticed. "We did eat good Jewish food in this Yemenite restaurant," he said. "They did have such a big pancake with a boiled egg in the middle. They did have such a salad what you do get in Israel, with chopped cucumbers and tomatoes and onions and, I think, some radishes."

"You had salad?" Ruth said. "You never eat salad."

"Off coss not," said Edek. "Zofia and Walentyna did have a bit of salad with their meat."

Ruth was startled. She had momentarily, very momentarily, forgotten that Zofia and Walentyna had been at dinner with Edek. The talk of salad had temporarily derailed her. She had drifted off. She'd thought the conversation was like old times. Edek regaling her with what he'd eaten. She realized that she'd become used to her father describing his solo lunches and dinners. She didn't think he'd be having too many more of them.

"The new restaurant what we did find makes a very good fried fish," said Edek. "The chicken soup was, for me, not so good. It did have some carry or paprika in it." Ruth restrained herself from pointing out that Yemenite food was as unlikely as Israeli food to contain any curry. She felt unreasonably irritated. "Zofia did say the chicken was very good," Edek said. "She does like such stuff what is hot. I did have kebabs which was pretty nice. And Walentyna did like very much her chicken."

Ruth's irritation turned into impatience. Was Edek going to list every item of food that each of them had consumed?

"Is something wrong, Ruthie?" Edek said.

"No," Ruth said. She knew it was not a very convincing no. But it was enough for Edek. He didn't seem concerned.

"This new restaurant does also have latkes," he said.

"What is the restaurant called?" Ruth asked.

"Could you hold on one minute, please?" Edek said. He always uttered that sentence slowly and clearly. With a formality in his voice. As though he was delivering a speech at Buckingham Palace. Could you hold on one minute please? Edek had said it that way since they'd first got a telephone when Ruth was six or seven. He always added *please*. Even if he was talking to her or to Garth or to one of the kids. Edek came back on the line. "I did write down the name of the restaurant because Zofia did say you would probably like very much the food in this restaurant." He paused, probably to try and decipher his handwriting, which was not easy to read. Possibly because he wrote everything in very small letters in a very small notebook that he kept in his pocket. He'd used the same sort of notebook for years. It was the standard five-by-three-inch spiral notebook available in stationery stores and supermarkets. When he finished one notebook, he transferred some crucial details to a new notebook and threw the old one away. Ruth often wished he'd saved all the notebooks. There would have been hundreds of them.

"The restaurant what we did eat at is called Rectangles," Edek announced.

Ruth pounced. "Rectangles isn't a new restaurant," she said in the tone of voice an unpleasant parent would use to show a child he'd been caught. Caught lying. Or caught being stupid. "Rectangles has been there for years," she said. "It's opposite the Second Avenue Deli. Just a few doors from where you live."

"Yes," Edek said. He sounded deflated.

"You are upset, Ruthie," Edek said, after a minute. "I can hear it in your voice."

"No, I'm not," she said.

"You are upset," Edek said. "You are probably upset about Zofia and Walentyna."

"No," Ruth said.

"I think that you are," Edek said. "Why does it make you upset?" he asked.

Ruth couldn't answer. She didn't have an answer. She couldn't really pinpoint why Zofia and Walentyna's arrival distressed her. But she felt she was right to feel distressed.

In Poland, she'd watched Zofia make a play for Edek. A direct and successful play. The words she was using, Ruth thought, were starting to sound as though she was referring to a Broadway production. Ruth thought she'd got rid of Zofia when she and Edek had left Poland. But it was very apparent that she hadn't. She'd thought that Zofia, and possibly Walentyna, were taking advantage of her father, but she didn't know exactly how.

"Zofia and Walentyna are very nice people," Edek said, "and they did come to New York. What is the big deal that does make you so upset?"

"How are they going to support themselves?" Ruth said.

"They got a bit of money of their own," Edek said. "And I will give them a help."

Ruth seized on the money issue. "You'll help them?" she said. "But I support you."

"Then you will support all of us," Edek said. "You can afford it."

Five

Ruth hadn't slept properly for nights. She found that her concentration was lapsing. She was drifting off into plans of how to get rid of Zofia and Walentyna when she was supposed to be composing letters. She was sitting at her desk trying to compose a condolence letter. She was feeling tired. And sorry for herself. The letter she was composing was becoming sadder and sadder. She read it. It was too sad. Condolence letters had to be very sympathetic and recognize the tragedy and enormity of the loss. But they also had to be uplifting. To have an uplifting note. The letter Ruth was writing was mournfully sad. It was so sad it stood a good chance of making the recipient wish they had also died.

She was halfway through trying to infuse the condolence letter with some sense of optimism, some sense of hope, when there was a knock at her door, and Zelda appeared.

"Hi, Roo," Zelda said. "I thought I'd stop by and say hello," she said. "I haven't seen you for ages. And I was just around the corner at the dentist."

Ruth got up and kissed Zelda hello. Zelda always smelled good.

She always smelled freshly washed. Even if she wasn't. Ruth kissed Zelda again. She loved the smooth planes of Zelda's face. And Zelda's curtain of strawberry blond hair. And Zelda's blue eyes. Ruth, like all Jews, was thrilled to have a blue-eyed child.

"How are you, Roo?" Zelda said. "You look a little tired. Are you okay?"

"I haven't been sleeping well," Ruth said.

"Is that still menopause?" Zelda said.

"I don't know," Ruth said. "It's probably just me."

"Why do they call it menopause?" Zelda said. "It doesn't pause and then return. You don't start menstruating again after a pause. The pause lasts forever. It should be called menostop."

Ruth started laughing. She felt cheered up. "Well I don't think it's either menopause or menostop," she said. "It's just me. I haven't been sleeping well. I begin forming a list of what's wrong and what could go wrong when I get into bed at night. Especially with Garth away."

"I think you're doing really well," Zelda said. "Zachary, Kate, and I all thought you might not manage as well as you have."

"You did, did you?" said Ruth.

She didn't know whether to be reassured or offended at the thought that her children were discussing and assessing how she was managing her life.

"I'm fine," Ruth said, firmly.

"It's really great about Grandpa, isn't it?" Zelda said.

"What's great?" said Ruth.

"Grandpa's new friends," Zelda said. "We met them."

"You met them?" Ruth said.

"Yes, Grandpa invited us all out to dinner with Zofia and Walentyna," Zelda said. "It's great for Grandpa to have them in New York. He seems really happy." Zelda looked at her watch. "I should go," she said. "I have to get back to work."

Ruth didn't like the notion of her father rushing to introduce Zofia and Walentyna to Zachary, Zelda, and Kate. It felt premature. The instant introductions could have imbued the relationships with a significance they may not have. Zofia and Walentyna had only just arrived. Why couldn't Edek have waited for a while? Waited for what? She thought. Waited till he was ninety-five? She chided herself. Edek wasn't a child. He was an elderly man introducing his grandchildren to two friends. Why should that agitate anyone? It wasn't agitating anyone. It was only agitating her. Ruth thought that she would leave the condolence letter until tomorrow. She felt less than clearheaded. And less than capable of giving any condolence letter an uplifting tilt. She attempted a thank-you letter for one of her most regular clients. She checked the previous thank-you letters she'd done for that client. She made a few notes, and then gave up. She looked at the fragments of her attempted thank-you letter. It was clear she was finding it difficult to summon up thanks, or gratitude. She decided to tidy her office. She felt that would make her feel better. Sorting and shifting documents and paper clips and pencils and erasers and ballpoint pens helped to put order into her thoughts. An hour later she felt much better.

One of the women who had agreed to join the women's group had e-mailed Ruth to say she had changed her mind. This morning she'd called Ruth. "I've just ended a very traumatic relationship," she said to Ruth, "and I don't feel ready to join a women's group."

Ruth didn't know Georgia, the woman, very well. She knew that she was an editor at a small publishing company. "What happened?" Ruth said. Georgia hesitated before speaking.

"We had a relationship that started out so wonderful," she said. "I just thought he was the second coming. And I was at a time in my life when I could have used the second coming of Christ.

"It took me a while to realize he had a problem. We'd make out and things would be quite erotic. And then nothing happened. No erection.

At first I put it down to nervousness. But it persisted. He would only get erections when we couldn't have sex. He'd suddenly get this raging erection when I was driving the car on the highway. And he'd say, 'I have this erection.' Or, just as I'd be leaving for work, or all packed and ready to go and catch a plane, he'd be lying there and he'd say, 'Guess what?' looking suggestively down at himself, and there would be this big erection.

"It made me feel guilty for thinking of sex as intercourse," Georgia said. "He helped me with that. He kept saying, 'There's more to sex than just intercourse. We can do lots of things.' And I had a girlfriend, a very old, good friend, who said, 'Oh yes, I never had such great sex as with one impotent guy once.' "

Ruth felt appalled. "Didn't any of your friends tell you to think about getting out of the relationship?" Ruth said.

"Not really," said Georgia. "I had one friend who said, 'At least you're at the table. Don't complain about the dinner.' Another woman said that my partner's inability to have sex with me was because he loved me so much, and I was failing to acknowledge this great sign of devotion." Ruth gasped. "I felt guilty at every step," Georgia said. "Guilty for not wanting to get married. Guilty for wanting to have intercourse, specifically. One girlfriend was just very flip. She said it was great to try to have sex with an impotent man. It was such a different dimension." Georgia sounded as though she was going to cry. "My cousin did say, 'He can't get an erection, he's got no money. What else do you want from a man? Just get rid of him. It's a bad deal. Dump him.' But that felt too crass and too brutal to me at the time.

"We started going to a therapist. We were doing all these exercises. The exercises didn't lead anywhere, and I became less and less able to feel aroused. Our relationship really started to unravel. I started to feel that I had a problem. That I couldn't have sex. I had not had intercourse for a long time by then. I started to feel like a virgin. Frightened and anxious about sex. That was the worst part. I couldn't get wet anymore."

She was brave, Ruth thought, to talk about getting wet. Ruth knew she should say something. After all, part of her reason for forming the group was to have a more intimate group of women friends. Women who were more connected to each other's lives. "I had a real problem getting wet," Ruth said. "I developed vaginal dryness, just when I thought I'd sailed through menopause. I tried using egg whites as a moisturizer. My gynecologist suggested it. It didn't work. Anyway, who wants to start separating the yolks from the whites of eggs before they have sex? It was impossible to use, too. You should try taking a handful of egg white and inserting it into yourself. More egg white ends up on the carpet and on the sheets than in you. Maybe if I'd beaten the egg white first, it would have been easier. It also felt a bit weird sharing that part of my life with a chicken I'd never met."

There was a silence on the phone. Ruth was glad that she hadn't mentioned that vaginal dryness was sometimes called vaginal atrophy. Vaginal atrophy sounded even worse. If you had to have any part of you atrophy, why couldn't it be your navel or something that didn't seem of much use, Ruth thought.

"I ended up taking a very small dose of estrogen in the form of vaginal tablets," Ruth said quickly to Georgia. She felt embarrassed. She wished she hadn't talked about vaginas and dryness and egg whites. She tried to steer her conversation in a more clinical, palatable direction. "The vaginal tablets, which each come in a disposable single-use applicator, are one twenty-fifth of the strength of the average daily hormone replacement pill. You insert one tablet twice a week. It's really easy," she said cheerfully, in an effort to bring the conversation to a squeaky-clean end.

"What have you got against Zofia?" Sonia said to Ruth. Sonia and Ruth were having dinner together. Ruth was glad to be having dinner with Sonia. She hadn't wanted to go home after work. She felt like being out in the world. Her own world had become too insular. Too circular. Too centered around Zofia and Walentyna.

"I don't know," Ruth said. "There was something about the way she pounced on my father, in Poland."

"Why shouldn't women pounce?" said Sonia. "And how do you know who pounced on whom?"

"I was there when she met him," Ruth said. "I was having breakfast with him in the dining room of the Mimoza Hotel in Kraków. I saw her look at him from the moment we arrived."

"I still don't get what's wrong with that," said Sonia. "She seems independent and direct. I think the two of them are courageous, adventurous, and brave women. True feminists. It can't be easy for two widows to leave their country and move somewhere else."

"How do you know they're widows?" Ruth said.

"Your father told me," said Sonia.

Why did two widows sound predatory? As though they should be preceded by a sign that said, "Beware of Widows," not unlike the "Beware of Dog" warnings. Widowers weren't viewed like that. Two widowers conjured up an entirely different image. Two widowers seemed a charming, attractive, and possibly desirable proposition.

Ruth sighed. It seemed that everyone in her orbit had met Zofia and Walentyna. Sonia had bumped into Edek and Zofia and Walentyna on Thirteenth Street, near the Quad Cinema. Sonia was on her way to see a client and Edek and the two women were coming out of a movie.

"Your father looked very happy," Sonia said. "He didn't look as though he minded being pounced on."

"I thought there was an ulterior motive behind her pounce," Ruth said. "She seemed like a predator to me."

"A predator?" Sonia said. "You're not showing a lot of sisterly solidarity."

"I sound like a misogynist, don't I?" said Ruth. She felt a bit ashamed of herself.

"You sound confused," said Sonia. "First, you treat your father as though he's a small child. You were trying to find him hobbies and wanting to enroll him in clubs. Now you sound as though he's a delinquent teenager. Your father is old enough to make his own decisions," Sonia said.

"I think he's been swayed by those breasts," Ruth said.

"Why shouldn't he be?" said Sonia. "Why shouldn't he be swayed by her breasts, sway with her breasts, have her breasts swaying wherever he wants them to sway. Or whenever she wants them to sway."

"Ugh," Ruth said. Why did Sonia have to invoke the image of Zofia's breasts swaying? Swaying and encircling the earth? Swaying and encircling Edek?

"I think you're probably a prude at heart," Sonia said.

Did Sonia say prune? Or prude? Ruth thought. Neither of the words could be considered complimentary. She decided Sonia had said prude.

"You're right, it's not very sisterly, is it?" Ruth said to Sonia.

"No," said Sonia. "You don't sound like an advocate for equality for women, for power for women. You don't sound like someone who talks about women banding together and attaining strength and influence through unity. You sound like a bitch. A bitch in a sulk."

Ruth was shocked. Why was Sonia calling her a bitch? A bitch was definitely worse than a prude. Or a prune. A bitch in a sulk was even worse. A sulking prude of a bitch was the pits.

Sonia's cell phone rang. "It's Michael, I'll take it outside," Sonia said, getting up and walking away from the table.

"Do you think lesbians dislike, like, or feel indifferent to penises?" a well-dressed man in his mid-thirties said to his friend. Both of the men looked like bankers or stockbrokers. They were sitting at the bar.

Ruth looked at them and frowned. It seemed like such a stupid question. How could you generalize about whether a group of women, lesbian or heterosexual, liked penises. And how could you ask a question about penises in general? Most people didn't think about penises in general. Or multiple penises. Penises didn't come in batches. They came in single units. And attached to a human being. Usually a man. Penises didn't come in collections or compilations. Or in bundles. Or bunches. Tied with bows. Like roses or tulips. You didn't think of clumps or clusters of penises. Or packages and parcels of men's appendages. You didn't think of penises in numbers or portions. Ruth was disturbed by the notion of penises in bulk. She flinched. She shouldn't have used the words *bulk* and *penis* in one sentence. Not only were the two words in the one sentence, they were only separated by one word. Penis and bulk raised the notion of bulky penises. Raised the notion? Why did she have to use the word *raise*? Bulky penises or penises rising were not thoughts she wanted to entertain right now. Entertain? She had to stop herself. Her head was starting to fill with bulky raised penises being entertained. Sonia came back.

"Those two guys at the bar were generalizing about lesbians and penises," Ruth said. "You can't generalize about lesbians and you can't generalize about penises. Penises don't come en masse." She stopped. The notion of penises coming en masse was too much for her. "I'll rephrase that," she said. Sonia laughed.

"I don't think of penises as disembodied, or as a group," Ruth said. "I think penises have to be attached to a brain and a body. If you're thinking about a penis it should belong to a person. Preferably someone you know."

"I can think about penises without worrying about who they belong to," Sonia said. "I just think about somebody sticking it in and how good that feels."

"You can think about somebody sticking it in and how good it feels while you're eating dinner?" Ruth said, looking at the medallions of lamb and mashed potatoes on Sonia's plate.

"Sure," said Sonia. "I love the rush of feeling of a penis being pushed into me."

Ruth ate a few mouthfuls of her steamed mussels. Maybe Sonia was right. Maybe she was a prude. She wondered if it was too late to change. She wondered if instead of feeling worried about whether the mussels were fresh or not or whether each mussel shell had opened properly, she could think about Garth sticking it in.

"I don't have that heady, almost giddy pleasure with Michael," Sonia said.

"That's sad," said Ruth.

"It probably is," said Sonia.

Ruth was surprised. She'd rarely seen Sonia be reflective about that aspect of her life. It was a little disconcerting. There was something endearing about Sonia's proclamations and declarations. Something endearing about her dictums and edicts. Ruth didn't want Sonia to become too reflective. She liked Sonia's certainty that she was right.

"I'm not getting very far with the women's group," Ruth said. "One of the women who said she'd join has just dropped out."

"You're not getting very far?" Sonia said. "You're not getting anywhere."

Edek called Ruth. "Hello, how is my daughter?" he said. He sounded bright and cheerful. He sounded, as Sonia had said, happy.

"I'm fine," said Ruth. "How are you?"

"I am very good," Edek said. Ruth looked at the handset of the phone she was using. Had she heard what she thought she'd heard? Had Edek said, "I am very good"?

Ruth knew something was wrong. Edek never said, "I am very good." His standard reply to the question of how he was, was, "As good as can be expected." She had never heard him say, "I am very good." She felt alarmed. She told herself to calm down. Change was not an immediate cause for alarm. Change could indicate improvement. What had changed in Edek's life? The arrival of Zofia and Walentyna. She didn't think that Zofia and Walentyna's arrival constituted an improvement. It felt more like an intrusion.

"I been busy, Ruthie," Edek said. "I did organize a bank account for Zofia and for Walentyna. I did talk to the bank manager to make sure that the money what Zofia and Walentyna got in the bank in Poland will come to the bank in New York. It does come with a telegram."

"You mean a telegraphic transfer," said Ruth.

"That is right," Edek said. "A telegram what does transfer the money."

"Zofia and Walentyna wanted to transfer their money to New York?" Ruth said.

"Off coss," said Edek. "I did also organize a Social Security card for the two women. I did go to the office what does such Social Security cards with Zofia and Walentyna. And we did answer the questions on the forms and now the people what does the Social Security will post to us the Social Security cards."

"You have been very busy," Ruth said. Edek had orchestrated all of this with maximum efficiency. As though he'd had it planned for a long time.

"I want you should do me a favor, Ruthie," Edek said. "I want for you to organize the health insurance for Zofia and Walentyna."

"Health insurance is very complicated," Ruth said. "It took me long enough to get health insurance for you."

"I know it is not easy," Edek said. "That is why I did ask you. You do know everything."

"Who's paying for it?" Ruth said.

"Naturally I got to help them out a bit," Edek said. "They are coming from Poland and in Poland nobody does have a lot of money."

"Some people do, now," said Ruth.

"But Zofia and Walentyna are not one of those some people," Edek said, "So I am helping a bit."

Edek seemed oblivious to the fact that it was not he who was help-ing Zofia and Walentyna a bit. It was Ruth. She had already mentioned that more than once. She didn't want to mention it again. She didn't want to take his helpfulness away from him.

"I'll look into the health insurance," Ruth said.

"I did know you would fix it, you are a good girl, Ruthie," Edek said.

Ruth didn't feel like a good girl. She didn't feel like a girl. And she didn't feel good. She was so agitated about Zofia and Walentyna. She'd been clenching her jaw and tensing her neck throughout the call. Now her jaw and neck both ached.

"Why can't we use song lyrics in our cards?" Max said to Ruth. "Why can't we have a card that says, 'Baby let me light your fire'?" Max looked fired up by her idea. Excited.

"I think we can have Jim Morrison singing that to us," Ruth said, "but we can't say, 'Baby let me light your fire,' in a card to Jim Brown or Jim Rosenblatt. That line in a card from a woman could sound provocative if not promiscuous. And from a man it might seem less than sensitive, or cerebrally deficient. Anyway we can't use lyrics be-cause we'd have to pay for them. And that's if the person who holds the copyright is willing to let us use them. It's too complicated. And lyrics don't really translate into cards."

Max looked deflated.

"Can you imagine sending someone a card that says, 'Shall we dance?' " Ruth said. "Actually, that would be brilliant. We could just have one word on the inside of the card. It could say, 'When?' "

Max cheered up. "I thought it would be a good idea," she said.

"It is," said Ruth, "but we can't do it. We'd either have to pay a fortune for permission to use the lines or we'd be refused permission. Do you know where the line 'Shall We Dance?' comes from?" Ruth said to Max.

"No," Max said.

"I didn't think you would. It's a generational thing. It comes from the Rodgers and Hammerstein musical *The King and I,*" Ruth said.

Shall we dance? Ruth had always seen the line as an invitation. An invitation to freedom. An invitation to undo limits and strictures and boundaries. An invitation to happiness. An invitation to love. She thought about it. *Shall we dance?* It was only composed of three words. Three ordinary words. She thought you probably couldn't copyright these three words. She made a note to ask Sonia.

Ruth was experimenting with a card. A card that could be sent by recent graduates still looking for a job, to their parents. A card that could be sent to a roommate, to a partner. There was a gap in the market for this sort of card.

Working Hard Is Time Well Spent

Thank you for paying my rent.

She usually tried not to rhyme her cards. She didn't like rhymes. But sometimes they were unavoidable. Ruth didn't feel entirely comfortable with this card. It had a different tone from most of her other cards. She knew it was cheeky. She hoped it came across as sincere. She also hoped it wasn't glib. She'd decided to use a less expensive paper for this card. You didn't want to be seen as making extravagant purchases if someone else was paying the rent. She'd also priced the card more cheaply than her other cards.

Ruth's Direct Text cards were displayed in their own stand. They were not interspersed among other cards. The stands could sit on counters or on shelves. Direct Text was embossed in pale gray print on all four sides of the white stands. It had taken Ruth a long time to find a white that wasn't too harsh. A white that looked inviting. And classy. So far, Ruth had twelve cards on the market. One of her newest cards:

Congratulations

Your success is spreading happiness.

was already being reordered. Ruth often felt guilty for making money
in such a relatively luxurious and indulgent way. She didn't have to
stand all day, or lift boxes or report to bosses. She didn't have to have
monthly or quarterly or biannual assessments. She sat in her own office
and put words together.

She had been looking for a sublet for Zofia and Walentyna. Edek
had said they were looking for an apartment. Ruth wasn't sure who
"they" were. She hoped that this particular "they" didn't include Edek.
Edek's sentence was ambiguous. It could have meant all three of them
were looking. Or it could have meant the apartment they were looking
for was for the three of them. The "they," in this case, had been the critical element of the sentence. Ruth thought a six-month sublet would be
a start. That way Zofia and Walentyna didn't have to buy furniture.
And wouldn't be committed to more time in New York than they may
have planned or may want. Ruth had been looking at the far east part
of the East Village. Around Avenue D. That area hadn't yet been entirely gentrified. Ruth had found herself half harboring a hope that the
area would be off-putting. She'd tried to push that uncharitable hope
into the background. She told herself she was choosing the area because
it was still good value.

She'd found a sublet on Avenue D when Edek announced they had
found an apartment. Ruth had been having dinner with Edek, Zofia,
and Walentyna at the Ukrainian East Village Restaurant, on Second Avenue. Zofia and Walentyna loved the Ukrainian East Village Restaurant.

"The goulash here is very, very good," Zofia said.

"They have very, very good piroshkis," said Edek.

"Everything is very, very good," Walentyna said.

Edek himself looked very good, Ruth thought. She noticed he had on a new shirt. And new trousers. Edek never bought clothes on his own. Zofia must have chosen them. Edek usually had to be forced to buy new clothing. Ruth wondered how much force Zofia had had to use.

Ruth, up until then, had avoided having dinner with Zofia and Walentyna. That also meant she hadn't seen much of her father. Walentyna was beaming at Edek as she ate. So was Zofia. Ruth looked at Walentyna. She was dressed in a white blouse with a round Peter Pan collar and sleeves gathered at the shoulder. A wide frill of white nylon lace ran down the front of the blouse. The frill was almost as broad as Walentyna. It just about dwarfed Walentyna's narrow frame. It went from the center of her rib cage to the outer edges of her chest. The blouse was perched on top of a voluminous, muted, floral-patterned skirt. Walentyna all but vanished inside her outfit. Walentyna didn't look uncomfortable or awkward about the clothes she was wearing. She clearly felt at home in the ensemble. Zofia was wearing a green Lurex skirt. Ruth didn't know they had Lurex in Poland. The skirt sparkled and shimmered every time Zofia moved. Zofia had already moved quite a lot. She'd stood up, tugged at the skirt, and sat down. This was an effort to stop the skirt from traveling halfway up to her hips. But the skirt was resilient. Every time she tugged at it and sat down, it rode right up again. Zofia's breasts, which were barely contained in a short, tight black top, moved when Zofia moved. They almost sprang out without any help, several times. As though they were determined to escape their environment.

Ruth was about to describe the Avenue D sublet when Edek interrupted her. "We did find an apartment," he said.

"You've found an apartment?" Ruth said.

"Yes," said Zofia, Walentyna, and Edek simultaneously. This was not good news. Ruth felt that acutely. "We did find an apartment what has got two and a half bedrooms," Edek said.

"We do not have half a bedroom in Poland," Walentyna said.

"This is America," said Zofia. "America has got everything."

"That is right," said Edek. "Here you can get half a bedroom and half a bathroom. Half a bedroom is still the same what is a whole bedroom but not so big. And half a bathroom does mean a bathroom what has not got a bath or a shower."

"We have many such bathrooms in Poland," Walentyna said.

Ruth looked at Edek. When did he develop his real estate expertise? When he was being busy? It seemed as though he'd really been very busy.

"It is a very nice apartment on the Lower East Side," Edek said.

"A very, very nice apartment," Zofia said, and patted Edek on the head.

"We got it already," Edek said. "I did sign a lease for two years. I did do everything myself. All the papers, all the documents, everything."

Ruth suddenly felt horrified. "You didn't take that apartment with the irrigation system on the terrace, did you?" she said.

"Are you crazy?" said Edek. "Off coss not. I did find a plain place. It does not even have an elevator. We have to walk up two such flights of steps."

"But it is very nice," said Zofia.

"Where is it?" Ruth said. Her head was reeling.

"It is on the Pitt Street," Edek said.

"Near Delancey Street," Zofia said.

Shit, Ruth thought. Zofia already knew her way around. Zofia already knew Delancey Street. Ruth wished she'd never given Edek any credit cards or set him up with his own checking account.

"We are very happy there," Walentyna said.

"We have been there for two days," said Zofia.

"You're living there?" Ruth said.

"Yes," said Zofia.

"We like it very much," Walentyna said.

Who was the "we"? Ruth wondered. Had Edek already moved in? Was she paying three thousand dollars a month for an empty Second

Avenue apartment? And who was going to have the half bedroom? How had Edek done this? How had he done this so fast? It took some people months to find an apartment. And weeks to get approved by landlords and boards.

"Edek has been very good to us," said Zofia, putting her arm through Edek's. Her breasts were resting against the sides of Edek's chest. Ruth tried not to look at them.

Edek has been very good to you? Ruth wanted to scream. *Edek* has been good to you? It hasn't been Edek. It's been me. Me paying the bills. My credit cards. My money.

"Edek has been very good to us," Zofia repeated. Ruth looked at Zofia. She thought Zofia knew that if it had been up to Ruth, they'd be on their way back to Sopot.

"We are very happy," Walentyna said to Ruth. Walentyna had a quiet modesty. A modesty that combined with her eclectic, uncoordinated, quite strange, and hardly flattering dress sense made her very endearing.

"I'm glad you are happy," Ruth said to Walentyna.

"What are you going to eat?" Zofia said to Ruth. Ruth had lost her appetite.

"My daughter does not eat," Edek said.

"I do eat," said Ruth.

"She does eat such funny stuff," Edek said. "She does eat such green vegetables in a plastic bag."

Both women looked at Ruth.

"It is not worth to try and talk to her," Edek said. "I did try many times."

"Will you have some soup?" Walentyna said to Ruth.

"I'll have some soup," Ruth said. Edek looked at her and raised his eyebrows. Ruth hoped her expression said, "Drop it."

They ordered their food. Edek ordered a platter of mixed piroshki for an appetizer and cabbage rolls with tomato sauce and rice for his main course. Ruth was about to suggest that this might be too much when Zofia said she would have the same. Walentyna ordered soup and a roast chicken. Ruth stuck to soup. Hot borscht. Zofia and Edek had finished their piroshki before Ruth had even started her borscht.

Zofia put her arm around Edek's shoulder and squeezed him toward her. She couldn't stop touching him. She patted his arms, his knees. She smoothed his hair back and wiped some piroshki with a napkin from the side of his mouth. Her touching irritated Ruth. It clearly didn't irritate Edek.

"New York is very interesting," Zofia said to Ruth. "It is more interesting than Poland."

"Most places would be," said Ruth.

"It is not so necessary to say this, Ruthie," Edek said.

"Edek darling, do not get so offended," Zofia said. "We are all friends."

"Ruthie is right," Walentyna said. "New York is much more interesting than Sopot."

"I think so, too," Zofia said.

Ruth felt uncomfortable. Zofia and Walentyna had rushed to her defense. She didn't want to be defended by them. How did she get herself into this?

"Sopot has a very nice beach," Zofia said. "But here I can get on the B, D, F, or Q train and go straight to Coney Island or Brighton Beach where I can swim. It is a trip of approximately one hour."

"You get the train to Coney Island?" Ruth said.

"Or Brighton Beach," said Zofia.

"She does do this swimming every morning," Edek said with pride.

"I did this every morning in Sopot," Zofia said.

"I know," said Ruth.

"She did this every morning in summer and in winter," said Walentyna.

"Swimming is very good for the blood," Zofia said, patting her arms and chest. "It is very good for the skin," said Zofia. "It is very good for everything."

Zofia's arms and chest did look in good condition. Her arms were taut. Solid but firm. Her chest clearly impressed Edek. It was an impressive chest. Zofia's skin was clear and barely lined. Her blood was bound to be good, Ruth thought.

"Maybe when I have a business it is possible that I will go to a swimming pool," Zofia said. "A swimming pool is not so good for the blood."

"Business?" Ruth said. "What sort of business?"

"I don't know," said Zofia.

"Zofia has quite a few ideas," Edek said.

"I bet she has," Ruth said, and tried to stop the caustic inflection in her tone from flying out. "It's not simple to set up a business," Ruth said.

"But Zofia is very clever," said Edek.

"People in America get MBAs, a master's degree in business," Ruth said, "in order to understand the world of business." Ruth wished again that she hadn't given Edek credit cards and his own bank account.

"You do not have such a degree yourself, Ruthie," Edek said. "And you do have your own business. And this business is a business what makes a lot of money."

"Yes," Walentyna said. "Edek did tell us this many times."

"America is a land of opportunities," Zofia said. She said this with the solemnity and seriousness of a government official on an immigration recruitment drive. "In America it is still possible to establish and administer a business," Zofia said.

Establish? Administer? Ruth realized, with a start, that no one had spoken any Polish at the table. When she and Edek had met Zofia and Walentyna in Poland their English had been interspersed with Polish. Zofia, as though she had read Ruth's mind, said, "Walentyna and me are prepared. We did a course in English. A course for businesspeople in Sopot who need to do business in English. It was called English Immersion. It was six days a week. We did it for eight weeks."

Eight weeks! This move to New York had been planned. Carefully planned. Planned with the research, preparation, and precision of the Great Train Robbery.

"They did speak a good English before they did do this course," said Edek.

"It was not bad," said Walentyna.

"It was good," said Zofia. "Now it is very good."

Everything, it seemed, in Zofia's universe was very good. Her blood, her chest, her skin, her English. "You did business English?" Ruth said.

"Yes," said Walentyna. "We did learn words like negotiation, accomplishment, undertaking."

"And transaction," Zofia added.

This was some transaction, Ruth thought. It had all the strategies, ploys, tactical maneuvers, and secrecy of arrangements between heads of states.

"I don't think Zofia will need such words," Edek said. "You either got a head for business or you got no head for business. In any case plain English is enough."

"Except if you do want people to pay you hundreds of dollars for one letter," Zofia said.

Walentyna smiled. Edek roared with laughter. Ruth didn't think it was funny.

"You are right, as usual," Edek said to Zofia. As usual? What did Edek mean by *as usual*? You had to know a person for a long time before you knew what was usual for them and what was unusual. Ruth felt uneasy. More uneasy than she usually felt.

Six

Tara McGann, who was normally imperturbable, was sitting at her desk looking agitated when Ruth arrived at the office.

"I went to a four-hour seminar last night," Tara said when Ruth asked her what was wrong. "It was run by a young woman professor who's also an assistant dean, so she's successful. The seminar was about how to prepare and put together applications for a job in the academic world. She talked about her own experiences in the job market as though everything was just fortuitous. As though it was all just good luck. She prefaced nearly every anecdote with, 'I didn't plan it. It just happened this way. It just fell into my lap.' She didn't mention asking for a letter of recommendation from someone important who just happened to be in the audience when she was presenting a paper. She didn't mention taking advantage of opportunities like that. Here she was, a female dean who couldn't say to a roomful of female graduate students—because the room was mostly made up of women—she couldn't say, 'You should be strategic too, like me.' She presented it all as a fluke. Strategy can be repeated. Luck can't. I was fuming.

No wonder that even in the humanities where women make up the majority of graduate students they still make up the minority of tenured professors."

"It is infuriating, isn't it?" Ruth said.

"I'm still fuming," Tara said. "I think the women who make it to the top, or look as though they are going to, want to buy into the notion that they are special, that they are extraordinary. They want to stand out. They don't want crowds of successful women around them."

"It's very hard for women to see that they would actually benefit from comparing notes, from sharing experiences and connections," Ruth said. "You couldn't prize a connection out of most women with a large pair of pliers."

Tara laughed.

"It's true," Ruth said. "Most women have murderous thoughts toward other women."

Ruth thought about it. She herself probably had more murderous than benign thoughts about Zofia. Sonia was right. Ruth wasn't being very sisterly.

Ruth realized that she hadn't seen her father alone since Zofia and Walentyna had arrived. She'd asked him to meet her several times. She'd suggested they have dinner or coffee together. But Edek always seemed unavailable. He always had an excuse. Ruth felt she would almost have to beg in order to see him alone. She'd complained about this to Edek. "I never get to see you alone," she said. "We always have to have Zofia and Walentyna with us."

"What should I do?" Edek had said. "Tell them that they are not welcome to be with me with my daughter? They are foreigners here. They do not know anybody. When they do know more people it will be different." He paused. "What is it that you do want to say to me what is so private?" he said.

"It's not a matter of having something to say that is so private," Ruth said. "It's just a matter of us being together."

"We are together," Edek said.

Ruth rang Sonia. "My father is always with those two women," she said. "They come as a trio."

"So what?" said Sonia.

"They're like triplets," Ruth said. "They're inseparable."

"Isn't this better than when he was coming into the office every day?" Sonia said.

"No," Ruth said. "At least then I knew what he was doing."

"What's wrong?" Sonia said. "You think Zofia is after your father?"

"She is," said Ruth.

"What's wrong with that?" said Sonia. "He's eighty-seven. It's great for him to have someone after him."

"I wouldn't mind him being with someone," Ruth said. "But not Zofia."

"What's wrong with Zofia?" said Sonia.

That was the third time Sonia had said, "What's wrong." The third time in less than a minute. Couldn't Sonia see what was wrong?

"There's nothing wrong with Zofia," Ruth said. "She's just not suitable for my father."

"You sound like one of those Jewish women in Melbourne who thought that every girl was 'not suitable' for their son," Sonia said.

Ruth was annoyed. She didn't want to be lumped in with the Jewish mothers of her childhood. She was a Jewish mother. But she wasn't "one of those" Jewish mothers.

"You sound like Mrs. Glicksman or Mrs. Dittman or Mrs. Feldman," Sonia said.

"I didn't know Mrs. Glicksman or Mrs. Dittman, or Mrs. Feldman," said Ruth. "I knew Mrs. Hoffman, Mrs. Friedman, and Mrs. Kleinman."

Sonia laughed.

It was clear that Sonia couldn't see anything wrong with the fact that Edek was sharing an apartment with two single Polish women. An apartment Ruth was paying for. Ruth decided to change the subject. "I need to ask you a copyright question," she said. "I want to use the phrase 'Shall we dance?' on a card. Could the estate of Rodgers and Hammerstein own the copyright to those words?"

"You know I'm not an expert on copyright matters," Sonia said. "I do trademarks, but I'll give you a basic opinion. 'Shall We Dance?' is a copyrighted song and falls within the scope of copyrighted works. Use of the song, including the lyrics and music, are the exclusive rights of the owner. But there may be some limitations to the exclusive rights of the owner. I think your use of the title most likely falls within one of the exceptions."

"So I might be able to use it?" said Ruth.

"I think so," said Sonia. "One of the limitations of copyright is the doctrine of fair use. Fair use is use of the copyrighted material in a rea-sonable manner, without the owner's consent, but there's no generally agreed-upon definition and as it's a judicial doctrine the scope varies widely among jurisdictions."

"How do you remember all this stuff?" Ruth said.

"That's what being a lawyer is," Sonia said. "It's remembering stuff. What else is going to be on the card?"

"Just the word *When* on the inside," said Ruth.

"So the copyrighted material does form a substantial part of your work?" Sonia said.

"It forms three-quarters of the card," Ruth said.

"I'll check with one of my colleagues and get back to you," said Sonia.

Ruth put the "Shall We Dance?" card into the Probable Card file. There was a Possible Card file and a Probable Card file. The difference eluded Max, but Ruth knew what constituted possible and what con-stituted probable. At least she did in her working life. Out of the office she couldn't get it straight. She knew that a brain tumor being the cause of a headache was possible but not probable. And that someone ringing her late at night could possibly spell trouble but probably didn't. These were the sorts of things Ruth inverted. She often thought of brain tumors when she had a headache and always thought a late-night call was cause for alarm. Self-inflicted anxiety and fear, self-inflicted suffering, Ruth thought, was something children of survivors often sought. It somehow validated their life. Allowed them to live. There seemed to be a need to pay a price for any sense of well-being. And made a life with too much happiness seem perilous. Ruth wondered how she could know these things so surely, and still be in their grip.

Ruth was walking up West Broadway. It was a Saturday. And SoHo was crowded. Packed with tourists. From everywhere. It was hard to move through or around the crowds. Ruth felt as though she had inadvertently arrived in a city she'd never intended to visit, as a member of a tour group she was horrified to have joined.

Someone called out to her. Ruth looked around. A dark-haired woman was waving wildly to her. It was Frida Arbol. Frida lived two blocks from Ruth. They sometimes had coffee together. Frida was Brazilian. And strikingly beautiful. She was a documentary filmmaker. She had made several well-received documentaries. She was currently working on a film about gay Hasidic Jews. She was thinking of calling it *More Miserable Than You*. Ruth thought that that was a great title.

"Where are you going?" Frida said to Ruth.

"I'm just walking," Ruth said.

"I'll walk to Houston Street with you," Frida said.

"I've been thinking of forming a women's group," Ruth said to Frida. "A group of women who get together regularly and talk. Talk about things that aren't easy to talk about. Like how awful women are to each other."

"Women are shocking to each other," Frida said. "They are ruthless." Ruthless sounded even more ruthless with Frida's Brazilian accent. Ruth tried not to let herself be distracted by how close the word Ruth was to ruthless. Words could always distract her.

"Sure, it is always another woman who puts you down, who is rude to you, who is jealous of you," Frida said.

"It's a myth that women are closely connected to each other," Ruth said. "They are very connected when you're down and out. If your husband leaves you, or you lose your lover, mother, father, or job, they're right there."

"That is true," Frida said. "When I was very upset for the few first weeks after I left my husband, everyone called. But then I wanted to go out dancing again, and not one of my women friends was available. So I started going out dancing on my own!"

"You go out dancing on your own?" Ruth said.

"Yes," said Frida. Ruth felt envious. She wished she was the sort of person who could just go out dancing, let alone go out dancing on her own.

"I couldn't go out dancing on my own," Ruth said.

"I would love to love to dance," Ruth said. Frida laughed. Ruth felt a bit flat.

"I'm going to Brazil for two months," Frida said. "I'll call you about that women's group thing when I get back."

When Ruth got home she called Helene. She hadn't seen Helene for years. Helene used to have a house on Shelter Island. Helene was in her late sixties. Ruth thought that it would be good to have someone older in the group.

"A women's group?" Helen said. "I'm not sure the husbands would be happy about that."

"Not all women have them," Ruth said. "And who cares?" she added in a tone that was more strident than she'd intended.

"A women's group?" Helene said, again. "What would we do?"

"Talk," Ruth said. "Talk about things we don't usually talk about."

"What sort of things?" Helene said.

"Anything," Ruth said. "By being able to talk about anything we might learn to become more comfortable talking about uncomfortable subjects."

"Why would anyone want to talk about uncomfortable subjects?" Helene said.

Ruth and Helene said goodbye.

Ruth walked around the loft feeling uncomfortable. She looked at a large box from International Wholesale Liquidators that had been delivered to her yesterday. The box had been outside the door of her loft when she got home from work.

She'd never heard of the International Wholesale Liquidators. She assumed the box must have been meant for one of her neighbors.

She looked closely at the label on the top of the box. It was addressed to her. She opened the box. It contained ten packets of toilet paper. Each packet contained twelve rolls of toilet paper. Quilted-two-ply-with-ripples toilet paper. Ruth could see the ripples. They looked like fine wavy lines running across the quilting. Ruth wondered what effect the ripples were supposed to have. She also wondered who had sent her the toilet paper.

Ruth called Edek on his cell phone. She hadn't spoken to him for a few days. She found it hard to catch him at home. He never seemed to be there. He always seemed to be out. Edek answered.

"Hi, Dad," she said.

"Hello, Ruthie darling," Edek said. "Can you hear me?" He always asked that question whenever anyone called him on the cell phone. It was as though he still couldn't believe they really worked.

"Yes, Dad," she said.

"That is good," Edek said. "I can hear you too." He usually followed that statement with, "I can hear you very good," or "I can hear you not so good."

"I can hear you very good," Edek said.

"Did you send me a box of toilet paper, Dad?" Ruth said.

"Off coss," Edek said.

"You sent me a hundred and twenty rolls of toilet paper," Ruth said.

"I do know this," Edek said.

"Why did you send me a hundred and twenty rolls of toilet paper?" she said.

"Because everybody does need toilet paper," Edek said. "And this toilet paper is out of this velt."

Out of this velt was the highest compliment Edek could bestow on anything.

"It has got such special lines on it what I did never see before. It is not so easy to find a toilet paper like this. If you did go to look for such a toilet paper with lines you would be running like a ghost what is wild," Edek said.

"I'd be what?" said Ruth.

"You would be running like a ghost what is wild," Edek said. "It is an expression what people do use in Australia and in America."

"An expression?" Ruth said.

"A ghost like what everybody likes to eat," Edek said with impatience.

Suddenly, Ruth got it. "You mean a goose," she said. "You mean a wild-goose chase."

"That is what I did say," Edek said. "You would be running and running and now it is not necessary."

Ruth tried to sound pleased about the toilet paper. She had been running her hands through her hair while she talked to her father. She probably did look like a ghost who was wild.

"What are you doing?" Ruth asked her father.

"Oy, I am trying to find a spot what would be good for a small restaurant what is not very expensive," Edek said. "It is not such an easy thing to find."

Ruth was speechless. She seemed to have lost the ability to speak. She was mute. She couldn't say anything. "What?" she finally said.

Her normally low voice sounded high-pitched, squeaky, and possibly queasy.

"Zofia does know what is missing in New York," Edek said. "And we are ready to go into business."

Ruth didn't reply. She didn't know what to say. What did Edek mean? Were the two things related? The issue of what was missing in New York? And the fact that they were ready to go into business? It was easier to take on board the notion of things being missing in New York than the thought of Zofia and Edek going into business.

"Zofia does have a plan," Edek said. "Can we have a meeting with you Ruthie to discuss the business proposition what Zofia does have?"

After two weeks in New York, Zofia had a plan. And a business proposition.

"Can you hear me, Ruthie?" Edek said.

"I can hear you," she said.

Seven

Ruth was sitting in Caffè Dante on MacDougal Street. She was waiting for Zofia, Walentyna, and Edek to arrive. She had suggested Caffè Dante because it was always quiet in the late afternoon. She felt she would need the quiet to deal with whatever plan it was that Zofia had. She'd ordered a cup of chamomile tea, in case chamomile did what it was reputed to do, quiet you down, soothe your nervous system. Her nervous system needed more than soothing, she thought. It needed heavy sedation.

The unpredictable and erratic aspects of Edek being in charge of the Stockings Department now seemed benign. Harmless. Almost amusing. This turn of events felt chaotic. And dangerous. She knew the danger wasn't real danger. Not the sort of danger that endangered people's lives. But her nervous system was having trouble delineating and quantifying the danger level. Her heart was racing. Zofia, Walentyna, and Edek arrived. Zofia had her arm through Edek's arm. It wasn't just a casual link of an arm. This linking had a proprietorial air. There was a determination and firmness about the way Zofia's arm curved and moved and looped itself through Edek and right back to Zofia. There was a defiance in the gesture. A defiance almost as audible as a shouted statement.

The trio saw Ruth, who was sitting at the back of the café. Edek disentangled himself from Zofia, and started to run toward Ruth. He looked like a man in a hurry. His short, quick, little steps imbued his rush with a sense of urgency. Edek clearly had something on his mind.

"Hello, Ruthie," he said. "I did tell Zofia and Walentyna that you would be already here. I did tell them that you do come early for everything."

"It is a very good thing to be always early," Zofia said as she kissed Ruth hello.

"Yes," said Walentyna. "Me and Zofia are also always early."

Ruth nodded. She didn't say anything. She'd already greeted Zofia, Walentyna, and Edek with what she hoped was warmth. She didn't want to invite a discussion about the virtues of punctuality or the problems associated with perpetual tardiness. She wanted to get to the point of the meeting. And punctuality was a complicated question for her. She was trying to be less punctual. She was tired of thinking that being ten minutes early was being on time. She'd been practicing trying to arrive closer to the correct time. She hadn't made much headway yet.

Edek pulled out a chair for Zofia and a chair for Walentyna. When both of the women were seated, he sat down himself.

"You look very nice, Ruthie," Zofia said.

"Thank you," said Ruth.

"Yes," said Walentyna. "You look very well."

Ruth was surprised. Maybe tension and apprehension suited her. Maybe tension made her look radiant? In much the same way that happiness affected other people. It made sense. Most people searched for happiness. She scratched and scrounged around for misery. No wonder she appeared to glow when she found it.

"You look like your mother, Ruthie," Walentyna said. "Edek showed us photographs of Rooshka."

"Edek showed us photographs of him and Rooshka," Zofia said. She sighed. "Edek did love his Rooshka very much."

"Like me and Zofia," Walentyna said. "I did love my husband, God rest his soul very much, and Zofia did love her husband, God rest his soul, very much."

"Rooshka was very beautiful," Zofia said. "Much more beautiful than me." Zofia said this with no bitterness, no envy, no judgment. She just stated it as fact.

"You are very attractive, Zofia," Walentyna said.

"Yes, I am very attractive," Zofia said, "but I am not beautiful."

Zofia was attractive, Ruth thought, but not very attractive. Then she felt mean. What was she doing evaluating and grading Zofia's appearance?

"Zofia is very, very attractive," Edek said. That seemed to settle things and bring an end to that conversation.

There was a momentary silence. "Okey dokey," Edek said. Okey dokey? Ruth thought. Where was Edek dredging that expression up from? From his days as a drover on a cattle ranch in outback Australia? Hardly. The closest Edek had come to a cow or a sheep had been a proximity to their assorted refrigerated body parts in butcher shops. Edek cleared his throat. "Okeydokey," he said, again. "Let us get down to the business." Edek paused. "Please listen carefully," he said. He enunciated each of the three words with care. There was a serious, somber tone to his voice as though he was issuing an edict at a United Nations conference.

"I'm listening," Ruth said.

"Zofia is going to make bolls," Edek said. "There are no bolls in New York. No bolls what are good, I mean. There are a few such Italian bolls but there is not one boll shop."

Zofia and Walentyna looked expectantly at Ruth.

"What is a boll shop?" Ruth said.

"A shop what does sell bolls, off coss," said Edek.

"And what are bolls?" Ruth said.

All three of them looked at her. They looked at her both in amazement and as though she was retarded.

"Ruthie, are you stupid?" Edek said. "You do know off coss what is a boll. Everybody does know what is a boll." Edek was agitated. "Even a person what does not eat bolls, what does eat such food with leafs like you, does know what is a boll," he said.

"I don't eat leaves," said Ruth. "I eat a variety of fruit and vegetables and grains and fish and nonfat dairy products, and sometimes chicken. I eat a pretty healthy diet."

"Pheh!" Edek said. "You do eat food what is not normal."

"Edek, Ruthie is right. The food she does eat is very good," Zofia said, patting Edek on the head.

Ruth, too, was now agitated. And perplexed. Why did Edek have to bring up her eating habits? And what was a boll?

"A boll is a boll what is made from meat," Edek said.

"Oh, a meatball," said Ruth.

"Yes, a meatball," Zofia and Walentyna half shouted, with a degree of relief.

"Off coss," Edek said, with a touch of annoyance.

"Zofia makes a very good boll," Walentyna said. Edek and Zofia nodded in agreement.

"A very good boll," Zofia added.

Why were they all calling them bolls? Ruth wondered. Were they emulating Edek? Maybe Edek had laid down the law. Maybe Edek had told them that boll was the way it was pronounced in America, or in New York. It probably wasn't far from the truth, Ruth thought. Edek's version of ball was possibly closer to the way Americans pronounced ball than the way Ruth did. Australians put a long-drawn-out and rather flat *a* into the center of ball.

"Zofia makes a very good boll," Walentyna repeated reassuringly. "My husband, may he rest in peace, and Zofia's husband, may he also rest in peace, said that Zofia's bolls were the best in the world."

How far out of Sopot had the two men traveled? Ruth wondered.

"Maybe the best bolls in Poland," Zofia said, after seeing Ruth's expression.

"In Poland people does know what is a good boll," Edek said. "In Poland people do eat a lot of very good meat. Poland does have the best sausages and hams and other meat from pigs and from cows." Edek paused and sat up straight. "Zofia does have a plan to open a small restaurant with maybe only six or eight or ten tables," he said. "Zofia will make the bolls and people what wants to can eat the bolls in the restaurant and people what wants to take the bolls home can take the bolls home. It is called takeout. I will be a partner with her and I will work in the business."

Ruth was astonished. "You know nothing about the food business," she said. "You know nothing about restaurants or takeout places."

"Excuse me," Edek said, in a tone that indicated he was annoyed at Ruth. "Excuse me," he said, again. "We do not know nothing about the restaurant business. We do know that all restaurants does do such takeout. Maybe not the posh, posh restaurants what my daughter does go to, but we are not going to make a posh, posh restaurant."

"Bolls are not posh, posh," Walentyna said.

Ruth wondered if *posh, posh* was a phrase they taught in Sopot's English Immersion course.

"Off coss bolls are not posh, posh," Edek said.

Ruth was stumped. She didn't know what to say. The whole venture, the whole plan, was absurd. You couldn't just fly in from Sopot and decide that meatballs were the missing ingredient of life in New York City. You couldn't just arrive and decide, with no experience and no money, that you could set up a restaurant in Martin's Creek, Pennsylvania, or Morrisville, Vermont, or Athens, Ohio. It wouldn't work in Martin's Creek, or Morrisville, or Athens, Ohio. It wouldn't work in Mesa, Arizona, or Duluth, Minnesota, or Petaluma, California. And it couldn't, Ruth knew with absolute certainty, work in New York.

"This is an absurd idea," Ruth said. "This is New York. The vast percentage of restaurants that open, fail. They don't stay open. They close," she added, for extra emphasis. "It's a very risky business," she said.

Zofia and Walentyna looked flat. Walentyna's small shoulders sank. And even Zofia's breasts seemed to slump. Or slump slightly. Ruth looked at Edek. He didn't look flat. He looked angry.

"You do think that we do not know what we are doing, Ruthie darling. I can see that," Edek said.

Edek's "darling" hadn't been infused with warmth. It had exuded annoyance.

"Yes, I think you don't know what you're doing," Ruth said. "You have to have had some experience to know what you are doing. It's like playing the piano, or doing cartwheels or flying a plane. You can't just start and expect to succeed."

Ruth immediately saw the flaw in her argument. She shouldn't have included cartwheels. That had been stupid of her. For a start it would probably be hard to do cartwheels if you were over thirty. And cartwheels, if you were young, could easily be learned. Although that hadn't been Ruth's experience. Even as a child she'd been too frightened to fling herself upside down on the ground. The world had felt perilous enough to Ruth if you were standing the right way up.

"What is a cartwheel?" Walentyna said. Ruth knew she was done for. She knew that any attempt at an explanation of what constituted a cartwheel, short of a physical demonstration, had to be complicated. And would dilute the point she had been trying to make. A circular sideways handspring with arms and legs extended, might be how the *Oxford English Dictionary* would define a cartwheel. Ruth wasn't sure that Walentyna or Zofia would be able to envision a cartwheel from

that definition. She thought that if she didn't already know what a cartwheel was, she, too, might have trouble comprehending a cartwheel
from that description.

"It doesn't matter what a cartwheel is, at the moment," Ruth said.
"The point is that you have to have experience before you can open a
restaurant."

"This will be only a small restaurant," said Edek. "And part of the
business will be the takeout bolls. Takeout is just like a shop. You do
make bolls. And you do sell bolls. How much experience does a person
need to do this? And we got experience. Zofia did make a lot of bolls.
And a lot of people did eat Zofia's bolls."

"Where?" said Ruth. "In Sopot?"

"First of all, I did eat many of Zofia's bolls myself and they are out
of this velt. I did eat many of Zofia's bolls," Edek repeated, with a
flourish. Edek could hardly be considered to have an abundance of
culinary expertise, Ruth thought. Nor was he likely to be seen as pos-
sessing an extraordinary palate. He lived on lasagna, schnitzel, gefilte
fish, and chopped liver with latkes, chicken soup, and chocolate to sup-
plement his diet. The way Edek had made the announcement suggested that he saw himself as Jean-Georges Vongerichten or Julia
Child. Actually, Edek was highly unlikely to have heard of either Jean-
Georges or Julia Child.

"We did invite many people to try the bolls what Zofia does
make," Edek said with a note of triumph. "We did invite the butcher
what is on Grand Street, the man what does own the dry cleaners, and
some young people what lives in our building. And everybody what
did have the bolls did say that the bolls was very, very good."

The whole thing was starting to sound like a farce. A worrying farce.

"What did you do?" Ruth said. "Take meatballs around the neighborhood?"

"Off coss not," said Edek. "We did have already two such buffet
dinners."

"You invited all those people to your apartment?" Ruth said.

"Yes," said Walentyna, "Zofia made veal, potato, and kielbasa bolls, she also made the veal and beef bolls she is famous for."

"Because we are in America," Edek said, "Zofia did make such turkey bolls. In America everybody does eat turkeys. There is not a person what doesn't eat a turkey."

Ruth had an image of Americans all across the country grappling with and devouring an entire turkey. Or large turkey legs and wings and carcasses. It wasn't a vision of Americans anyone would want to export.

"Zofia did make turkey and bratwurst bolls," Walentyna said. "The bolls were very good."

"It was the first time I cooked with a turkey," Zofia said. "In Poland people do not eat many turkeys."

"Everybody did eat oll the bolls," Edek said. Oll the bolls. Oll the bolls, Ruth thought, sounded like the name of a Cossack dance or a song sung by Russian boatmen on the Volga River.

"The man who owns the dry cleaners came to dinner?" Ruth said.

"Yes," said Walentyna. "And his wife."

"And the people who does work for the architect what is on Ludlow Street," said Edek.

"And a woman who has got a small dress shop on Essex Street and her boyfriend," said Zofia.

"And Zofia did tell this woman to bring her friends, so she did bring four friends," Edek said. "And they was very nice people."

"Very nice people," said Walentyna.

Ruth was still trying to assimilate the notion of inviting virtual strangers to dinner. Few people in New York invited people they knew well to dinner. Most people met in restaurants. And here were Edek, Zofia, and Walentyna hosting dinner parties for half the neighborhood.

"Zofia did put oll the bolls on such big plates what is called platters," Edek said, "and people did help themselves. Every person what did come did say the bolls was better than any bolls they did ever eat."

"Yes," said Zofia. "And in Sopot, too, everybody liked my bolls very much. People did know I make very good bolls."

"I am not a good cook," Walentyna said. "But I am a very good assistant. I am going to be Zofia's assistant, and a partner in the business."

Walentyna was going to be Zofia's assistant? And a partner in business? To Zofia, Walentyna, and Edek the proposed business seemed to be a done deal, a fait accompli. Ruth had no idea how they thought the proposition was going to be able to become more than a proposal.

"You are not a bad cook, Walentyna," Zofia said. "You make a very good cheesecake. And I make very good bolls."

"You do make very good many things," Edek said to Zofia. Ruth hoped that Edek was referring only to food. She didn't want to know what else Zofia might be very good at.

Ruth couldn't quite believe what she was hearing. Edek, Zofia, and Walentyna thought that being able to make a meatball was going to translate into a business. A business that made money.

"This is not a great idea," Ruth said. "People with years of experience in the restaurant business don't open their own restaurant. Owning a restaurant is not like having a dinner party."

All three of them looked at her.

"Why not?" Edek said. "It is exactly like having a big dinner party but you do do it every day."

"And you give the extra guests bolls to take home," Walentyna said.

"But you do charge money for the guests to take the bolls home," said Edek.

Ruth was lost. She thought the dinner party analogy had gone astray. Edek and Walentyna had failed to see the difference between inviting guests and having paying customers. It seemed a relatively large oversight. Most restaurants weren't full of guests. They either had customers or they folded.

"You do not give extra guests bolls to take home," Zofia said. "You give bolls to take home to those guests who do want to eat their bolls at home."

"Zofia is right," Edek said.

"Yes," said Walentyna. "Zofia is right."

"The children did eat Zofia's bolls," Walentyna said with a quiet smile of pride.

"What children?" Ruth said.

"Your children, off coss," said Edek.

"My kids," said Ruth.

"We did invite them to have a dinner with us," said Edek. "And they did enjoy very much the bolls what Zofia did make."

So they had all been enjoying a dinner together, Ruth thought. All of them, except her. "So the kids know about the restaurant plan?" Ruth said to Edek.

"Off coss not," Edek said. "We would not say something to them before we did talk it over with you."

Ruth took a deep breath. This was what Edek thought constituted talking it over with her? No one had asked her what she thought.

"Okeydokey," Edek said for the third time, "we did talk enough today about the restaurant. You think about it, Ruthie. Don't rush. You think about it and we will talk in a couple of days."

Ruth knew that a couple of days meant the next day or possibly later that night. Edek's version of "Don't rush" meant that he could tolerate, with great restraint, not having an answer straightaway. Edek stood up. "I love you, Ruthie," he said. Ruth knew he loved her. But, she wondered, what had moved him to make the declaration at this particular moment. There was something poignant in the way he'd said it. As though he was grateful to her. Grateful in a way that made her want to cry.

"I love you, too, Ruthie," Zofia said. That "I love you" jolted Ruth right out of her emotional state.

"I love you, too," Walentyna said.

Ruth felt hemmed in by love. Backed into a corner. An uncomfortable corner. Something irritated her throat. She started to cough. This much love could clearly cause choking. This much love could possibly kill you. Edek, Zofia, and Walentyna left Caffè Dante looking pleased. As though they'd accomplished what they'd set out to achieve. Ruth shook her head. She sipped the last of her chamomile tea and left.

Images of Zofia knee deep in meatball mixture dogged Ruth. She kept seeing Walentyna molding hundreds of bolls or cleaning the floor. And Edek in a white chef's hat managing the cash register. She saw Edek and Zofia and Walentyna surrounded by yards of bolls. And no customers. Yards of bolls and no one to eat them. She envisaged them having to auction off whatever equipment they'd bought, and closing shop. Ruth had gone straight to the end without addressing the question of how they were going to get the money they needed to begin. So far, no one had mentioned money. It was lunchtime the day after they'd met in Caffè Dante. Ruth was surprised Edek hadn't called her yet. She decided to go outside and get some fresh air. Or at least inhale what passed for fresh air in New York.

Ken Kennedy, an Australian architect who had offices in the Sanger Building, was in the elevator. She knew he'd designed a small restaurant in Mott Street.

"A friend of my father's wants to start a restaurant in New York," Ruth said to Ken Kennedy. "I think she's crazy to even think about doing it."

"What school, what culinary institute did she go to?" Ken Kennedy said.

"She didn't," Ruth said. "She comes from Sopot, in Poland, and I'm not sure Sopot has one."

"Does she have contacts in the food industry?" Ken Kennedy asked.

"No," Ruth said. "She's only been in the country for three weeks."

"I wouldn't advise her to proceed on that basis," Ken Kennedy said.

"Thanks," said Ruth.

Ruth decided to ring the aptly named Patricia Biscuit. Patricia Biscuit ran a public relations company that specialized in restaurants and chefs.

Ruth didn't know Patricia Biscuit well, but she knew her well enough to call her. Ruth and Patricia Biscuit had Geoffrey Firth in common. Geoffrey cut both their hair. Sharing a hairdresser was a close bond in New York. When Ruth and Patricia Biscuit met socially, usually at an art exhibition opening, they always admired each other's haircut, and discussed Geoffrey with great affection.

"I know this might be an impossible question," Ruth said to Patricia Biscuit, "but could you give me a rough idea of what you think would be the crucial factors to take into account if you wanted to set up a restaurant?"

"Do you want to go into the restaurant business?" Patricia Biscuit said to Ruth.

"No," Ruth said. "A friend of my father's does and she is convinced she can do it."

"Two things you have to think about in order to get a restaurant up and running are concept and location," Patricia Biscuit said.

Ruth wondered if meatballs could be considered a concept.

"A successful restaurateur has to be wedded to either a concept or a location," said Patricia Biscuit. "You either have your heart set on a location, find a place in that location, and then figure out the concept, or you have a concept that is amazing and hasn't been done before and then find a location."

If meatballs were a concept, could they be considered an amazing concept? Ruth didn't think so.

"Some well-known restaurateurs and chefs have put restaurants in a more remote location," Patricia Biscuit said. "And this being New York, there is some mystique in putting a restaurant in a remote location. If you're successful, you become a destination restaurant."

Ruth couldn't imagine people going to the other side, or the other end, of Manhattan to pick up a meatball.

"It's important to know your demographics, know who you're trying to reach," Patricia Biscuit said.

Zofia was trying to reach meatball eaters, Ruth thought. How could you tell what demographic meatball eaters fell into?

"And you've got to price your product for the right market," said Patricia Biscuit.

"What do you mean?" Ruth said.

"Look," said Patricia Biscuit. "In Soho nobody's going to buy a one-dollar latte but they'll buy a four-dollar latte. You're selling an image and that image has to be priced correctly."

Ruth wasn't at all sure that Edek, Zofia, or Walentyna would know their demographics. Or understand why a one-dollar latte wouldn't sell in SoHo.

"Is their finance in place?" asked Patricia Biscuit. Their financing plan probably was in place, Ruth thought. Her place. Her bank account.

"I don't think so," Ruth said.

"Well they'll have to go to their bank with a projected profit and loss statement," Patricia Biscuit said. "And the bank will want to know that they have invested a certain amount of their own money or their family's money, in the project. Because a restaurant is such a risky business the bank needs to know that if the business fails, you will lose proportionally more than they will."

Ruth made a note to tell Edek, Zofia, and Walentyna that even banks saw a restaurant as a very risky business. She wasn't sure it would have any impact on them. The three of them might just think a platter of balls would sway the bank.

"You have to have enough cash to float the business for a year," Patricia Biscuit said. "And then you have to expect that it will take five years to begin to break even. Not to make a profit. To break even."

Edek would be ninety-two before the venture would even begin to pay for itself, Ruth thought. Maybe even Edek would see that that didn't make sense.

"You have to expect to expend ten years of your life on the project," said Patricia Biscuit.

Ten years, Ruth thought. That would make Edek ninety-seven. That would possibly make Edek the oldest restaurateur in the world.

"They've probably taken that into account," Patricia Biscuit said. "Most people do."

Most people, Ruth thought. If only Patricia Biscuit knew how removed from most people Edek, Zofia, and Walentyna were. They had a certainty about the future of their endeavor. And it didn't involve breaking even or ten-year projections.

"Opening a restaurant would daunt most people, wouldn't it?" Ruth said to Patricia Biscuit.

"You'd think so," she said. "But it doesn't."

Ruth had a sinking feeling that Edek and Zofia and Walentyna fit ted right into the scores of the undaunted.

"Do they have a well-known chef?" asked Patricia Biscuit. "A well-known chef can carry a location or a concept."

"No, they don't have a well-known chef," Ruth said. Her voice sounded flat. She was starting to feel oppressed by the probable pitfalls of running a restaurant. Or maybe she was depressed at the thought of trying to explain the potential disasters and calamities of their plan to Zofia and Walentyna and Edek.

"If you don't have a well-known chef, there are other things you can do to create a buzz around a restaurant," said Patricia Biscuit.

Ruth's head was starting to buzz. Zofia probably had enough buzz to launch ten restaurants if buzz was all that was required. She had enough bust, as well. And if bust wasn't a prerequisite it was probably a bonus. Ruth felt exhausted thinking about Zofia's buzz and her bust.

"You can hire a public relations firm, like mine, to create a buzz," said Patricia Biscuit.

"We hire models to sit in restaurants when they first open. We throw parties for beautiful people, we have press receptions. Publicity is a huge aspect of having a successful restaurant."

Ruth didn't think the sale of a few meatballs would cover the cost of a PR budget.

"A good publicist is invaluable. If you're a good publicist and the *New York Times* tells you they've noticed a trend of vegetables in desserts," Patricia Biscuit said, "you tell the *New York Times* that the chef, at whatever your client's restaurants is, has a rhubarb and squash dessert. Then you ring your client and say you better create a rhubarb and squash pie."

"Really?" Ruth said.

"Of course," said Patricia Biscuit. "If you're a good restaurant owner or a good publicist, you'll do whatever it takes to stay in the press to keep your restaurant going."

Ruth made up her mind to write a list of the perils and expenses of opening a restaurant, to present to Edek, Zofia, and Walentyna.

"What if you hadn't been trained at a culinary institute or any-where else," Ruth said, "and you set up a restaurant on a shoestring budget, with not much equipment and not enough money to last more than three months without bringing in an income." Ruth had imagined that scenario would be the bare minimum for Zofia, Walentyna, and Edek to set up their business. And the best the trio could hope for. And that would be with Ruth funding the venture. "What would you say to somebody who was going to do that?" Ruth said to Patricia Biscuit.

"I would wish them the best of luck," Patricia Biscuit said. That sort of luck didn't sound promising, Ruth thought.

Ruth called Edek. He sounded overly excited to hear from her.

"Hello, Ruthie," he said with a mixture of enthusiasm and excitement, if not hysteria. "Did you notice that I did not call you?" he said. "I did want to give you plenty of time to think about our proposition. I was going to wait a bit longer. I did tell you not to rush." He paused. "Could you hold on a moment, please?" he said. "I will just tell Zofia and Walentyna that it is you."

"It is Ruthie," Edek shouted. Ruth heard the sound of footsteps.

"Hello, Ruthie," she heard Zofia say, in the background.

"Hello, Ruthie," Walentyna echoed.

Ruth took a breath. She didn't quite know how to proceed. She'd expected to be able to speak to Edek alone. She hadn't expected an expectant audience of three.

"What do you think, Ruthie? Our plan is a very good idea, isn't it?" Edek said.

"It's a good idea under certain circumstances," said Ruth.

"Ruthie does think it is a good idea," Edek shouted to Zofia and Walentyna. Ruth could hear general sounds of rejoicing.

"Dad, Dad," she said. "I said it was a good idea under certain circumstances,"

"Circumstances," Edek said. "We do not need circumstances. We got already our plans."

"Circumstances are not things you need or don't need," Ruth said. She hesitated. That wasn't strictly true. There were circumstances you needed and circumstances you didn't need. "Circumstances are conditions relevant to events or actions," Ruth said.

"We got already our actions," Edek said. "We do not need to buy circumstances."

"You can't buy or borrow circumstances," Ruth said. She grimaced. That wasn't strictly true either.

"I do not want to buy some circumstances or to borrow them," Edek said. "You do know me, Ruthie, I do not like to borrow anything.

I prefer to give what I have got. I do not like to borrow what someone else has got."

How did they get so lost, Ruth wondered.

"The main thing," said Edek, "is that if you do not need such circumstances then we do not need to worry about them."

"Yes, you do," said Ruth.

"Ruthie, you do worry too much," Edek said. "You do not need to worry about circumstances, we do not want them."

Ruth gave up. She couldn't bear to spend any more time wrestling with the definition or explanation of circumstances. Especially when Edek was adamant he didn't want any.

"Listen, Dad," she said. "I talked to someone in the food business."

"She did already talk to somebody in the food business," Edek shouted to Zofia and Walentyna. He sounded triumphant.

"Thank you, Ruthie," Zofia called out.

"Dad, will you listen to me," Ruth said.

"I am listening to you, Ruthie, and I am very happy with what you are saying," Edek said.

"The person I spoke to was somebody with a lot of experience in the business," Ruth said.

"The person what she did speak to is a person what has got a lot of experience in the business," Edek shouted.

"Dad, just listen to me," Ruth said.

"I am listening. I am listening," Edek said.

"The person I spoke to told me how difficult it was to be successful in the restaurant business," Ruth said. "I didn't feel good about the whole idea to begin with. After talking to her I felt much worse."

"Off coss things are going to get verse," Edek said. "Things do get verse before they do get verse," he said.

"You mean things are going to get worse before they get better," said Ruth.

"No," said Edek. "I did mean what I did say. Things are going to get verse before they do get verse." Edek sounded agitated. "Why do you think always that I do mean something what is not what I am saying?"

Ruth thought about it. Of course, as things got worse, they were, by their very definition, getting worse. Getting worse was a gradual progression. So things were getting worse before they got worse. The more common notion of things getting worse before they got better was actually quite spurious. It was hypothetical and contained a possibly unwarranted optimism.

"Sorry, Dad," she said.

"That is okay," he said. "Anyway nothing could be verse than not to try to do something what you do know will be a big success."

"A lot of things could be verse," she said. "I mean worse."

"Ruthie, what is wrong with you," Edek said. "Off coss a lot of things could be verse. To be dead, off coss, would be verse. You cannot sell bolls in a boll shop if you are dead already."

Zofia called out something. "It is okay, Zofia," Edek said loudly. "We will not have a dead person selling bolls."

She hadn't made much progress with this call, Ruth thought. It was ending with Zofia, Walentyna, and Edek still selling balls. And no dead men helping them.

"It is okay," Edek called out to Zofia and Walentyna. "Ruthie is such a nervous type. She does always have to worry about things."

"Ruthie, when you can see what Zofia can do with a boll, you will feel much better," Edek said to Ruth.

Edek, Ruth thought, probably knew very well what Zofia could do with a ball. That thought made her feel nauseous.

"Don't worry, Ruthie darling," Edek said. "Zofia does know what she is doing."

Ruth was sure Edek was right. She was sure Zofia knew exactly what she was doing. If only Ruth knew exactly what that was.

Eight

Ruth was in the office trying to remedy a rather mangled mess Max had created. Ruth had had James King, the real estate lawyer, on the phone. James King had been furious.

"Scout was the dog, not the dog's owner. The dog's owner is called Willie," James King shouted. "You wrote a condolence letter to Scout, the dog, about the death of the dog's owner, Willie. Willie is still alive. The dog is dead. And I've sent the dead dog an insane letter telling him that Gus and I will think of his owner every day. And that the park won't be the same without him. I didn't read the letter before I posted it," James King said. "And then I had to suffer the acute embarrassment of bumping into Willie. He looked at me very strangely before thanking me for my letter. One of my neighbors, who's also got a dog, called me to tell me what had happened. Willie had shown her the letter. I'm so angry," he'd said.

Ruth apologized profusely. "I'll write a letter to Willie," she said, "explaining that because the passing away of Scout was so important to you and Gus, and you wanted to express your sympathy as fully as possible, you commissioned me to write the letter. I'll apologize to him profoundly and tell him that the sentiments expressed were genuine and heartfelt. And that I was horrified to find that my secretary had inadvertently switched the names."

James King had agreed to that. But it hadn't calmed him down. When he said goodbye, he was still fuming. Max had been creeping around the office trying to appear invisible. She looked very visible. And glum. "I'm sorry," she said, every time she saw Ruth. Ruth was now writing a letter to Willie to try and explain and apologize for the debacle. She also had to write James King a letter of apology. She buzzed Max.

"Max, don't under any circumstances charge James King for the stupid Scout/Willie fuckup," she said. "And don't charge him for the letter of apology to Willie, or for the letter of apology I'm writing to him."

"I wouldn't have," Max said.

"I'm just making sure," said Ruth.

"I'm sorry," Max said, again.

Ruth felt agitated. She hated making mistakes, let alone making enormous blunders like that. She felt angry with Max.

"Call up Delectable Edibles and order a fruit and wine basket," Ruth said to Max. "Tell them you'll bring a letter around to be delivered with the basket. And ask if the basket can be delivered this afternoon."

"Is this for James King?" Max said.

"Yes," said Ruth. "Who did you think it was for? The pope?"

By the time she had finished the dog fuckup letter she felt calmer. She still felt angry with Max.

"I promise I won't do that again," Max said, when she saw Ruth.

"Good, because I don't pay you to have me writing letters to a dog expressing condolences over the death of his owner when the owner is alive and the dog is dead."

"Would you have done the letter to the dog if the owner had been dead?" Max said.

Ruth started to laugh. "Probably," she said, "if that was what James King had wanted."

Just as Ruth was about to leave the office, Edek called. He sounded breathless. "Ruthie, Ruthie, I got some very big news," he said. Ruth steeled herself. Zofia couldn't be pregnant, she thought. Zofia was at least sixty-five. Not even Zofia and her daily swim and her unlined skin and her invigorated blood could still be capable of conception. Why did she jump to that conclusion? Ruth wondered. No one else would expect news from their father to contain the fact that a sixty-five-year-old woman was pregnant. She still felt tense. Big news from Edek at the moment, she felt, could not be good.

"Ruthie, Ruthie, can you hear me," Edek shouted.

"Yes, I can hear you, Dad," she said.

"I can hear you, too, Ruthie," he said.

"I got very big news."

"What?" said Ruth. She was getting edgier.

"I did find a spot what is perfect for a restaurant," Edek said.

"You've what?" said Ruth.

"I did find a spot," Edek said. "I was with Zofia and Walentyna and we did find it."

How could they have found a spot for their restaurant? Didn't they know spots cost money? No one had mentioned money. There had been no talk about money. Money for a spot? Money for a pot? Money for a sock or a rock? The question of money hadn't come up.

"The spot is in Attorney Street," Edek said.

Ruth knew Attorney Street. It was a small street off Stanton Street. Just minutes from Zofia, Walentyna, and Edek's apartment. Attorney Street was a very inauspicious street.

"Ruthie, do you want to have a meeting with us to discuss the location?" Edek said.

Maybe a discussion of the location would lead to a discussion of the money, Ruth thought. "When do you want to meet?" Ruth said.

"Now?" said Edek. "Would that suit you?"

"I guess so," said Ruth.

"It is no use to meet at the spot because the shop is locked up," Edek said. "Shall we meet at Noah's Ark?"

"Can we meet at Brown?" Ruth said. "At Brown I can have a salad."

"Off coss," said Edek. "Where is Brown?"

"It's on the same street as Gertel's Bakery," Ruth said. "It's on Hester Street between Ludlow and Essex. It's closer to Ludlow."

"Okay," said Edek.

"I'm going to walk," said Ruth. "So it will probably take me twenty to twenty-five minutes. I'll walk past Attorney Street on my way."

"The shop is 102," Edek said. "It does not look so good, Ruthie, but Zofia does say it is better that it does not look so good."

Ruth wondered if Zofia thought the price would be less for a less-than-attractive space. Or whether she was thinking of developing a plain, down-at-the-heels, no-frills meatball palace.

"You will see our spot," Edek said. "It is a shop what is in between two garages."

A spot that was between two garages was hardly a selling point, Ruth thought. She was sure the shop hadn't been pitched like that.

"We did meet already the owner," Edek said. "He is a very nice chappie." Ruth's head was whirling. They had found a spot and met the owner who was a nice chappie. A nice chappie. Who did Edek think he was, Prince Philip? She didn't think Prince Philip would be looking at a shop wedged between two garages.

Ruth walked through the Lower East Side. The area was bustling with people. The streets were vibrant with stores and stalls. Except for Attorney Street. Attorney Street was empty. There were no people. No cars. That part of Attorney Street was short. It ran for one block between East Houston and Stanton streets. There was a warehouse, open to the public, which sold an assortment of alcoholic beverages, disinfectants, dishwashing liquids, candy, cookies, and toilet paper. That was empty, too. Diagonally, across the street, Ruth saw Edek's "spot." The vacant shop may not have been wedged between two garages. Wedged, perhaps, suggested a squeezed appearance. The spot didn't look crushed by its neighbors. It just looked out of place. One of the garages contained a car repair business. Ruth saw half of a car mechanic. The other half of him was under a car. The garage on the other side of Edek's spot was closed. Ruth wondered what you could sell from Edek's spot. Spanners? Jacks? Car accessories? Tire repair kits? No one seemed to have flat tires anymore, she thought. When she was a child, people were always changing tires on the side of the road. Ruth thought no one would describe Edek's spot as a prime location. Prime food locations rarely abutted car repair yards. How many people wanted to eat meatballs feet away from blackened grease, metal shavings, and soot deposits?

Ruth arrived at Brown. She'd given up thinking about what she would say. She had nothing to say. There were too many incomprehensible, if not lunatic, aspects of what they were planning. She said hello to Alejandro, who owned Brown and a catering company that mostly catered for photo shoots. He also designed, manufactured, and distributed handbags and skateboards in Europe and America. He was intelligent, articulate, and multilingual. This sort of skill overkill was not uncommon in New York.

"Did you see the Attorney Street?" Edek said as soon as he saw her.

"Yes," said Ruth.

All three of them kissed her hello. She sat down.

"I am very happy that you did see it, Ruthie," Edek said.

"Yes," said Zofia.

They looked at Ruth expectantly.

"It's a very small street," Ruth said.

"Yes," Edek exclaimed, as though they were talking about the discovery of a diamond mine.

"There is no one in the street," Ruth said.

"Yes," said Edek triumphantly.

"There's no pedestrian traffic, no road traffic," Ruth said.

"That is right, Ruthie," Edek said. "It is very quiet."

"I'm not sure very quiet is the right requirement for a food outlet," Ruth said.

"A food cutlet?" Edek said. "We do not plan to make a food cutlet. We do plan to make bolls. Bolls is not cutlets."

"I said outlet, not cutlet," Ruth said.

"I think outlet is where you do sell the food," Zofia said to Edek.

"You do sell cutlets in an outlet?" Edek said, looking bewildered.

"An outlet is a point from which goods are sold," Ruth said. "And the goods you are planning to sell are balls, not cutlets."

"I do know this," Edek said. "We was never going to sell cutlets."

"Dad, what I'm saying," Ruth said, "is that Attorney Street is not a great position to sell meatballs or cutlets or chickens or spaghetti from. It's not a good location."

"Maybe it is not a good location for cutlets or chickens or spaghetti," Edek said. "But it is a good location for bolls."

Walentyna had started to look a bit nervous. "Maybe Ruthie is right," she said. "Maybe it is the wrong street."

"Walentyna," Edek said gently, "Zofia does know what she is doing."

"You are right, Edek," Walentyna said, cheering up. "I did not think we would win a green card. Zofia was sure we would win one."

Something was wrong with Walentyna's logic, Ruth thought. There was no correlation between being able to set up and run a restaurant and making a haphazard guess about the outcome of a green-card lottery.

"This spot is the right spot for us," Edek said.

"Why, Dad?" she said.

"Because it is very cheap," he answered.

"It is cheap because not a lot of people want to occupy that space," said Ruth.

"That is true," Edek said. "Nobody does want to be next to a motor mechanic. People what do fix cars do always have such a dirty place. That does not mean that a restaurant what is next door will be dirty."

"I think it would be very off-putting," Ruth said. "Even if the street was crowded with people and cafés and restaurants, which it isn't, being next door to a motor mechanic would still be off-putting."

Edek looked at Ruth, and with barely contained glee, pulled out his trump card. "I did have a talk to the motor mechanic what is next door," he said. "And the motor mechanic did say that he is finishing up. He did say he is closing his business and he is going to move to Brooklyn."

"In three weeks," Zofia said, nodding her head, as though the motor mechanic moving had removed every obstacle to their empire.

"It is a perfect size," Edek said. "We will have only seven or eight or maybe nine or ten tables. Is that right, Zofia?" he said.

"That is right, Edek," said Zofia.

"How much is this cheap location?" Ruth said to Edek.

"Cheap," said Edek.

"How cheap is cheap?" Ruth said.

"Very cheap," Edek said.

"Dad, do you mind telling me the cost in dollars, rather than using adjectives," Ruth said. "An adjective is a descriptive word used to describe nouns," she added.

Edek looked offended. "I know what is a adjective," he said. "And it is better for me for the moment to use a adjective. We can talk more in a few days."

"I just want to know how much the rent is," Ruth said. "Can you just tell me?"

"I did tell you," said Edek. "I did say it is cheap."

Ruth sighed. It was a sigh of impatience.

"I will write down everything what we will need, and then I will talk to you about how much," Edek said.

"How much for what?" said Ruth.

"How much for everything," said Edek.

Ruth was trying not to think about Edek or Zofia or Walentyna. She was trying not to think about balls or bolls. She wasn't succeeding. She was also restraining herself from calling Garth. She didn't want to call him every time something went wrong. She didn't want to call him too often. She had begun to find that she felt better if she didn't keep calling Garth. If she didn't keep trying to keep track of him. And she didn't want to call him every time something went wrong. Technically nothing had yet gone wrong. The boll program was still merely a proposition. Boll program. This didn't feel like a boll program. It felt like a boll pogrom. She called Sonia.

"That could be a great idea," Sonia said after Ruth had explained the concept of boll central or boll heaven.

"A great idea?" Ruth said. "A great idea for three people, one of whom is eighty-seven, to go into a business they've had no experience in? And the basis of that business is the fact that a few people in Sopot, and my father and my kids, and a few people on the Lower East Side think Zofia's meatballs are out of this world."

"It really could be a good idea," Sonia said. "Meatballs are so straightforward. They're not pretending to be something else. Most of the prepared food you can buy at halfway decent places is in disguise. Lettuce isn't even lettuce anymore. Lettuce is now being fried. It's being fried and masquerading as pastry. Suddenly everything in upscale food stores is wrapped in fried lettuce. And if I see one more thing with truffle oil or truffle shavings or foie gras, I'll scream. I don't want to eat bison meat either," Sonia added as an afterthought, "or have my beef stuffed with blue cheese, or wasabi through every dish."

"I didn't realize it was such a volatile issue for you," Ruth said.

"Neither Michael nor I have time to cook," Sonia said. "I buy food on the way home, unless I'm going out to dinner. And then Michael buys his own."

"Who makes the girls' dinner?" Ruth said.

"The babysitter," said Sonia. "They eat at six o'clock."

"I'd buy meatballs if they were really good," Sonia said. "They sound so wholesome. Everything today seems to be stuffed or marinated or sautéed in ingredients you've never heard of and never eaten."

"I'll tell my father that you're a customer he can definitely count on," Ruth said. She had a headache. "You've given me a headache," she said to Sonia. "I should never have brought the subject up."

"Lots of things give you a headache," Sonia said. "You should be more discerning about what you allow to make your head ache."

"Thanks," said Ruth.

Nine

Ruth had spent the morning looking at sheets of card paper. She had looked at whole sheets, and swatches and squares and strips. She had looked at hundreds of textures and colors. She had felt cocooned in a world of textures and densities and half shades and whole tones and matte, glossy, and semi-matte finishes. It was the sort of world where, Ruth felt, nothing unpleasant or uncalled for occurred. She hadn't wanted to leave. She was sitting in her office looking at the swatches of the card paper she'd ordered. One of them was a reddish, muted maroon. The color was almost red. And almost maroon. It was a color that cut across genders. A color she felt men and women would be comfortable with. She was going to use it on a card that seemed, in this era of e-mail exchanges, almost old-fashioned:

Last Night Was Great

Can we have a second date?

Ruth hoped that teaming the text with the dark red would give it a contemporary boldness. A contemporary confidence. The boldness and confidence of e-mail exchanges.

Zachary called her. "Just checking in, Roo," he said. "How are you doing?"

"I'm fine," she said.

"How's work?" Zachary said.

"Work's okay," she said.

"Are you sleeping, Roo?" he asked her.

"Zelda asked me yesterday if I was sleeping well," Ruth said. "And Kate asked me last week. I don't want you to get together and talk about my insomnia. I don't want you to get together and talk about me. Anyway, it's not insomnia, I'm just not sleeping well."

"We all know you don't sleep well if anything's bothering you. And Garth being away is a big deal," Zachary said.

"If I didn't sleep when things bothered me," Ruth said, "I probably wouldn't have had an uninterrupted night's sleep in my life."

Zachary laughed.

"Zelda asked me if I was managing," Ruth said. "It made me feel infantile. I am managing. Well, sort of. I am missing Garth. And Grandpa is driving me around the bend."

"Hey, isn't Grandpa's idea for a restaurant great?" Zachary said.

"What?" said Ruth. "He told you about it?"

"He told all three of us," Zachary said.

"Well, it's not great," said Ruth. "And it's not his idea. It's Zofia's."

"Why isn't it great?" Zachary said. "Zofia makes a mean meatball. Last night she made Bolognese balls. Not meatballs with a Bolognese sauce. Meatballs with the sauce through them. They tasted like meatballs and like the sauce."

"You were there last night?" Ruth said. "I haven't seen you for weeks."

"Roo, Grandpa is my grandfather," Zachary said.

"I know that," she said.

"I think you're missing Garth more than you know," Zachary said to her.

"I haven't spent a fortune lying on analysts' couches for you to fill in what's missing in my self-awareness," Ruth said. "I know I'm missing Garth."

"Roo, do you want me to move into the loft with you for a while?" Zachary said.

"No," Ruth said. "Thanks, anyway. I'm fine. Maybe you could move in with Grandpa and distract him from Zofia?" Ruth said.

"I don't see what you've got against her," Zachary said. "It's great for Grandpa that she's here. And it's great for Grandpa to be having sex."

"How do you know Grandpa is having sex," Ruth said.

"Roo, of course he's having sex," said Zachary.

Ruth had arranged to have breakfast in the morning with Edek, Zofia, and Walentyna. She hoped she'd be able to focus on something other than the thought of her father and Zofia having sex. The breakfast had been set up to discuss money. Money for their project. Edek had insisted that they meet at Noah's Ark. He said he'd heard they had pickled herring for breakfast. Edek, Zofia, and Walentyna all looked nervous when Ruth arrived. They looked tense. As though they were preparing for a meeting with the head of the World Bank. Edek was scratching his hands. She hadn't seen him do that for years. The last time had been when the foreman at the factory he'd worked at had told him to retire. Zofia was a slightly paler shade of herself. And Walentyna was white. Ruth was relieved to see that Zofia's outfit was not remotely less subdued. She was wearing a black and green tartan skirt, a lime green top, and a black emerald-rhinestone-studded belt with a heart-shaped buckle. Zofia's ensemble lifted Ruth's spirits. All three of them leapt up from their chairs as soon as they spotted her. The speed

with which they rose from their chairs bothered Ruth. They had
jumped to attention as though she was the head of the Mafia. As
though one wrong word, one gesture in the wrong direction, and they
could be shot. She kissed each of them effusively. She wanted them to
see she wasn't a monster.

"Shall we order some food?" Ruth said. There was definitely something wrong if she had to be the one who suggested they needed to eat.
Edek ordered a small portion of pickled herring. Zofia and Walentyna
ordered pancakes and maple syrup.

"I like the American pancakes very much," Zofia said.

"I do, too," said Walentyna.

"They're very good," Ruth said, in an overly eager manner. She
hated American pancakes. And loathed maple syrup.

"You do like such American pancakes?" Edek said to her, looking
suspicious.

"Yes, I quite do," she said.

"I did not see you eat such a pancake once," Edek said.

"Maybe I haven't had one in a while," she said.

Edek looked at her. "When did you eat a pancake?" he said.

"I can't remember the exact date, Dad," she said. Why had she got
herself into this mess? There had to be other ways to appear agreeable.
"Anyway I think they're very good," she said.

"They are not so good what the pancakes what is for blintzes,"
Edek said.

"That is true," said Zofia. "The pancakes we make for blintzes in
Poland are much better."

They had three and a half Jews left in Poland, but they had blintzes
in Sopot? Ruth had thought you could only get blintzes in the bigger
Polish cities. The cities that catered to the Holocaust tourist industry.
Jews touring Poland looking at death camps, ghettos, and neglected
Jewish cemeteries. Jews searching for their former homes, factories,

shops, and office buildings. Or the homes, factories, shops, and office buildings that belonged to their parents or grandparents. Ruth didn't know you could get blintzes in Sopot.

"The pancakes what is on blintzes is out of this velt," said Edek. Ruth was happy that the conversation seemed to have regained a degree of normality. Edek talking about what food was out of this velt was a good sign that things were settling down. She started to feel less like Mussolini or Stalin. She started to feel more like herself.

"You want a piece of my pancake?" Zofia said to Ruth.

"No thanks, Zofia," she said. "I'm very happy with my fruit salad."

Edek ate his pickled herring at lightning speed. He put his empty plate on another table, and pulled out some papers. There were three sheets of paper. They looked as though they had been folded and un-folded several times. Edek had been carrying them in his pocket. Zofia rushed to finish her pancakes, and Walentyna stopped eating. Edek spread the papers out. Ruth saw that they were filled with lists of items, written in Edek's European-style handwriting. Although Edek's hand-writing was neat, it had a bit of a flourish, the y's and the g's, the f's and the p's all had impressive loops. And every i was dotted.

"I got all the paperwork, Ruthie," Edek said. "I got the money what we will need. I got everything."

Ruth couldn't bear to look at the sheets of paper. She didn't want to scrutinize each line. She didn't want to slip back into being the war-lord or the despot.

She saw several headings on the lists. There was Furniture, Kitchen Stuff, Fridges, Toilet. Each of the headings was in capital letters. And underlined. Not much was listed under any of the headings. Edek didn't appear to have itemized too many things. She thought that rent must be somewhere on the sheets. Rent couldn't have been thrown in with kitchen stuff. Or maybe it could. She saw Rent on the last page. It had its own category, as did Meat Grinder, Stove, and Dishwasher. Ruth couldn't read the details without her glasses. She didn't want to take them out. She didn't want to appear imperious. She wanted to keep the whole thing low-key. She squinted at the figures.

"You do not need to read it, Ruthie," Edek said. "I will tell you what is on the papers."

"Okay," she said.

"What is on the papers is all the stuff what we do need to start the business," said Edek. "Me and Zofia and Walentyna did sit down to think of everything what we would need. We did think of everything."

Zofia and Walentyna were nodding. They were looking intensely at Edek. They clearly thought he was doing a good job.

"We did also think that the restaurant would not straight away make a profit," Edek said. "Because we do have to wait a bit till more people does know about Zofia's bolls."

Did he mean more people than the man who owned the dry cleaners and his wife, and the butcher on Grand Street and Zelda, Zachary, and Kate?

"It doesn't happen so quick that people will learn about Zofia's bolls," Edek said, "so we did put down on paper enough money so we can make bolls for three months. After three months we will for sure have plenty of customers."

This was Edek's pitch? This pitch wouldn't have gone down well with the head of the World Bank. Ruth straightened herself up to point out a few flaws.

"And when we do have plenty of customers we will pay you back every penny what you do give us," Edek added.

Every penny that she gave them? Clearly Zofia and Walentyna didn't have any money. She was not sure why she thought they would.

Zofia looked at Ruth. "Walentyna and I did bring all our money to New York. We have got nearly fifteen thousand dollars in the bank."

"They do need their fifteen thousand dollars," Edek said. "They can manage like this because I do pay the rent."

Ruth opened her mouth to say, "I pay the rent," then she stopped. Zofia was looking at her.

"Ruthie, I know that you do help Edek with rent," she said, and gave Ruth a semiwink. It was a wink that said she knew Ruth paid the rent.

Ruth kept quiet. "Ruthie, what do you think?" Edek said. "Do you want that I should tell you how much money we do need for everything. I did already add up all the expenses."

"Okay," she said.

"Good," Edek said. He put the sheets of paper back into his pocket. He took a deep breath, straightened his shirt, and looked at Ruth. "What we do need, Ruthie, is thirty thousand dollars," Edek said.

Ruth looked at him. "You think you can open a restaurant in New York for thirty thousand dollars?"

"Off coss," said Edek.

Thirty thousand dollars. Some New Yorkers paid thirty thousand dollars to rent a house in the Hamptons for a month. And Edek, Zofia, and Walentyna thought they could get a restaurant up and running for that amount?

"What does the thirty thousand dollars cover?" Ruth said.

"Everything," said Edek.

"It can't," said Ruth. "It's not enough money."

"I did tell you that to Ruthie thirty thousand dollars is not such a lot of money," Edek said to Zofia and Walentyna. "Ruthie does have to write less than one hundred letters and she can earn thirty thousand dollars."

What had Edek been busy calculating? Her income? He didn't seem to have calculated a fraction of what it would take to open a restaurant. And what did he mean thirty thousand dollars was not a lot of money for her?

"Thirty thousand dollars is a lot of money to me, and to most people," Ruth said. "It's just not a lot of money to start a restaurant. It's not enough money to start a restaurant."

"Ruthie, do you think I am stupid?" Edek said. "You do know nothing about the restaurant business. I do know already quite a lot."

Ruth looked at Zofia and Walentyna. They were both nodding.

"We are going to buy old tables, old chairs, old stoves, a old sink, and even a old toilet," Edek said.

"An old sink and an old toilet?" Ruth said.

"And old pots what you do cook in and old things what do you bake on in the oven," Edek said.

"Edek means secondhand," said Zofia.

"Secondhand is still old," said Edek.

Edek ran through a list of what other old things they were buying. The restaurant was beginning to sound very old.

"And that thirty thousand dollars includes the rent?" Ruth asked.

"Off coss," said Edek. "We did tell the owner that we are going to fix it up and he did say that in this case he would not charge us anything for the first three months."

Ruth was starting to feel overwhelmed. The project was taking on surrealistic dimensions. Ruth had images of old meatballs being cooked in old saucepans and served on old plates. And an old toilet for people to shit in.

"How will you know how to fix the store up?" Ruth said. "You've never run a restaurant. How will you know what to put where?"

"Two of the girls what does work for the architect what is on Ludlow Street did do plans for us." Edek said. "They did tell us that this shop did once used to be a small restaurant so we do not need too much special permission to also have a restaurant in this spot."

"You've got plans drawn up?" said Ruth.

"Yes," said Edek, in a loud voice, as though he was already the CEO and he was addressing his shareholders.

"We have a plumber and a carpenter from Poland," Walentyna said. "And they did give us a very good price."

"And we do have a painter what is Polish, too," Edek said. "Not a painter what is like Gut, a painter what does paint walls."

Ruth didn't want to ask any more questions. She was tired. She'd already asked too many questions. She was starting to feel like a Gestapo interrogator. A tired Gestapo interrogator.

"You can be a partner, Ruthie," Edek said.

"I don't want to be a partner," she said. "You can be a partner," she said to Edek.

"I am going already to be a partner," Edek said. "I think Ruthie will give us the money," Edek said to Zofia and Walentyna.

Ruth thought about it. She thought she had probably wasted far more than thirty thousand dollars in her life. Possibly just in the last few years. When appliances broke, she just replaced them. When the fridge didn't work she bought a new one. When the almost new washing machine broke down she ordered a new one. When fax machines and answering machines and cameras proved too complicated for her to use, she ditched them. She never had anything repaired. Or returned faulty items. Returning things took too much time. And having anything repaired in New York was too difficult. Garth was no good with equipment either. He hated anything with buttons to press or sets of directions. He haphazardly pressed, twisted, and prodded buttons and levers and hinges, so that any possibility of whatever it was ever functioning was completely eliminated. The loft had had an entire closet of barely used equipment until she'd arranged for the Salvation Army to take it away.

"Did you make the decision, Ruthie?" Edek said. Edek sounded hesitant. He'd lost some of his CEO polish and confidence. He sounded more like the assistant manager of a grocery store. "Are you going to give us the thirty thousand dollars?" he said.

"Yes," said Ruth. "I have to, really."

It was true. She couldn't face telling Edek that he didn't know what he was doing. She couldn't bear quashing the prospect of a bolls shop or a bolls empire or a bolls nation. Edek banged the table with his fist. "I did tell you she was a good girl," he shouted. Edek looked elated. He kissed Ruth, and then he kissed Zofia and Walentyna. Zofia and Walentyna kissed Ruth simultaneously, on different cheeks, and then they kissed Edek. All the kissing and banging had given Ruth a headache.

"I am going to order some more pickled herring," Edek declared.

"I will have some pickled herring, too," said Zofia.

"I think I will have some more pancakes," Walentyna said.

Ruth was surprised. Walentyna was not a big eater. Zofia and Edek were also surprised.

"Maybe two such plates of pancakes will be too much for you," Edek said to Walentyna.

"It will be too much, Walentyna," said Zofia. "Maybe you should have something else."

"I want pancakes," said Walentyna.

"Okay, okay," said Edek.

"I'll have some more fruit salad," said Ruth.

Ruth called Garth. She'd spoken to him on the weekend and told him about Edek, Zofia, and Walentyna's plans. He wasn't surprised.

"Nothing your father would do could surprise me," Garth had said. "He's just wonderful. How many other people would be thinking of going into any business, let alone the restaurant business, at eighty-seven. This will occupy him for weeks."

"So you don't think anything's going to come of it," Ruth had said.

"No," said Garth. "You have to know what you're doing to open a restaurant in New York. And somebody has to fund you."

Now Ruth had to call Garth and tell him that while Edek, Zofia, and Walentyna may well still not know what they were doing, they did, now, have a backer. Her. Ruth wondered whether Garth would be shocked. He was pretty unshockable. She herself had been a bit shocked at her decision to hand over thirty thousand dollars. Then she'd recovered. Even if Edek, Zofia, and Walentyna's plan resulted in an attempted plan, an aborted plan, or a failed plan, which was more than highly likely, it was worth it. Edek was so excited about the possibilities. And to be excited about possibilities at eighty-seven was not bad. She didn't want to take that away from him. And when their plan of selling thousands of balls didn't pan out, she was sure Edek would bounce back. He would have dozens of theories and explanations and thoughts about why the plan didn't work. None of the reasons would be based on any missteps or mistakes the three of them might have made. Edek's faith in the plan would remain unshakable. Her father was resilient. What if he bounced back with too much force, she suddenly thought. What if he came up with another scheme? This one had been thought up and proposed in record time. She had a short fantasy about having to grapple with a series of wildly improbable business proposals. She decided to deal with one at a time.

Garth answered the phone. Ruth steadied herself. She told Garth that Edek had come up with a sum that they needed for their meatball emporium. "It was thirty thousand dollars," she said.

"Thirty thousand dollars to open a restaurant?" Garth said. "You can probably buy a thirty-thousand-dollar bottle of wine in New York. You can't open a restaurant for that."

"My dad had all these figures written down on three sheets of paper," Ruth said.

"What were they?" said Garth.

"I don't know. I didn't want to look too closely. One of the categories was called Kitchen Stuff. And there was room in the budget for a toilet. My dad had the three sheets spread out in front of him. I think he'd spent a lot of time compiling the figures."

"Oh no," said Garth.

"They've found a Polish plumber and a Polish carpenter," Ruth said. "And some architecture students have drawn up plans. I gave them the money."

"You gave who the money?" said Garth.

"I gave my father the thirty thousand," Ruth said. Garth started laughing. "You think it's funny?" she said.

"I do think it's funny," said Garth.

"I think it's probably crazy," said Ruth.

"I can't imagine your father as a chef," Garth said.

"He's not going to be the chef," said Ruth. "He's probably going to be the maître d' of their proposed seven- or eight- or ten-table meatball palace. You don't mind the money?" Ruth said.

"Not at all," said Garth. "We've spent far more than that on totally useless stuff."

"Who's we?" said Ruth. "Me? Are you talking about the excessively large number of TV sets and VCRs and DVD players and phones and fax machines and sound equipment we've gone through?"

She knew that she was the one who'd wanted all that stuff. Garth would have been happy with one black-and-white TV, one telephone, and a radio. The cassette player he had in the studio was eight years old, covered in paint, and cost about thirty dollars in the first place.

"No," Garth said. "I'm not talking about you. I'm talking about us. We're hardly the most financially responsible people in the universe. We don't search for the best interest rates on any money we have. We never look for the best deals on whatever it is we're looking at or doing. We fly business class when coach wouldn't kill us."

"It would kill me," said Ruth. "I'm sure my varicose veins must make me prone to blood clotting. And blood clotting produces embolisms. And embolisms obstruct your arteries."

Garth started laughing again. "I'm not saying we shouldn't do any of those things," he said. "I'm just saying we do. This project," Garth said, "is going to keep your father very happy and very occupied. It's going to stretch his brain and keep him alert."

"He's having no trouble keeping alert," Ruth said. "You should see Zofia's necklines. They'd keep anyone braced and alert."

"It's going to keep your father young," Garth said.

"What?" said Ruth. "The possible restaurant? Or Zofia's breasts?"

"Both," said Garth. "You're a bit preoccupied with Zofia's breasts, sweetheart."

Ten

Ruth looked at the new card she'd written.

You Are Part of My Heart

A large part.

She was pleased with the card. She liked the way it looked. The card was on matte white handmade paper. The text was embossed in a semi-matte black. The message was simple. And direct. The distributor had told her that more and more stores were ordering Direct Text cards. Ruth was thrilled. She hadn't really expected the greeting-card line to do well. It had started as an experiment. She enjoyed doing the cards. She found it relaxing. And much less taxing than writing letters.

Max buzzed her. "Willie, Scout's owner, is on the phone," Max said.

"Who?" said Ruth. Then she remembered the fuckup.

"I don't want to talk to him," Ruth said. "Just apologize again on my behalf." "I don't think he wants an apology," Max said. "He sounds very cheerful. His name is Willie Sonoma."

"Okay," said Ruth.

"You wrote a letter to my dead dog about my death," Willie Sonoma said to Ruth.

"I know," said Ruth. "I'm sorry."

"That's fine," said Willie Sonoma. "It's easy to be confused when they both sound like dogs' names. My name could have been Scout and my dog could have been Willie."

"But you weren't Scout and he wasn't Willie," said Ruth.

"I know," said Willie Sonoma, "but it didn't bother me. I was really moved by the condolence letter and I wanted to thank you."

Ruth almost began to explain that she wasn't the sender of the condolence letter, she was the writer. There was no need to thank her, she wanted to explain. The letter had been sent by James King. She stopped herself. There had been enough confusion about Scout and Willie. Or Willie and Scout. She didn't want to introduce another set of complexities about who the letter was from.

"I wanted to know if you could write a thank-you note for me," Willie Sonoma said. "Something I could send to a number of people. I got so many condolence cards about Scout's death."

"Yes, we can do that," Ruth said. "Do you want to give Max the details we need to know, and I'll do that with pleasure."

Ruth was surprised to hear that a large number of people were sending condolence cards to the bereaved owners of deceased dogs. She didn't think it was a market she would tackle. She thought her indifference to, if not dislike of, dogs would seep through the greetings.

"Thank you," said Willie Sonoma. "And I really loved your letter."

Just as Ruth was packing up and preparing to leave for the day, Edek, Zofia, and Walentyna arrived.

"Ruthie, I am happy that you did not yet leave," Edek said. "We did all want to see you. We did want to say thank you very much for the money. We are very happy with what we done so far and we are very sure that it is going to be a big success."

Edek's insistent use of the word "we" bothered her. How many "we's" had he already used? He sounded as though he was making a speech on behalf of the United States Congress. Then she felt mean. Why shouldn't Edek use the word "we"? There were three of them.

"Can we sit with you a few minutes?" Edek said. "We been working all day."

"Of course, Dad," she said.

"We done already a lot of work," Edek said. "Zofia does know already what bolls she will make. We will start with not too many such different bolls." He pulled a piece of paper out of his wallet. "This is the bolls what we will start with."

Zofia and Walentyna were looking at Edek intently. As though he was about to read out the Declaration of Independence. Zofia was nodding her head in the way that music lovers, at a concert, nod in anticipation of the notes that are coming up next.

"The bolls what we will start with will be," Edek began. He paused, and then in a more formal voice began reading from his list. "We will have turkey and bratwurst bolls, what we did already tell you about," Edek said. "And veal and beef bolls and veal, potato, and kielbasa bolls what you do also already know about. And we will have turkey and spiced coconut bolls, Bolognese bolls, chicken and bratwurst bolls, plain chicken bolls, beef and kielbasa bolls, and pork and sauerkraut bolls."

Edek looked at Ruth. "That is already nine such different bolls," he said. "And that is not everything. We will have also for those people what does not eat meat, separate bolls."

"Bolls for vegetarians," said Zofia.

"That is right," said Edek. "The bolls for people what does not eat meat will be carrot and honey bolls and potato and cheese bolls."

"The potato and cheese bolls have got a mixture of Parmesan cheese and gouda cheese," Walentyna said.

"They are very good," said Zofia.

"They are not bad," said Edek. "They are not so good what the veal and beef bolls or the chicken bolls or the veal and sauerkraut bolls."

Edek had plainly been tasting a lot of bolls. Ruth corrected herself. Balls. He had been tasting a lot of balls. Maybe bolls was better. Tasting a lot of balls sounded quite unsavory.

"And for those people what does not eat meat, we will have also chickpea and tomato bolls," Edek said. "To tell you the truth, I do not like too much the chickpeas, but Zofia does say that in New York there are plenty of people what do not eat meat."

"Especially downtown where we will be," Walentyna said. "Zofia says that there are more vegetarians who do live downtown."

Ruth looked at Zofia. How did Zofia know this? How had she figured that out? Ruth was sure she was right. Downtown Manhattan was certain to have a higher percentage of vegetarians than the Upper East Side. Or the Upper West Side. How had Zofia known that?

"Zofia and me did go to more than thirty restaurants and we did count how many meals was on the menu for people what does not eat meat," Edek said. "And Walentyna did go to nearly thirty restaurants herself to look at the same thing. I can tell you we was pretty tired when we did finish."

"You counted the vegetarian meals that are being served in restaurants?" Ruth said.

"Only the restaurants what are between the Fourteenth Street and where we do live," said Edek.

"Walentyna looked at the menus of quite a few restaurants in uptown," said Zofia.

Edek looked back down at his list. "We will have also, to eat with the bolls, cucumber salad, what is very good."

"It is made from very thinly sliced cucumbers which are marinated in vinegar and sugar," said Zofia.

"And we will have cooked red cabbage and raisins what you can eat hot or cold," said Edek. "And some small bolled potatoes."

Did Edek mean ball-shaped potatoes, or potatoes that were boiled?

"Zofia is very clever," Edek said. "She does boll all the potatoes first. Then when you do want to eat them she does put them in the bolling water for just a few minutes."

"If we want to make money," Zofia said, "then we have to know what we are doing."

"Off coss," said Edek.

"The bolls do all have eggs, onions, breadcrumbs or flour, and spices," said Zofia. "Eggs do stay fresh for more than a few days and the rest of the things are not perishable."

"Nonperishable," said Walentyna.

The English course in Sopot must have been pretty comprehensive, Ruth thought. The difference between nonperishable and not perishable was not enormous.

"Nonperishable," said Zofia.

"Then you do order the things what need to be fresh," said Edek. "Things like the meat and the chicken and the sausages and the vegetables. These things you do order two or three times a week. Zofia does have a very good system for the bolls. All of the bolls are very different but Zofia does make them in such a way what does make it very easy to make all the different bolls."

"I am very efficient," Zofia said. "All the onion is grated or finely chopped. For some bolls I use raw onions in the mixture and for some bolls I do fry the onion in a little bit of oil to make them nice and sweet before I put them in the mixture. All the vegetables we will use are grated too. The meat is put through a meat grinder. I do like to grind my own meat. In Sopot I did always grind my own meat."

Suddenly the phrase *grind my own meat* slipped from its place in the kitchen into something decidedly more sexual. Ruth grimaced inwardly. Why did she have to do that? Why did she have to twist series of words into unpalatable images? And then have to struggle to get the images out of her head. Grinding your own meat was not an easy image to dismiss.

"We did already buy a quite big grinding machine for meat and a grating machine for the vegetables and the onions," Edek said. "Both of them was very cheap. They was owned already by other people but they was in very good condition, Ruthie."

"And we are looking at very good secondhand big dough-mixing machine to mix the boll mixture," said Walentyna excitedly. "In Sopot Zofia mixed all her bolls by hand, but in a restaurant you do need a machine."

"Mum did always make her meatbolls by hand," Edek said to Ruth. "Rooshka did make very good meatbolls," he said to Zofia and Walentyna.

"Of course," said Zofia. "Edek did tell me that Rooshka was a very good cook."

"She was a very good cook," said Ruth.

Zofia explained that most of the balls were baked. A few were boiled. And none were fried. That way, she said, the balls were healthier and less fattening. The baked meatballs were all cooked on large trays at 375 degrees. The ones that were boiled were boiled in water or broth. At the mention of less fattening, Edek nodded and looked meaningfully at Ruth.

"People can take the bolls home and put them in the freezer," Edek said.

"You can put the bolls straight from the freezer into the oven and they are ready twenty minutes later," said Walentyna.

Bolls expertise was spilling out and filling the room. Ruth looked around her to make sure she was still in the office. She was. She could see her cards. And her files. And her notebooks.

"With a menu like this you do not waste too much food," Walentyna said.

"Yes," said Zofia. "You do not have to buy hundreds of fresh in-

gredients every day. The fresh ingredients you do buy are the ingredients you know you will use. The rest of the ingredients are nonperishable or else do last a long time. I will give you an example, Ruthie
darling."

Ruth was getting used to being called Ruthie darling by Zofia. It
wasn't making her bristle as much. She was too tired to bristle, she
decided.

"If I do make my chicken bolls," Zofia said, "I do use chicken and
onions and eggs and breadcrumbs and salt and pepper. If I do make
chicken and raisin bolls, which I did make often in Sopot, I do use the
same chicken, onions, eggs and breadcrumbs and salt and pepper. And
I do add raisins and chopped garlic and cardamom and a little bit of
honey."

Ruth had to admit that the chicken and raisin balls did sound
very good.

"Zofia does make a very good pork boll," said Walentyna. "It is
pork with apple and raisins and smoked kielbasa."

"You can get a very good smoked kielbasa, in the Polish butcher on
First Avenue," Zofia said.

Zofia seemed to know more about New York than most New Yorkers. She knew where the swimming pools were and which beaches you
could swim at. She knew what meals were being served in different
parts of the city. And where to find Polish carpenters and plumbers and
Polish kielbasa. Ruth didn't know whether to feel impressed or
daunted.

"I do not like so much the smoked kielbasa," Edek said. "I do like
plain kielbasa. I do not like anything what is smoked."

"You probably had more than enough smoke in Auschwitz," Ruth
said, and then wondered how those words had slipped out of her
mouth. Zofia and Walentyna looked somber.

"Walentyna and me do feel very bad about what did happen to the
Jewish people in Poland," Zofia said.

"Most Poles didn't," said Ruth. "Most Poles were pleased to get rid of their Jews. Most Poles were pleased to see their Jews gone."

"Ruthie, Zofia and Walentyna are not such Poles," Edek said. "They was not even adults then."

"I'm sorry," said Ruth.

"That is all right, Ruthie," said Zofia. "Edek did suffer very much."

"And so did Rooshka," Edek said.

Everyone looked miserable. How had she leapt from kielbasa to Auschwitz? Ruth thought. She wished she hadn't. She felt desperate to get the conversation back to balls. To balls. Or old kitchen stuff. Or old chairs and tables. Or anything else.

"How do you bake the balls?" Ruth said to Zofia.

"Zofia does bake them on baking trays or in muffin trays," Walentyna said.

"We do not have muffins in Poland," Zofia said.

"Off coss not," said Edek. "Muffins is rubbish."

"I do not like muffins," said Walentyna.

"I do not like muffins," Zofia said.

"I don't like muffins," Ruth said in a rush. She was grateful for the opportunity to show some solidarity, to be part of the group. She wanted to remove the disaccord that she'd created. "I think muffins are disgusting," she said.

"Muffins is definitely rubbish," said Edek.

"In Poland I bought trays for small cakes to bake my meatbolls," Zofia said.

"Well, muffins are basically cakes," said Ruth. "Bad cakes."

"Terrible cakes," said Edek.

The muffins had brokered a peace between them. Everyone seemed relieved. The accord over muffins had given them a bond. Unified them.

"We did find very good muffin trays," said Zofia. "They do have round not straight sides. And they are just the right size."

Even in a more subdued state Zofia's "just the right size" contained a lustiness. It was not a quiet lustiness. It was the sort of lustiness that announced itself with trumpets. The sort of lustiness you could be arrested for.

"The bolls are very good for sandwiches, too," said Zofia. "We will make boll sandwiches in the restaurant."

"The beef and veal bolls with some of the purple cabbage is out of this velt in a bread roll," said Edek. "I think we are going to sell many such bolls in rolls."

Bolls in rolls. Ruth liked the sound of that. She went into a rhyming reverie. Polls of bolls in rolls, lots of bolls in rolls, pots of bolls in rolls. She stopped herself. She was becoming bowled over by bolls. Her mother used to make balls. Meatballs. They had called them by their Yiddish name, *Cotlatten*. Rooshka used to grind her own meat and mold the balls by hand. Each ball was the same size and came out perfectly round. Thinking about her mother made her feel sad. Last week, she had taken a red purse that had belonged to her mother down from the top shelf of her closet. It was a red leather purse, with tortoiseshell handles. Ruth had never used the purse. She had had it, along with four pairs of her mother's shoes and two of her mother's dresses, in her closet for the eighteen years since her mother had died. Ruth couldn't wear the shoes. Her feet were too big. The dresses didn't fit her. She was too tall. She had opened the purse gingerly. As though it was still attached to her mother. Clutched in her mother's hand, or held under her mother's arm. Inside the purse were two sheets of paper toweling. They seemed to have been used as padding to keep the purse in shape. Ruth had no memory of putting paper toweling in there. It was not something she'd do. She'd never padded any of her own purses or bags to make sure they retained their shape. She took the paper toweling out and caught a faint whiff of her mother's scent. She put her face close to the inside of the purse. She was shocked. The purse smelled of her mother. Surely people's scents couldn't remain for so long after the persons themselves had gone? She had to steady herself. Scent was a pretty powerful thing. It could summon up people who were not present. People who were not in the same room, not in the same building. Not in the same hemisphere.

Ruth often walked into Garth's closet. Garth's closet smelled of Garth. Ruth found the scent reassuring. Soothing. She would walk into the closet and breathe deeply. She would close her eyes and breathe as deeply as she could. As though she was inhaling Garth. Garth had only been away from New York for just over ten weeks. It made sense that you could still smell Garth if you were standing in the middle of his shirts and trousers and jackets and socks. But surely an object couldn't retain its former owner's perfume, its former owner's scent, for over eighteen years. Ruth had picked up one of the sheets of paper toweling, and sniffed it again. It definitely smelled of her mother. So did the purse. She had felt unnerved. She looked at the bag as though part of it was alive. As though it might begin to talk to her. As though her mother was still living. She'd put the bag carefully back in the closet. Now that the purse appeared to contain traces of her mother, she felt she should keep it somewhere very secure. A bank vault wouldn't be any good. She didn't want to think of her mother locked in a blank, airless bank vault. She stopped herself from thinking about her mother, or whatever still remained of her, disintegrating in black, airless earth.

"We will have a special sweet pickled apples and tomatoes and onions mixture," Walentyna was saying. "Zofia does make this herself with apples and tomatoes and vinegar and sugar and ginger and mustard and raisins."

"We will also have horseradish," Zofia said. "Little pots of both these things will be on each table for customers who would like to have them with their bolls."

"Zofia will not make the horseradish," said Walentyna.

"No, we will buy kosher horseradish," said Zofia. "We did already find the best brand."

"Zofia is not going to charge the customers extra for those things," Edek announced. He announced this with a tone of ambivalence Ruth didn't often see in her father. She could see Edek was conflicted. Torn between seeing this decision of Zofia's as a magnanimous, benevolent gesture worthy of Bill Gates or Mother Teresa, and viewing the giving away of condiments as an unnecessary way to cut into their profits.

"In the future we will maybe charge for those things," Edek said, authoritatively, looking at Zofia.

"In the future we will also try new bolls," said Walentyna.

Ruth looked at them. They were planning a future. They hadn't yet started. Who knew if they ever would start. Let alone have a future. They had no experience. Their budget was ludicrous. Impossible, really. And they had to navigate the city's complex, incomprehensible, and sometimes nonsensical health department and building code requirements.

"The Polish carpenter did send already someone to clean up the shop," Edek said. "We do need to throw out the rubbish what is in the shop before the carpenter and the plumber can start."

"You've started the demolition?" Ruth said. She was shocked.

"Yes," said Edek. "He will finish it quickly. There is only three walls what we will take out and a lot of rubbish."

"Wouldn't it have been better to not touch the building till you had your plans approved?" said Ruth.

"We do need to get such a approval only for a few of the things what we will build," Edek said. "We got already a person what is called a expeditor what is doing this for us."

"The young people from the architect's office did organize this for us," Zofia said. "The expeditor did say we can pay him in bolls when the restaurant does open."

"He did come to our apartment for a dinner," Edek said. "And he did say that Zofia's bolls was very good."

Ruth was flabbergasted. "Is the expeditor Polish?" she said.

"No," said Edek. "As a matter of fact he is Irish."

The three of them got up to leave. Ruth felt exhausted. "We are going to eat now," Edek said to Ruth. "Would you like to join us?"

"Zofia does force me to go to such different restaurants," Edek said, before Ruth could answer. "Restaurants with carry. Restaurants with paprika. She does say we do need to see what food people is eating."

"My darling Edek," Zofia said. "Is it true that I do find you something you do like to eat at every restaurant?"

"That is true," Edek said. "And it is usually not too bad."

Ruth tried not to feel irked by the "my darling Edek." She was too tired to feel irked. The expeditor, the demolition, the sweet pickled apples and tomatoes and vinegar, sugar, ginger, mustard, and raisins, and the plans for more balls had worn her out.

"Will you join us?" Edek said, again.

"No thanks, Dad," she said. "I think I'll go home."

Eleven

Ruth hadn't seen much of Zofia or Walentyna or Edek for the past couple of weeks. She'd been relieved. She'd been experiencing Edek, Zofia, and Walentyna overload. Edek had phoned her a few times. Mostly from his cell phone. He seemed to be constantly on the move.

"Are you going to the gym regularly?" she'd said to him.

"Off coss," he said. "It does nearly kill me the weights what I do lift." He'd sighed exasperatedly on the other end of the line. "Now I got three people what does make sure I do go to the gym." He stopped. "No, I got four people," he said. "Zachary does phone me from time to time to check that I am still going to the gym. So I got Zachary and Zofia and Walentyna, and my daughter."

"I'm pleased," Ruth said.

"I myself am not so pleased," Edek had said.

Edek never suggested that they see each other alone. Just the two of them. Unaccompanied by Zofia or Walentyna. Maybe he didn't want to be questioned by her. Or interrogated. Or advised. He had dropped into the office briefly about a week ago. He'd wanted to borrow the self-navigating vacuum cleaner. Ruth had helped him to pack the vacuum cleaner into a box. She had tried to talk to Edek about his relationship with Zofia. She had tried to dissuade him from seeing the relationship as permanent. She thought he should wait, take his time. A permanent commitment was a big decision, Ruth had said. Edek had stopped what he was doing and looked at her.

"How much permanence have I got?" he said. "I have not got such a lot of permanence. If I was thirty or forty or fifty maybe I would have a permanence. It is crazy to talk to a person what is eighty-seven about a permanence." Edek had looked agitated. "What is the opposite of permanence?"

"Transient, fleeting, transitory, ephemeral," Ruth said.

"What is a plain word what someone what does use a plain English would speak?" said Edek.

"Passing," Ruth said.

"That is a good word," said Edek. "Because when you are a person what is eighty-seven, the things what got to pass will pass much more quickly."

Ruth looked perplexed.

"There is not so much to pass, Ruthie," Edek said. "Nearly all the things which is going to pass did pass already." He looked at her as though she was retarded. She had felt stupid.

Last night Ruth had gone for a walk with Zelda. She had walked with her arm through Zelda's. They had walked through SoHo and Tribeca down to Battery Park City. They hadn't talked much, most of the time. They had just walked. The weather was warming up. The evening air felt almost balmy. Ruth felt happy. She felt happy to be holding Zelda's arm. Happy feeling the sides of their bodies touch. Happy smelling Zelda's hair. At Battery Park, they caught the ferry to New Jersey and walked around Hoboken.

"I really like Zofia," Zelda said, when they were almost back in

SoHo. "She's really very nice. Zachary and Kate think so, too. And Walentyna is so cute. Walentyna offered to teach me to sew."

Walentyna could sew? Ruth thought. Maybe that explained Walentyna's strange clothes? They did have that homemade look. If Walentyna's clothes were evidence of Walentyna's sewing skills, Ruth thought that Zelda might as well give the sewing lessons a miss.

"I love the clothes she wears," Zelda said. "She makes them herself."

"You love them?" said Ruth.

"Yes," said Zelda. "They've got that childlike, innocently put-together look. They're so unself-conscious. They're just draped on her. Nothing is tight."

"Nothing is tight?" Ruth said. "It's not that they're not tight. Not tight is not the problem. The problem is that they're ill-fitting."

"Roo, you used a double negative in two consecutive sentences," Zelda said. "Wait till I tell the others."

"I think it was my astonishment at the fact that you like Walentyna's style of dressing. Or that you even see it as a style," said Ruth.

"I don't want to look that way myself," said Zelda. "I just want to know how to make a basic skirt."

Under instructions from Walentyna, Zelda's skirt might not be as basic as Zelda was envisaging, Ruth thought. It might be missing some basic necessities. Like the need to fit.

The other two previously confirmed members of the women's group had e-mailed, separately, the next morning, to say they had to drop out. One said that she suddenly realized that she worked late most nights, and the other woman didn't offer an explanation. Ruth felt dismayed. And then annoyed. No one suddenly realized that they worked late most nights. It was not one of the things you suddenly realized. If you worked late most nights, you almost certainly knew that you worked late most nights.

Late in the afternoon, Edek had called. He'd asked her if they could have a meeting. A meeting about the business. "We can meet at the café what you do like," he said. "The Caffè Doughnut."

For a moment Ruth was bewildered. She didn't know a Caffè Doughnut. "It's not Caffè Doughnut," she said. "It's Caffè Dante." Caffè Dante was the opposite of a Caffè Doughnut. Some of its cakes were made by Mario, the owner, and the rest were air-freighted in daily from Milan. Although this being New York, Ruth thought, there was probably a store selling handmade doughnuts that were packed in dry ice and air-freighted from Antarctica. Anything that came from a long way away sold well in New York. If a camel had to carry the item across a desert and then pass it on to a donkey, that item would be hot, in New York.

"It does not matter what is the name of the café," Edek said. "Me and Zofia and Walentyna do know where it is."

"When do you want to meet?" Ruth said.

"Today after work?" said Edek.

"Okay," Ruth said.

Zofia and Walentyna and Edek were already at Caffè Dante when Ruth arrived. All three of them were eating gelati.

"We do have to choose a name for the restaurant," Edek said, before Ruth had even sat down. "We do need your help, Ruthie."

"What do you think of Restaurant Zofia and Walentyna?" Edek said.

"That's not bad," said Ruth. "Zofia and Walentyna are unusual and exotic names. The name could be different enough to attract people."

"I think we should have bolls in the name of the restaurant," Edek said. "Otherwise how will people know that they can buy bolls?"

"They will see the bolls when they do come inside," said Walentyna.

"We do need to tell them that we got bolls," Edek said. "*Oy cholera,*" he said, and hit his head with the palm of his hand. "I got a name what is perfect."

Ruth and Zofia and Walentyna turned to Edek. "I got what is a perfect name," he said. "In America they do have a saying what means you do have to have some bolls. They do say, 'You have got to have some bolls.' "

Zofia and Walentyna looked at Edek, perplexed.

"It is an expression what they do say in America and it is perfect for us. 'You have got to have some bolls.' "

Zofia and Walentyna still looked bewildered.

"I know what you mean, Dad," Ruth said.

"Thank God Ruthie is here," said Edek.

"You mean the saying, 'You've got to have balls,' " Ruth said.

"That is right," Edek shouted. "My neighbor a nice chappie what was upstairs in the Second Avenue he did say not you've got to have bolls. He did say, 'You gotta have bolls.' "

"Balls are a slang word for testicles," Ruth said to Zofia and Walentyna. "The saying means, you've got to be strong and courageous. Well that's more or less what it means."

"Aha," said Zofia, so we will be saying two things, you do have to have our bolls and you do have to be strong like a man with testicles."

"I think so," said Ruth.

"It is perfect," said Edek. "Everybody does know what you gotta have bolls does mean."

"You gotta have bolls," said Walentyna. "I do like that name."

"You gotta have bolls," said Zofia.

"You gotta have bolls," said Edek.

Ruth wrote it on a napkin. You Gotta Have Balls. Edek put the napkin in his pocket.

The next time Ruth heard from Edek, he was shouting into his cell phone. "Hello Ruthie, hello Ruthie," he was shouting. Ruth could hear the sound of heavy traffic in the background.

"I am on a street, Ruthie, what is called the Bowery," Edek shouted.

"Here you can buy everything what you do need for a restaurant. I did buy glasses very cheap. Do you want some glasses? I can buy for you a box of twelve glasses what costs ten dollars for the whole box."

"No thanks, Dad," Ruth said.

"Maybe you do need the glasses for the office, Ruthie?" Edek said. "I don't think we do," said Ruth.

"Do you want some plates or some knives?" Edek said. "They got plates and knives. And off coss they got forks and spoons."

"I've got plenty of cutlery, Dad," Ruth said. "But thanks anyway."

"Everything is so cheap," Edek said. "They have got a oven what does cook pizzas. They have got saucepans. They got big saucepans and small ones. Do you want a saucepan, Ruthie?"

"I'm sorry, Dad, I've already got too many saucepans," Ruth said. She wondered whether Edek would go through the entire inventories of the restaurant supplies stores he was visiting. "The saucepans what they got here are very good," Edek said. He sounded a little crestfallen as though he was about to give up on her as a prospective purchaser of kitchen equipment. Then he rallied himself, "Ruthie they got such big spoons what are for mixing," he said. "I think you would like a couple of those spoons."

Ruth relented. "Okay," she said. "Get me a couple."

"Okeydokey," Edek said, "They got a box of twelve such big spoons for thirty-five dollars."

Ruth was about to say that she didn't need twelve large mixing spoons, she only needed two. But Edek had moved on.

"I got things for salt and peppers," he said. "I got things what do hold napkins. You can buy things what are old and things what are new. You can buy a old cash register what is nearly new. It is half of the price of the same thing what is new."

Edek, Ruth thought, was clearly in charge of the Stockings Department of You Gotta Have Balls. Sonia's office had registered the name You Gotta Have Balls, for the restaurant, for Edek, Zofia, and Walentyna. Ruth had been surprised that no one else owned it.

"It's a brilliant name," Sonia said at the time, after she'd stopped laughing.

"Ruthie, they got some very good chairs here," Edek said. "They are made from wood. They are very comfortable and they do only cost thirty dollars for one chair."

"Is that what you're buying for the restaurant?" said Ruth.

"No," said Edek. "The young woman what does work with the architect did buy us chairs at an auction. They did cost fifteen dollars a chair. I am telling you about the chairs because the chairs what you got is not too comfortable."

The chairs Edek was referring to were the fourteen chairs around her dining room table. The chairs were 1950s metal chairs with different-colored backs and seats. They were beautiful. And comfortable. They had come from a school cafeteria.

"I love those chairs," Ruth said. "They'd now cost over two hundred and fifty dollars each."

"That is crazy," said Edek. "The chairs what they got here on the Bowery is much more comfortable."

Twelve

Ruth finished working on another card. She really enjoyed writing the cards. They were less prescriptive than the letters. And she'd been writing letters for a long time. She'd been writing letters for so long that she no longer wrote any letters of her own. She sent people she knew short notes. The first two or three cards she had written had been quite wordy. She felt she was fine-tuning the cards. Becoming more succinct. She was trying not to use more than twelve words. Her new card used twelve words.

I Want You to Know

Your presence adds immeasurably to my existence.

Ruth saw this as a card that cut across gender lines. And sexual orientation. She felt that men would be as comfortable sending this card as women. It was understated and unsentimental enough for a man. And it didn't have a big heterosexual stamp across it. Ruth thought it could be used as a birthday card, a friendship card, an anniversary card, or a card for a new or an old lover. The card was not inspired by or linked to Zofia and Walentyna's arrival in New York. A card she might be more likely to send to Zofia might read: Your Presence/Is presently not quite a pleasure. She wondered, briefly, if there was a market for a card like that. Probably not, she thought. It was probably too nasty. Ruth thought she had scribbled the lines out in jest. But she felt bothered by the lack of joviality, conviviality, or generosity contained in the message.

Patricia Biscuit called Ruth. "I wanted to know how your friends are going with their restaurant plans," she said to Ruth.

"They're planning to open on a thirty-thousand-dollar budget," said Ruth.

"Oh God," said Patricia Biscuit.

"Where?" she asked.

"Attorney Street," Ruth said.

"Oh no," said Patricia Biscuit.

"Attorney Street is off East Houston," said Ruth.

"I know," said Patricia Biscuit. "I know the street."

Ruth didn't think anyone could interpret "Oh God" or "Oh no" as an enthusiastic response.

After lunch Ruth decided to walk to Attorney Street. She wanted to see what was happening. Edek had been strangely quiet. She got to the store. The door was open. She looked in. There were clouds of dust from the floor to the ceiling. There was carpentry equipment and plumbing equipment and ladders. And several men in overalls. A couple of them shouting in Polish to each other. Toward the back of the store she saw Edek, Zofia, and Walentyna. All three were wearing overalls. And masks. Ruth was stunned. Taken aback. She hadn't expected this. And she had never, in her wildest dreams, imagined she'd ever see Edek in overalls. Ruth called out, but no one heard her. One of the carpenters had started up a chain saw. She stepped back out into the street.

She felt a bit dazed. She noticed a large note addressed to the phone company tacked onto the front door. "Please do make a lot of noise. We cannot hear," the note said. It was in Edek's handwriting. Ruth went back to work.

Max came into Ruth's office. "We've got a delivery from A and B Printing Company. It's for your father," Max said. "It's two boxes and they're both very heavy."

"I'll tell my father," said Ruth.

She called Edek. He sounded in a rush. "Can you please open a box?" he said. Ruth opened it. It was full of stationery. She saw letterhead. And envelopes. "Does it have business cards?" Edek asked.

"Yes," she said.

"Thank you very much," said Edek. "We will pick the boxes up in a couple of days."

Before she could say goodbye, he was off the phone. Two minutes later, Edek rang back. "Zofia did say to remind you that you are coming to our place for a dinner tomorrow night," he said.

"I haven't forgotten," Ruth said. She was still getting used to Edek saying "our place." She'd only been to the apartment twice. She'd avoided making an excessive number of visits. She still found it strange to see Edek's possessions in the middle of things that belonged to Zofia or Walentyna. Ruth had studiously avoided going into the bedrooms.

She looked into the box of stationery she'd opened. There was enough stationery to run half a dozen McDonald's franchises for the foreseeable future.

Edek called again. "Ruthie, do me a favor please," he said. "Can you look into the boxes to see if one of the boxes does have boll point pens?

"Ballpoint pens?" said Ruth.

"Yes," said Edek. "Boll point pens. Boll point pens are things what every restaurant does need to write things with."

Ruth was still in the storeroom. She opened the second box. "These boxes are way too heavy for you to pick up," she said to Edek. "I'll have to have them sent over."

"Okay," he said. "Did you find the boll point pens?"

A list of the contents of both boxes was on top of the box she'd just opened. She looked through the list. One of the items was two hundred engraved ballpoint pens. Edek was very pleased.

Edek and Zofia and Walentyna's apartment looked very cozy. They'd put more photographs on the walls. They had also bought two new lamps and a rug. Ruth looked at the photographs. There were photographs of Edek and Rooshka and photographs of Ruth and Garth, and a series of photographs of Edek with Zachary, Kate, and Zelda. There were photographs of Walentyna and her husband, a tall, thin, sensitive-looking man. And a photograph of Walentyna with her mother. And Walentyna with two of her sisters, and three of her nieces. There were photographs of Zofia and her husband. Zofia's husband looked solid and cheerful. He had his arm around Zofia and a large smile on his face. He looked like a happy and well-fed man. A photograph of Zofia's parents was also on the wall. And a photograph of Zofia and her two brothers. Zofia looked quite striking. She had short, spiky hair even then, when most of the other girls' hair would have been waved or curled. She looked boldly at the camera. As did her breasts.

"I was sixteen in that photograph," Zofia said from across the room.

"You don't look much different today," Ruth said.

"Thank you very much, Ruthie darling," said Zofia.

Ruth looked at the bottom of the photograph. It was dated 1952. That made Zofia sixty-nine. Ruth was amazed. How could sixty-nine-year-old legs, arms, and breasts look so good? Ruth looked down at her own body. There was much more evidence of wear and tear. Maybe anxiety and tension made more than one's psyche sink. Maybe breasts drooped in despair and thighs and bums just gave up. She thought it was probably too late for her to convert to cheerfulness. Her body parts would be in shock. They'd think they'd been officially acquisitioned by someone else.

Zofia brought out a plate of mini potato and kielbasa balls.

"Ruthie, these small bolls Zofia does call croquettes," Edek said. "Croquettes are what people does eat at cocktail parties. You do eat them with your fingers."

"The croquettes will be very easy to serve at cocktail parties," Zofia said. "You can eat them at room temperature or heat them in the oven. And you do not need anything else. Two or three croquettes and a glass of wine is perfect for each guest."

Ruth admired Zofia's certainty about what was perfect. Ruth, herself, was much more well-versed in what was not.

"Try a potato and kielbasa croquette, Ruthie," said Zofia.

"No thanks," said Ruth.

"Ruthie did used to be a fatty," Edek said to Zofia. "Till today she does think that if she does eat something what is not stuff what she does eat every day she will be a fatty again." Edek paused. "It is not so easy to have parents what was in concentration camps," Edek said to Zofia and Walentyna. "I think if her mum and me did not experience this, then maybe my daughter would be a bit more normal."

Ruth hadn't ever heard her father acknowledge the possibility that the brutality and horror that he and Rooshka had experienced may have had an effect on her. She thought she would like to talk to him about it. Not this evening. Another day.

"I am normal," said Ruth. "I'm very normal." She knew that you couldn't be very normal. You were either normal or not normal. But she'd felt the need to assert a degree of normalness, more normal than normal.

"I do think that if Rooshka and me was not taken to the ghetto and to Auschwitz, and Ruthie did grow up in Poland, things would be easier for her," Edek said.

"I'm glad I wasn't brought up in Poland," Ruth said. "The place is full of anti-Semites." The words had erupted from her with no notice. She was surprised at the force with which they came out.

"Ruthie, there are probably plenty of Polish people what are not anti-Semites," Edek said. "Very many Poles was anti-Semites and I am sure there are Polish people what are still anti-Semites. But Zofia and Walentyna are not those people."

Ruth felt embarrassed about her outburst. It was so out of place. She wished she'd talked about croquettes and how good they'd be at cocktail parties. She wished she'd talked about anything other than Poland.

Zofia brought out the food. There was a bowl of beets and a potato and ham salad, a mushroom and rice dish, some of Zofia's cucumbers in sugar vinegar, and a platter of chicken and fried onion balls.

"I have something special for you, Ruthie," Zofia said. "I have been experimenting with spinach. I know you like spinach."

Ruth felt twice as bad.

"Ruthie does like that spinach stuff very much," said Edek.

Zofia came in with a bowl of steaming green balls. "Wow," said Ruth. "Those balls look beautiful." They did. They were very green. Almost a dark emerald green. Zofia put two spinach balls and some beets on Ruth's plate. She placed several slices of the cucumber against the spinach. The pale and dark greens against the red of the beets looked dazzling. "This plate looks so beautiful," Ruth said.

"It is going to taste even more beautiful," Edek said. "Not for me, because I do not like such green things what you do."

Ruth put some of one of the spinach balls on her fork. Edek, Zofia, and Walentyna stopped eating. They were all looking at her. And looked as though they were holding their breath. She put the food into her mouth. The spinach ball was delicious. It was moist and tender and tasted mostly of spinach, with a surprising hint of assorted curry spices.

"These are fabulous," Ruth said.

Edek slammed his fist on the table. Ruth was staggered that nothing on the table, including the glasses, fell over or broke. "Ruthie does like the spinach bolls," he shouted.

"I love them," said Ruth.

"She does love them," said Edek, beaming. "It is not so easy to please Ruthie."

"I am very happy that you like them," Zofia said.

Ruth suddenly felt like a spoiled child, who had everyone around her overjoyed at the smallest sign that they had pleased her.

"I don't like them, I love them," she said to Zofia. "What's in the balls?"

"Plenty of spinach," said Edek.

"They are made from spinach and egg whites and a little bread, and onions and garlic and some coriander and cardamom and cinnamon," Zofia said. "The coriander and cardamom and cinnamon are from a very good Indian shop on First Avenue. In Sopot it was not so easy to get fresh cardamom."

"You were cooking with cardamom in Poland?" said Ruth.

"Yes," said Zofia. "But it was not so fresh."

"Zofia can cook with everything," Edek said.

"That is true," said Walentyna. "Zofia does cook with everything. She does make new bolls late at night."

"She does invent them," said Edek.

Edek, Zofia, and Walentyna were so sure of the success their balls would bring. They had no comprehension of how it would be almost impossible for their plan to succeed. Ruth hoped that they would manage the disappointments that were almost inevitable. Ruth looked at Zofia. The black-and-silver-flecked top Zofia was wearing had an even lower neckline than most of the others. Ruth had a brief fantasy of Zofia's breasts keeping them all afloat when the venture sank.

Ruth ate everything on her plate and asked for more. Zofia and

Walentyna and Edek looked very happy. Edek's happiness seemed to have enlarged his already capacious appetite. He kept piling more and more food on his plate.

"Zofia is not going to make such spinach bolls for the shop," Edek said.

"It does take too much spinach for one boll," said Zofia.

"We would have to have a whole room just for the spinach," said Walentyna, laughing.

"I will make spinach bolls for you, Ruthie," said Zofia. Ruth was about to protest. "I am going to make you a few dozen spinach bolls to keep in your freezer," Zofia said. "It will be a pleasure for me."

"Thank you," said Ruth.

The evening had gone well, Ruth thought, apart from her own insistence on bringing up Polish anti-Semitism. She wished she hadn't. She had enjoyed feeling at ease with Zofia, Walentyna, and Edek. She had enjoyed enjoying Zofia's food, and seeing Zofia, Walentyna, and Edek's pleasure. It had been a nice evening. She looked at her watch. It was 10:30 P.M.

"I think I should go home now," Ruth said. "It's been a very, very nice evening."

"Stay a little bit more," said Edek.

"Yes, stay a little bit more," said Walentyna. "Me and Edek will make a cup of tea."

Edek and Walentyna went into the kitchen. Ruth was left with Zofia. Ruth felt a bit uncomfortable. She hadn't spent any time alone with Zofia. She didn't know what she was worried about. Her worry, she told herself, was absurd. And anyway, she wasn't alone with Zofia. Edek and Walentyna were in the next room.

"Are you still swimming every day, despite the fact that you're up late cooking?" Ruth said to Zofia.

"Yes," said Zofia. "I do swim now every day at a swimming pool which is on Seventh Avenue near Carmine Street. It is not as good as swimming in the ocean but it does take me five minutes in a taxi or twenty minutes on the F train to get there. The pool is not bad. It is sixty-nine feet long and is very clean. And very cheap. It does cost twenty-five dollars a year."

Zofia probably knew the dimensions, the cost, and the state of cleanliness of every swimming pool in New York City, Ruth thought. Ruth felt daunted by the ease with which Zofia did things. She researched restaurants during the day, entertained guests in the evening, cooked balls at night, and swam early in the mornings. And didn't complain. Ruth had never heard Zofia complain. She didn't say she was tired. She didn't say she missed Poland. She just didn't complain.

Ruth was suspicious of people who had no complaints. She didn't understand how they couldn't see what was wrong. There was always something wrong. And something wrong with people who couldn't spot what that was.

"I do not need so much sleep," Zofia said. "When you do get older you do not need so much sleep. You do not sleep in the same way. You never sleep like a baby again. When you do get older you wake up, go back to sleep, wake up, go back to sleep."

Zofia's explanation was so matter-of-fact. She wasn't tormenting herself with anxiety about insomnia. Ruth hadn't thought about the fact that once you were over thirty or forty, you'd probably never sleep like a teenager or a baby again. Zofia had accepted the change in sleep patterns as the norm. She wasn't going to sleep clinics to see if she had sleep apnea or thrashed in her sleep or had some other sleeping disorder.

"I can still swim like a young girl," said Zofia. "I cannot sleep like a young girl. It is better to swim."

Ruth thought about herself lying in bed panicked about not sleeping. Lying in bed panicked about being sleep-deprived. Listing symptoms of sleep deprivation. She would definitely be better off swimming.

"Your father and I have very good sex," Zofia said. Ruth nearly fell off the chair. How had they moved from swimming to sex? And sex with her father?

"When I wrap my legs around him, I feel very happy. And he feels very happy," said Zofia.

Wrap her legs around him? Why did Zofia have to tell her that? And why did she have to add how happy it made him? Wrapping your legs around someone seemed a very personal detail to discuss with anyone other than the wrapped person. The wrapee. Ruth thought she'd probably never talked about wrapping her legs around anything, even the sheets.

She felt a bit shaken. Why did Zofia have the need to share this information with her, Ruth thought. It was going to be hard for her to get the image of her father wrapped in Zofia's legs out of her head.

"We eat well together," Zofia said. "And we have sex well together." Her father ate well before Zofia was in New York, Ruth thought. She did think that he probably hadn't had anyone's legs wrapped around him, for a while at least, before Zofia's arrival.

"Sex is very good for a woman," Zofia said. "The chemistry in the body of a woman changes when she has sex and it is very good for the heart and the liver and the kidneys."

How come Zofia was an authority on hearts, kidneys, and livers? She should set up a practice as a cardiologist, a gastroenterologist, or a nephrologist. Zofia's advice to patients would be more palatable than the advice dished out by most specialists. Zofia would probably advocate sex as a solution for heart disease, kidney failure, or liver malfunction. And suggest sex as a preemptive measure to ward off all ailments.

Zofia hadn't seemed to need any commentary or response from Ruth. She seemed to be happy doing the talking. Ruth was pleased. She wasn't sure that she had a lot to say about her father being wrapped in Zofia's legs or sex being good for hearts, livers, and kidneys. Ruth looked at Zofia. She was glowing. Ruth was sure that Zofia had never suffered from vaginal dryness. She was sure that Zofia had never tried to lubricate herself with raw egg whites.

"Sex is very good for the skin, too," Zofia said. Zofia had already advocated swimming as being very good for the skin. Now, sex was good for that and everything else. If Zofia's opinions and certainties ever reached a larger audience, it could decimate the beauty industry, Ruth thought. Instead of buying expensive creams and miracle lotions and undergoing dermabrasions and detoxifications, legions of women would be out there swimming. Swimming up and down pools, crowding the oceans, joining health clubs. And having sex. As often as possible.

Thirteen

Ruth had just finished telling Sonia about Zofia's legs being endlessly wrapped around Edek. She'd had to wait until the end of the day. She hadn't wanted Max to overhear her. She had been in and out of Ruth's office all day. Max had decided to use the electronic desktop labeler. Everything in Ruth's office was receiving long-lasting, laminated, adhesive-backed labels.

"Lucky Zofia," Sonia said.

"What?" said Ruth. "How can you think her lucky because she's got her legs wrapped around my father? He's my father. And he's eighty-seven. It doesn't sound very attractive to me. It's lucky that she told me after the meal. I wouldn't have been able to eat after that conversation. It was too off-putting."

"I think she's lucky to feel sexually satisfied. Sexually alive. Sexually living a full life," Sonia said.

"With an eighty-seven-year-old?" said Ruth.

"With the right eighty-seven-year-old," said Sonia. "And for Zofia that seems to be your father."

"You don't want to have sex with an eighty-seven-year-old man, do you?" Ruth said.

"No," said Sonia. "An eighty-seven-year-old isn't at the top of the list of men I'd like to have sex with."

"Who is?" said Ruth.

"Someone a bit younger," said Sonia.

"Michael isn't even sixty," Ruth said.

"But I don't feel that way about him," said Sonia. "I'm married to him, I love him, but I don't want to wrap my legs around him."

Ruth wished she hadn't mentioned Zofia and her wrapped legs to Sonia. She'd always been disturbed by Sonia's attitude to her husband and Sonia's desire to have sex with other men. It seemed so traitorous, duplicitous, and disloyal. Far worse than hating your in-laws. Or being dishonest about money. Or telling friends that your husband did pirouettes around the house, in ballet shoes and a tutu.

"I have sex with Michael," Sonia said. "But it's not the leg-wrapping sort. I want to wrap my legs around someone. Someone else."

"But you don't want to leave Michael?" Ruth said.

"No, not at all," said Sonia. "I just want to have better sex."

"Why can't you have better sex with Michael?" said Ruth.

"I just can't," Sonia said. "I can only have mediocre sex with him. I don't feel at all excited about the possibility of sex with Michael. Sex with Michael never feels outrageously sensual, or even primal. It feels pleasurable. But then anyone, short of a rapist, sticking his dick in me would probably feel pleasurable."

Ruth sighed. She hoped she was sighing at Sonia's inability to have good sex with her husband and not at Sonia's ability to experience pleasure with anyone other than a rapist.

"It's neurotic to feel that way about Michael," Ruth said. "Well it's neurotic to feel that way and not even try to find a solution that doesn't involve someone else's penis."

Ruth was pleased to be talking about Sonia's neurosis. Sonia was always pointing out Ruth's. "I think you should see a couples therapist," Ruth said to Sonia. "Really, you're squandering your marriage dreaming of wrapping your legs around someone who's not your husband. And envying a woman whose legs are wrapped around an eighty-seven-year-old man."

Ruth arrived home from work at the same time as one of her neighbors. Marvin lived on the sixth floor. Marvin was a very successful businessman. He was on the board of several prominent museums and charities.

"What would you say to someone who wants to start up a restaurant in New York, with thirty thousand dollars?" Ruth said to Marvin.

"I'd say one word. 'Don't,'" said Marvin.

"What if the restaurant was small and the rent was very cheap?" Ruth said.

"I'd say the same thing," Marvin said. "'Don't.'"

Ruth had surprised herself by asking Marvin the question. She thought that she'd half harbored a hope that Marvin would say it could be done. She hoped her father would be okay. She hoped he wouldn't feel depressed when the whole thing fell apart. She'd been worried about what her father was getting himself into. She rephrased that in her head. She knew what he was getting himself into. She'd been worried about how he would feel when the whole endeavor fell apart.

She called Garth. "I'm worried about my dad," she said.

"I spoke to him yesterday," Garth said, "and he was in great spirits."

"It's his spirits that I'm worried about," said Ruth. "How is he going to manage when this whole restaurant thing collapses? It's going to collapse before it's even opened. I want them to at least be able to open the place. And maybe stay open for at least a month. I really think they won't even be able to do that. They haven't asked for any more money," she said to Garth. "And they haven't asked for advice. Not that I could give them any advice. I gave them my advice when I first heard of their plan. It told them it was a lunatic idea. They've been in high-speed production mode ever since. They're making balls day and night. Experimenting with the menu and planning new additions, new varieties of balls to serve when the business is in full swing. They're going to feel terrible if they don't even open." She paused. "Maybe I shouldn't have given them the money in the first place," she said.

"You did the right thing," Garth said. "Think of the excitement and passion they've already experienced. Your father is out in the world doing real things."

Excitement and passion were certainly part of Edek's life, Ruth thought. She didn't want to talk about Edek being regularly wrapped in Zofia's legs. She didn't want the image she had in her head of her father's body and Zofia's legs to be any more vivid than it already was. Edek was certainly doing real things.

"How many people will have had the experience of opening a restaurant at eighty-seven?" Garth said.

"Not many," said Ruth. "Which is just as well. The entire restaurant industry could have gone down the drain. People would have been eating at home again and half the people employed in the service industry would be out of work."

"This is going to be fabulous for your father," Garth said. "Even if it doesn't work, your father will spend months working out what went wrong."

"Well they've started on their path to things not working out," Ruth said. "I walked past the store. The place was covered in construction supplies and equipment. And Polish carpenters and plumbers."

"I know," said Garth. "Your father has called me with regular updates on how cheaply everything is being done. I've been on the phone to him for hours. He's told me the cost of each item and what a bargain it is."

Garth had been on the phone to her father for hours? Garth never spoke to anyone on the phone for hours. He'd never spoken to her on the phone for hours. Ruth started to feel agitated. It probably just felt like hours to Garth, she decided.

Suddenly she realized that she didn't mind if in fact Garth had talked to her father for hours. She didn't mind if he'd talked to her father for hours, minutes, or days. She didn't know why she didn't mind. But not minding made her feel good. She realized she'd stopped counting how many times Garth called her. Or how frequently he called her. This realization almost shocked her. And pleased her. It made her feel more normal.

"Is my father calling you from his cell phone at a dollar fifty a minute to tell you about all these bargains?" Ruth said.

"Possibly," said Garth. "You know they got quotes from about twenty plumbers. Their guy's quote came in at half the price. The same for the carpenter. Your dad is nearly hysterical with happiness. He just loves a bargain."

"He does adore a bargain," said Ruth. "He's told me more than once about the price of bottled water and toilet paper in Chinatown."

"He's told me, too," said Garth.

"At least there's a correlation between those two items," Ruth said. "If you drink a lot of water, you'll definitely need more toilet paper."

"Your father also told me that the greeting cards are doing well. He said he's read a few of them and he thinks they're very good," said Garth.

"So now he's an expert on meatballs and greeting cards," Ruth said.

"How does he know they're doing well?"

"He said he asked Max," said Garth. "He also said you're working too hard and that you ate Zofia's spinach balls when you came to dinner. And had two helpings."

"Was working too hard connected to the number of spinach balls I ate?" Ruth said.

"He didn't say," said Garth.

Ruth paused. "Can I ask you something?" she said. "Have I ever wrapped my legs around you?"

Garth laughed.

"I was just thinking about it," Ruth said. "Do I wrap my legs around you when we have sex? I'm not sure exactly what it is that I do."

Garth was still laughing.

"I'm serious," Ruth said. "I want to know if I've ever wrapped my legs around you. I must have, mustn't I?"

"Sweetheart, we've had sex so many times," Garth said. Ruth did a quick calculation in her head. If they'd had sex, on average, twice a week, over twenty-five years, that would be two thousand six hundred times.

"We've had sex thousands of times," Garth said.

"Probably around twenty-six hundred times," said Ruth.

Garth started laughing again. "I'm impressed by that," he said.

"But have I wrapped my legs around you?" Ruth said.

"Of course you've wrapped your legs around me," Garth said.

"When?" said Ruth.

"I can't give you the exact date and time," said Garth. "Sometimes you wrap your legs around me, sometimes you lie flat, sometimes you have your legs in the air."

"Really?" said Ruth. "I feel much better knowing that."

Edek called Ruth. He sounded almost breathless with excitement. "Ruthie darling, can you come for a few minutes here to Williams-burg?" he said.

"You want me to come to Williamsburg? Now?" Ruth said.

"Yes, please Ruthie," Edek said. "It is not so far. Where we are is very near to the Williamsburg Bridge. It will take you maybe ten minutes in a taxi."

It suddenly struck Ruth that Edek, Zofia, and Walentyna were navigating their way around New York with more dexterity and famil-iarity and ease than she did. She rarely left Manhattan. And felt lost the minute she crossed a bridge or went into a tunnel that led to New Jersey or Brooklyn or the Bronx or Staten Island.

"I can't come now," Ruth said. "I've got about twenty letters to do." Tara McGann had left. She was still working at night, handwriting the letters that had been typed, but she no longer worked for Ruth during the day. It had interfered too much with her Ph.D.

"It will take you only a few minutes, Ruthie," Edek said. "I know you are even more busy than before because Terra did leave."

"How did you know that?" said Ruth.

"Because Max did tell me," said Edek.

Was there anything about her that her father didn't know? Ruth thought. Possibly that she'd had sex with Garth two thousand six hundred times, she decided.

"Me and Zofia and Walentyna do want to show you some furniture what we got for the restaurant," Edek said. "We are where the Polish carpenter and the painter does work. It is a warehouse what they do call a workshop but it is not a shop. Should I give you the address?"

"Okay," Ruth said, "but it will take me at least an hour. There are two letters I have to finish."

"We will wait here for you, Ruthie darling," Edek said.

Ruth caught a cab to Williamsburg. When she arrived at the building, it was clear that Edek had been waiting for her. He was hanging out of a window, on what looked like the fourth or fifth floor, waving to Ruth.

"Ruthie, Ruthie, I am up here," he was shouting. Ruth walked up the stairs. Edek was waiting for her. "We got here the tables what are for the restaurant, Ruthie," he said. "They are in the room at the back. Come with me," he said, and started to run.

Why did her father have to run everywhere? There was a sense of panic that had never left him. Panic about getting things done. Panic about being late. Panic at having to wait. Panic about missing a cab or a plane or an appointment, or a meal. It was as though the panic that

had set in, when he was imprisoned in the ghetto, had never left. Everything had to be done at high speed. In case there wasn't much time. He
was like that when Ruth was a child, and he was like that now. Edek
had, between the ages of twenty-two and twenty-eight, definitely and
with good reason, thought that he had no time left. That he would be
killed or drop dead, any minute. Since then, he had been on the run.
Ruth remembered him running up and down flights of stairs in factories, with large, heavy parcels in his arms. He was still doing that when
Ruth was in her twenties.

Ruth followed Edek. In the back of the back room she could see a
collection of small, square, straight-legged wooden tables. The size that
could seat four people. And be put side by side to accommodate larger
numbers. Zofia and Walentyna were standing next to the tables. They
beckoned Ruth over, and pointed to the tables. Ruth looked at the tables and gasped. The top of each table had, across the edge of each of its
four sides, like a frieze, stenciled in thick enamel paint, the words "you
gotta have balls." The enamel paint was so dense that the words, in almost innocently plain lowercase print, looked three-dimensional, and
as though they were set into the tabletop. Each of the signs was painted
in one of four very 1950s colors. There was a dusty tangerine pink, a
muted canary yellow, an eggshell blue, and a pale, almost lime green.
Some tables had combinations of yellow and pink. Some tables had
green and yellow. Some tables had three colors, others had all four.

"These tables are spectacular," Ruth said.

"Spectacular," Edek shouted. "I did tell you that Ruthie would like
them," he shouted to Zofia and Walentyna. "I am so happy that you do
like them," he said to Ruth.

"So are me and Zofia," said Walentyna.

"They are stunning," said Ruth.

"These was old tables what they did buy very cheap," Edek said.

"Who?" said Ruth.

"The young architects what do work on the Ludlow Street," Edek said. "They did also tell the painter what to do. And he did do a very good job."

"Walentyna, show Ruthie the tablecloths which will go on top of the tables," said Zofia. Walentyna unfolded a clear plastic tablecloth and put it on one of the tables. The table looked delicious. Almost edible.

"It looks perfect," Ruth said. "Just perfect."

Ruth left Edek, Zofia, and Walentyna beaming. She felt happy, herself. She couldn't believe how beautiful the tables looked. The young architects or architecture students—Edek hadn't been clear about whether they were students or graduates—were very clever. Ruth had walked about half a block away from the building when she thought she heard her father call out. She looked back. Edek was leaning out of the windows shouting. Ruth walked back toward the building. "You do need to get for yourself another Terra," Edek shouted. Back in the office, Ruth looked at the pile of letters and notes for letters on her desk. She'd been working late most nights since Tara had left. Her father was right. She'd have to get another Tara.

Ruth was late. She was due to meet Sonia and Therese, a colleague of Sonia's, for dinner. Ruth had met Therese before. She liked her. Therese, a lawyer, was in her early thirties, single, and gay.

Ruth was almost twenty minutes late by the time she got to the restaurant. She was proud of herself. It was the first time she had arrived late for any meeting or to meet anyone. She kissed Sonia and Therese hello, and took off her coat.

"I've ordered for you," Sonia said. "Therese and I were starving."

"What did you order?" said Ruth.

"Roasted monkfish with a baked fava bean and ricotta frittata," said Sonia.

"That sounds fabulous," said Ruth.

"I made sure the frittata was baked, not fried," Sonia said.

"Thank you," Ruth said quickly before Sonia could say anything more on the subject of fried versus baked. Or baked versus fried.

"Why are you late?" Sonia said. She turned toward Therese. "Ruth is never late. She's pathologically incapable of being late."

"I'm just late," Ruth said. "It's the new me. The new me is able to be late."

"What else can the new you do?" Sonia said.

"I'm not sure," Ruth said, sitting down. "What were the two of you talking about?" she said. "What have I missed?"

"We were talking about love," Sonia said. Sonia had extended the *o* so that the word came out sounding like luuurve. Luuurve rhymed with curve.

"Ruth is in luuurve," Sonia said. "She's in luuurve with her husband. I'm not in luuurve with my husband. I love my husband, but it's just love. Not luuurve."

"I've been in luuurve," Therese said. "I was madly in luuurve with my ex. But she wasn't madly in luuurve with me."

"Well I hope my husband still luuurves me," Ruth said. "I've been a bit of a pain since he's been in Australia."

The food arrived. Ruth was glad to have a diversion. She hadn't wanted to explain exactly how she'd been a pain.

"One of the senior partners was a real pain to me today," Therese said. "I've never got on well with him, but today he was so rude to me. I swear he was on the verge of calling me a fucking dyke."

"He's too smart to do that," Sonia said. "He knows that that would be actionable."

"Do you feel you experience a lot of prejudice against you because you are a gay woman?" Ruth asked Therese.

"Sure," said Therese. "Particularly from women. Women no longer thought of me as a woman once I came out. Somehow you lose your rights to being seen as fully female if you are not interested in a man. As if femaleness or femininity is in some way connected with your sexual choice or orientation. It's absurd. There's an assumption that to be a lesbian is to be aggressive. To not want a man is seen as rejecting and aggressive. Choosing one's sexuality or being willing to buck the system for one's sexuality is definitely seen as less than feminine. And mainly by other women."

Ruth looked at Therese. She was wearing a beautifully cut dark navy suit. The jacket was nipped in at the waist and flared out slightly over her hips. The pencil-line skirt ended at her knees. It was as feminine as a business suit could be. Therese had thick, shoulder-length, wavy light red hair and very pale skin. She had a delicate look about her and a definite femininity.

"Therese is trying to get pregnant," Sonia said.

"I'm about to try," Therese said. "I've just decided which sperm bank I'm going to use."

"Therese has been researching sperm banks for months," Sonia said.

"The whole sperm-bank thing almost started to gross me out," said Therese. "After looking at what felt like thousands of sperm-bank sites, the information started to feel like an onslaught. It started to feel almost beyond human. There are women who find that sperm banks really suit them because you can have so much apparent control over things. But I thought, I don't know if I want that much control."

"What sort of control?" Ruth said.

"For a start, sperm banks do a lot of screening. They reject all but five percent of the sperm that's given to them. They use the sperm that's the most likely to get you pregnant," Therese said. "They look for the best morphology, the best motility, a high sperm count, which if you're going to spend the money, and it's a lot of money, makes sense."

Ruth had an image of a mountain of rejected sperm. The rejected sperm looked slumped and dejected. They seemed flattened and forlorn. Ruth wondered how they disposed of the dejected, rejected sperm. Did they shovel it out into some earth? Or did they parcel it up for the garbage? She felt a bit sorry for the sperm that didn't make the grade.

"It's such an industry, and in the end, that's what's started to gross me out," Therese said. On one of the sites you can look at the donor's handwriting samples. You can buy the guy's baby picture for twenty five dollars. You can pay for Ph.D. sperm. There is something so consumer-driven about so much of it."

"What other details do they give you?" Ruth said.

"They give you race, ethnicity, hair color, hair texture, eye color, skin tone, blood type, height, weight, occupation, interests, religion," said Therese. "They give you statements. You can get an audiotape on some of these sites."

"So you do see the man," said Ruth.

"No, it's an audiotape, not a videotape," Sonia said. "You never get to see the guy."

"Do they have the Tiffany's of sperm banks and the Kmart of sperm banks?" said Ruth.

She knew that if there was a Tiffany's of sperm banks, that's where she'd be shopping. She'd like to choose sperm that seemed buoyant and well balanced. She didn't want sperm that lacked self-esteem or flagged easily or was easily bored. She'd like curious sperm and even-keeled sperm. She wouldn't want a depressive type. Or sperm that complained.

"Yes, you can get the Tiffany's and the Kmart version of sperm banks," Therese said.

"How does the Tiffany's equivalent differentiate itself from the Kmart?" said Ruth. "What does the Tiffany's have to offer?"

"I can see that you've already discarded the Kmart in favor of Tiffany's," Sonia said to Ruth.

Ruth looked at Sonia. "You haven't flown coach for years," Ruth said. "You almost sneer at business class. I'm allowed to inquire about Tiffany's."

Therese started to laugh. "You've made me feel better about all of this," Therese said. "The Tiffany's of sperm banks offer you more," Therese said. "You can get the audio recording, the baby picture, the handwriting sample, the donor's favorite foods and colors, his reasons for becoming a donor. Some of these sites have so much data. You can get the whole medical history, the donor's medical history, the donor's mother's medical history, the donor's father's medical history, you can see if there is a history of alcoholism in the family. You can study the Tiffany's donor file and look for diseases like cancer and heart problems and genetic problems like dwarfism and color blindness."

"Dwarfism and color blindness are hardly equal," said Ruth. "I'd prefer color blindness, wouldn't you?"

"We're not going shopping," said Sonia.

"There's a lot to shop for," said Therese. "There's so much data. A girlfriend would often come over and help me go to the sperm-bank sites. We'd have dinner and say, 'Yeah, let's go to the sperm bank.' And we'd go to the sperm-bank sites, and I'd look at my girlfriend and she was falling asleep. There's so much data."

Ruth understood too much data. She found it difficult to buy from catalogues, let alone go online. When she looked through office supplies catalogues, she went into a stupor. The sheer volume of products and variety of choices brought her to a standstill. She spent more time in a state of indecision over hole punchers and pencil sharpeners than if she'd walked to a store to purchase them. And she would end up buying useless items like pencil pillows, which happened to be on the same page as pencil sharpeners.

"You can ask for the guy's post-thaw motility count," Therese said. "That's important because multiple sperm work together to penetrate the egg but only one sperm is going to get in there and penetrate the egg. So the more sperm that are trying, the better your chances are. If you're going to the Tiffany's of sperm banks you can ask a lot more questions. You can ask if the donor has produced other live children, and how many?"

"Would you consider having sex with a live donor?" Ruth said. She paused for a moment. "I don't know why I said a live donor," she said. "You could hardly get pregnant having sex with a dead donor."

"Oh, I don't know," Therese said, laughing. "Maybe there's a way. Maybe there's one last erection left in the guy even though he is dead.

"I know a lot of lesbians who've had sex with a guy in order to get pregnant. It's not a big deal for some and for others it's a horrifying thought," Therese said. "I wouldn't be averse to having sex with a guy. Not as a lifestyle, but as a short-term project with a clear aim."

"A very clear aim," said Sonia.

Ruth thought that most penises probably had a good aim. A good sense of direction. Few penises wandered or took the wrong fork or made a wrong turn, or exited in the opposite direction. You saw very few penises lost in the wrong place or poring over a road map, or buying a compass. Or consulting aeronautical charts or checking out latitudes and longitudes or the pattern of stars. Most penises weren't studying atlases or encyclopedias, or carrying their own portable radar stations. Most penises knew where they were. How they got there. And where they were going.

"It's hard to find a donor who will just give his sperm," Therese said.

"How is the frozen sperm shipped to you?" Ruth said.

"It comes in a small vial packed in dry ice," said Therese.

"More and more women are using sperm banks," Therese said. "Women who don't want to miss out on their chance of having a child because they've been waiting to meet Mr. Right, or Mr. Semi-Right."

"If more women start using sperm banks men could start to feel displaced or superseded," Ruth said.

"They'd probably feel in demand as sperm donors," said Sonia. "It could spawn an entire industry. Sperm as the perfect birthday present. Sperm catalogues and sperm gift vouchers. There could be sperm sales and discounts. And sperm wholesalers. And sperm Internet auctions and bids."

The three of them started laughing.

"Sperm farming could become the next big thing," said Ruth, when she managed to stop laughing. "People could invest in sperm shares and sperm futures," she sputtered.

"The Dow Industrial Index could go up and down depending on the rise and fall of the penis population," Sonia half screamed while holding her sides.

Ruth suddenly realized that the noise around them had abated. Had muted itself to a murmur. She looked around. Most of the people at the other tables had stopped talking. Heads were turned in their direction. Necks seemed to be craned and twisted. Some people had their backs turned to their own table.

Therese looked at Ruth to see what Ruth was looking at. "Shit," said Therese. "Everyone in the restaurant has been listening to us." Therese started laughing again. "I've had a great time," she said. "I hope they have too."

"Let's have dinner again," said Sonia.

"Can we form a women's group?" Ruth said. "We could meet once a month?"

"Okay," said Therese.

"Okay," said Sonia. "We're on!"

"We're on," said Ruth. "We've already got three of us. Let's look at our schedules and set a date."

Zofia called Ruth. Ruth had just arrived at work. She was surprised to hear Zofia on the phone. Zofia rarely called her at work. Or at home. Edek made most of the calls.

"Ruthie, will you do me and Edek and Walentyna a big favor," Zofia said. "Will you come to tai chi with us?"

"What?" said Ruth. "The three of you are doing tai chi?"

"Yes," said Zofia.

"You're doing tai chi?" Ruth said as though if she repeated it she might get a different answer.

"Yes," said Zofia. "We do try and do it two mornings a week. It is very important to do something like this when you work very hard. Tai chi in the morning does make you very calm."

"Where do you do it?" said Ruth.

"In Chinatown. In the Sara Roosevelt Park near Grand Street," said Zofia.

"Does my father enjoy the tai chi?" Ruth said.

"He is learning to enjoy it," Zofia said.

"Okay, I'll come with you," Ruth said. Things were changing at a very rapid pace, Ruth thought. She was now the daughter of a would-be restaurateur. And she was about to do tai chi. With her father.

Edek came to the phone. "You do not need to speak Chinee to do this," Edek said. "You do just look at what everyone else is doing and you do do the same thing yourself."

"What do people wear, Dad?" Ruth asked.

"Just some old pajamas," Edek said.

Ruth decided he meant sweatpants or loose clothing.

When Ruth arrived at the Sara Roosevelt Park the tai chi group was just assembling. There were about forty people. Everyone was Chinese except for Zofia, Walentyna, and Edek. Nobody seemed bothered by Edek, Zofia, and Walentyna's presence. The tai chi began. Ruth had trouble following the movements. She looked at Edek and Zofia and Walentyna. They were raising one arm at a time, and turning to the right and turning to the left. Ruth was the only one out of step. She became more tense. She decided she'd have to buy a book and study the moves. The rest of the group had their arms in the air, pointing to the east. Ruth, who thought she was starting to get a grip on the movements, was turned to the west.

As silently as it had started, the class ended. People picked up their bags and left the park. "Okeydokey," Edek said to Zofia and Walentyna. "We do have to go. José and Juan will be already at the restaurant."

Edek rushed to the street to look for a cab. He stood, almost in the middle of the street, waving his arm. He didn't look calm. The calming benefits of tai chi seemed to have left Edek seconds after the session had ended. "We got work to do," he shouted to Zofia.

A few days after the tai chi experience Ruth had coffee with her father. It was just the two of them. Zofia and Walentyna weren't there. Edek and Ruth had met at the Second Avenue Deli. It was like a reunion. Ruth felt happy to be out with Edek. To be just the two of them. She ordered cheesecake for Edek. He loved the Second Avenue Deli's cheesecake. And she had a small piece of cheesecake herself.

In the middle of their conversation Edek looked at her and said, "I do love you, Ruthie, and I do miss you. I will be able to see you more when we are not so busy. Maybe I will even have a bit of time to help you out with the business now and then."

"That would be great," Ruth said. "The Stockings Department hasn't been the same since you left."

"You do probably mean that you have not got so much stuff what you did not need," said Edek, laughing.

"We're using it all," said Ruth. "Or most of it."

Edek told her that he and Zofia and Walentyna had talked to two young Mexican men, Juan and José, about coming to work for them when the restaurant became busy.

"They did come to our place for a dinner and they are very nice young men," Edek said. "They did like Zofia's bolls very much."

"You're already planning to hire people?" Ruth said.

"Off coss," said Edek. "We cannot have a restaurant what is busy with just me and Zofia and Walentyna."

"What if it's never busy?" said Ruth.

"Off coss it will be busy," Edek said.

"What if it's not?" said Ruth. "Will you be all right?"

"I am all right now," Edek said. "I was all right before. I will be all right if the restaurant is busy. And I will be all right if the restaurant is not so busy."

Ruth didn't have the heart to ask him if he would be all right if the restaurant closed after a few weeks.

Two weeks after she had coffee with Edek, she went over to Attorney Street. Edek had asked her to drop in. The change in the place was astonishing. Most of the construction equipment had gone. There was a counter and shelves and chairs and tables. The painted enamel "You Gotta Have Balls" signs on the top of each table looked joyful and whimsical. The place was looking like a restaurant. Rose-tinted Plexiglas sheets hung suspended from the ceiling, in front of each of the three main walls of the restaurant. Behind each of the rose-tinted Plexiglas sheets was a series of lights. It was the sort of indirect lighting that was very flattering. The Plexiglas covered the broken edges of bricks and crumbling mortar and remnants of framing timber and old electrical conduits that had been left on the walls. A piece of clear corrugated Plexiglas that looked as though it was floating, hung just below the ceiling. At one end of an old zinc counter was a small bar with three 1960s pink, plastic-backed barstools. Everything about the design was inviting. There was a flirtatiousness in the fittings and the colors. And a warmth and an excitement. Ruth looked around her. She wanted to move in. Edek, Zofia, and Walentyna appeared from the kitchen at the back of the restaurant.

"I just love it," Ruth said. "I just love it."

"It is very nice, Ruthie, isn't it?" said Walentyna.

"It's wonderful," said Ruth.

"To tell you the truth," Edek said, "it is not exactly the style what I do like, but Zofia did say that the young people what works in the architect's office do know what they are doing."

"It is wonderful," Ruth said. She was almost in a state of shock. How could a run-down, completely inauspicious space be transformed, with a few Plexiglas sheets, into this?

"Zofia, show Ruthie the kitchen," Walentyna said. Ruth followed Zofia into the kitchen.

The kitchen, which was small, had a twelve-burner stove with two large ovens. A smaller convection oven was attached to the wall. There was a large fridge and a freezer and an industrial dishwasher. A meat grinder and a dough mixer were on a bench not far from the multiple sink unit. Two stainless steel tables were in the middle of the kitchen. Pots and pans and strainers and ladles, and whisks and mixing spoons and other utensils, were hanging from ceiling hooks, above the tables. And an entire wall of metal shelving looked as though it was ready to house ingredients for cooking. The stainless steel tables had the matte sheen, the smoothed patina, of well-used equipment. Quite a few of the pots and pans had the dents and bumps and scratches of years of cooking and scrubbing and washing. Ruth thought that there was something very touching about seeing them all cleaned up and ready to start a new incarnation. There was no wasted space in the kitchen. The equipment had been chosen, installed, and arranged with the precision of an instrument panel on a space shuttle.

"Who planned this kitchen? Who worked out what went where?" Ruth said to Zofia.

"Me," said Zofia.

"How did you know what to do?" Ruth said.

"Ruthie darling," said Zofia. "I have been cooking for a long time. I know what things should be in what places. I am sixty-nine. I have been cooking since I was twenty."

"You don't look sixty-nine," Ruth said. "You look much, much younger than that." Zofia looked pleased.

"Ruthie darling. I have been swimming every day since I was ten years old. And swimming is very good for everything."

Ruth was sure swimming couldn't give you unlined skin and firm breasts. If swimming were that effective, women all over the world would be spending half their lives submerged in water.

"I am sixty-nine," Zofia said. "And Walentyna is sixty-seven. I think I was the oldest person in the food-protection classes that me and Walentyna did do," Zofia said. "We did have to pass an examination to get a certificate from the Department of Health in order to be able to run a restaurant. We did go to classes each day for three hours, for a week. You must get seventy percent on the final exam to get a certificate. I did get ninety percent and Walentyna did get eighty-five percent." Ruth was amazed. Zofia and Walentyna and Edek had done everything. They had permits to run a restaurant. They had a kitchen approved by the health department.

"You did all this on thirty thousand dollars?" Ruth said to Edek, when she came back out of the kitchen.

"No," Edek said. "We still got five thousand dollars left."

Ruth was feeling calm. Soothed by a new series of cards she was writing. She called them the Can We/Can I series. She had been in her office all day, composing the cards. She hadn't taken any calls. And she hadn't gone out for lunch. Writing cards, Ruth thought, was a very peaceful occupation. You had a few words and you kept moving them around. Until they pleased you. And hopefully pleased someone else. The cards were doing well. Almost sixty outlets across America now stocked Direct Text cards. The cards were being sold in New York, Chicago, Boston, Minneapolis, Washington, D.C., New Orleans, Atlanta, Seattle, Kansas City, St. Louis, and San Francisco. They weren't being sold in huge numbers, but the numbers were growing. The Can We series had a short question on the cover of the card and a short sentence on the inside.

Can I Shout Out Loud?

I love you.

Can We Continue?

To make love together.

Can We Laugh Together?

Forever.

Written out all together, the lines read like a bad poem. Separated into cards, they seemed much more moving. Ruth also had a reconciliation card in the series. She'd noticed that there were no cards for people who'd had an argument or a disagreement or a fracture in a relationship. Her reconciliation card was simple. Ruth hoped it wasn't too simple. It said:

Can We Talk?

Please.

Garth thought it had too pleading a tone. Ruth didn't agree. She'd felt irritated and tired when she'd been talking to Garth, and wished she hadn't read him the card. She'd felt tired of being on her own. Tired of being without Garth. Tired of thinking about Edek and the imminent meatball disaster. She had been sitting on her anxiety about Edek's venture into the world of food. As a vendor. Not as a consumer. As a consumer, Edek was fine. Better than most. But as a vendor his venture was going to be a botched fiasco. Ruth didn't think you could sit on anxiety or botch a fiasco. Anxiety wasn't a piece of furniture and fiascos were already botched occurrences. You Gotta Have Balls was not far away from opening. And Ruth was feeling very anxious. Garth kept saying everything would be all right. Garth always thought everything would be all right.

Ruth had wanted to talk to someone who felt as anxious as she did.

She didn't want to talk to someone who thought everything would be all right. She needed to find a Jew to talk to. Jews always knew that things were never all right. Nothing was ever all right for a Jew. It couldn't be or the person wouldn't be Jewish. Jews were genetically predisposed to spot what was wrong. And most Jews could. The sandwich wasn't quite right. The soup lacked salt. The portion was smaller than it used to be. The weather was too hot or too cold or too humid or too dry. The air-conditioning was on too low or too high. The crowd was too big or there were not enough people. The list of imperfections and blemishes and blots and complaints was endless. And contagious. If a Jew heard another Jew complaining, he joined in immediately. Even Jews who had, briefly, ceased to complain, started up again. Ruth didn't know how Garth could think that everything was all right. Or would ever be all right.

Patricia Biscuit had called Ruth late in the day yesterday. Patricia Biscuit had deliberately walked past Attorney Street. "The place looks good," she'd said to Ruth, "but no one's going to know they're there. They don't have a well-known chef. They've got very little chance of making it. They're going to languish in that street." Patricia Biscuit paused. Ruth hoped that Patricia Biscuit had said all she had to say on the subject.

"And they've got a very weird name," Patricia Biscuit said.

"They're going to be making a variety of balls. Meatballs and vegetarian balls," said Ruth.

"I don't know that balls of any sort are going to be the hot-ticket item of the moment," said Patricia Biscuit. "Spaghetti and meatballs had their heyday long ago, but not long enough to be making a comeback as a nostalgia dish. And Swedish meatballs came and went."

Ruth's spirits sank. She really wanted Edek and Zofia and Walentyna to sell more than a few balls. She wanted the enterprise to last for a while. She didn't want to think it was doomed from its first moment. She didn't want it to sink before it had started.

"How much would it cost to retain your company for a short period?" Ruth said to Patricia Biscuit.

"A basic PR package begins at five thousand dollars a month," said Patricia Biscuit. "Who owns it?" she added.

"My eighty-seven-year-old father and two of his friends," said Ruth.

"Oh God," said Patricia Biscuit.

Ruth had arranged to meet Sonia after work, at the restaurant. Sonia hadn't seen it yet. Edek had told Ruth that they hoped to open next week. Ruth had tried not to feel an enormous trepidation. Edek was outside the restaurant when Ruth arrived. He looked as though he had been waiting for her. He looked a little bothered, Ruth thought. Maybe he was tired. Ruth went to walk toward the entrance to the restaurant. Edek stopped her. "Ruthie, I do want to show you something," he said. "Come with me." Edek walked to the garage on the left of the restaurant. The garage that hadn't housed the car mechanic. Edek bent down to open the garage door. Ruth made a move to help him, but he waved her away. He pulled the garage door up as though he was a man of twenty. He brushed some dust off his clothes and stepped inside. "Come in, Ruthie," he said. Ruth followed him. Inside was a medium-sized, rectangular-shaped space. The walls were painted white. The place was empty. A sheet of white plasterboard was propped against one wall.

"How come we can just walk in here?" Ruth said to Edek.

"Because it is ours," said Edek. "We are the tenants. We did rent this at the same time what we did rent our place next door."

"What?" said Ruth. "You rented this place as well as the shop the restaurant is in?"

"Yes," said Edek. "We did rent it straight away when we did rent the restaurant."

"You've had them both for all this time?" said Ruth.

"Yes," said Edek.

Ruth couldn't believe it. She looked at Edek. Things were going from bad to worse. "To tell you the truth, Ruthie, it was my idea," Edek said. "I did say to Zofia that it is stupid to put such a lot of money into a restaurant which will be a big success. And then when we are a big success we will have nowhere to put more customers. The man who does own the garage is a very nice chap. He did say that the garage was already empty for three years. I did tell him that we was going to clean it up and paint it. It did already have a toilet. We did only have to make it bigger for wheelchairs. Every toilet what is in a new restaurant does have to be big enough for wheelchairs. The toilets what are already in restaurants do just have to fit people."

Ruth looked at her father. He was now quoting New York City Department of Health and Mental Hygiene regulations. Ruth had never understood what the mental hygiene issues in restaurants could be. She didn't understand what mental hygiene was. Was it brushing or flossing your psyche? Did you have to do frontal lobes or cerebral hemispheres yoga? Pilates for the unconscious?

"I am very happy, Ruthie, that we got this garage," Edek said. "We did have already many people what did come in to ask when we was going to open."

"How many people have come in to ask you?" said Ruth.

"A minimum of five or six people a day."

Ruth felt flat. Five or six people a day asking about when they were opening. And they were paying two lots of rent.

"The rent is very cheap," Edek said as though he knew what she was thinking. "We got already the extra tables and the extra chairs," said Edek.

"But you're not even open," Ruth said. "This is lunatic. Five or six people come in to inquire about when you're opening, and you're already expanding."

"Five or six people, minimum, every day," said Edek.

"But you're expanding before you're opening. It's crazy."

"Ruthie, Ruthie, column down. We do know what we are doing," Edek said. "The Polish plumber did say it was more cheap to do everything at once. The Polish painter did say the same thing." Edek paused. "Ruthie, I did mean to tell you that I did spend a bit more money. I did put it on the credit card. It was six thousand dollars. I hope you don't mind.

"I don't mind," said Ruth. The six thousand dollars seemed much easier to comprehend than the plans for the expansion of the restaurant.

"Thank you," said Edek.

Ruth felt light-headed. "Is Sonia here yet?" she said to Edek.

"She is in the restaurant," Edek said. "And so is one of the young architects. She is a very nice girl."

"Let's go and see them," said Ruth. She started to walk toward the garage door. She should have something to eat, she thought. She was feeling quite unwell.

"I will show you one more thing," Edek said, beckoning her back. He picked up the sheet of plasterboard that had been leaning against one of the walls, and moved it. Behind the plasterboard was a rectangular three-foot-wide floor-to-ceiling opening that led into the restaurant.

Ruth felt quite dizzy. As though she might keel over. She took a deep breath. She looked at her father. "So, you've already expanded," she said. "You've expanded before you've even sold half of a meatball."

"Yes," said Edek. "I think it was very clever. To tell you the truth, Zofia and Walentyna was a little bit nervous, but I did say not to worry. I do know what I am doing."

"How do you know what you're doing?" Ruth said. "You've never owned a restaurant before."

"It is not such a hard thing to know, Ruthie," Edek said. "A restaurant does have food. And we got very good food. And people does need to eat."

Edek should be lecturing at Harvard or Yale, Ruth thought. Few people could condense a course in how to run a business into three sentences.

Ruth could hear Sonia talking to Zofia. "Let's go in there," she said to Edek.

"Isn't this fabulous?" Sonia said as soon as she saw Ruth.

"It looks good, doesn't it," said Ruth. "Have you seen the other half?"

"Yes," said Sonia. "Edek showed it to me. It's brilliant. In summer they're going to roll up the garage door and put extra tables and chairs out on the sidewalk."

They were going to have extra tables in the new space, extra tables outside. All these extras. And they hadn't opened. They hadn't had one customer yet.

"We did get already a permit what does say we can have six tables outside," said Edek. "Small tables like we got already here."

Ruth shook her head.

"It is no harm to be prepared," Edek said. "Maybe people will not want to sit outside but if people does want to sit outside then they will be able to."

"Edek is very clever," said Zofia.

Edek was nuts, Ruth thought to herself. Edek was preparing to open a meatball emporium in an old former restaurant and an old garage, in an out-of-the-way location, on the Lower East Side. And with no experience.

A young woman came out of the kitchen. Walentyna was behind her. "Ruthie, I do want to introduce you to Rose," said Walentyna.

"Rose is the very nice girl what did do all the architect stuff with her friends what are in the Ludlow Street," Edek said.

Rose was dressed in a T-shirt and jeans. She looked about twenty-five.

"You've done a brilliant job," Ruth said to Rose. "I love the look of the place."

Edek beamed. "My daughter is not so easy to please," Edek said to Rose. "If she does say it is a brilliant job, it must be for sure very, very good."

"Do you want me to show you what we're doing in the new space?" Rose said to Ruth. "It's very simple. It's only going to take a couple of days."

Edek raced ahead of Ruth and Rose. "Rose is going to put such pink stuff on the walls, but not so much what is what we got in the restaurant," he said.

"That's right," said Rose. "We're going to run two two-and-a-half-foot strips of the rose-tinted Plexiglas down each wall, and have the lighting behind them. These walls were in much better condition so we didn't have to cover the entire wall. The strips will be perfect. And we're doing the same clear corrugated Plexiglas just below the ceiling."

"I think it will look beautiful," Ruth said.

"I did know Ruthie would be happy with this," Edek said. Ruth nodded and tried to look as though she was happy.

"I'm very glad you like it," Rose said. "The three of us who've worked on this project only graduated last year. This is our first project. It's been a dream job. Edek and Zofia and Walentyna are dream clients."

"Thank you darling," Zofia said, and rushed over to hug and kiss Rose. Walentyna hugged her, too. Edek gave her a big hug, and kissed her goodbye.

"Do we have something to eat?" Ruth said. "I need to eat something."

"Off coss we got something to eat," Edek said. "Zofia has prepared a dinner for us."

"It will be ready in five minutes," said Zofia.

Ruth felt dismal. This was going to be even more of a disaster than she thought. Instead of Edek, Zofia, and Walentyna standing in a small restaurant with a kitchen full of meatballs and no customers, Edek, Zofia, and Walentyna would now be standing in double the space, feeling worse, and looking more alone.

Ruth took Edek aside. "What do you think of us hiring a public relations company to help get the restaurant off the ground?" Ruth said to Edek.

"We do not need help," Edek said. "People will see what good bolls Zofia does make and they will want to come and eat them."

"This sort of help, helps," said Ruth. "That's why people use public relations companies. They invite important people to the restaurant, they call journalists, they talk about the restaurant."

"How much does this cost?" Edek said.

"About five thousand dollars a month," said Ruth.

"Are you crazy?" Edek screamed. "Five thousand dollars a month? For not even a quarter of that price we could have the garage what the car mechanic was in."

Ruth's head started to swim. "Let's eat," she said to Edek.

Ruth felt better after eating. Zofia had made turnip balls for her. The turnip balls were now part of Zofia's vegetarian range. The balls were flecked with green and orange. Parsley and carrots, Zofia explained. Ruth, who wasn't crazy about turnips, thought that even turnip haters would like these balls. The others had eaten chicken balls and pork and bacon balls. Pork and bacon seemed like pork overkill to Ruth. But Sonia ate three of them. Sonia and Zofia got on exceedingly well. They both loaded their plates. They both had good appetites. Probably for more than one thing, Ruth thought. Food and sex, for a start.

Zofia served two sauces with the balls. A roasted butternut squash and garlic sauce. And a chickpea sauce. Both sauces were dense.

"I do not like the chickpea sauce so much," Edek said, at the end of the meal. "But the other sauce is not too bad."

"They're both delicious," said Sonia.

"We will sell these sauces frozen or fresh," said Zofia.

"Zofia does make the sauces very thick," Walentyna said.

"When they are very thick you can use them to spread on a piece of bread or a cracker. If you add a little water to them and heat them you can use them as sauce, and if you add a bit more water you have got a soup. And if you want to you can cook some fish or chicken or meat in them," Zofia added.

"That is brilliant," Sonia said. "I'll definitely be one of your customers."

"With us the customer is always the king," Edek said.

"You can't say the customer is the king," said Ruth. "It's sexist. It's offensive to women. Women aren't kings. Men are kings. Women don't want to be kings."

"That is a stupid thing to say," Edek said. "Everybody does want to be a king."

"Maybe some women don't. Maybe some women are happy to have what they've got, and very happy at the thought of having a king," Sonia said suggestively.

Zofia nodded knowingly and Edek slapped the table. "You got a very good point," Edek said to Sonia.

"You've probably got one, too," said Sonia.

Zofia laughed uproariously. And so did Edek. Even Walentyna smiled. Ruth looked grim. And glared at Sonia.

Sonia took another spoonful of the roasted butternut squash and garlic sauce. "This is so good," she said.

"It has roasted butternut squash," Walentyna said. "And roasted onions, roasted garlic, a little olive oil, white wine, sage and thyme, and a very little bit of sugar."

"Walentyna is Zofia's assistant," Edek said.

Ruth went on to add that Walentyna was also a partner in the restaurant, but Walentyna seemed perfectly happy to be called Zofia's assistant.

"And what's in the chickpea sauce?" Sonia said.

"It has got chickpeas, onions, garlic, fresh ginger, a little peanut oil, cumin, turmeric, some red chili flakes, and paprika," said Zofia. "I do call it Burmese chickpea dip, sauce, or soup."

"The roasted butternut squash and garlic is also called dip, sauce, or soup," said Walentyna. "All of our sauces will be dip, sauce, or soup so that people will know what they can do with them."

"That's very clever," said Ruth.

"It's brilliant marketing," said Sonia.

"Zofia does also make Burmese chicken and chickpea bolls," Walentyna said. "The Burmese chickpea sauce is very good with the Burmese chicken and chickpea bolls."

"How do you know how to make Burmese balls?" Ruth said to Zofia.

"Zofia does know this because Zofia is very good with bolls," Edek said. Before Ruth could envisage any balls, and in particular Edek's balls, Edek said, "Zofia does read many Burmese recipes and recipes from many other countries and then she does make up her own recipes for bolls or loafs or a sauce." Edek paused. "She is like a top musician," he said. "She is like a Daniel Barenboim with bolls."

"You mean like a Daniel Barenboim of balls," Ruth said. "That's a better way to say it."

"Zofia is like a Daniel Barenboim with bolls," Edek repeated.

Jim Redding was on the line. Ruth knew she would have to speak to him. Jim Redding always refused to give Max the details of whatever letter he required. "Put me on the phone to the boss," he always said to Max. He wanted, he explained to Ruth, her to write a letter to his fiancée. It would accompany a prenuptial agreement prepared by his lawyers. "Prenuptial agreements are very common now. Everyone has one," he shouted. Jim Redding always bellowed. Ruth often put him on the speakerphone and turned the volume down.

"I'm having a clause inserted in this prenup," he barked. "It's just the standard legal jargon. It tells her what she already knows. I don't want any children. It's a no-children provision.

"I'm a straight-talking, straightforward man," Jim Redding said.

"I've laid out the negotiables and the non-negotiables to her. She either wants to get married or not."

"So she's expecting this clause to be in the prenuptial agreement?" Ruth said.

"She's agreed to it," Jim Redding said. "These no-child provisions are becoming more popular. They're legally dubious, of course, but it lets her know where I stand. If I hear, 'Oops, I'm pregnant,' I'm out of there."

Ruth thought that it would be a bit late for Jim Redding to be out of there. If he hadn't been in there in the first place, his fiancée wouldn't have been pregnant.

"She's agreed to no children," he shouted. "She knows how I feel. She's said she doesn't want them either. But the trouble is she's thirty-four. I've been in this position before. Three times with women in their thirties. I've told them I don't want children. And in each case it was a deal breaker.

"I love the girl," he said. "I want this letter to be romantic. I want to let her know that this marriage is about love." Ruth had written down *Romantic*. All about love. No children.

"The key word is *romantic*," Jim Redding said.

"I understand," said Ruth.

Jim Redding's call had depressed her. She called Sonia. "Do the women in your office talk about love when they discuss their relationships?" Ruth said.

"They do," Sonia said. "But it's in transactional terms. They talk about sex and relationships as a transaction. As if a man is an investment. The conversation is almost always about trying to make the right investment in the right man. Like how much time should they put into a man before getting what they want. You hear things like, 'Well, we went out for dinner, but I think he could have taken me to a nicer restaurant, so I made sure I went straight home and didn't linger at his door.' Or, 'I didn't let him kiss me because I felt he could have taken me to a nicer restaurant. I don't want to put in the time if it's not going to work out.' It's like they're saying. 'I'll pull my investment out of that one and put it somewhere else if this one isn't going to pay dividends.' "

"How old are these women?" Ruth said.

"From their twenties to their forties," Sonia said. "There's a punishment-reward system that they operate on with men. Maybe we all do."

Ruth hung up the phone. She thought about Jim Redding and his no-children provision. Sonia had recently asked Ruth if Zofia or Walentyna had any children.

"No," Ruth had said. She knew this from Edek. "They were both not able to have children," Edek had said to her. Ruth hadn't asked why. "It does happen to some women," Edek had said.

Sonia had asked Ruth the question at the second meeting of their newly formed women's group. The group still consisted of only Ruth, Sonia, and Therese. At the first meeting Sonia had announced that there would be no agendas and no formal structure to the meetings. Therese had agreed. Ruth, who was outnumbered, had had to agree.

"I didn't think Zofia had children," Sonia said. "She's too sexually alive to be a mother."

"I plan to be a very sexually alive mother," Therese said.

"You're pregnant?" Ruth and Sonia had chorused simultaneously.

Therese nodded. "I had an intrauterine procedure," she said. "The doctor separated the sperm and fed it through a tube through my cervix and into my uterus. It cut the sperm's traveling time to my uterus by about five hours. And I'm pregnant."

Therese patted her stomach. She looked happy. "I explained to my mother that this isn't artificial insemination," she said. "It's alternative insemination."

Sonia, Ruth, and Therese had spent most of the rest of that second meeting discussing pregnancy, childbirth, and motherhood. And office politics. How to counter the inevitable, almost punitive measures that come into play when female lawyers become pregnant.

The women's group was on the verge of expanding. A colleague of Therese's was coming to the next meeting. And Frida, who had returned early from Brazil, had called to say she would like to join the group.

Ruth was happy. She felt that the women's group was under way. She thought that maybe when there were more members they could institute a few guidelines about the group's goals and have a flexible formula about the format of the meetings.

Edek called Ruth in a state of high excitement. "We are not yet open and we did already have today some customers," he said.

"That's great," Ruth said.

"Me and Zofia and Walentyna are very happy," he said. "They was very nice people. We did explain that we are not officially opened, but we got food because we will open tomorrow. They was very nice."

"Do they live locally?" said Ruth.

"Ruthie, how should I know where they do live?" Edek said.

"I thought they might have said something," said Ruth.

"They did," said Edek. "But they did not say where they do live. They did say they are making a film. As a matter of fact the whole street was full of such big trucks. Every truck did belong to the people what is making the film."

Ruth hated film crews filming in her street. They could block entire neighborhoods with huge trucks. And flotillas of enormous caravans, and cameras and lights and endless equipment and assistants.

"Film crews, with all their trucks and equipment, can be so annoying," Ruth said. "I hope they don't stop customers from coming in."

"Ruthie," Edek said exasperatedly. "Off coss they did not stop the customers. They was the customers."

Two days later, Edek called again. The restaurant was now officially open. Edek was almost hysterical. Ruth had trouble understanding what he was saying. Half of it was in Polish and the other half was in more-mangled-than-usual English. Ruth knew that it was not something worrying. Edek's hysteria had a happy, if desperate, edge to it. Edek finally calmed down. "The film people did come back," he said. "They will be making this film in this street for two weeks." He stopped to catch his breath. "They did cancel the company what was making their lunches," he said. "And they did ask us to make bolls for them. They did say the bolls what they did buy was very popoolar."

Edek had always pronounced popular that way. It was a particularly idiosyncratic pronunciation, with the emphasis on the poo.

"They did say that the bolls what they did buy was very popoolar," Edek repeated, his excitement rising, again.

Ruth called him a few days later. "How are things?" she said.

"The film people are very happy with their lunches," he said. "And we did get a few more customers. One man did come already three times."

"You wouldn't believe what Zofia is making," Max said when she came back from lunch one afternoon. Ruth was frazzled. Max had been gone for over two hours. The phone hadn't stopped ringing. There had been four deliveries. And Ruth's head was aching.

"I'm sorry I'm late," Max said, when she saw Ruth's expression. "I've just been to the restaurant," she said. "I got there in time to see Zofia taking a Happy Birthday curried beef meatloaf out of the oven. It was huge. Somebody ordered it for a surprise birthday party for their husband. It had 'Happy Birthday Larry' baked into the top of the loaf, in caramelized onion lettering. It looked fabulous. I told Zofia that I wanted one. Zelda was there," Max said. "She said she'd called in because she was worried about how they were managing."

"And how were they managing?" Ruth said.

"They seemed fine," said Max.

"Were there any customers?" Ruth asked.

"There were a few," said Max.

Ruth had been trying not to be anxious about Edek. And Zofia and Walentyna. She'd been trying not to think about the trio. Or the restaurant. Zelda had told her that Zofia had baked a congratulations meatloaf for the film crew when the filming was finished. "It was humongous," Zelda said. "It had 'Congratulations' in caramelized onions and carrots in huge capital letters baked across the top. I caught a cab over from work when Grandpa told me about it."

"How does he look?" Ruth asked Zelda.

"He looked a bit tired," Zelda said.

Ruth was on the treadmill when Edek called her. She'd been treadmilling longer and longer in her effort to allay the growing anxiety she felt about her father and the restaurant venture. When Edek called, she'd already been running uphill for an hour and twenty-five minutes.

"How are you, Dad?" she said.

"To tell you the truth, Ruthie, it is not so easy."

Ruth wound down and got off the treadmill. "Of course it's not easy. Most of the restaurants that open in New York fail. It's a very tough business. You sound tired," Ruth said.

"I am a little bit tired," said Edek. "I did not sit down for a minute all day."

"I've been worried about you," Ruth said. "Opening a restaurant is very difficult. And very stressful. It's very hard for a new restaurant to get customers."

"We are getting quite a few customers," Edek said. "The problem is that with the customers we must order food every day. Zofia does tell Walentyna what we do need. Walentyna does write it down. I must order the things what we do need and then me and Zofia must pick up the things what cannot be delivered. I am going to call José and Juan. Zofia does need help in the kitchen and help with other stuff."

"Maybe you should wait a little while before hiring people and see if things settle down. It's not easy to work out a routine and know the best way to do things when any business opens," said Ruth.

"Ruthie, you do not know what you are talking about," said Edek. "You did never own a restaurant. You did never work in a restaurant. You did only eat in a restaurant."

Ruth felt mean for suggesting that they wait before hiring José and Juan. Edek was eighty-seven. She should have been paying José and Juan to come in and help.

"Ruthie, I got to go," Edek said. "I do have to find José and Juan."

"How many customers are you getting?" said Ruth.

"Plenty," Edek said.

"How many?" said Ruth.

"I do not know how many," Edek said. "I do not sit and count the customers what we got. I am too busy."

Later in the afternoon, Garth called. Ruth was still feeling bad about suggesting that Edek wait before hiring José and Juan. "Do you think we should hire a public relations company to help my father and Zofia and Walentyna out?" she asked Garth.

"It will agitate your father," Garth said. "It will make him feel as though he doesn't know what he's doing. As though he's not in control."

"He's not," Ruth said.

"He called me, and told me he'd hired José and Juan, the two Mexican men they had lined up, and that he was now talking to Juan's friend, Vincente," said Garth.

"He must have called you minutes after he hung up from me," Ruth said. "Enough minutes later to have called José and Juan first. They're planning their global expansion with a few customers, a few hundred meatballs, and no money."

Ruth walked home. She'd left the office early. The sky started to darken. As though it might rain. Ruth hated the sky darkening. She knew that there was a massive restless ocean of air above. It extended upward for possibly a thousand miles. This restless ocean was far more tempestuous than the watery ocean that covered three-quarters of the globe. Ruth didn't like the knowledge that a massive restless ocean of air was above her. Whenever the sky darkened Ruth saw it as a reprimand or a threat. A missive or a directive or a warning from above.

Kate called Ruth from the restaurant. It was a Friday night. You Gotta Have Balls had been open for less than four weeks. Ruth could hear a lot of noise in the background. She had had lunch at the restaurant, several times, since it opened. The restaurant had never been noisy.

"Roo, it's fucking bedlam here," Kate said. "Grandpa is causing chaos. He's spending ten minutes talking to each customer, so no one's getting seated. Then, when people are seated, Grandpa's telling them what to eat instead of asking them what they want. And he's giving José and Juan half the orders in Polish. And teaching them English. He's dementing everyone in the kitchen. He's getting a lot of the orders wrong anyway, whether they're in Polish or English. And Zofia is pacifying the customers. And Walentyna looks terrified."

"There are that many customers?" said Ruth.

"The place is teeming with people," said Kate. "The restaurant is full. There are people waiting to get in. And people waiting to be served. Grandpa keeps walking out into the street offering meatballs to the people who are waiting to get in. He's desperate for them not to leave. It's like a lunatic asylum," Kate said. "Zelda's on her way to help."

Zelda and Kate had both, when they were students, worked as waitresses on their summer vacations and sometimes during the rest of the year, at night.

"It's lucky he's got you," said Ruth.

"He needs more than us," said Kate. "He needs to be sedated." Ruth laughed. "Hey, Roo," Kate said. "We're all of us, me and Grandpa and Zofia and Walentyna, wearing white aprons with 'You Gotta Have Balls' across our chests. Grandpa ordered fifty of them."

"Grandpa, that table," Kate shouted. "Grandpa was about to deliver the wrong food to the wrong table," she said to Ruth. "He's done that about ten times. Zofia never blows up at him. She's the only one in the place who knows what she's doing. José and Juan would be fine if we could keep Grandpa away from them." Kate's voice had been steadily rising. She was shouting in order to be heard. "After we close tonight, or first thing in the morning, I'm going to teach Grandpa how to be a maître d'," Kate shouted. "And I'm writing out a list of what's missing. We need waitresses for a start. José says his wife has worked in restaurants. I don't know if she speaks English. But it doesn't matter. Grandpa has already hired her. He got on the phone as soon as Zofia said they needed more staff. I think José's niece is coming too. I'm going to help out for the next few days," said Kate. "And I told Zelda to take Monday off. We'll need her to get through the weekend. And then we've got to spend Monday training the staff. And restraining Grandpa." Ruth heard a large crash. "Shit," Kate said, and then started laughing. "Grandpa has dropped a platter of meatballs into the cash register. It was the mixed meatball special. I've got to go, Roo," Kate said, still laughing. Ruth leaned back in her chair. She was so glad she was not there. She was so glad she'd stayed at the office late.

Sonia called Ruth. "We've been eating Bolognese balls," Sonia said. "Michael went to the restaurant to pick some up on the weekend. They were installing a new cash register. Your father said they'd had an accident with the old one."

"They did," said Ruth.

"The Bolognese balls were a big success," Sonia said. "Michael loved them, the girls loved them, and I loved them. You have to try them. You can't spend your life eating turnips and spinach."

"Thanks, Sonia," Ruth said.

Max interrupted the call to say Garth was on the line. "I'm going to remove myself from any more talk about turnips," Ruth said to Sonia. "Garth's on the line."

Ruth picked up her other line. "Hello sweetheart, how's my girl?" Garth said.

"I'm okay," she said. She was okay, she thought to herself. She was enjoying being able to be alone. She wasn't enjoying being alone. But being able to be alone had given her a calmness. It couldn't have been an enormous calmness. No one else had noticed.

"How about your father and Zofia and Walentyna?" Garth said. "I knew they were getting quite a few customers, but Kate told me they were packed last Friday."

"It was hilarious," said Ruth. "Well, hilarious if you weren't there. I think Kate and Zelda were nearly at meltdown by the end of the weekend. They closed on Monday for staff training. Kate and Zelda conducted the sessions."

"Kate told me that a lot of the customers live in the neighborhood," Garth said. "One of them told her that if anyone paused outside the place for more than ten seconds to see what was going on, your father would come rushing out to introduce himself and tell them about the restaurant."

Ruth started laughing. "My father's a maniac," she said. "No wonder I've needed decades of analysis."

After another week, there was more order and there were fewer casualties in the day-to-day workings of You Gotta Have Balls. Edek's duties were clearly defined. He had to meet people, greet people, and seat people. He was the maître d'. Kate had written his duties on a card for him. They had employed two waitresses, José's wife Evangelina and José's niece Angelica. Both of them were good. Kate said that Evangelina could, when the restaurant ironed out more of its teething problems, become the manager and take over the morning shift. "It's going to kill Grandpa and Walentyna, if not Zofia, if they keep working these hours," Kate said to Ruth. José and Juan had their friend Vincente helping them in the kitchen. And Walentyna had regained her equilibrium. Business was reasonable at lunchtime, Kate said. But it was the evenings that were busy. "Most nights we have had very few empty tables," she said. They had also made the decision to close the restaurant on Mondays.

Edek was not quite an oasis of calm. When Ruth had last seen him, he was still greeting every customer with a tinge of hysteria. She had eaten at the restaurant with Zelda and Zachary and Kate. Edek had rushed by her table to say "Another customer" each time he seated someone. Ruth was quite stunned at what was taking place. People were ordering, eating, and paying for their food. You Gotta Have Balls had turned into a real restaurant with real customers. Zofia seemed to be taking everything in her stride. Nothing seemed to faze her. Or surprise her. She came out of the kitchen at regular intervals to see if Edek was all right.

"We have to work very hard to make sure that we keep the customers that we have got," Zofia said to Ruth at the end of the evening. "People have to come back," she said. "If they come back we will have a good business."

"That is very clever," Edek said to Zofia.

"She really has got balls," Zachary said when Zofia left.

"Zofia did decide to have a small party to say thank you to the people what did help us," Edek said to Ruth. "We will make the party on a Monday night."

"Zofia is brilliant," said Kate.

"She is a very good cook," said Zelda. Zelda was eating a chocolate, almond, and prune ball, one of two desserts on the menu. The other dessert was a freshly baked Granny Smith apple.

By the time Ruth arrived at the party, You Gotta Have Balls was crowded. A handwritten sign on the front door said, "We are closed for a small private party."

Ruth could see Zachary and Zelda talking to Max. Then she saw Edek. Edek was kissing people. Ruth saw him kiss José, Juan, and Vincente. Edek had nearly dislodged the tray of food Vincente was carrying. She watched Edek kiss Kate and then kiss Sonia, who was standing next to Kate. Sonia put her arms around Edek and gave him a very boisterous kiss back. Edek kissed a few more people. Ruth had no idea who he was kissing. Walentyna saw Ruth and made her way through the crowd to hug her. "I am so happy to see you, Ruthie," she said. "This is a very nice party." It did seem like a nice party, Ruth thought. People seemed relaxed and friendly, which couldn't be said for all New York parties. Often the atmosphere was as tense and agenda-driven as a board meeting. There were about fifty or sixty people at the party. This was not Ruth's version of a small party.

Ruth's heard Edek's voice. "Ruthie, Ruthie, Ruthie," Edek was calling out. He was coming toward her clutching the hand of a thickset man in his forties or early fifties. "Ruthie, this is Peter, the butcher what does have his shop not far from where we do live," Edek said. "The one who did come to our home with his wife for a dinner. Peter," Edek said, "I do want you to meet my daughter, Ruthie. Ruthie does write letters and she does make a lot of money."

Edek introduced Ruth to half a dozen people. He told everyone more or less the same thing. "This is my daughter, Ruthie, and she does earn a lot of money." There were small variations. To some people, he pointed out the price of the letters she wrote, and to others he said that she earned a lot of money, but she worked too hard. Ruth started to feel wealthy, overworked, and embarrassed. She excused herself and walked away before Edek could begin another introduction. She walked straight into Zofia. Zofia embraced Ruth. The embrace was so tight, Ruth's chest started to constrict. Zofia embraced her again, and beamed. Ruth stepped back and greeted Zofia. Zofia was wearing a bright green dress. It was the sort of dress young girls wore in skating rinks. It was closely fitted in the bodice and the sleeves, flared out at the waist, and ended just above the knees. The neckline and the hemline were both fur-trimmed. Zofia looked as though she was representing Kazakhstan at the Winter Olympics. Except for the neckline. And her cleavage. Zofia's cleavage overshadowed the very bright green of the dress, and the fur trim.

"Ruthie darling," Zofia said. "I was looking for you." I want you to meet John and Virginia. They do live in our building. John and Virginia, this is Ruthie, who is nearly my daughter."

Ruth tried not to look disconcerted or distracted by Zofia's statement. She didn't feel she was nearly Zofia's daughter. She wondered how near nearly was. She thought the proximity was probably variable. That thought made her feel better.

"We love having Zofia and Walentyna and Edek in the building," John said.

"Half of the people in the building have put on weight since Zofia arrived," said Virginia.

Ruth laughed. So did Zofia. "That is not true," Zofia said. "Look at John and Virginia. Are they fat?"

Are they fat? was not usually a question hosts or hostesses in New York asked when introducing their guests. Maybe in Poland it was polite to ask one of your guests if another guest was fat. But not in Manhattan.

"No, they're not," Ruth said, too quickly. And then wished she hadn't said anything. She sounded like someone who was overly eager to reassure perfect strangers that they were not overweight.

Zofia turned to greet somebody else. Ruth saw Prudence Price, the restaurant critic and food writer, in one corner of the room. She recognized her from photographs she'd seen in newspapers and magazines. Ruth was astonished. How did Prudence Price hear about this? She walked toward her and introduced herself.

"So you're Edek Rothwax's daughter?" Prudence Price said.

No one had said that to Ruth since she was about twelve or thirteen. "How do you know my father?" Ruth said.

"He accosted me in the street as I walked past, one day a few weeks before the restaurant opened," Prudence Price said.

"Oh no," Ruth said. "My father is very partial to blondes."

"He was accosting everyone," said Prudence Price. "He stopped everyone who walked within half a block of the restaurant, to tell them about it and tell them when it would be open. He offered me a five percent discount if I lived in the neighborhood. When I told him I didn't he said I could have the discount anyway. I ate here twice last week. When he saw me here yesterday, he invited me to the party. This restaurant is a unique concept," Prudence Price said. "And it's very focused. There's been nothing like it in New York, or in any city I've been to. They're using a very eclectic and creative blend of ingredients. I've just had a curried beef and raisin ball, and I'm going back for more."

Ruth contemplated telling Edek that Prudence Price was a well-known food writer, then decided against it. Edek was out of control as it was. He was still kissing people.

Ruth saw Zofia walk past Edek and pat his bum. It was more than a pat really. It was a prolonged pinch. A squeeze. Ruth was appalled. No one behaved like that in public anymore. People didn't pinch or squeeze each other's bums. Ruth reached for a glass of water and tried to get the image of that pinch out of her head. Max, who'd been kissed multiple times by Edek and Zofia and Walentyna, introduced Ruth to her new boyfriend. The new boyfriend looked much nicer than most of Max's previous boyfriends. Maybe Edek's talks to Max about choosing better men had had some effect. Ruth made her way over to Sonia.

"Watching Zofia makes me want to jump into an affair," Sonia said.

"With Zofia?" said Ruth.

"No," said Sonia. "With a man. There's something about the way Zofia uses her body that tells you she's using all of it," Sonia said. "And that's how I want to feel. I feel as though I'm only using a part of myself."

"Sonia, whatever Zofia is using," Ruth said, "she's using it on my father. And that's something I'd rather overlook at the moment."

"It's hard to overlook Zofia," said Sonia. "And your father's not too bad, himself," Sonia added.

Ruth rolled her eyes.

Someone starting tapping on a glass. Gradually, the room quieted. Edek was standing, with a glass of wine in his hand. "I would like to propose a toast," he said. A series of toasts followed. Edek made a toast to José, Juan, and Vincente. A toast to Evangelina and Angelica. A toast to Rose and her colleagues. A toast to Kate and to Zelda. A toast to Zachary, who, he told the guests, was a doctor. And a toast to Ruth, who he said was "very successful in her business." Ruth was relieved and grateful that he hadn't included a list of the prices she charged for letters. "I would like also to propose a toast to my wife Rooshka, who is no longer with us," Edek said. "Rooshka is the mother of my daughter Ruthie. And I would like to propose a toast to the late husbands of Zofia and Walentyna." Each of the toasts was greeted with cheers and applause. The deceased recipients of the toasts were applauded just as loudly as those still living. By the time Ruth left, hundreds of balls had been eaten. And half of the guests were calling them bolls.

That night Ruth dreamt about Zofia. Zofia was in one skating outfit after another. She was wearing dresses with halter-neck tops, dresses with V-necklines, and dresses with shoestring straps. Dresses edged in diamantés or beading or sequins. One of the dresses was trimmed with fake, plastic seashells. All of the dresses flared out at the waist and ended above the knees.

Fourteen

Ruth opened the *New York Times*. She had had a leisurely breakfast. She had bought herself fresh strawberries and some melon. And a richer yogurt than she usually had. She had made herself a pot of coffee and some thick whole-grain toast. She was feeling good. She had set the table with orange napkins that matched the dark red of the coffeepot. She had been setting the dining table for herself for breakfast, and for dinner when she ate at home. She no longer ate at the small side table under the window. She felt much more at home in her home.

Ruth finished reading the news pages of the *Times*. She read the Metro section, and flicked through the Dining Out pages until she stopped, in shock. There, on page 6, under the heading "Bowling Them Over with Balls," was a photograph of Edek. "The most charming eighty-seven-year-old maître d' in New York is at a new restaurant on the Lower East Side, called You Gotta Have Balls," the article said. The article went on to say that not only was You Gotta Have Balls a new restaurant, it was a new experience in New York dining. "If Edek Rothwax isn't enough to lure you back," the article said, "the food will.

There are balls, balls, and more balls. But what balls." The article described eight or ten varieties of balls. And then went back to Edek. Edek seemed to have told the reporter his life story, including his stint as manager of the Stockings Department of Rothwax Correspondence.

Ruth called Edek. She didn't usually call him this early. "I can see that you did already see what was in the newspaper?" Edek said.

"It's unbelievable," Ruth said. "Who told the reporter from the *Times* about you?"

"I did," said Edek.

"You did?" said Ruth.

"I did ring the *New York Times* and I did explain that Zofia did come from Sopot because she and Walentyna did win green cards. And that Zofia did see straight away that the people what is in New York does not have bolls," Edek said. "I did tell him that she does make many, many different bolls. Bolls like he did never have in his life. I did tell him that Zofia's bolls are out of this velt."

"And he listened to you?" Ruth said.

"Off coss," said Edek. "He did come the next week after I did speak to him. He was a nice chappie. He did explain that he was busy and couldn't come before then. I did say that is fine with me and with Zofia and with Walentyna."

When Ruth got to work, there were already six messages from clients who'd seen the article. All of them congratulated her. "I didn't know you had such an interesting father," two of her clients said in their messages. And another client wanted to know if he could use her name to make a booking. Zachary, Zelda, and Kate called one after another. They were all ecstatic.

"Can you believe Grandpa is in the *New York Times*?" Zelda said.

"Half of the people I work with have asked me if he's my grandfather," said Zachary. "Grandpa is amazing."

"He is pretty amazing," said Ruth.

When Kate called she was hysterical. "Roo, did you see the article?" she half shouted. "Isn't it brilliant? Grandpa has come a long way. He hasn't dropped anything on the new cash register, and now he's in the *New York Times*."

Two hours later Kate called back. "Grandpa called me," she said. "He asked me what someone who answers the phone and takes reservations is called. He said the phone hasn't stopped ringing. I told him they needed a receptionist. I told him that two weeks ago, but he said they were managing."

Ruth found it hard to work. She had calls all day. Mr. Bregman of Bregman Capital Ventures, Ruth's client whom Edek had accosted when delivering a letter for Ruth, rang. Ruth rarely heard from Mr. Bregman himself. It was usually his assistant who called. Mr. Bregman had clearly forgotten Edek berating him for not having visited Israel. Mr. Bregman wanted to know if Ruth could organize a table for eight for the coming weekend. Ruth said she would try. Mr. Bregman said to send his best regards to her father.

The first thing Ruth saw when she walked into You Gotta Have Balls was her business card. It was attached to one corner of the restaurant's cash register, with sticky tape. She flinched. She wasn't selling hot dogs or homeopathic lotions or customized T-shirts. She was writing very expensive letters. She was sure that Rothwax Correspondence's client base didn't come from people who glanced at cards stuck on cash registers. Part of her felt as though she was being a snob. Being elitist. But she didn't care. She didn't want her business card stuck on anyone's cash register. The card was taped at an odd angle so that half of it stuck out. The skewed way it was taped gave the card more prominence than if it had been carefully placed. It was a Monday, and the restaurant was closed.

Edek, who'd been sitting at one of the tables, saw Ruth looking at the card. He came running up. He looked very excited. He was wearing his You Gotta Have Balls apron, and something about the combination of the apron and his eagerness made her want to cry. Her father was beaming. He had the full-fledged, almost innocent eagerness of a child. Ruth thought about what her father had experienced. He had experienced the barbaric and base nature of human beings. The murderousness of ordinary people. People who were not psychopaths, people who were somebody's husband, somebody's son, son-in-law, father, somebody's father-in-law or cousin. People who were somebody's neighbor, people who were members of somebody's congregation. And Edek had experienced the murdered. He had lain among them. So many of them had belonged to him. Ruth wondered why all of that hadn't extinguished all eagerness from his system. And why she herself had so much trouble dredging up minuscule amounts of optimism or exuberance or eagerness.

"Ruthie, I can see that you did see already my good idea," Edek said, giving her a kiss. "To tell you the truth, I did think that maybe you would not be too happy about it. I did say to Zofia, 'If Ruth is not happy we will take off the business card what we did put on the cash register, straightaway.' "

"I'm happy about it, Dad," Ruth said. Edek looked at her quizzically. "I am happy about it," she said.

"Ruthie, darling, I think you are more column than what you was," Edek said.

More calm than when? Ruth wondered. She wasn't sure that she was more calm. She wasn't sure she'd ever be more calm. She wasn't sure she'd ever be calm. Although calm did seem to be acquired with age. Most old people seemed to be more relaxed, more tranquil. Ruth thought that she'd probably be one of those rare, jittery geriatrics.

"You was never such a column type," Edek said. "But you do take a few things more easily now. I think you are not so worried about some things."

Ruth tried to think of a list of things she was not worried about. She couldn't think of many things. Maybe she was more calm about Garth being away. She had stopped seeing the loft as empty without Garth. She wondered what things Edek thought she was less worried about. She thought he was probably referring to Zofia. She wondered if he was right.

"How are you, Dad?" she said.

"As good as can be expected," he said, giving his usual answer. "As a matter of fact, I am a little bit tired," he added. "And Walentyna is, too, a little bit tired."

It was no wonder that Edek was a bit tired. He was eighty-seven. He was the maître d' of a new restaurant. And possibly still in charge of its Stockings Department. The last time she had inquired Edek was still phoning through orders and making sure that deliveries arrived. Ruth couldn't believe that her father and Walentyna were only a little bit tired. She herself was tired. And she just sat behind a desk. And worried. And composed letters. Zofia, it was clear, was not tired. Ruth hadn't expected Zofia to be tired. Zofia didn't seem like a person who would ever get tired. Maybe swimming did that for you, too.

"We got a new person what will start next week," Edek said. "She will answer the phone and make all the bookings. This will make things easier. Zofia and me and Walentyna are very happy with the girl what is coming to answer the phone."

Ruth was pleased to hear that they'd found a receptionist. "How did you find her?" Ruth asked.

"I did ring up Dr. Blechner," Edek said.

"Dr. Blechner?" Ruth said. "Dr. Blechner is a dentist."

"Off coss he is dentist," Edek said. "But he does have a girl what does answer the phone. And the same girl does make the bookings for people what do need to see Dr. Blechner."

"They're two different jobs," Ruth said. "One of them is making dental appointments and the other is taking table reservations."

"They are both bookings," Edek said. "One is for teeth, and one is for food. Food is not so different from teeth. You do have teeth in order to be able to eat."

Edek looked pleased with his reasoning and logic. Edek's logic floored Ruth. She contemplated trying to explain that there were a few links missing from that series of statements and deductions and conclusions. But she decided against it.

"Dr. Blechner did say that one of the girls what used to work for him was looking for a job," Edek said. "So I did call her. As a matter of fact she was very happy. She did come to see us straightaway."

"What did you say to Dr. Blechner?" Ruth said.

"I did say that I got a small business and we do need a person what can answer the phone," Edek said. "And Dr. Blechner did say that this girl was very good."

"So you've got a dentist's receptionist coming to work in the restaurant?" Ruth said.

"Yes," said Edek. "And she is very happy and we are very happy." Ruth shook her head. "It is not such a different job, Ruthie," Edek said. "In one job you do make appointments to fix teeth and in the other job you do make appointments for people to eat."

Put like that, it sounded almost reasonable.

Ruth wondered what Patricia Biscuit would have to say about Edek's methods of staff recruitment. She thought that Patricia Biscuit probably had a firm set of requirements, a list of the qualities, qualifications, and credentials restaurants should look for in a receptionist. Patricia Biscuit had called Ruth during the week. "You didn't give me the full picture," she had said, sounding peeved. "You said nothing about the marketing strategy for the restaurant."

"I didn't know they had one," said Ruth. "Neither did they."

"That was a great story about the green-card lottery," said Patricia Biscuit.

"It's true," said Ruth.

"If they need my help," Patricia Biscuit said, "could you tell them it would be a pleasure?"

Zofia came out of the kitchen. "Zofia my darling, come and sit down for a few minutes," Edek said. "Ruthie is here."

Ruth was startled. *Zofia my darling.* That's what Edek had said. He hadn't said Zofia darling, he had said *Zofia my darling.* Zofia darling sounded casual. *Zofia my darling* was an altogether different matter. The *my* had a possessiveness, an ownership, a togetherness, embedded in the two letters. Ruth had never heard Edek call Zofia *Zofia my darling* before. Ruth felt uncomfortable. She took a deep breath. She knew the unease she was feeling was unreasonable.

Ruth was walking home from work. It was pouring rain. Rain was pelting down from the sky in sheets. Ruth was holding a clear plastic umbrella she'd bought over her head. Clear plastic umbrellas were not easy to find. Ruth liked to hold umbrellas low and close to her head. That way she stayed as dry as she could. The disadvantage was that she couldn't see where she was going. With a clear umbrella she knew where she was.

A fierce wind whipped her umbrella inside out. Ruth stepped into a doorway and tried to pull the umbrella back into shape. The shaft of the umbrella snapped in half. Ruth dumped the umbrella into a trash bin and walked on, clutching her rain hat to her head. Her coat was drenched. So were her shoes. She hated the turmoil that weather could create.

Ruth got home, changed, and called Edek. "How are you getting home tonight?" she said. "It's pouring."

"Don't worry, Ruthie," Edek said. "José is going to give us a lift home."

Zofia got on the phone. "Ruthie darling, rain is very good," Zofia said. "I like rain very much. I like rain on my face and rain in my hair. Rain is very good for you," Zofia said, in an emphatic, almost exultant voice. Clearly Zofia thought that being waterlogged, in any form, was beneficial.

"I'm glad you're getting a lift home," Ruth said. She hoped she didn't sound damp and unresponsive about the exhilarations of rain.

Ruth called Garth. "It's pouring here," she said.

"Is it, sweetheart," he said. Garth didn't sound too concerned about the rain.

"It's really heavy," Ruth said.

"It's just rain," Garth said.

Just rain. It wasn't just rain, Ruth thought. Nothing was just anything. Chocolate wasn't just chocolate. Chocolate made you fat. Cheese wasn't just cheese. Cheese could cause constipation, and clog your arteries. Sun wasn't just sun. Sun produced melanomas and heat rashes and heatstrokes and sunburns and blisters. Nothing was just anything. Everything had a consequence. And so did rain. Rain bothered her.

"My father thinks I'm more calm," Ruth said to Garth. "He didn't say more calm than when. He did add that I wasn't such a calm type. Would you have preferred a calm wife?" she said.

"You're not that uncalm, sweetheart," Garth said.

"If I was more calm, you might have to find some agitation of your own," Ruth said. "You might have to lose some of your equanimity if I wasn't providing enough agitation and tension for the two of us."

"So, you're doing me a service, really," Garth said.

"I think so," said Ruth.

Garth was coming home soon. Ruth hadn't asked him exactly when he was coming home. Maybe she was more calm.

Ruth's client James King called her. He seemed to have forgiven her for her dog cock-up. Her Scout/Willie fuckup. Not only did he seem to have forgiven her. He was groveling. Some people could grovel well. Some people were exceedingly good at groveling. James King wasn't. It suited him much better to be brusque. And angry. When James King groveled, he sounded greasy. Ruth had had to hold the receiver away from her ear while James King delivered a ten-minute monologue on how proud she must be of her father. James King wanted Ruth to arrange a table for ten for him, on his birthday. "I've heard the chef does meatloaves as birthday cakes," he said. I'd like to order one of them. I'd like it to say 'Happy Birthday Jimmy.' " Ruth didn't want to know that James King called himself Jimmy. Not in a conversation where he'd already become unrecognizable. "We're going to have a ball," James King said. Ruth grimaced. She didn't like James King trying to be funny. Or chummy. Her father's restaurant was changing her relationship with her clients. More of them had started chatting to her. She was spending more and more time on the phone. She'd told Max to try and vet anyone who wanted to chat. "I can't afford to chat to every client who rings up," she said. "And neither can you," she added, "or we'll go out of business."

Edek called Ruth. "Zofia did just send something over for you," he said. "She did send some bolls in a box what does keep them hot. They should be there any minute. Zofia did say to tell you that they got no fat. I got to go, Ruthie," Edek said. "We are very busy." A messenger from Portable People arrived with a large box. Inside was a vacuum-sealed hot food container. Edek called again. "Zofia did say to tell you that the bolls what she did send to you are made from a fish what is called a striped bass. They do have also sweet corn, red peppers, red onions, and a thing what is called cilantro," he said. Ruth opened the container. Inside were ten of the striped bass with sweet corn, red peppers, red onions, and cilantro balls.

Ruth tried one. It was superb. She called Sonia. "Do you want to come over and share my lunch?" she said.

"What a fabulous idea," Sonia said. "It's been decades since anyone asked me to come over and share their lunch. I can pretend I'm in high school and not in a New York law firm. I'm coming over."

Sonia hadn't even asked what Ruth was having for lunch. Few high school students, even in New York, could be eating striped bass, sweet corn, red pepper, red onion, and cilantro balls for their lunch, Ruth thought.

"This woman can cook," Sonia said, eating the last of the striped bass balls.

"Zofia can cook, can't she," said Ruth. "She can cook. She can swim. She can wrap her legs around men. And her breasts could probably float an entire Olympic swimming team."

"I can't swim or cook," said Sonia.

"I'm a reasonable cook," said Ruth, "an average swimmer, and can't recall wrapping my legs around a man. Garth says I have." Ruth sighed. "My breasts probably wouldn't be buoyant enough to float a cork."

Sonia laughed. "Zofia is pretty good," said Sonia. "And I think she loves your father."

"Do you think so?" said Ruth.

Ruth's phone rang. It was 7:00 A.M. She was still in bed. She'd had trouble sleeping, and when she'd slept she'd had a very bothering dream. In her dream, Zofia had been swimming in the sea. Making one powerful, smooth movement after the other with her arms and her legs. Her head had moved rhythmically, taking in air. Ruth was behind her. Losing ground. And floundering. When Ruth woke up she was so relieved to be in her bed, in SoHo, and not in the middle of the Atlantic Ocean. Ruth picked up the phone. It was Kate.

"Roo, you wouldn't believe who came into the restaurant last night," Kate said. "Steven Spielberg." She repeated it, in case Ruth hadn't heard. "Roo, Steven Spielberg was in the restaurant last night. He had that baseball cap on, the one he always wears. He was with two guys who work with him. He talked to Grandpa but Grandpa had no idea who he was. And neither did Zofia or Walentyna."

"That's very funny," said Ruth.

"Apparently, Spielberg is filming in the area," Kate said. "Grandpa said he was a very nice chap. When I told Grandpa who he was, Grandpa just said again that he was a very, very nice chap. I asked Grandpa what they were talking about and he said they were talking about the Holocaust and being Jewish. I've got to go and ring Zelda and Zachary."

Later in the day Ruth called Edek. "Kate told me that Steven Spielberg was in the restaurant last night."

"Yes," said Edek. "As a matter of fact he is a very nice chappie. I did like him very much. He speaks like a plain man. He doesn't speak like he is Steven Spielberg. To tell you the truth I did get a surprise when Kate did tell me he is Steven Spielberg. I think he is a religious man," Edek said.

"Really?" said Ruth.

"I think so," said Edek. "He did wear a hat the whole time he was here."

"He may be religious, Dad," Ruth said, "but that's not why he wears a baseball cap. He wears it so people won't recognize him. He's famous."

"Off coss he is famous," Edek said. "When Kate did tell me his name, I did know straight away that he was the person what did make *Schindler's List.*"

"How did Steven Spielberg hear about the restaurant?" Ruth said.

"You remember the people what was filming in the street what we did make bolls for? They did tell him," said Edek. "They did tell him that the bolls was very good. He is coming next week back to New York and he will come for a lunch with us."

"He is coming back next week?" said Ruth.

"Yes," said Edek. "He is a very, very nice chappie. His mother Leah does own a kosher restaurant in Los Angeles. It is a kosher restaurant but it does only have dairy. They do not have chopped liver. But they do probably have cheese blintzes."

Iris Lord came into Ruth's office. She was there to pick up a letter Ruth had written for her. "I tried to get a booking at your father's restaurant," Iris said, "and I couldn't. So, I went there and explained that I was a friend of yours and a client. I spoke to your father. He's a doll. He looked as though he was going to rupture something when I said I was a client of yours and couldn't get a table. He looked desperate. And then he had a brain wave. He asked me if I wanted to eat in the kitchen. I went to say no, but he'd already dragged me in there and was carrying a chair. He put me in a corner and served me himself. Can you believe that?"

"Actually, I can," said Ruth. "I've known my father for a long time."

"You must adore him," said Iris.

"I think I do," said Ruth. "How long were you in the kitchen for?"

"Over an hour," said Iris. "Your father insisted that I try half the menu and finish my meal with the chocolate balls. Is Zofia your father's girlfriend?"

"Sort of," Ruth said. "Or more than sort of."

"You can tell by the way she keeps her eye on him every time he comes into the kitchen," Iris said.

"She's got trays of meatballs coming out of the oven. Meatballs boiling on the stove. Sauces being poured. And when he walks in, she doesn't lose sight of the fact that he's in the kitchen. She smiles at him and blows him kisses." Iris Lord paused. "Have you noticed her breasts?" she said to Ruth.

"I have," said Ruth. "Many times. They're hard to overlook."

"They were even harder to overlook when I was there," Iris said. "The kitchen was very hot. Zofia was wearing nothing but a black bra and skirt under her apron. She went into the restaurant like that," Iris said. "The restaurant was in chaos. Two sets of people were arguing over one table."

The relative peace of the previous chaos was shattered when, in the one week, the *New York Post*, the *Daily News*, and the *New York Observer* all came out with articles on You Gotta Have Balls. The *Jewish Monthly Press* began the flood. Their piece, titled "Mending a Fence with Balls," was a treatise on how Edek Rothwax, an Auschwitz survivor, and his two Polish partners were healing the relationships between Poles and Jews. Their venture into the restaurant business, the *Jewish Monthly Press* said, was a project of partnership and peace. A photograph of Edek and Zofia accompanied the article. Edek was seated. He looked almost dwarfed by, and very much at peace with, Zofia's breasts. The other headlines were less politically ambitious. "What a Ball," "Have They Got Balls," "Balls to Die For," they shouted. Ruth was dazed. How had all of this happened? She had no idea. One minute her father was driving her mad ordering cardboard tubes for the office that they'd never use. And she was desperate for him to have a hobby or find a friend or join a reading group. And, two minutes later, he was running a crowded and sought-out restaurant. And living with Zofia. And Walentyna.

Zelda called Ruth. "Isn't this the most amazing thing? All those articles about You Gotta Have Balls?" Zelda said. "Kate is crying, she's so happy for Grandpa. And Zachary said everyone he works with at the hospital has seen the articles."

The only people who were unperturbed were Edek, Zofia, and Walentyna.

"Isn't this amazing?" Ruth said to her father.

"I did tell you Zofia's meatbolls was very good," he said.

It now became almost impossible to get a dinner reservation at You Gotta Have Balls.

"No table is available for at least four weeks," Cheryl the receptionist said to one caller after another. They were already taking reservations for the month after next. Every night they had to turn people away.

Edek was negotiating for the former mechanic's space. "He does want a lot of rent," Edek said to Ruth. "He does see all the people what does come to the restaurant and he does think we are millionaires. I did say to Zofia that if we do have to pay a little more, then we do have to. The mechanic's place is perfect for us because we will be able to make the kitchen bigger. The plumbing what he has got is in the same place as the plumbing what we got. The Polish plumber did explain that to me."

Ruth hadn't wanted to ask Edek if they were making money. Ruth knew that a lot of apparently successful businesses failed to make a profit.

"Can you afford the higher rent?" she said to Edek.

"Off coss," said Edek. "We did already speak to the accountant. He did say we are nearly in a position to give you back your money. All of it, Ruthie."

"I don't want it," she said, tears welling up in her eyes.

"What is the matter, Ruthie?" Edek said.

"I think I'm happy for you," Ruth said.

"You are a funny girl, Ruthie," Edek said. "You did never complain once about giving me money. Now, I do want to give you money and you do start to cry." He looked at Ruth. "Ruthie I do know that you are happy for me," he said. They were standing in the street, outside the restaurant.

"Let's go inside, Dad," she said.

"Cheryl is very, very good," Edek said. "Me and Zofia and Walentyna are very happy with her." Edek pronounced the *Ch* in Cheryl in the way it was pronounced in *chain* or *chance* or *chapter* or *chant*. Cheryl didn't seem to mind.

Inside, Cheryl, the former dentist's receptionist, was dealing with the customers. She had the warmth and concern and patience of someone used to dealing with people in pain. Or people in a state of fear. Or tension. Cheryl stayed calm in the most unruly or unpleasant circumstances. When people insisted that they had made a reservation, kindness poured out of Cheryl. When someone was unhappy with their table, she exuded enormous sympathy. She placated anyone who was irate. Nothing flustered Cheryl.

Ruth's neighbor Marvin, who lived on the sixth floor, had called Ruth. "Tell your father not to let go of that receptionist under any circumstances," Marvin said. "Someone's bound to want to poach her. She's priceless. I can't believe I said 'Don't, Don't, Don't,' when you asked my advice. There's always something surprising in the restaurant business. There's always something that works when everyone says it won't. And thousands of things that don't work when everyone agrees that they can't fail. Don't forget," he added, "to tell your father not to let anyone poach that receptionist."

Ruth made the mistake of using the term poached when she gave Edek Marvin's advice. Edek only associated the word poached with an egg. Or several eggs. She and Edek had a long, protracted, and incomprehensible conversation about Cheryl's choice of breakfast dishes. Neither of them had ever had breakfast with Cheryl. Edek then progressed to his own preference of egg-cooking methods. "I do like fried eggs and scrambled eggs," he said. "But a poached egg is not for me. Rooshka did like a poached egg," he added.

"Mum liked boiled eggs, too," Ruth said.

"That is right," said Edek.

They were both quiet for a while. Edek looked as though he might cry. Ruth felt tearful herself. "Mum was a good girl," Edek said.

"She was," said Ruth. "She'll always be part of us," Ruth said. "Part of you, part of me, part of the kids, part of Garth."

"I hope so," said Edek. "It is a very big shame that she did not see what a big success the grandchildren is. And what a good daughter you did grow up to be."

"I'm glad you think I'm a good daughter," Ruth said.

"Off coss you are a good daughter," Edek said.

Ruth put her arms around her father. He looked as though he might cry, again. Ruth brought the subject back to eggs. Edek jumped right in. Another very scrambled conversation ensued. Finally, Edek understood. "Why did you talk about poaching," he said. "If you did tell me that somebody would try to steal her, I would understand straightaway. You did use the wrong word," he said to Ruth, with more than a degree of glee in his voice.

Zofia had begun to send some of their customers to Ruth. "Zofia does only recommend you to customers what are rich," Edek told Ruth. Ruth wondered how Zofia could divine who was rich and fit in a sales pitch for Rothwax Correspondence while juggling balls and loaves and sauces. Zofia divided the customers into types. Zofia's categories were quite specific. "He is the type who is nice to you if you are important," she said. Or "the type who is not nice to his wife." Or "the thin type." There was the type who was a very nice person. The type who did not like to spend money. The type with a good appetite. The type who was generous. The type who pretended he was nice. In Zofia's lexicon, everyone was a type. Zofia was right, Ruth thought. Everyone was a type. Ruth thought about herself. She hoped she wasn't the miserable type.

One of the clients Zofia had sent to her was a clairvoyant.

"I don't believe in psychics or fortune-tellers or clairvoyants," Ruth had said.

"I do not believe in these things myself," Zofia said. "But people pay her a lot of money. She must give them something that they are looking for."

The psychic Zofia had sent to Ruth couldn't make up her mind about what she wanted in the letter Ruth was writing for her. Ruth thought that that was a bad sign. The psychic called Ruth several times with changes or additions to the proposed letter. Maybe psychics had too much information coming from too many sources. Maybe they had too many options and possibilities, Ruth thought. Ruth knew how that felt. It could make your head feel very crowded.

Ruth was at You Gotta Have Balls having dinner in the kitchen.

There had been no empty tables and Zofia had wanted her to stay. Ruth had protested that the kitchen was already overcrowded. But Zofia had insisted. Zofia was wearing a skirt and bra. And her apron. That seemed to be her new uniform. The bra she was wearing was bright green. She didn't look undressed. In her bright green bra, she looked more East Village than partially naked. José and Juan and Vincente didn't seem fazed. They were too busy. They were cooking and plating food, and stacking plates and washing dishes. They worked with an almost wordless coordination. Ruth was eating turnip balls.

"Luciano Pavarotti came into the restaurant today," Walentyna, who had come in and out of the kitchen, several times, said to Ruth.

"Luciano Pavarotti was here?" Ruth said.

"Yes," shouted Zofia. "He did come with his wife."

Edek came into the kitchen. "His wife is quite a bit younger than what he is," Edek said.

"It is good to have a wife who is younger," Zofia said, turning to look at Edek, with a very coy smile on her face.

Wearing an apron and covered in sweat, Zofia could still look coy. Zofia could look coy. And sultry at the same time. Edek looked at Zofia for a long time. Ruth looked at one of her turnip balls.

"I did ask Mr. Pavarotti if he did know Mario Lanza," Edek said when he stopped looking at Zofia. I did say that Mario Lanza was Mum's favorite singer. Mr. Pavarotti did say off coss he did know who Mario Lanza was."

"Luciano Pavarotti came into the restaurant and you asked him about Mario Lanza?" Ruth said.

"Yes," said Edek.

"Edek did want to know," Walentyna, who was carrying half a dozen used glasses, said.

"I think most people would want to know about Pavarotti," said Ruth.

"Then it is good for him that Edek did ask him about somebody else," Zofia said.

"Zofia is right," said Walentyna. Walentyna always thought Zofia was right. Ruth had never heard Walentyna really disagree with Zofia.

"I think Zofia is right, too," Edek said. Edek also seemed to think Zofia was always right. In this particular case, Ruth thought Zofia probably was right. Celebrities couldn't help but be accustomed to being the center of attention. Maybe it was good for Luciano Pavarotti to be asked if he knew Mario Lanza.

Ruth was reading an article about toilet seats. She was supposed to be writing a letter of complaint for one of her clients. The letter was a complaint from Ruth's client, to a friend, about the manner in which property they'd jointly owned had been sold. This was Ruth's client's attempt to avoid legal action. Ruth felt letters of complaint should be calm and clear. With an unmistakable goodwill and a certainty that the issue could be resolved without fracturing any relationship or friendship. Ruth didn't like writing letters of complaint. Sometimes she wanted to drop the conciliatory tone and just say, "You've been an asshole." Ruth wondered if *you've been an asshole* would fly as a greeting card. It would depend on what was inside, she decided.

She didn't want to write anything this morning. She had a headache and hadn't slept well again. She had dreamt about her mother. In her dream she was going through her mother's drawer of bras and underpants. When she woke up, Ruth realized that Rooshka had possibly possessed more bras than Zofia. Rooshka had had backless bras, strapless bras, bras made for halter-neck necklines. She'd had lace bras and satin bras. Bras with their straps centered and bras with their straps on the side. Ruth wasn't sure what to make of the bra connection between Zofia and Rooshka. She didn't like to think of them both in one sentence. One of them was very alive. The other was probably an assorted mixture of disintegrated bones and teeth. Ruth flinched. She had to keep images like that from coming into her head. They felt unbearable.

The article Ruth was reading was about a professor of pharmacology who had invented a portable toilet seat. The hinged seat folded in half and had four adjustable legs. You could alter the height of the legs to accommodate different toilet heights. The portable toilet seat was designed to hover about an inch above the real toilet seat. The portable toilet seat came in its own case and weighed just over six pounds. Ruth didn't think she'd buy one. She'd feel stupid carrying her own toilet seat around. And it wouldn't feel all that hygienic to eat out with a toilet seat on your lap. Or hanging off the back of your chair.

Ruth dropped into You Gotta Have Balls. She wanted to see Edek. She'd had a growing feeling of unease since she'd dreamt about her mother's bras. It was 4:00 P.M. The restaurant was almost empty. Zofia, Edek, and Walentyna were sitting at one of the tables near the counter. They were all eating. And immersed in their food. They looked so cozy. Like a family. Ruth tried to push that thought out of her head.

Zofia saw Ruth. "Hello, Ruthie darling," she said, and stood up and pulled a chair out for Ruth.

"Have something to eat, Ruthie," Edek said. "We do have something to eat at this time every day," said Zofia.

Ruth looked at their plates. Zofia and Edek's plates were laden. They had two or three slices of what looked like a beef and veal loaf, a couple of carrot and honey balls, some cabbage salad, and some boiled potatoes. Even Walentyna had a lot of food on her plate.

"Have something to eat, Ruthie," Edek said. "It is very good."

"I know it's good," Ruth said, "but I had a late lunch and I'm not really ready for dinner."

"We do have to eat now," Walentyna said, "because it does get very busy from six o'clock."

Ruth looked at them. They all looked so calm. So unruffled. It was as though this sort of thing, this rush of customers, this sort of attention, was just what happened when you opened a restaurant. Some newspaper articles were on a table beside them. Ruth looked at the clippings. A New York Polish newspaper declared, in bold print, "Polish Balls Better Than All Others." "Zofia is very, very good with balls," the *Downtown Press* proclaimed on page 3. "Edek Rothwax, the eighty-seven-year-old part owner of You Gotta Have Balls, says that his chef and partner, Zofia Zebrzydowska, is very, very good with balls," the article began. There was a photograph of Edek. Edek was beaming. His quote was repeated in the caption under the photograph. *Kitchen* magazine had an interview with Zofia. The article was accompanied by a full-page photograph of Zofia, working in the kitchen. Zofia, whose hair was spikier than usual, was wearing her green bra.

"Zofia does not look bad," Edek said, looking at the photograph.

"Zofia looks very good," said Ruth.

"Thank you, Ruthie darling," Zofia said.

All three articles mentioned Zofia's croquettes, the mini version of her balls. Most of the articles had mentioned the croquettes. The croquettes were the only appetizers on the menu. The appetizer was a sample dish of three or four croquettes. You could order a vegetarian or vegan or meat or mixed croquette appetizer. The croquettes were served with a small pot of Zofia's sweet pickled apples, tomatoes, onions, raisins, vinegar, sugar, ginger, and mustard mixture and a small pot of horseradish. The appetizers were free. They came with the meal. Samples of croquettes as an appetizer had been Edek's idea. His initial ambivalence about not charging for food items had given way to a firm conviction that handing out samples would be good for business. "I did think that it would show people that all the bolls what Zofia does make are very good," he'd said. "Not just the bolls what they would anyway choose." Edek had been right. Cheryl confirmed that a large number of customers said they'd tried food combinations they wouldn't ordinarily have ordered. Zofia's dip, sauce, and soups had also been a big success. The Food Store had just begun to stock them at their two Upper East Side locations. Ruth was disturbed by how undisturbed Zofia and Edek and Walentyna were by everything that was happening. None of them looked tired. All three of them looked as though they were thriving. Walentyna seemed less shy, less retiring, although her wardrobe had remained unchanged. Her dresses were still too large and too many of them had puffy sleeves and a voluminous skirt. Walentyna's ankles looked tiny coming out from under volumes of fabric.

Last week Walentyna had demonstrated how the dips turned into sauces and soups at the Food Store's Madison Avenue branch. Edek had accompanied her. Ruth had gone along to watch. Walentyna had handled the event with confidence and élan. At the end of the demonstration Edek had come up to the microphone.

"I do want to say that my daughter Ruthie, who does have a very successful business, is here with us today." He pointed toward Ruth. "Ruthie is a very clever girl," he said. "She does write letters for people what needs them."

Several people who'd been watching the demonstration clapped.

"Are you single, Mr. Rothwax?" a woman called out to Edek.

Edek turned toward the woman. "No madam, I am sorry. I am not," Edek said.

Ruth looked at Edek. He avoided her gaze.

Edek, Zofia, and Walentyna were becoming socially desirable. Customers were inviting them to their homes. Customers who had butlers and drivers. Ruth had been surprised that people with butlers and drivers would go to a restaurant on Attorney Street. Those sorts of people, Ruth thought, never left the Upper East Side for anything other than an international destination.

"How do you know they've got butlers and drivers?" Ruth had asked Edek.

"They do tell me," Edek said. "They do think it does make them more important."

"One chap was not very happy when I did say that me and Zofia cannot come to his home for a dinner," Edek said. "I did explain that we was very busy. He did say that in that case he would not come back to the restaurant." Edek laughed. "Zofia did tell him that it was very lucky that we did not need his business. And I did say that we do not need such posh, posh types. We got plenty of normal people what we do like.

"It is not so good to be rich," Edek said. "To be a person what does have a butler and driver. When you are such a rich type, everybody does only say nice things to you, and that is not good."

"That is right," said Zofia, who had joined Edek and Ruth. "It is not so good to be so rich that everybody only says nice things to you."

"It's possibly better than having everybody be nasty to you," Ruth said.

"Maybe not," Edek had replied.

"I've acquired a cachet I've never had before in the office," Sonia said to Ruth when she called her at home. Ruth was glad that Sonia had called. She had been sitting in her living room feeling sorry for herself. It had been a long day. She'd woken up that morning permeated by fearfulness. It was a nebulous fearfulness. It just arrived and didn't seem connected to anything in particular. Nothing she could isolate. She'd experienced it many times. It always brought with it an ominous sense of doom. Sometimes she had to get out of bed to shake the fear off. Sometimes it stayed with her all day.

Sonia sounded in a very good mood. It was quite late. Sonia obviously wasn't tired. "Half of the young attorneys and associates are so impressed that I know Edek," Sonia said. "I'm milking it for all it's worth."

"I've lost a couple of clients, I think, because I couldn't get them reservations," Ruth said. "And I have had a few who've groveled. It's really strange. I thought things were strange enough when my father bought the self-navigating vacuum cleaner, but now every second person I speak to seems to have heard of my father. It leaves the self-navigating vacuum cleaner in the dust."

"So to speak," said Sonia. "I rang to see if you wanted to have breakfast with me in the morning. We could go to Balthazar and have soft-boiled eggs and toast fingers."

"And pretend we're still children," said Ruth.

"Children can't afford Balthazar's prices," said Sonia.

"I can't come tomorrow morning," Ruth said. "I'm trying to buy two burial plots."

"Two what?" said Sonia.

"Two burial plots," Ruth said.

"For whom?" Sonia said.

"For me and Garth," said Ruth. "Except I've run into a snag. There are only two burial plots left in the Shelter Island cemetery. And there's a waiting list of three."

"Why are you buying burial plots?" Sonia said.

"I'm buying them for when we die," Ruth said.

"I didn't think you were going to live in them," Sonia said. "I meant why are you buying them now?"

"I don't know," said Ruth. "I started feeling anxious about being buried in a noisy, overcrowded, carbon-monoxide-filled cemetery. And I thought being buried on Shelter Island would be much nicer."

"Much nicer than what?" Sonia shouted. "You'll be dead. Nothing will be much nicer. Nothing will be much nicer than anything else."

Ruth ignored her. "I put our names on the waiting list," she said. "We're number four. But I want to talk to the woman who's in charge, in the morning. I want to make sure she got all our details right."

"You really are strange," Sonia said. "You're either buying a burial

plot or reading something really morbid, like the transcripts of the
Nuremberg trials or how many people died a day at Bergen-Belsen."

"Buying burial plots isn't morbid," Ruth said. "It doesn't fit into
the category of the things about me you call morbid. It's not morbid.
You could look at it as expanding your property portfolio. And your
options."

"Options?" said Sonia. "There are no options when you're dead."

"Can't you have breakfast with me and ring the woman at the Shelter Island cemetery later?" Sonia said.

"Okay," Ruth said.

Ruth wasn't sure why she was thinking about her own burial. Her
previous thoughts about her own death had been limited to a fear of not
having enough time to say goodbye. She had contemplated and composed her final words to Garth, and to each of the children. Many
times. She had endless tracts of what she wanted to say. What she
wanted to include. She had concluded that her death would have to take
a long time. Her final words were not that final. She had too many re-
minders and rejoinders and pointers and codas. She had told Zachary
and Garth that if she suffered any brain damage through illness or accident she didn't want to hang around. "Just pull the plug," she'd said.
"Even if I'm smiling," she'd added.

"If you're smiling I'll know there's something wrong," Zachary
had said.

A few weeks later she'd called Zachary. "Check me out, even if I
look cheerful," she'd said.

"If you look cheerful," he said, "we'll know there's something really wrong."

She'd wanted to call Garth earlier and ask him if he'd like to be
buried on Shelter Island. But she'd thought it was too morbid a thought
to make an international call about. Most people wouldn't want a call
from a wife or husband inquiring about where they'd like to be buried.
Maybe Sonia was right. Maybe she was morbid.

Ruth called Garth. "I miss you," she wailed into the phone. "I miss you. I can't handle everything that's happening. It's all too much for me. Half of my clients ask me about my father. I know that's not a bad thing. They ask about Zofia, too. I nearly slipped the other day, and said she was very busty. Usually I say she's a great cook. I'm not sleeping well. I look exhausted. My dad looks a decade younger. He looks like a badly dressed version of Clark Gable. He's still wearing those old parkas that all old Jews wear, and short-sleeved shirts. And Zofia looks wonderful. No, she doesn't look wonderful. She looks fabulous. She's cooking in her underwear. She's wearing bras under her apron. So far I've seen her green bra, her red bra, and her rather lurid purple one, as well as her black bra. She says it's hot in the kitchen. Soon she'll be cooking in matching underpants." Ruth could hear Garth laughing. "It's not funny," she said. "I think I'm in a state of shock. Not about the bras or the possibility of seeing her in her underpants. I think I'm shocked about everything that's happened. I'm really shocked, although no one else seems to be. My dad and Zofia and Walentyna are acting as though what's happened is perfectly normal. The kids all think it's very exciting."

"It is," said Garth.

"It could be too exciting," Ruth said. "Too much excitement unnerves me. Too much of anything makes me nervous." She paused. "Well, not too much sadness," she said. "I take that in my stride."

"This is the best thing that could possibly have happened to your father," Garth said. "It's more than the best thing that could possibly have happened because it's so implausible."

"I thought it was impossible," said Ruth. "That's not quite the same as implausible. Or improbable. Implausible is not probable. Improbable is not likely. But impossible is not able—" she said.

Garth interrupted her delineations and deliberations. "I've got good news," he said. "I'm coming home."

"You're coming home?" Ruth said. "I thought you were going to be away for about another two weeks."

"No," said Garth. "I'm coming home. I'm almost on my way. I'll be there in two and a half days."

Ruth felt elated. "I'm so happy," she said. "I hope I'm not hysterical when I see you."

Max buzzed Ruth, who had been on the line to a new German client, Günter Eckert. Günter wanted her to write a letter he wanted to send to one of his British clients. He wanted the letter to be businesslike, but have a tone of warmth and optimism and subtlety. Ruth had spent an hour talking to Günter. Germans were very fussy. As fussy as Jews.

Max had buzzed her as soon as she got off the line. "Your father called," Max said. "He said that if you can, he'd love you to come over for a cup of tea."

"For any particular reason?" said Ruth.

"No," said Max. "He sounded quite casual. He just said to come over and have a cup of tea with them if you had the time."

Ruth looked at her watch. It was three-thirty. She wouldn't mind leaving the office, she thought. It was a nice day outside. The sky was blue and inviting. She decided to walk over to Attorney Street. The sunshine was irresistible. New York had very few days when the sky was a clear, bright blue and the weather was mild. In New York, the weather was either too hot, too humid, too cold, too cloudy, or too overcast. She felt in good spirits. She had had two soft-boiled eggs, at Balthazar, with Sonia that morning. She had dipped toast fingers into each egg. Sonia had toasted her in orange juice. Ruth had been proud of herself. Being able to eat two soft-boiled eggs instead of her All-Bran and yogurt had made her feel less rigid. And the fact that she'd eaten them with toast fingers made her feel almost carefree.

Edek and Zofia and Walentyna were expecting her. Max had told them she was coming. They were sitting at a front table of the restaurant when she arrived. The three of them were looking at a magazine. "Come here, Ruthie darling," Edek said. Ruth walked over to them. She looked at what they were looking at. It was *New York* magazine. And Edek and Zofia and Walentyna were on the cover. They were standing together. Edek was in his beige-colored parka and his sneakers with Velcro fasteners. Walentyna was wearing an oversized dress with a pattern of pink rosebuds all over the fabric. And Zofia was in magenta and yellow. With her hair spiked and her bust making a statement. Across the upper half of the front cover, in large print, was the heading, "The Coolest Gang in New York." Ruth was stunned. Totally stunned.

"I don't like too much the photograph of me," Edek said. "Zofia does look very good and Walentyna, too."

"Edek you look very good," Walentyna said.

"Edek darling," Zofia said. "You look very, very good."

"Wait till Garth sees this," Ruth said when she could speak. She looked at the photograph again. To one side, in smaller type, it said, "Spielberg flying in for the wedding." "Steven Spielberg is flying in for the wedding," Ruth said. She paused. "You're getting married?" she almost shouted.

"Yes, Ruthie darling," Edek said.

"Yes," said Zofia.

"Yes," said Walentyna, looking flushed and happy. "Zofia and Edek are getting married."

Ruth felt sick. The boiled eggs started repeating on her. "When?" she said.

"Next Sunday," Edek said.

"Does anyone other than the millions of people who read *New York* magazine know about this?" Ruth said.

"The magazine is not yet in the shops," Edek said.

"It will be in the shops tomorrow," said Walentyna.

"Well, does anyone other than the millions of people who'll tomorrow know about this know?" Ruth said.

No one answered her question.

"Garth knows, doesn't he?" Ruth said. No one said anything. "He knows, doesn't he?" Ruth said. "That's why he's coming back early, isn't it?"

"I did have to tell Gut," Edek said. "I did want to make sure he would be there."

"What about me?" Ruth said.

"I did know you would off coss be there, Ruthie darling," Edek said.

Ruth took a packet of Rolaids out of her bag. She put four of the antacid tablets in her mouth. She chewed them slowly. Her heart was pounding. José, Juan, and Vincente came into the restaurant. José proposed a toast. Evangelina and Angelica and Cheryl joined in. Evangelina poured glasses of seltzer water for everyone.

"To Edek and Zofia," José said.

"We wish you a very happy life together."

Zofia hugged Edek. Then she hugged José and Juan and Vincente and Evangelina, Angelica, and Cheryl. And Walentyna and Ruth. Edek hugged and kissed everybody. And so did Walentyna. The phone kept ringing. Everyone was still hugging and kissing.

"I should answer the phone," Cheryl said eventually, after several more toasts. José, Juan, and Vincente made one last toast and went back into the kitchen. Zofia and Walentyna stood up. They both looked flushed.

"New York *Newsday* is on the line," Cheryl called out. "They want to know if they can schedule an interview."

"Tell them not until next week, please," said Walentyna.

Ruth looked at Edek. "How are you, Dad?" she said.

Edek looked at her. "I cannot say that I am as good as can be expected," he said. Ruth felt a flutter of anxiety. She looked at her father.

"I cannot say that I am as good as can be expected," Edek repeated. He took her hand. "Who could expect this, Ruthie darling," he said. He shook his head and started laughing.

"I'm very happy for you, Dad," Ruth said.

"I do know this," Edek said.

Ruth hugged him. And started crying.

You Gotta Have Balls Recipes

Beef and Kielbasa Balls

2 small onions, finely chopped
½ pound kielbasa, cut into chunks
1½ pounds lean ground beef
2 heaped tablespoons plain breadcrumbs
2 large eggs
1 teaspoon salt
½ teaspoon coarsely ground black pepper
Olive oil

Preheat the oven to 375°F. Lightly brush a nonstick baking sheet with olive oil.

Put the onions in a large mixing bowl. Using a food processor fitted with the blade attachment, pulse the kielbasa until thoroughly ground; it should have a paste-like consistency.

Add to the onions in the mixing bowl. Add the ground beef, breadcrumbs, eggs, salt, and pepper and mix thoroughly with hands until well combined. The mixture should have a firm consistency.

Form the mixture into balls approximately 1½ inches in diameter. Lightly brush the balls with olive oil and place on the oiled baking sheet. Bake until golden brown, 35 to 40 minutes. Remove from the oven. Using tongs or a spatula, transfer the balls to a platter and serve.

Serves 6 to 8, approximately 20 balls

Chicken and Raisin Balls

2 small onions, finely chopped
1½ pounds bratwurst, cut into chunks (raw or cooked)
1½ pounds lean ground chicken
2 heaped tablespoons plain breadcrumbs
5 ounces golden raisins
2 large eggs
1 teaspoon salt
½ teaspoon coarsely ground black pepper
Vegetable or canola oil

Preheat the oven to 375°F. Lightly brush a nonstick baking sheet with vegetable oil.

Put the onions in a large mixing bowl. Using a food processor fitted with the blade attachment, pulse the bratwurst until thoroughly ground; it should have a paste-like consistency.

Add to the onions in the mixing bowl. Add the ground chicken, breadcrumbs, raisins, eggs, salt, and pepper and mix thoroughly with hands until well combined. If using the raw bratwurst, the mixture will feel a little sticky.

Form the mixture into balls approximately 1½ inches in diameter. Lightly brush the balls with vegetable oil and place on the oiled baking sheet. Bake until lightly browned, approximately 35 minutes. Remove from the oven. Using tongs or a spatula, transfer the balls to a platter and serve.

Serves 6 to 8, approximately 20 balls

Turkey and Spiced Coconut Balls

  2 small onions, finely chopped
  3½ ounces sweetened coconut flakes
  2 pounds lean ground turkey
  2 heaped tablespoons plain breadcrumbs
  2 large eggs
  2 tablespoons hot curry powder
  1 teaspoon ground cardamom
  1½ teaspoons salt
  ½ teaspoon coarsely ground black pepper
  Vegetable or canola oil

Preheat the oven to 375°F. Lightly brush a nonstick baking sheet with vegetable oil.

Put the onions in a large mixing bowl. Using the food processor fitted with the blade attachment, process the coconut until thoroughly ground. Add to the onions in the mixing bowl. Add the turkey, breadcrumbs, eggs, curry powder, cardamom, salt, and pepper and mix thoroughly with hands until well combined. The mixture should have a firm consistency.

Form the mixture into balls approximately 1½ inches in diameter. Lightly brush the balls with vegetable oil and place on the oiled baking sheet. Bake until golden brown, 30 to 35 minutes. Remove from the oven. Using tongs or a spatula, transfer the balls to a platter and serve.

Serves 6 to 8, approximately 20 balls

Potato, Parmesan, and Gouda Croquettes

1½ pounds new red potatoes

3 tablespoons butter

1 teaspoon olive oil, plus extra for oiling the muffin pan

2 small onions, finely chopped

9 heaped tablespoons all-purpose flour

8 ounces grated Parmesan cheese

5 ounces grated aged gouda cheese

4 large egg whites

2 large eggs

½ cup skim milk

1¼ heaped teaspoons sweet Hungarian paprika

½ teaspoon cayenne pepper

2 teaspoons salt

¾ teaspoon coarsely ground black pepper

Preheat the oven to 375°F. Lightly brush a nonstick mini muffin pan with olive oil.

Cook the potatoes in a pot of boiling water until tender, about 15 minutes. Peel, transfer to a mixing bowl, and mash the potatoes. Set aside to cool.

In a nonstick sauté pan over medium heat, add the butter and olive oil. When the butter is melted, add the onions and cook, stirring, until lightly browned. Set aside to cool. When the onions are cool, add them to the mashed potatoes. Add the flour, Parmesan and gouda cheeses, egg whites, whole eggs, skim milk, paprika, cayenne, salt, and pepper and mix thoroughly with hands until well combined. The mixture should be quite firm.

Drop rounded teaspoons of the mixture into the oiled muffin tins. Press lightly to smooth the top. Bake until golden brown, approximately 35 minutes. Remove from the oven and set aside to cool for 10 minutes. Using tongs or a spatula, transfer the croquettes to a platter and serve.

Serves 20 to 30 for appetizers, approximately 60 croquettes